A FAIRE Affair

A FAIRE

Affair

ROSE PRENDEVILLE

First published by Eridani Press.

Cover illustration and design by Jessica Khoury

Lifebuoy art by BraveSpirit

Heart flourish art by Timonko

Names: Prendeville, Rose, author.

Title: A Faire Affair / Rose Prendeville.

Description: First edition. | Nashville, Tennessee : Eridani Press, 2026.

Identifiers: ISBN 978-1-955643-20-7 (trade paperback) | ISBN 978-1-955643-21-4 (ebook)

Subjects: LCSH: Tennessee—Fiction. | Hebrides (Scotland)—Fiction. | Barra Island (Scotland)—Fiction. | Man-woman relationships—Fiction. | Romance fiction. | Renaissance fairs—Fiction. | Phobias—Fiction. | BISAC: FICTION / Romance / General | BISAC: FICTION / Romance / Friends to Lovers | BISAC: FICTION / Romance / Small Town & Rural | GSAFD: Love stories.

Classification: LCC PS3616.R452 | DDC 813/.6—dc23

LC record available upon request.

For Grandma Ruth and Grandma Jet.
I wish we'd had more time.

And for my mom.
I'm sorry I covered your mouth when you sang.

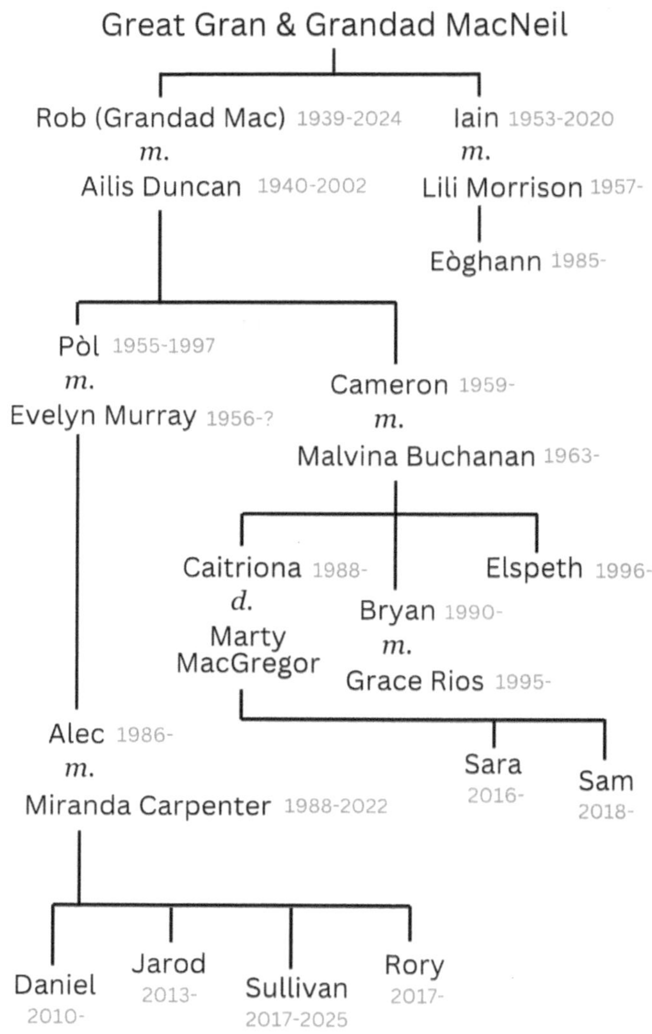

MacNeil Family Tree
Great Gran & Grandad MacNeil
Rob (Grandad Mac) 1939-2024
m.
Ailis Duncan 1940-2002
Iain 1953-2020
m.
Lili Morrison 1957-
Eòghann 1985-
Pòl 1955-1997
m.
Evelyn Murray 1956-?
Cameron 1959-
m.
Malvina Buchanan 1963-
Caitriona 1988-
d.
Marty MacGregor
Bryan 1990-
m.
Grace Rios 1995-
Elspeth 1996-
Alec 1986-
m.
Miranda Carpenter 1988-2022
Sara 2016-
Sam 2018-
Daniel 2010-
Jarod 2013-
Sullivan 2017-2025
Rory 2017-

Buchanan Family Tree

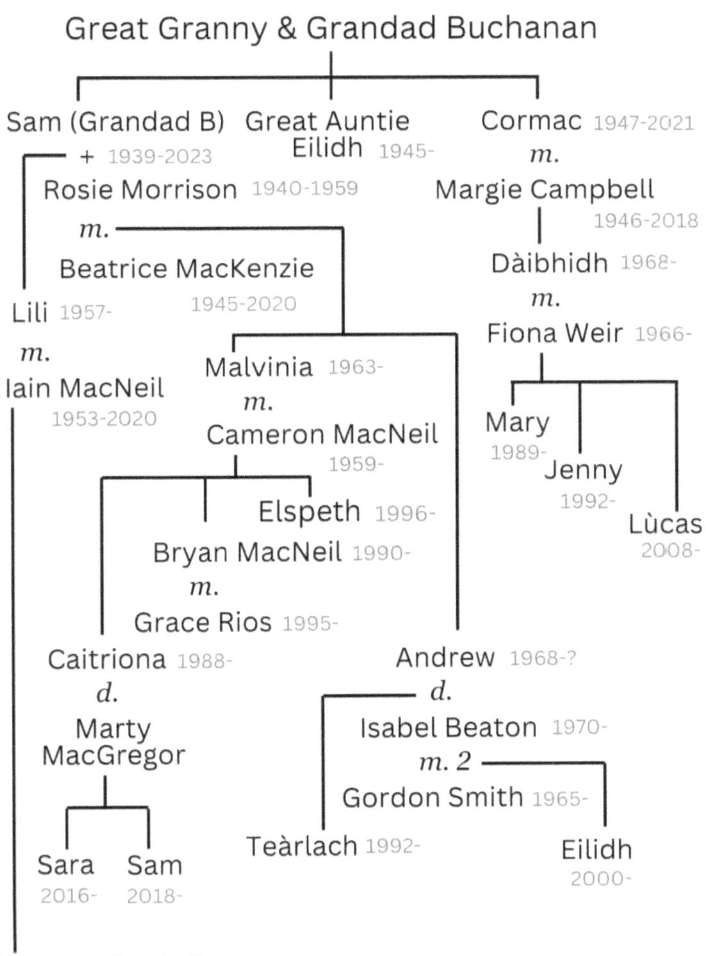

Guide to Gaelic Name Pronunciation

Eòghann - O-wen (Owen)
Pòl - POhl (Paul)
Teàrlach - CHAR-lugh (you can call him Charlie)
Eilidh - AY-lee
Ruairidh - ROO-ry (Rory)
Dàibhidh - DAH-vee (David/Davy)

Prologue

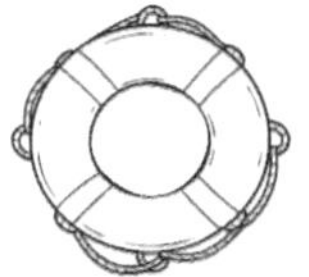

1 YEAR AGO... BARRA, SCOTLAND

Eòghann should have brought a longer ladder. At six feet and two inches, he still needed to stretch to reach the top-most crack above the arched doorway, his charcoal cable knit riding up and dragging his shirt-tail with it so a chill nipped his low back. But the last time he used his tallest ladder inside Our Lady, Star of the Sea, he'd come dangerously close to taking out an ancient chandelier—and Father Murphy's heart right along with it. Since then, he'd stuck with a middling ladder if he was working anywhere near the church out of an abundance of caution.

He rolled his neck and let his limbs go loose before stretching the last little bit to spread plaster into the cracks with his trowel, smoothing it along the archway. Another draft tickled his skin, and this time traveled all the way up his spine until his scalp tingled.

Finished with this part of the repair, Eòghann dropped the trowel into his bucket of plaster and hitched up his jeans.

That was when he noticed her.

With hair the color of dawn's first rays and wide, expressive eyes of forget-me-not blue which Eòghann knew without a doubt he wouldn't forget as long as he lived, the young tourist seemed to have tumbled into the church like a windswept woodland sprite. Now she wandered up the aisle, still looking around in awe—and very much in danger of colliding with his ladder as she gazed at the stained glass and intricately carved ceiling.

For his part, Eòghann realized he wasn't breathing. How could he, watching her glide around as though she were the holy lady herself, the eponymous Star of the Sea?

He'd probably go to hell for blasphemy, and if not for that, then for the raging tightness growing in his jeans and threatening a most uncomfortable descent.

"Help you?" he rasped.

She jumped, blinking rapidly, and searching the ceiling as though it were Jesus himself come down from the cross to speak.

He cleared his throat to make it less raspy, drawing her gaze. A trick of the light made it seem as though her eyes flared at the sight of him. Probably, she was merely startled all over again.

"Sorry. I didn't know anyone was here," she drawled.

The American Invasion, his cousin had called her and her companion last night when the women had entered the pub.

An alarm bell clanged loudly in Eòghann's ears. He knew better than to get mixed up with tourists, especially American ones.

She glanced around in delight, smiling and nodding her head to each bong of his internal alarm, until he realized with some mortification it was simply the tower bell chiming the hour.

"Your church is beautiful," she said, her words like laughter on a summer breeze despite the way she hugged her bare arms into her body against the ever-present chill.

"Thank you," he said, burning with a surge of pride for his

part in the church's appearance—years of maintenance and gentle restoration.

"Not even close to being a ruin," she added.

"Were you expecting ruins?"

"I hiked over to Borve Point to see some this morning."

"Not impressed?"

"Not sure I ever found them," she laughed.

"They can be hard to spot if you don't know what you're looking for."

"I found this place, so at least it wasn't a wasted trip."

"Do you fancy churches, then?"

"I like old things," she answered, sliding into a pew.

Eòghann glanced back up at the wall he'd been repairing. "What sorts of old things?" he asked, suddenly dizzy. Taking a deep breath, he made his way down the ladder to set aside both bucket and trowel.

"Besides churches? I love old ladies." She grinned. "Old ladies with no f—"

She caught herself mid-swear, and Eòghann raised his eyebrows.

"Fear," she settled on, as though she hadn't been about to say *no fucks* right there inside a church. "And I like old recipes. Interesting inscriptions on ancient grave stones. Cranky old cats."

"A regular antiquarian," he teased.

Smiling, she shrugged a little. "If you say so."

"Are you on your own?" he asked.

"Indeed I am." Her smile faded as she nodded her head. "I broke up with my boyfriend a couple of weeks ago. What gave it away?"

Eòghann swallowed. That wasn't at all what he'd meant by the question, but he filed the information away for later. "His loss," he managed to rasp.

She nodded. "I like to think so. He is, of course, telling all his friends I'm afraid of commitment, since I broke up with him after he proposed."

"And what do you tell your friends?" Eòghann wondered aloud.

She took a deep breath and let it out heavily, staring straight ahead rather than at him. "The truth. Or part of it. He's... to put it kindly he's completely uninspired in bed."

Eòghann laughed out loud as heat surged through him to parts he ought not be contemplating inside church walls.

She laughed too, then snapped her mouth shut, as though realizing what she'd said, and craned her neck to look around for other witnesses.

"Forgive me, Father, for I have sinned. Isn't that how I'm supposed to start?"

Mouth dry, all he could do was nod at the crack about his age—at least ten years her senior. And what did that mean, given her penchant to appreciate old things?

"It's been *never* since my last confession, but yes. We lived in *sin*."

She made air quotes when she said the word, and Eòghann's parts-uncontemplated stirred once more. He didn't know why she was telling him all this, but he didn't want her to stop talking.

"Honestly, after seven long years I feel like I've done my penance already."

"Time served," Eòghann said softly.

"Exactly."

"And good behavior?" he teased, and sweet Mary, Star of the Sea, he was definitely going to hell for flirting with a tourist on the rebound in church.

In response, she shrugged, not only her shoulders but her whole body, her face too. "Mmm..." she intoned, and he would bet everything he owned she tread a razor thin line when it came to good behavior.

"Do you suppose there's any hope for me?" she asked, rubbing her arms against the chill once more, and instinctively he stepped forward, stripping off his cable knit jumper and offering it to her.

What had she said? Any hope for her? He had plenty of those, and he was trying to squash them one by one.

She reached for the sweater gratefully, and Eòghann was hit with a waft of honeysuckle and something sweeter, something he couldn't quite discern.

"He only proposed out of some skewed sense of obligation. And I get it, I mean, I did waste some of the best years of being able to appreciate beautiful things stuck looking at him every day. *Wow*. Those are inside thoughts. That sounded really awful out loud. I didn't mean he was ugly."

"It's all right," Eòghann said, feeling vaguely confused but still utterly charmed.

"He was fine. He was hot, at first, I guess."

Eòghann nodded.

"What I meant was, in addition to time-served, I'm going to be legally blind. Probably soon. Hell—sorry—can you say that in church?"

"Some brands of theology encourage it," Eòghann replied, but his brain was caught in a record scratch. *Legally blind?*

She smiled at his joke. "We just weren't well matched in any way. I try to be optimistic. He's more of a pessimistic pragmatist. I love to travel. His idea of vacation is rotting away on the same old golf course year after year. I love museums. And churches, obviously, and art. For years my friend Beatrix and I talked about jetting around the world to see all the Vermeer paintings together. Pierce laughed, bought me a book, and said,

Now you can look at them anytime you want without ever leaving the couch."

"Not quite the point," he commiserated. As someone who'd never traveled anywhere, he could appreciate her disappointment better than most.

"Thank you! So as far as penance goes, perhaps I made up for the sin of living together by setting both of us free."

"That's one way of looking at it," Eòghann agreed.

"Now I suppose you'll ask if I'm sorry for living with him. In the beginning, no. By the end, very much so."

"Noted."

"And before you ask if I'll do it again..." She sighed deeply, as though she'd been wrestling with these thoughts a long time. "It depends what you're asking. Living together? Probably not. Sex outside of marriage? Definitely, yes, and hopefully as soon as possible."

"Oh," Eòghann said very cleverly.

"I'm a tactile person, Padre," she said, and even if she was teasing him for working in the old church, he found he didn't mind the nickname.

"I have needs the same as anyone," she went on. "But when I do lose my vision, I don't know how much I'll retain. Will I be able to see faces clearly? Read non-verbal cues to know if someone's actually attracted to me? You probably know as well as anyone—you can't believe a word that comes out of a man's mouth, especially not when he wants to get in your pants. I mean—not—I didn't mean to insinuate you know about the pants part."

Eòghann didn't know quite what to say, so he said, "You're shivering," and nodded to the sweater in her hands.

She held his gaze for a long moment before pulling it over her head, closing her eyes and taking a long inhale. It probably smelled terrible, some combination of plaster and Eòghann's sweaty musk. He held his breath, waiting for the tell-tale nose wrinkle.

Her eyes crinkled as she smiled instead.

The jumper pooled in her lap, easily long enough to cover her bum once she stood, which meant her height was all in her legs. Eòghann had no business thinking about her bum or her legs or the way the sleeves fell to her fingertips, which she seemed to enjoy as she snuggled down into the cozy wool.

"Thank you…?"

"Eòghann," he replied, a bit tongue-tied after her confession.

"Wesley. Teal."

"Pleasure," he replied truthfully.

He shuffled backwards to lean against another pew as an excuse to adjust his black work jeans while he tried to think of something witty to say. If he had been a priest, he supposed he'd ask her a question. *Do you promise to repent from wickedness and vow to not have any more relations outside of wedlock? Unless it's with me?* No, definitely not that.

"Are you here with your friend Beatrix then? Has Barra taken possession of a Vermeer I'm not aware of?"

The woman—Wesley—laughed. "Wouldn't that be hilarious? If we found the stolen one here in your local pub? No, Bea's probably doing something busy and important in Boston."

"Are you from Boston?"

"Tennessee. I'm tagging along with my friend Grace." Her eyes widened as she remembered this fact. "Who I should probably get back to before she sends out a search party. She'll think I've fallen off a cliff by now."

"We frown on that here."

She laughed again, and her whole face was like a summer sunset, the kind you wait around all night for, bright and cheery.

It warmed him right down to his toes, and he didn't ever want to stop basking in her light.

"Thanks for the..." she gestured between them as she got to her feet.

Was she keeping his sweater then? "It was lovely chatting to you," he said.

"Likewise," she grinned, and it was pure honey. He wanted to lap up every drop.

When the door closed behind her, Eòghann slid down into a pew, and then kept going until he was lying flat on his back, staring up at the wood-paneled ceiling. He exhaled slowly and threw a cool arm over his flushed face.

He quite liked that jumper, but he supposed she could keep it. He wasn't sure he could resist her a second time, and as a rule, he tried very hard to resist tourists.

Not that he was a saint any more than he was priest. In forty years, he'd never set foot off the island. Of course, he had dabbled with tourists. But this one–she was dangerous. From the moment she'd blown inside Our Lady, Star of the Sea like some kind of sentient summer squall, the left side of his brain had been screaming out all the reasons he should put as much distance as possible between them—as much as one could while confined to the same tiny island. Meanwhile the right side of his brain kept repeating, "Home" over and over on a loop.

And somehow, that single word scared him most of all.

Chapter One

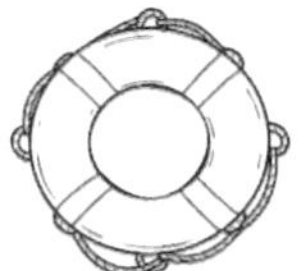

KNOXVILLE, TENNESSEE

WESLEY TEAL. INTERIOR AND SET DESIGN.

Who was she kidding?

Doodling business cards on her iPad while she was on the clock was a definite no-no, but somedays it was the only thing keeping Wes sane, even though they would never be printed. She'd missed her window for all that.

Forgive me, Father, for I have sinned, she thought to herself with a chuckle. The phrase, which had begun as a bit of a joke last year, came to mind so often nowadays, she was practically Catholic by association.

It was an entirely inappropriate little game she liked to play, imagining what penance Father Eòghann MacNeil might give her for each minor transgression. If there was a hell, she was definitely bound for it. Hopefully there were different floors— like, one for people who were fun but a little naughty and a totally different one for dictators and murders and private equity bros.

Wes changed the font to bold black over a lemonade yellow background with honey-golden stardust and shivered despite the warm cable knit pullover she was wearing to ward off the institutional A/C of the office. *His* cable knit pullover.

She ought to text him a flirty little message about how she was wasting company time, so he could text back a flirty little penance, each of them safely on their own side of the Atlantic. Maybe she'd confess how her greatest sin had been lying to herself about not catching feelings last summer.

Is the celibacy thing a hard and fast rule? was another question she could ask, waiting anxiously while three dots appeared and then vanished and then appeared again as he tried to explain why he'd seemed so awfully into her at the midsummer ceilidh, right up until they'd kissed and he'd runaway like some kind of terrified Bambi, making excuses about needing to get home to bed.

The next morning, she'd fantasized about putting on her most scandalously short skirt, and sitting—legs open—right in the front pew, watching him suffer through his wretched sermon. To keep herself from following through on the desperate fantasy, she dragged Grace off on an ill-advised adventure instead, commandeering an inflatable dinghy unfit to survive a summer storm.

Served her right, nearly drowning, but the relief in his stormy eyes when they'd arrived back on dry land safe and sound had been mostly worth it.

Yeah. She was definitely going to hell.

Her cell phone buzzed, startling her from the daydream as she slapped the cover of her iPad closed and sat up straight, looking around at the other cubicles. A tingle ran down her spine at the idea he might be calling to chastise her. That would be a welcome turn in their textual relationship.

But the caller ID showed LT COL TEAL, and her heart began to race for an entirely different reason.

"Mom? Are you okay?" she demanded as she headed for the nearest stairwell to take the call in semi-privacy.

"Of course. Why wouldn't I be?" her mother asked. "Why do you sound hysterical? Are you having trouble with your vision?"

Wes rolled her eyes petulantly. "You never call unless something's wrong."

Her mom was silent for a long moment before she said, "I don't think that's true." She sounded fine, at least.

"Okay," Wes said, trying to also sound fine. "What's up? How's it going? You want to go to a movie or something?" she asked, knowing full well the last movie her mother had gone to see in the theater was *Memento*. She'd declared it a perfect film, and had never seen the point in going back because nothing would ever top it.

Another long pause while her mom probably tried to decide if she was joking. "I was wondering if any of your friends were realtors."

"No. None of my friends are anything so practical, as you've often pointed out."

"College is expensive—"

"Why do you need a realtor? Are you being transferred away from Oak Ridge?"

Her stomach tightened, which was honestly pretty silly. Oak Ridge National Laboratory was less than an hour away, and she still only saw her mom once or twice a year. They were both pretty happy with the arrangement.

"Goodness, no. It's for your grandmother."

"What?" Wes asked, gripping the banister.

"She seems to have gotten herself into some kind of financial pickle."

"Financial pickle? Wait—what?"

"I suppose she didn't say pickle exactly, but she's decided to sell that big old drafty house at last and move somewhere more practical. I thought maybe you'd know someone who could help do it quickly."

"Does it need to be done quickly?" Wes asked, keeping her voice level despite her mounting panic. She loved the old Tudor house on the edge of Knox County more than any other place in the world, and Grandma Ruth was her very favorite person.

"We didn't go into specifics. She only called to see if I wanted anything from the house. I gather she still has some of your dad's old things."

"Sure," Wes agreed, wondering why Grandma Ruth hadn't called her with the same offer.

"How's work?" her mom asked in a distracted sort of way before Wes had a chance to shift gears.

"Are you asking because you care or because it's the only way you know to make small talk?"

"I'm sorry I asked."

"Work is work. How's yours?"

"Classified."

"Glad we caught up."

"If you think of a realtor, let your grandmother know."

"You bet. Bye—"

The line went dead before she could add *Mom*.

Wes hurried back to her desk and threw the laptop and iPad into her backpack. "Family emergency. I'll work remote the rest of the day!" she called to her boss, not waiting for permission before taking the stairs two at a time, speed-dialing her grandma's number on the way down.

"What did your mother tell you?" Grandma Ruth asked after the second ring.

"Some kind of financial crisis is forcing you to sell Warwick Hall as quickly as possible."

Her grandmother burst out laughing, thank goodness, and Wes felt a tiny bit better before she'd reached the crosswalk on the corner.

Unfortunately, her mom had gotten the pertinent details absolutely correct. Grandma did intend to sell Warwick Hall, and Wesley's best childhood memories along with it. But there had to be something else going on. Grandma Ruth loved the old house as much as Wesley did. Maybe she really was in some kind of financial trouble and didn't want to say—or worse, maybe she was sick.

The thought froze Wesley's heart and made her stumble. She'd almost lost her grandma when the old lady developed pneumonia a couple of winters ago on the heels of a previous infection. It had been sudden and scary, but this—planning and preparation, and not saying a word to Wes? Somehow this was worse.

Back at her apartment, she put on a swimsuit, too keyed up to sit still. Ever since boarding school, swimming lap after lap had been the best way to snap out of a panic spiral and turn her thoughts somewhat productive. After about sixty laps of the small apartment pool, however, the only thing that was clear was she needed to visit her grandma.

The thing was, whatever was going on, if it were Wesley in trouble, she wouldn't tell anyone either and she'd never have called her own granddaughter for help. But Wes *had* to help. She might not be able to fix anything, but she wouldn't let Grandma Ruth face it alone.

A few hours later, Wesley's thoughts were still miles away in Stratford, Tennessee, when she met her best friend Grace for pizza.

"Know any realtors?" Wes asked, gazing darkly into her beer.

Grace frowned and shook her head. "You want to move?" she asked.

"What, and disrupt my carefully curated walkable five block radius of a life?" Wes teased, forcing a smile she didn't feel. "No, it's for my grandma."

"Grandma Ruth?" Grace asked, nearly choking on her pizza.

Wes nodded, biting her lip.

"Is she okay?"

"The Lieutenant Colonel thinks she's in some kind of financial trouble, but all Grandma would tell me is that Warwick Hall is too much for her to maintain on her own anymore," Wes said, guilt stabbing at her brain for not making more of an effort to visit and help out the last year or so. "Says she's going to take an apartment in one of those retirement communities."

"And what—learn to play pickleball?"

"It's probably mandatory."

"Damn. But I guess if that's what she wants," Grace said.

"I guess."

"You don't believe her?"

Wes shrugged.

"Wow. End of an era."

It was the end of several eras, in a way. "I'm going to take off the rest of the week and go see her. Make sure that's all it is."

"Can I come?" Grace asked. Without missing a beat she added, "I'll drive."

"Don't you have school?"

"It's finals week. I don't have to do anything but unlock the library. Jen can do that. I have vacation time I was going to lose anyway."

Wes hesitated. It was one thing to show up on her grandma's doorstep unannounced—quite another to bring a friend. And if there was some financial situation that needed fixing—or worse—she didn't want to drag Grace into all that.

"Please? I'd love to see the old place one last time."

"Of course you can come," Wes relented. "But I'll rent a car."

"Don't be dumb. You know I get car sick as a passenger princess. Pay me for gas if you want, but I'm driving. It isn't that far."

"Gray—"

"I was going to Stratford tomorrow anyway—"

"Oh really?"

"For the... peaches."

Wes raised an eyebrow.

"I *love* Stratford Farmer's Market peaches. You can tag along if you want."

"Liar."

Grace shrugged.

"Are you this bossy with your boyfriend?"

A soft, secret smile hitched up Gray's lips on one side. "Hard to be bossy when you're an ocean apart," she said demurely.

She'd been long-distance dating Bryan the Stoic Scot, Father Eòghann's cousin, since returning from Barra at the end of last summer.

"What time should I pick you up?" she asked Wes. "Nine too early?"

"I'll be ready," Wes agreed.

It wasn't that she minded Gray's company. She was glad to have it, and the house in Stratford had been a haven for their whole gang—the self-ascribed Shakespeare Syndicate—back in their college days when they were young and idealistic, each of them running away from one thing or another.

But Wesley knew her friend's sudden eagerness to skip work and visit Grandma Ruth wasn't about peaches. Grace was perceptive, and it didn't take a genius to realize Wes didn't love driving anymore. She also knew Wes would sooner suffer a thousand paper cuts in the ocean than ask for help from anyone.

And Grace was right. On both counts

Wesley preferred not to drive anymore if she could help it. She hadn't actually told Grace yet, but her Stargardt disease was progressing more rapidly these days. The blind spots, which had previously been an ever-present annoyance, were much worse than even a year ago. She'd first realized it when she struggled to read her magazines despite wearing glasses during the flight over to Scotland. At work she'd been blaming eye strain, blue light, glare.

All of that may be true, but it was also the big M: macular degeneration.

The thing she'd been out-running for almost twenty years was finally catching up. Soon it would overtake her and level off, and then she'd know the extent of the change and what her new normal would look like.

For now, it meant she still carried a driver's license, but she was afraid to use it.

Still, that's what taxis and ride-shares and her own two legs were for. Unlike Blanche Dubois, Wes had never depended on the kindness of strangers—or friends, for that matter.

She was the only daughter of an only daughter. She was the dependable one. The self-reliant one.

So self-reliant she was actually spiraling over Gray's offer of a ride. But showing up for Grandma Ruth was too important, and Grace knew that too—knew Wes would accept the help because it was in aid of her grandmother. So Wes thanked her friend, declining the additional offer of a ride home from the pub, and walked back to her apartment to pack a bag, still fizzing with tension.

She needed to get laid, was the trouble. She hadn't experienced a dry spell this long since she was a teenager.

Wes had been with Pierce for more than seven years before they broke up last spring, and twelve months was a veritable drought. Hell, a year ago she thought twelve days was a drought. It was why she'd let her hormones drag Eòghann MacNeil, a *priest* for Christ's sake, down to a dance party on the Barra beach.

He'd looked handsome and vulnerable and hungry, and she'd figured what with being a priest on a tiny island, his drought had probably been far longer than hers.

They had danced barefoot under a sky that never slept, mindlessly grinding to the pulsing beat of some Celtic rock band. Eòghann had kept his back to the ocean so Wes could enjoy the view, but she'd been more intent on the whorls and eddies in his sea green eyes.

She'd been attracted to him from the very first moment they met. He was sexy and intense and awkward and kind. And completely unavailable. As a priest, he was perhaps the one person of her acquaintance less likely to commit than she was.

And that, of course, was part of the allure.

It was the reason she hadn't gone out to a club or a party on the prowl for a one-night stand this past year—because feelings were too easily caught and Wes had turned over a new leaf. She didn't need a man. She was a strong, independent, competent woman.

Instead, each time she felt the need for a shag, she found a reason to flirt with Eòghann long distance.

Sighing, Wes picked up her phone, scrolling back through a year's worth of messages.

JULY 6

> **Wes**
> Forgive me, Father, for I have sinned.

Eòghann
Not an auspicious start, Teal. You only just left.

> **Wes**
> I'm very talented and have a great capacity for sin. Especially when there's no one to keep me in line. 😆

Eòghann
What on earth have you done?

> **Wes**
> I imagined stuffing a whiny 6 year old in the overhead luggage bin for the duration. I may have wished a pox upon his house.

Eòghann
For shame! On a child?

> **Wes**
> And that was BEFORE he barfed on me.

Eòghann
ON you on you?

> **Wes**
> That was my penance, wasn't it? I'll spare you a description of the horrific smell that has been my constant companion for the last 6 hours.

Eòghann
Time served, certainly.

Wes
Pray for me?

Eòghann
Seems like the people sitting close enough to
smell you need prayers more.

JULY 7

Wes
Finally home. 🌙 Thanks for the memories. I'm
going to scald off my skin in the shower.

Eòghann
Try and stay out of trouble. Come back again
soon.

Wes
No. You come here.

Eòghann
Goodnight, Wes.

Wes
How do you say it in Gaelic?

Eòghann
Oidhche mhath.

Wes
Oidhche mhath, Padre.

Wes cringed looking back at her blatant flirting, but to be fair, it'd been an excruciatingly long travel day.

Reading through their messages now stirred up all the same old fluster and yearning. The problem was, text messages couldn't hold her. They couldn't touch her. They couldn't stroke her hair or kiss her forehead while they told her not to worry because everything was going to be okay.

But neither would a one night stand, and at the end of the day, Wes wasn't starved for sex so much as she was starved for touch. She was starved for connection. And that was why she'd held on a little too long when she hugged Grace at dinner.

She wanted to text him anyway, but she didn't like to appear needy, and she couldn't think of any funny repartee, and so, with a huff, she tossed the phone aside and reached in her night-stand for Pablo, her favorite vibrator.

Chapter Two

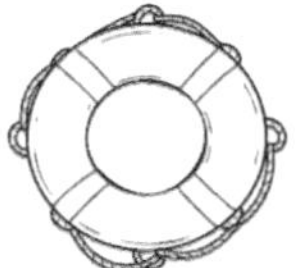

As she waited for Grace to pick her up the next morning, Wes kept scrolling through Eòghann's old text messages to make her heart beat fast with arousal instead of anxiety.

It was becoming a problem. But she wasn't going to stop.

In three weeks, it would be a year since they met in that old church on the Isle of Barra and she was already trying to draft something witty—and maybe a little naughty—to say about it. Humor was the best way to take the pressure off, to make it clear she wasn't hanging by a thread waiting for his next reply. Because she wasn't.

AUGUST 16

Wes
Forgive me, Father, for I have sinned.

Eòghann
You really have to stop starting conversations
this way. What have you done now, ye wee
devil?

> **Wes**
> I was jealous of Gray staying behind to
> fornicate or what-have-you.

Eòghann
I have not.

> **Wes**
> Exactly—nor have I! And now I've no patience
> for her moping around like she lost her best
> friend.

Eòghann
Understandable. Bryan's much the same. It's
very annoying.

> **Wes**
> Tell me about it! I'm the only best friend Grace
> is allowed to mope about losing.

Eòghann
Has she lost you?

> **Wes**
> She's about to if she doesn't stop acting like
> Bryan's more important. 😗

Eòghann
Cold, unfeeling woman.

> **Wes**
> What penance would you suggest for such a
> selfish lack of empathy?

Eòghann
You must take Grace out at once and try to
cheer her up.

Wes
Tacos or pizza?

Eòghann
Why not taco pizza?

Wes
Gross.

Eòghann
It IS supposed to be penance.

    Wes
    Can't I say 3 Hail Jesus's or something?

Eòghann
We should probably steer clear of that.

    Wes
    Fine. Make sure the Stoic Scot doesn't get too
    deep in his feelings. Let him know she misses
    him like crazy?

Eòghann
Make sure she knows it's mutual.

Grace pulled up outside the apartment complex right on time, and when Wes tossed her suitcase into the back of the Subaru, she was surprised to see her friend had brought a suitcase of her own.

"Is that bag to carry your peaches or are you planning to stay a few days?" she asked, settling into the passenger seat and typing Grandma Ruth's address into the GPS.

"What did you think I was going to do, kick you out at the end of the driveway and pull a U-turn to hightail it back here?"

"Kind of."

"I would never. Road trip snacks?" Grace offered, pulling a bag of sweet and savory gas station treats from the back seat.

"Stratford's forty-five minutes away. An hour if we hit

construction," Wes said. "Or, you know, a bunch of geese decide to take their time crossing the road."

Grace shrugged. "Better eat up then," she said, turning up the music.

"You sure listen to a lot of Pink these days," Wes teased around a mouthful potato chips.

"She's the voice of a generation."

Wes laughed. "And how is the Stoic Scot?"

The first day they met Bryan, he sang a Pink banger in the karaoke bar, and Wes was half-tempted to fall in love with him herself. Ever since, Grace had kept the singer's albums on a more steady rotation than ever, but considering Wes had been obsessively rewatching season two of *Fleabag* on a loop since meeting her own hot priest, she had precious little room to talk.

Her friend's whole face lit up at the mention of Bryan. "He's good. Great, actually. Ardbeg is doing a re-release of his Rionnagach whisky and plans for the Finnbar Distillery are rolling along."

"Amazing!"

"Yeah. He's going to try to spend part of the summer here."

"What? When?"

"TBD. We haven't ironed out the details yet."

"Clock's ticking. I'm surprised you didn't have it planned months ago."

"I mean *I* would have. Bryan's a little more..." She took a deep breath.

"Free spirited?" Wes suggested.

"I was going to say last minute."

"Spontaneous?"

"Flies by the seat of his pants."

Wes grinned. "It vexes you, doesn't it?"

"Vexes? Who are you, Lady Catherine de Bourgh?" Grace asked.

"She might be my *favorite* old lady in literature. She could take Miss Havisham in a fight."

"Ugh, and you call yourself an honorary English major."

"Listen, I remember exactly three works from British lit class: *The Tempest, Pride and Prejudice,* and *Great Expectations.*"

Grace gasped. "We studied *Beowulf* in that class! And Oscar Wilde—and the Brontës!"

"I'm vexing you right now, aren't I?" Wes teased.

Her friend sighed dramatically. "Sometimes, it does vex me, okay," Grace said honestly. "And sometimes it's perfect. Bryan actually pays attention and reads the moment and knows instinctively what I need."

Wes smiled. "It's good to see you so happy."

"I really am."

"How's his cousin?" Wes asked with as much disinterest as she could manufacture in three very interested words.

Grace glanced at her and back to the road. "Which one? He's related to half the island."

"Lùcas," Wes lied.

"Lùc's good. He applied to a university program in the fall."

"For his art?" Wes asked with a little stab of jealousy. Oh, to be young and fresh and just starting out. *Forgive me, Father, for I have sinned...*

Nodding, Grace added, "University of Edinburgh."

"Wow, big steps," she said. "And Teàrlach?" she asked, naming another cousin she'd met last year.

"He's all right. Embroiled in some kind of law suit."

"What?"

"He's taking on the bigger airlines for not allowing accommodations to hire disabled pilots."

"Good for him," Wes said, nodding.

The next few miles passed in silence, and then Grace

cautiously offered, "Eòghann's doing fine. Maybe a little bored, it sounds like, but healthy and helpful as always."

Wes nodded. So she was that transparent. They flirted constantly, but it was a tightrope. He didn't say much about himself unless prompted, and she tried not to appear too eager to know everything lest he—like Grace—see right through her. "That's good to hear."

"Do you not talk to him anymore?"

"Oh, you know," Wes hedged. "Nothing real. Mostly memes."

SEPTEMBER 22

Eòghann
Happy Autumnal Equinox, heathen.

> **Wes**
> How are you celebrating?

Eòghann
Standing in a corner at the ceilidh with Bryan.

Will you mark the day?

> **Wes**
> Suppose I should write down my thoughts and feelings and burn them in a bonfire?

Eòghann
A fitting way to pass the time.

> **Wes**
> Tragically, my landlord frowns on bonfires in the living room.
>
> But luckily I have neither thoughts nor feelings to write down.

Eòghann
Jealous.

What would you write down if you did have
such fits of humanity?

> **Wes**
> Probably some mundane variation of "I need a
> new job. With better insurance." Or something
> maudlin like, "I miss my dad."

Eòghann
Does autumn make you miss him more?

> **Wes**
> It's sharper then. Do you miss yours all the
> time?

Eòghann
No.

> **Wes**
> So tell me why you're hiding in the corner
> instead of dancing?

Eòghann
Moral support for Bry. His one true love is far
across the sea. You might've heard.

> **Wes**
> A tragic tale...

Eòghann
Also there's no one here for me to dance with.

> **Wes**

IN NO TIME THEY REACHED THE TURN-OFF FOR WARWICK

Hall, Grandma's Tudor-style farmhouse. A handwritten poster was duct taped to the no through traffic sign pole.

RENAYZANTS FAiRE → THiS SATURDAY.

The women looked at each other. "Um..." Wes said.

"What else is down this road?" Grace asked.

"This road is Grandma Ruth's driveway. Pull over?"

Wes got out and ripped down the sign, tossing it in the floorboard with the empty bag of snacks.

The long drive up to the house brought back memories of early summer holidays, Wesley in the passenger seat holding her breath as the big house came into view.

This time was no different, except the vast lawn, which used to be a field of wildflowers, had become dramatically overgrown with tall grass and weeds and whatnot. It reminded Wes more of Miss Havisham's withered garden in *Great Expectations* than the vibrant Klimt-painted landscape of her youth.

"I almost forgot how cute it is!" Grace trilled, beaming up at the house as she parked behind Grandma's Miata.

For the most part, Warwick Hall was exactly as Wes remembered it. Maybe a little more frayed around the edges—in need of a power wash and fresh paint—though even with sunglasses on it was a little hard to make out what was faded and what was merely the blurring of her central vision. But it was still the same magnificent home with its half-timbered facade, steep gables, and partial turret. English ivy climbed the walls, and an overgrown hydrangea hadn't bloomed in years.

"I guess it is a lot for one old lady to be keeping up with," Wes murmured.

It was also the stuff of midsummer night daydreams.

Wes had spent every vacation there as a little girl, until she told her mom she didn't want to go anymore. The part she never said out loud was that it wasn't fair of her to be a summertime burden on her widowed grandma. Her Air Force engineer mother never thought to question her motives, and from then on, a series of summer camps and art camps and academic acceleration programs had monopolized Wesley's time, setting her grandmother free to travel and date and live her best AARP life.

A big black bird flew overhead, swooping and cawing what sounded like, "Intruders! Intruders!" the moment they stepped out of the car.

Grandma Ruth met them in the driveway, and Wes breathed a sigh of relief that she at least looked healthy enough. "Sakes alive, I thought I was going to have to chase off my first ticket holders," she said.

"Intruders!"

"Is that a raven?" Grace asked.

"Settle down, Duncan, this is family."

"Family!" the bird repeated, to Wesley's astonishment.

"What on earth are you girls doing here?" Grandma asked, going in for a hug before Wes could answer.

"Ticket holders?" Wes repeated, squeezing her grandmother tight. "That sign was real?"

"Sign?"

Wes got out the poorly spelled poster.

"They actually put up a sign?" Grandma Ruth asked, shaking her head.

Wes sighed. "Who's *they*? What's going on, Grandma? Is this why mom thinks you need money?"

"I'm a foolish old lady, that's what's going on."

Wes shook her head. "But for the record, you're not sick or anything?"

"Fool!" the bird cawed.

"No, sweetheart, I'm not sick. But I'm good with a slingshot though," she threatened the bird, making Grace snicker. "Come inside, both of you. We might as well drink while you hear my tale of woe."

Grace grinned at Wesley, and Wes had to smile too, giddy with relief. It was good to be home.

"Don't mind Spencer," Grandma said, as they stepped inside, past a grizzle-bearded man in a moth-eaten shirt, who sat on the porch tuning a... weird violin?

"Who's Spencer?" Wes tried not to sound too alarmed.

"Is that a lute?" Grace asked him.

"Hurdy-gurdy," Spencer replied.

Wes wasn't sure it was possible for her eyebrows to lift any higher. "Is he speaking Muppet?"

"Hurdy-gurdy is the instrument. Spencer's the entertainment."

"Entertainment. For your Ren faire? Where is he sleeping?"

"Ren-ay-zants," Grace corrected.

"In a tent out back," Grandma said, waving vaguely over her shoulder. "Iced tea?"

"I thought for sure you meant something stronger," Wes said. "But okay."

Grandma Ruth grinned and poured three glasses. When Wes took a gulp she sputtered.

"Long Island," she explained to Grace, coughing into her sleeve.

Grandma cackled and set out a bowl of potato chips and another bowl of green onion dip. She yanked several times on a drawer before it opened for her to retrieve three coasters, and then seemed to give up on ever getting it closed again.

"So this faire," Wes prompted.

"Ren-ay-zants," Grace repeated.

Grandma grimaced. "You know how I always wanted to host one here."

"You did?" Wes asked. *Had* she known that? She supposed Grandma Ruth had made jokes about it over the years, but Wes had never taken them too seriously.

"From the first second of the first minute I laid eyes on this place I could see it all so clearly. I never told your grandfather that's why I wanted to buy the property, but I never forgot."

For a moment she seemed to disappear into the same rabbit hole of memories Wes had fallen down on her way up the drive. They used to take nature walks through the woods behind the house, and when they'd come to a clearing, Grandma Ruth would say, *"Wouldn't a life-sized chess match be perfect right there?"* or *"We could set up stages here, and invite our favorite musicians."* Then she'd take Wesley's hands, and they'd dance around in a circle as if there was a maypole.

Wes hadn't thought about any of it in years.

"When I decided it was time to bite the bullet and sell this place, the only way I could make myself do it was if I got to host my faire first. But I'm old. And I'm tired. And I knew the only way it would actually happen was if I hired an event company to do the hard work."

Wes sighed. "They ripped you off?"

"It certainly seems that way."

"You paid up front?"

Grandma nodded. "A few thousand towards expenses—"

"A few?"

"Ten. For permits, toilets, advertising. Then they were supposed to keep fifty percent of ticket sales."

"And they...?"

"They put up a crappy poster, apparently, and hired Spencer. I suppose *hired* is doing a lot of heavy lifting. They told him the wrong date to show up and he did."

"And ticket sales?"

Grandma shrugged. "They said sales were great. Then they stopped returning my calls. And emails. I haven't seen a penny. I have no idea how many disappointed people are going to show up on Saturday demanding refunds."

"This might actually be worse than the Willy Wonka Experience," Grace whispered.

"Helpful, as always." But Wes had to agree. "Were you counting on that money? From the ticket sales?"

"No. I used my rainy day fund. Any profit was going into sprucing this place up before I try to sell it, but no, I don't need the income. I also can't cover too many refunds if it comes to that. They might not have sold any tickets at all, or they might've sold thousands. There's no way to know."

Based on their other efforts, Wes was inclined to suspect the former.

"How did you find this company?" Grace asked.

"How does anyone find anything these days? I typed it in the search bar and clicked on the first link—Exemplary Boiled Events.

Grace burst out laughing. "Okay, in her defense, I'd have clicked on that link too," she told Wes.

"It was silly, I guess, thinking I could put on my little faire. Like we used to go to, remember?"

Wes and Grandma Ruth had been to every faire in driving distance: outside Nashville and Charlotte, Florence and Atlanta. Now that Wes thought about it, Grandma Ruth was practically a rennie back in the day.

"I ordered a new costume and everything," she said sadly.

"You didn't," Wes replied with a grin.

"Fashion show, please," Grace demanded, clapping her hands.

When she offered a feeble, flustered protest, Wes prompted,

"Come on, Grandma, you know you want to," and that was all the encouragement it took besides a gulp of liquid courage before Grandma scurried off her to her bedroom to change.

Wes turned to Grace.

"This is amazing," her friend said.

"Except for the part where she got scammed."

"Obviously except for that."

"Why didn't she ask me to help?" Wes whispered. She'd have been disappointed about the plan to sell, but she would've understood.

Grace sobered and offered a little one-shoulder shrug. "Maybe the apple doesn't fall far from the tree."

Wes wanted to demand what Grace meant, but she wouldn't insult her by pretending that if the shoe were on the other foot she'd have asked for help either.

They held each other's silent gaze until Grandma's footsteps padded back across the living room and into the kitchen.

Her dress was crimson velvet, parting in the front to reveal an underskirt of richest gold. At her shoulder there was a modified, white ruff collar edged in yet more gold.

"Oh Grandma," she breathed.

"Isn't it resplendent? I suppose I could put it on this Saturday and stand out front writing checks to refund tickets."

But Wes couldn't let that happen. The costume's sparkly gold accents reminded her of her gold speckled business cards that would never be. She'd let that dream fade long before her vision had—hard to run your own design business with vision loss—but her grandmother's dream could still come true.

Grandma Ruth had sacrificed time and time again: for a husband in the Air Force and a granddaughter whose only constant had been her home. Now she'd been brave enough to try something new, and Wes would be damned if she let some shitty scammer steal that dream out from under her.

"What if you didn't? Issue refunds on Saturday? What if you stood out front in this amazing dress and proclaimed, as Queen, that there'd been some mistake and everyone was two weeks early? That they should hold onto their tickets until the first weekend in June, when you'll be happy to welcome them back to Warwick Hall for the first ever Stratford Renaissance Faire?"

A huge grin was spreading across Gray's face, and they both gazed expectantly at Grandma Ruth, whose eyes twinkled despite being filled with doubt.

"I'm not sure what difference a few weeks can make."

"It'll make all the difference," Wes said. "I know exactly how to organize a Renaissance faire."

"You do?" Grandma and Grace asked at the same time.

"What, like it's hard?" Wes quipped, with more bravado than she was feeling, but fake it 'til you make it, right? Anyway, hard or not, she kind of felt like she owed it to Grandma Ruth.

May 20

> **Wes**
> Forgive me, Father, for I have sinned. Sorry, I know you're tired of that bit. The TLDR is this: my grandma tried to organize a Renaissance faire and got scammed.
>
> No, that's not an Onion headline. It really happened.

> **Wes**
> But this is her DREAM, Padre! So I may have lied and told her I can pull it off. (Not a euphemism.) Pray for me!

For the first time in a year, he left her message on Read.

Chapter Three

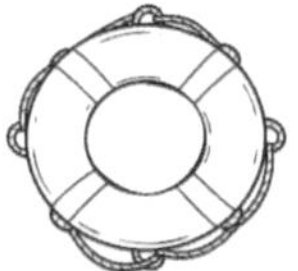

BARRA, SCOTLAND

The water was definitely, without a doubt, most assuredly going to be the end of him. Eòghann was born drowning, and there was some kind of poetic justice in the fact that he'd die drowning too. It had stalked him like a carnivore his entire life, and one day it would carry him home.

He drew a deep breath—or tried to. His watch beeped anxiously to warn him that his heart rate was through the roof. No kidding. His chest was already beginning to constrict, and he hadn't reached the surf yet. He was spinning, trapped in a whirlpool dragging him down, down, down.

He snapped his eyes open, staring hard at the sun and then down at his bare legs, his toes burrowing into the sand, grounding him.

"Eòghann? Are you still there?" The voice was tinny and far away. "Look at me, Eòghann."

He looked down at the phone in his hand. One earbud had slipped out of his ear. He raised his phone to block out the scenic view, squinting against the sunlight at the concerned face of Dr. Patel, whose spiky black hair and horn-rimmed glasses made a stark contrast to his soothing, lilac dress shirt. The therapist was frowning, but his eyes were gentle behind his specs.

"What are you feeling, Eòghann?"

"I thought we agreed cataloging my symptoms only exacerbated them?"

"Give them voice, and then let them go, like a balloon in the wind."

"Bryan would hate that. Terrible for the environment."

"A bubble then."

"What sort of bubble?"

"An environmentally friendly one. How do you feel?"

"Dizzy. Faint. Like vomiting. Profusely. Linda Blair."

"A joke. That's progress."

"Is it though?"

"Have you visualized putting those feelings into bubbles and releasing them to the sky?"

Eòghann did something with his head that was a combination of nodding yes and shaking no as he tried to imagine a dizzy-filled bubble spinning off into the atmosphere and a breathless one imploding in on itself like some kind of black hole.

"Good. Now I want you to take one step forward."

Eòghann didn't respond.

"One tiny step. Not into the water, merely towards the water. We'll do it together."

This time Eòghann choked on a laugh.

"You know what I mean," Dr. Patel said.

Eòghann glanced down at the foam flicking the beach antagonistically a few feet away. Bile surged up his throat and he closed his eyes tight. "No offense, Pat. But I live on a fucking island. If exposure therapy were going to work, don't you think I'd be cured by now?"

"Avoidance isn't exposure."

In a way, Patel had a point and in a way, he was one hundred percent wrong. After all, it wasn't as though Eòghann could truly avoid the water. Not really. It was always there, taunting him every time he left the house. He could hear it, like the rumble of a purring jungle cat, see it from practically any vantage point as he drove around the fifty-eight square kilometers that comprised the Isle of Barra. Stalking. Preying. Waiting.

No, there was no avoiding it. It was like a very large, vicious elephant inside the prison cell that was his life.

For the last seven weeks Eòghann had stood in this exact same spot every Wednesday at three, but as yet he hadn't managed to dip so much as a toe into the sea.

"Close your eyes and picture yourself somewhere safe and dry."

It sounded silly, but Eòghann closed his eyes. "I can still hear the surf, Pat."

His therapist didn't sigh. He was too professional for that. But something in his long-suffering silence *felt* like a sigh.

"All right. I'm picturing myself watching a rugby match at Auntie Eilidh's," Eòghann said, doing so begrudgingly, and okay, maybe the tightness in his chest loosened the tiniest bit.

"Who's winning?" his therapist asked.

"Glasgow Warriors, of course."

This time Patel did try to stifle a deep, guttural objection.

"Why? Who do you like?"

"Edinburgh. Obviously. Let's try a different approach," he suggested gently. "Let's talk about your why."

Eòghann groaned. "We've talked about that. The pool. My cousin Pòl."

"Not why you developed aquaphobia. Why you want to overcome it."

"Er..."

"There must be some reason you woke up at the age of forty-one and decided it was time to conquer your fear. I'd like to hear about it. But even if you aren't ready to share, the next time we come to this spot, instead of focusing on the physical symptoms of panic, I'd like you to focus on the reasons why you will step into the water despite those symptoms.

"Is it because you've developed a passionate desire to scuba dive the Great Barrier Reef? Or you're desperate to cruise the endless sunshine of the Caribbean?"

Dr. Patel's suggestions were making him feel faint again, blackness creeping into the edges of his vision.

"Eòghann? Remember to count your breaths."

A pair of forget-me-not blue eyes floated into his mind.

As though his thoughts had conjured her, a text message from Wes popped up on his screen and he tapped it, forgetting for a second that his therapist was on the line. But his eyes couldn't focus well enough to read it without his specs.

BEEP BEEP BEEP went his watch. He needed to figure out how to turn the heart rate monitor off.

"Do you have your why?" Dr. Patel asked, and he tapped back to the video call.

As if there were only one reason.

Overcoming his fear couldn't bring his cousin Pòl back to life. It couldn't change the memory seared into his brain since last summer of his cousin Bryan speeding off into a storm alone to rescue Wesley and Grace while Eòghann stood helpless on the shore.

He'd been avoiding her text messages that morning. The night before, after the midsummer ceilidh, they'd gone for a walk—just rambling to no place in particular—neither of them ready to say goodnight.

After stopping to admire the colors of the evening sky, he'd been overcome with a primal urge to kiss her. He had never in his life wanted to kiss anyone more.

Wes licked her lips, her bonnie blue eyes lighting every inch of his skin on fire before they skated across his own lips. And then she leaned up, because she was tall enough no tiptoes were required, and they kissed, and time stood still, and the universe stopped expanding in search of meaning.

It was like kissing sunshine, too hot and bright to face directly but life-giving all the same. He'd kissed plenty of tourists in his twenties and early thirties, plenty of party girls who'd come looking to be swept up in a Scottish fairytale for a night or two before they had to return to real lives far away. Most of them treated kissing like something elicit, to be giggled over with girlfriends, or else as an appetizer to be plowed through quickly on their way to the main course. Not Wes. She had kissed him like it was the whole entire meal.

Like the morning they met, a tiny voice inside Eòghann's heart had cried out for home.

In Welsh, the language Eòghann studied in secondary school as a way to irritate his father, the word was hiraeth, this homesick longing for a placed he'd never been. When they finally kissed, Eòghann had realized the desire surging within him wasn't merely a desire to have her. It was much more dangerous. He wanted to keep her. Somehow in a few short weeks he'd fallen too far down a point of no return.

And then he panicked.

Because Barra wasn't her home, and though it felt as if *she* were somehow *his home,* soon she would leave, while he'd still be stuck here.

Pining.

And more or less alone.

He'd mumbled an inane excuse about needing to get some sleep, and such a look of disappointment had burned in her forget-me-not eyes. It would be imprinted on his soul until the day he died. But once it was out he couldn't take it back, and he had scuttled off, disgusted with himself for abandoning her without an explanation, all in a misguided effort to protect his worthless heart.

His behavior and the whole unfair situation still stung the next morning, so he kept himself busy, ignoring the vibrations of text messages, afraid they would be from her, asking to pick up where they'd left off.

Then his phone began to buzz with an incoming call, and he ignored that too, but no sooner had it stopped than it started again.

The blood in his veins turned to ice when he saw it was Gavin, the lad who worked security at the ferry office.

"Gav?" he answered, not recognizing his own scratchy voice.

"Eòghann, mate, you wouldn't know the whereabouts of your cousin's American guests, would you? Only he's not picking up and the ferry cap says there's two idjits out on the harbour in one of those inflatable dinghies. Doesn't your Auntie Eilidh have one of them? Most of the other tourists have headed out, so I thought—"

Eòghann never heard the rest of what Gavin thought because he rang off and called Bryan, jumping into his truck and heading straight over to the cottage.

When he got there, the look on Bryan's face had told him Gavin's instincts were correct.

Standing frozen to the pier, Eòghann had been desperate to charge in after the two Americans as his cousin had, but instead he watched Bryan head off into the squall alone—a one man rescue mission—and if he was cast overboard, if he drowned like Pòl because Eòghann had been too useless to go with him, then Eòghann thought he might let the sea finally win because he'd never be able to live with himself after that.

He'd thrown up while he was waiting and vowed not to ever ignore her texts again. Then he commandeered the ferry office radio to check on Bryan. When Wesley's frightened, exhausted voice had answered him, he'd thrown up again with relief.

That was new.

So no. Overcoming his fear couldn't erase the bitter memories of last summer or the vinegar taste of shame that tainted his relief when they all arrived back on dry land, shaken and soaked to the skin, but ultimately unharmed.

But it would mean he never put a cousin in harm's way again.

"Yes," he rasped. "I have my why."

"Good," Dr. Patel said. "And my guess is you've had this reason for a while, so let me ask you a second question. Why now?"

Because eleven months ago had almost been eleven months too late.

Because two months ago as they'd sat in the pub, Bryan had shown him the ring he'd bought for Grace, and Eòghann had realized his cousin's American girl might want to get married back home in Tennessee, and he would miss it because he was trapped here by the goddamned ocean.

"Do you have it?" the therapist asked him again.

"Aye," Eòghann gasped, his own voice sounding muffled to his ringing ears.

"Excellent. Now look at me and only at me, and take one step forward. Good. One more. Can you do one more? Still not into the water, but towards it?"

Eòghann couldn't breathe, and his shirt was drenched in

sweat despite the brisk spring breeze, but he thought of Wesley Teal, her blue eyes dancing as she reached for his hand.

He took one more step, scrunched his toes in the sand. And then salty, foamy brine rushed in, grabbing at his ankles and dragging him to his knees. He tried to scream, but imagined the water rushing into his mouth, filling his lungs like the day he was born.

"Breathe, Eòghann," said a faraway voice. "You're safe, I promise," the voice lied if the heart-rate monitor on his watch was any indication because his heart was about to explode inside his chest. "Eòghann?" the voice called once more, and he hurled the voice as far as he could and fell backwards into the black.

Eòghann blinked open one sandy eye.

The tide was lapping at his shorts and he skittered backwards until he was well on dry land, his breaths coming in quick gasps.

Had he actually passed out? That was new, too. Wasn't therapy supposed to make him better, rather than worse?

Jesus, he could've landed face first in the water. Dr. Patel always said a panic attack only felt like dying, but he wouldn't actually die. *Jesus.*

He reached for his phone to give the therapist a snarky jab. How long had he been out for? Was Patel still on the video call?

Where was the video call? He looked down at the white sand, feeling along either side of his legs and twisting around in search of the phone.

Taking a slow, deep breath, he forced himself to look out along the beach towards the water, but his phone wasn't there.

He'd wanted to hurl it into the drink, but—no, surely he

hadn't actually done so? Maybe he'd simply dropped it right up close in the sandy shallow, but if he had, it was as good as lost. He wasn't going to look for it. The sea could have it and frankly, good riddance.

After brushing the sand from his clothes and skin, he slipped on his shoes and trudged back home, disappointed in yet another failed therapy session. Hopefully Bryan and Grace would favor a very long engagement.

Chapter Four

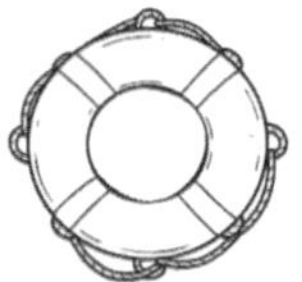

STRATFORD, TENNESSEE

It was surprising when Eòghann didn't text Wes back. Not that he owed her a response, but she usually got one by the time she woke up.

She scrolled back through her phone to make sure she hadn't missed it.

OCTOBER 18

Wes
Forgive me, Father, for I have sinned.

Eòghann
Seeing as I can't actually grant you absolution,
do I even want to know what you've done now,
ye wee devil??

Wes
Greed, I suppose? I couldn't decide, so I
bought two costumes. Should I dress up as
Glinda or a Zombie Statue of Liberty for
Halloween?

Eòghann
Which one has the shorter skirt?

Wes

Eòghann
Can you be a Zombie Glinda?

Wes
Not quite the same bold statement, but I like
where your head is at.

Eòghann
I live to serve.

Wes
YEAH you do! Always serving face!

Eòghann
Wrong number. Who's this?

Wes

So are you for or against the shorter skirt?

Eòghann
Samhain is meant to be terrifying. Glinda may
be too PoPuLaR.

Wes
I see what you did there, and you're right.
Dead Liberty it is. I can shorten the skirt.

Eòghann
Heading to a club?

Wes
A party with some of Gray's school friends. I'm her +1. She doesn't think I get out enough.

Eòghann
What, only 3 days a week?

Wes
Hah. If only. The sad truth is, Padre, she's right. I'm so stir crazy I'm actually looking forward to this boring teacher party. I hope I can keep up with them.

Eòghann
Why? Is it a dance marathon?

Wes
Nobody drinks like teachers and librarians.

It's a problem. Once, in Frankfurt, a conference of librarians drank the city dry.

They actually ran out of beer. IN FRANKFURT!

Eòghann
Good thing you don't like German beer.

Wes
I believe my exact words were, "I prefer Scottish beer when in Scotland."

Eòghann
Be safe, please.

Wes
Don't wait up!

Eòghann
Fine, but I want pictures.

She had indeed sent him pictures, even though it was rude of him to remind her she wasn't a member of his congregation. And the costume had been spectacular, proving she could pull a plan together when she tried. But Wes wasn't an event planner. Nothing like one. It would be a minor miracle if she could put on the Renaissance faire of her grandmother's dreams.

"Much as I hate to admit it, I think we need a spreadsheet," Wesley said to Grace as they sat on the big front porch swing drinking fresh squeezed orange juice with a little bit of vodka after scarfing down bowls of piping hot tater tot casserole.

"No spreadsheets," Grace moaned. "I'm on vacation."

"It's the only way."

"You pulled off one hell of a last minute double quinceañera last year," Grace said. "Did you have a spreadsheet for that?"

"No. That's why it felt last minute," Wes pretended to pout.

Grace rolled her eyes. "And weren't you the mastermind behind my twenty-first?"

"Panda-monium was a group effort. And seeing as how you didn't realize it was your birthday party until nine years later, I don't think we can count Panda-monium."

"Fair."

"I made a list of everything Grandma Ruth *thought* she paid for: advertising, tent rental, *toilet* rental—"

"Very important."

"Perhaps the *most* important. Organizing vendors. Construction of two stages. And hiring more performers in addition to Spencer."

"Oh, they didn't hire me," Spencer piped up from somewhere out of sight.

"So creepy," Wes mouthed to Grace, who nodded.

"I work for tips," he added. "And not on stage. I wander. I'm a wandering minstrel—" he began to sing.

"Got it. No stage for you," Wes called.

"Forget the stage for now," Grace suggested. "What else?"

"That's basically the list of things she thought she was

paying for. Then there's the general bucket of things she expected them to arrange."

"Like tickets."

"Tickets, parking, food."

"Like I tell the kids when they're writing their research papers: one step at a time. Bird by bird."

"Bird by bird," Wes repeated. It was the title of Grace's favorite book on writing, but her friend believed it could be applied to any situation. "There's an old barn behind the house. Maybe we could use that for the pub instead of renting a tent."

Grace mimed checking something off a list, and weirdly, it made Wes feel a tiny bit better.

She scrolled through her phone again. Still no reply from Eòghann. Maybe she inadvertently offended him the last time they'd texted?

APRIL 22

Wes
Happy Earth Day. I suppose it's appropriate that it's been raining for something like 10 days straight.

Eòghann

Wes
I know. Believe me. But at the risk of sounding as old as you—we needed it.

Eòghann
I'm going to ignore that rude comment and assume it's the demon rain causing you to act out.

Wes
Does it make you want to put me over your knee, old timer?

Eòghann
Obviously. Do you get the day off to celebrate Earth Day?

If it weren't raining would you walk through a forest in your bare feet and touch some grass?

Wes
I mean yes, there's nothing insurance companies care more about than the earth, so of course we get the day off. (lol)

Gray wants to go to a special pollinator exhibit at the zoo. She must be the only woman on the planet who gets hot and bothered over bees.

Eòghann
Is there a choking emoji? I need a choking emoji.

Wes
Kinky! And I'm serious! For obvious reasons, pollinators make her think of Bryan.

Eòghann
...Ew?

Wes
What "ew"? Bryan has a bee tattoo on his forearm!

Eòghann
OH. Yes. He does.

Wes
YOU HAVE A FILTHY MIND PADRE

Eòghann
A thousand pardons.

Do you forgive me?

Wes
I'll consider it.

Eòghann
🙏

Wes
IF you answer a question. 😈

Eòghann
😬

Wes
😇

Eòghann
What's your question, Teal?

Wes
If you got a tattoo, what would it be and where?

Eòghann
...

Wes
Don't overthink it. Clock's ticking.

Eòghann
I already have a tattoo.

Wes
👀 Say more.

Eòghann
No.

Wes
What?!

Come on!

Please?

Eòghann

...

Wes

I'll show you mine if you show me yours!

Eòghann

Happy Earth Day, brat!

Had she taken the flirting too far with the spanking bit? She should've asked if he wanted to put her in the corner. Then he could have replied, *Nobody puts Wesley in the corner* and she could've swooned and he wouldn't be ignoring her now.

"Intruder!" the raven cawed, startling Wes as he took off from his perch in a nearby oak tree to soar out over the grounds.

A vehicle had turned up the drive, a big pickup truck hauling a camper van. Wes squinted and saw a second truck following right behind it.

"Maybe she didn't get scammed after all?" she wondered aloud. "Maybe *Exemplary Boiled Events* is here to start setting up?"

"That will never not be funny," Grace laughed.

"Intruder!" the bird screamed again.

Standing and shading her eyes with one hand, Grace smiled. "It isn't the event people."

"Are you sure?"

"I'm sure. Don't get mad..." Grace warned.

"Famous last words, Gray."

"I called Andy."

"What, last night?"

"If you want to be precise about it, he called me Tuesday night after pizza, and I mentioned something was up with Grandma Ruth and the house."

"Okay..."

Grace scrunched her face. "I may have texted him an update yesterday."

"The second we arrived?"

"No. But about five minutes after Grandma Ruth put on that Elizabethan dress."

"Gray."

"They want to help. And I knew you'd never ask them to."

"That's not true!" she protested, even though they both knew it was absolutely true.

"Name one time you've ever asked for help."

"I asked Bryan to help with your double quinceañera."

"You did?" Grace asked, her eyes going all soft at the mention of her boyfriend.

"No," Wes sighed and shook her head. "It was his idea. He asked me."

Instead of gloating that she'd won the argument, Gray's smile turned all melty and sweet over Bryan, and Wes rolled her eyes.

"The point is, it was my idea to try to forge ahead with this thing. They have jobs and lives and—"

"Wes, we all have fond memories of this place. And Grandma Ruth! She's like my second abuelita. She's the only grandma Sadie's ever known!"

"I know but—"

"And they're actually in the Ren faire business."

"Which means they already had obligations on the calendar they've now canceled to fly to my rescue!"

"Which *means* their feelings would be irreparably hurt if you didn't let them help with this."

"They could be blackballed. Breaking their contracts could ruin their careers, and then they'll hate me."

"I don't think it's that serious," Grace soothed, as the two trucks pulled off into the grass so as not to block the driveway.

But it would be that serious when her friends began to resent having dropped everything to bail Wes out. It would be seventh grade all over again. She sighed deeply.

"I said don't get mad."

"Cause that's how it works? You know asking for help gives me hives."

"Oh, I know. But you didn't ask. They volunteered. And, it's going to be fine," Grace assured her before she skipped out towards the first truck, squealing, "Andy!"

The stocky figure of Andy Darwish jumped out of the back seat, tossing his ashy brown hair out of his eyes, and catching Grace as she threw her arms around him and hugged him tight.

Wes hadn't seen him since Christmas, when he spent the holiday with his sister in Knoxville, but it had been much longer since she'd seen his two companions.

Sadie was next out of the truck, her long box braids gathered in a ponytail that nearly reached the waist of her jean shorts. She made a beeline for Wes, folding her up in her warmth and jasmine perfume as they rocked back and forth in each other's arms, and despite Wes being uncomfortable with the reason for their visit, she melted into her friend's embrace.

Last but not least, Jack stepped around from the driver's side, his jet black hair hidden under a Bodes Abiquiu trucker hat. "My turn," he murmured, and so Sadie stepped back to make room for him.

"Jack," Wes sighed, overcome with emotion at the whole reunion.

"It's been too long, Teal," he said, pulling Wes into his arms. "I think you've grown."

Wes laughed out loud. "You always forget I'm tall."

"Not this tall," he argued.

"I've been 5'11" since my senior year of high school."

"You've definitely grown. How you been?"

The question made her throat catch as he squeezed her tight, and she was instantly transported back to college, when his hugs felt like he needed them as much as she did.

"I've been good," she assured him. "You know. Same old."

When Jack let go, Andy was waiting, his sweet anxious face peering at her sideways from under his bangs. "Is it okay we're here?" he whispered.

"It's always going to be okay," Wes said, and it was true. These were her people. She'd never be sorry to see them, even if they showed up to help where they weren't needed, even if they came because they thought they had to, even if they all ended up regretting it in the end. "What the heck possessed you to come though?" she demanded.

Andy shrugged one shoulder. "We got bored in Ohio."

"Bored," Wes repeated skeptically.

"So bored," Sadie echoed.

"I hope we never go back to Ohio," Jack added.

"That's good, since I'm guessing you probably had to piss some people off to get here this fast."

They all shrugged sheepishly.

"Drove through the night," Jack said. "No big."

"Worth it," Andy added. "And we brought friends!" He gestured to the other truck, where a tall, white man with reddish hair and three ginger kids were stepping out, stretching, and gawking up at Warwick Hall.

"I can see that. Who are they?"

"Danny and the Boys," Andy said. "They're a band. You're having a faire, right?"

"I guess we're going to need those stages after all," Grace said with a grin. "Is it me, or does he look a little like Bryan?"

"You think every handsome man with auburn hair looks like Bryan," Wes retorted.

Grace tilted her head like she was going to argue, but then

she said, "I can't help it if my man has all the best features of every other man."

Wes gagged and rolled her eyes, but it was actually pretty cute. She only hoped Danny and the Boys didn't end up hating her by the first weekend in June along with the rest of them.

A FEW HOURS LATER, WES LEANED AGAINST THE FOLDING table on the back porch, where her grandmother was dishing up bowl after bowl of gumbo from a pair of giant crockpots.

"This is great," Wes told her. "But why did you have so much in your freezer?"

"Because the recipe makes enough to feed the 412th Test Wing, and there's only me and Duncan here. Why do I suddenly have so many mouths to feed?"

"Well, you have all this space for a Ren faire, but no performers—"

"Except Spencer," Grandma Ruth reminded her.

"Except Spencer—"

"I don't need much space," Spencer piped up. "I'm a wanderer, remember? It's sort of my thing."

"And our friends all happen to be Ren faire performers who we haven't seen in years, and Grace and I thought isn't this situation ideal?"

"That's exactly what I said to her," Grace piped up. "Warwick Hall would be ideal."

"Cut the crap, girlies. I've seen *White Christmas*. I'm the one who showed you *White Christmas*. And I may be fool enough to get scammed, but how does this help?"

"I told you. We're going to postpone the faire until June."

"They're more than just the entertainment," Grace piped up. "They're here to help make it happen."

"Sweetheart, it's going to take more than some pretty faces to turn this place into a real faire."

Jack preened. "She thinks we're pretty?"

"Do you trust me, Grandma Ruth?" Andy asked, putting an arm around her shoulders.

"Don't answer that," Jack cut in before she could.

"You, I trust," she replied, patting Andy on the cheek. He'd always been her favorite member of the Shakespeare Syndicate, even more so than Wes, she secretly suspected.

"Good. 'Cause we've been at this a long time," Andy said. "I think we have the knowledge and business expertise," here he gestured to Sadie, "to help you pull off something special."

"Not to mention contacts," Jack added. "We have some of the finest musicians and artisans on speed dial and on the way. In the meantime—"

"We're at your disposal," Andy said, finishing his sentence with a little bow like the well-rehearsed duo they were. "You need stages? We can build stages...?" he said, casting a dubious glance at Jack, who nodded back uncertainly.

Grandma Ruth laughed. "You've certainly always had charisma, I'll give you that."

Andy grinned.

"We juggle fire now, too," Jack boasted.

"*Not* near the house."

"No, ma'am."

"And *not at all* if we're under a no burn order."

"Cross our hearts," Andy promised. "If it would make you feel better, we could ask Danny and the Boys to sing. Sort of an audition?"

"That's not necessary," Wes piped up, but Grandma looked intrigued.

"It's no problem. You'll love them. Gallifrey!" Andy shouted, and the father of the boys, or Wes assumed he was their father unless he was in the habit of picking up stray ginger children on the side of the road, turned his way.

"What kind of name is Gallifrey?" Wes whispered.

"A made up one," Andy whispered back. "How about a song for our hostess?" he called to the band.

"Of course," the man replied in a mild Scottish accent, as he set down his spoon and nudged the boy next to him to do the same.

"They can finish eating first," Wes said, glaring at Andy, who mouthed *It's fine*, and took the lens cap off his fancy camera to capture the moment.

Gumbo abandoned, the family gathered their instruments. The Scotsman took a guitar from the oldest boy, who carried a second one for himself. The middle son handed off a tambourine-like drum to his younger brother, who was still shoveling food in his mouth but accepted the drum reluctantly, while the middle boy settled into a set of bagpipes.

They started with a jaunty jig or reel or whatever kind of Celtic music made your feet tap right off your legs of their own volition. When they finished, the youngest boy set down his drum and went back to his food, but the father whispered something to the other two, and the bagpipe was set aside on a chair. They transitioned to a slower song that sounded almost mournful, no less so when the middle boy, tapping out a rhythm on his thigh, began to sing "The Fields of Athenry" in a melancholy treble.

Goosebumps ran down Wesley's arms despite the muggy late May heat.

"This makes me miss you so much," Grace crooned into her phone, where she'd been filming the audition.

"Fine," Grandma Ruth said, clapping her hands when they finished. "You can perform every set if you want to. As long as there's no child labor laws against it. When do we open?" she teased.

"One step at a time," Wes replied, laughing. "And say hello to the Stoic Scot for me," she teased her friend, trying to ignore the green-eyed pang of jealousy that struck her sideways as she remembered a certain dusty-blonde Scot of her own, Father What-a-Waste. Whoever let him take holy orders deserved a lifetime of damp socks and sodden sweater sleeves, not that she'd have let his title stop her if he'd been keen.

She'd probably come on a little too strong, to be honest—and if she *was* being honest, she had no right feeling jealous of Grace. She'd chosen Eòghann exactly because she didn't want a relationship and because he was unavailable. This way she could flirt, and she could pine, but no one was in danger of falling in love, and she could pour her emotions into platonic affection. Because no matter how fondly she texted her summer-fling-that-almost-was, no matter how real their *situationship* occasionally felt, at the end of the day, he was still a priest.

That was what she wanted, and that was what she'd chosen, and the fact that he hadn't texted her back simply served as a good reminder. They weren't dating. They never would.

Shaking her head to clear it, she bent close to her list and circled *stage*. Even without a stage, they had music and honestly between that and a queen, what more did a Renaissance faire need?

Glancing around at all of their cheerful, happy faces, Wes felt a little bit removed, like she was watching them through a television screen instead of being there with them.

She checked her phone for the millionth time, craving Eòghann's calm and soothing banter, but there was still no reply to her earlier message.

Wes
I truly am the worst.

When no bubble appeared indicating a response-in-progress, she paused to calculate the time difference. It wasn't late at all, but maybe he was busy.

Maybe he was busy with a woman. Hearing her confession. Or not. After all, he was only human, and Wesley wasn't sure what the rules were, but she was pretty sure there must be wiggle room.

She didn't like the thought of him wiggling with anyone because she actually kind of was the worst, and so she kept typing. Happy to interrupt.

Wes
I have the best friends in the entire world. They showed up like the cavalry to help with Grandma's faire.

I'm so happy to see them. And I wish they'd all leave.

Wes
Story time? Picture it: Sleepy Hollow, 2007. A middle school trip. Word got around that the boys' swim team was going to force a new scholarship kid to swim across the Hudson River to put him in his place.

Even at 12 I knew it was stupid. I asked a chaperone for help. She said boys will be boys and no one likes a tattle tale.

Wes

So I asked my friends. Not these friends,
different friends. Half of them helped the
other half of us sneak out of the hotel, and we
confronted the boys before anything bad
happened, but all the yelling on the riverbank
drew attention. Predictably, we got in a metric
ton of trouble. We were banned from
overnight travel for the rest of the school year,
which meant we were kicked off our sports
teams. My friends never forgave me. That's
not hyperbole. I had to start all over and find
new friends. Even the new kid never
forgave me.

Wes

So there. My greatest confession. I know this
isn't the same as that. These friends—they
aren't a bunch of fickle adolescents. But things
go wrong. And it's silly to ask for their help
when I don't need it, you know?

You don't have to answer, by the way. I
suppose my penance would be to accept the
help they want to offer. I'm not sure I can.

Chapter Five

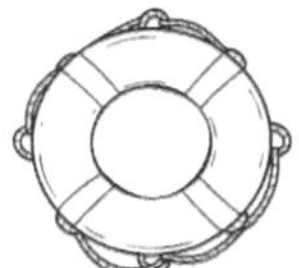

BARRA, SCOTLAND

The pub was busy for midweek, but Eòghann liked it busy. Somehow it made him feel a part of something so much larger than the tiny island in the middle of the sea.

He chuckled, because he reminded himself of Mrs. Bennett bragging, "We dine with four-and-twenty families," in *Pride and Prejudice*, but honestly, the Bennetts might've had a greater social network then Eòghann MacNeil did. He knew everyone, but he rarely felt a part of it all.

Karaoke at the pub helped.

"I'm bored," Lùcas Buchanan, his young cousin sighed, sliding into the seat across from him.

"Thought you'd be first in line to sing."

Lùcas shrugged glumly. "It's all the same songs, all the same people. Don't you ever get tired of it?"

"The island's swamped with tourists for the festival. What're you on about?"

"*You* always said not to get mixed up with tourists," Lùc

complained. "Even though you and Bryan ignore your own advice."

Before he could argue with Lùc, Father Murphy called, "All right, Eòghann?" and crossed the pub to shake his hand.

"Aye. Any jobs need doing?"

Father Murphy frowned, trying to think. "Not at the moment," he said, before sliding onto a bar stool in front of a pint of bitter. "The old Star of the Sea is ship shape these days thanks to you."

Eòghann nodded and disappointment must've shown on his face because the priest quickly added, "If I hear of any parishioners who need a hand, I'll send them your way."

"Ta," Eòghann told him, taking a long, slow sip of his Stornaway ale and then checking to see if the table would rock under the weight of his elbows. He could fix a wonky table leg, no problem and no charge. But the table stood firm against his attempt to make it shake. Maybe he was in a rut like his cousin.

Lùcas slid down in his chair. "I'm so bored," he repeated, rocking his head against the back of the chair and glaring a hole through the ceiling.

"Auntie Eilidh would say only boring people are bored."

"Pish off. She told me she was bored last week watching football."

"Rugby's more her game."

Lùcas tilted his head, lifting his eyebrows thoughtfully in a way which suggested he could get behind a bit of rugger.

"Why're you so bored then? Thought you were off to Edinburgh for the autumn term?"

The boy's face fell. "Haven't decided," he muttered. Homesick, and he hadn't set foot off the island yet. It was kind of sweet.

Eòghann tried to suppress a fond smile, wondering—if he himself had left home straight out of school, in the parallel universe where such a thing were possible—would he have been more like Bryan? Raring to go without a backward glance? Or like Lùcas, wistful hesitance tempering his enthusiasm?

The world would never know because Eòghann had never possessed the strength nor the ambition to overcome his fear.

"Haven't decided? Of course you must go. It'll be a grand adventure," he told his young cousin. "But I hear if you're a good lad, they let you come back time to time."

That earned a small smile.

"Go on now, give us a song. Some Kylie Minogue or Lewis Capaldi or summat."

"Fine," Lùcas sighed dramatically, and pushed himself up from the table, heading for the karaoke stage in the corner.

Hannah, the server, brought Eòghann another round, but maybe he'd had too much already because he found himself staring into the residual foam, contemplating it like the beer held the mysteries of the universe.

"Any wobbly tables need mending?" he called after her.

"Don't think so, love," Hannah answered on her way back to the bar.

Lùc's chair scraped shrilly against the stone floor as it was dragged back, but this time a different cousin dropped down, and Bryan was practically vibrating with excitement.

"All right?" Eòghann asked.

"Why aren't you answering your phone?"

Eòghann had prepared for this moment. He took a sip of his drink and calmly replied, "Lost it."

"Lost it?" Bryan repeated. "Where?"

Eòghann stared dumbly at him.

"Right. Apologies." He glanced around at the nearby tables as though the errant phone were misplaced in the last few minutes, and something about that action being so very Bryan made Eòghann smile.

"I lost it in the sea," he confessed.

Bryan froze, staring at him, a thousand questions flitting across his eyes, each of them failing to make it past his lips.

"Or at the beach anyway." Eòghann rubbed his sweaty palms on his trousers and then crossed his arms. "You tried to call?"

"Called. Texted. I was about to send a carrier pigeon. I've found someone," Bryan said, a huge grin spreading across his face.

Eòghann searched his memory for their last conversation. Bryan and his investor had broken ground on their eco distillery several months ago and they were itching to get their new still installed.

"Someone to operate the still?" Eòghann asked.

Bryan's auburn brow furrowed in confusion. "Oh. Yes. But no."

He passed his phone over, pressing play on a video. Eòghann squinted against the reflection of a nearby lamp. The video showed Grace Rios, Bryan's American girlfriend, and Eòghann flicked his gaze up to his practically giddy cousin who nodded back down at the phone. The bar was too noisy to hear what Grace was saying, but she quickly turned the camera around and after a bit of shaking, she zoomed in on a man in a baseball cap singing and playing guitar alongside three boys, one of whom held a bagpipe.

"You worried she's going to fall for a different Scotsman?" he teased.

Bryan's open, expectant face turned to one of exasperation. "Look at him, man," he demanded, nodding back to the video.

So Eòghann took his reading glasses from his breast pocket and peered down at the phone once more, but a clue would've been nice. He tilted his ear towards the phone speaker, hoping to hear anything which might help him give Bryan the reaction he was clearly expecting.

Bryan snatched the phone back, using his thumb and fore-finger to zoom in on the grainy video before angling it towards Eòghann again. "Look at his face and tell me that's not Alec."

Exasperated himself, Eòghann glanced back at the video, but then his eyes snapped back up to his cousin. "Our Alec?"

The glee returned to Bryan's eyes. So Eòghann looked down at the video again. The man stood a few meters away from the camera, his eyes obscured by the shade of his cap bill. It was probably wishful thinking on Bryan's part, right? It must be.

Eòghann squinted more. Shave Bryan's beard and add a few years?Bryan and Alec had always looked like brothers—like someone did a copy and paste of their Grandad Mac.

The middle boy set down his pipes, and Grace zoomed the video in closer. The child looked so much like Alec did at twelve, it was startling. Speaking of copy-paste. He started to sing, and Eòghann turned the volume all the way up, holding the speaker close to his ear.

When he heard the boy's voice, a chill ran down his spine and for a moment he was back at school, listening to Alec sing with the choir, looking daggers at any lad bold enough to snicker. His gaze drifted to Bryan's excited one, yanking him back to the present.

"You have to come with me," Bryan begged.

A cold wave sloshed over Eòghann, the past and the present colliding, and he shook his head, setting down the phone as the video continued to play.

"You've a p-passport, haven't you?"

"I have. Lord knows why." Wishful thinking a few years after Teàrlach got his pilot license.

"Because you hoped someday you'd use it. Come on," Bryan pleaded.

Eòghann kept shaking his head, like he was some kind of bobble head toy that couldn't stop.

"Eòghann I know, all right. But it's Alec!" His eyes were dancing. Glistening.

How could Eòghann tell him that it wasn't only the water that was insurmountable when it came to Alec, but everything else, too?

When Alec left, his aunties and neighbors had passed each other knowing glances. He'd wanted to study medicine, and so they'd urged him to go, but in their hearts they all believed the words they whispered later—that he was too much his mother's son to ever stay. Evelyn Murray MacNeil had a restless spirit, and when she couldn't convince Pòl to leave with her, she left them both behind, though Alec was only tiny.

They said it had always been a matter of time until Alec followed in her footsteps, but Eòghann knew the truth. He'd known it the day Alec left and every day that he never returned.

Bryan may have found their long-lost cousin, the missing musketeer who'd pissed off to Glasgow—to the mainland and then the world. But Eòghann was the reason he'd left as well as the reason he never returned. One by one those musketeers had left, first Alec, then Bryan, then Teàrlach. Sometimes Eòghann liked to pretend he'd stayed, not because the water kept him imprisoned like Elba or Alcatraz, but because the family needed him there. That he stayed so his cousins could be free. And for the most part, he'd been content confined to his little island jail. It was only the awareness he could never leave that made him claustrophobic.

"I know it's asking a lot. Too much probably," Bryan said, his voice gentler than Eòghann deserved.

Eòghann shook his head. "Alec went no-contact for a reason."

Now Bryan was shaking his head. "He didn't though. You

kept in touch for a few years and so did we. Then I got busy and self-centered and sort of lost track of him."

"He knows where we are. The island hasn't been swallowed up by the Bermuda Triangle for Christ's sake," Eòghann said, unpausing the video.

"Maybe he didn't know how to come home," Bryan replied, so earnest his voice cracked.

Looking up, Eòghann found himself locked in his cousin's steady gaze.

"P-please come with me. It has to be you and me. Together."

Impossible. If his last attempt at therapy had shown him anything it was the futility of trying to escape.

"You think he'll tell you to shove off and welcome me with open arms?" Eòghann asked, trying to understand why the usually independent Bryan was so insistent he come along.

"I'm afraid I'm not enough. But together we might convince him to come home." Bryan shrugged one shoulder. "Don't make me go alone," he pleaded.

"Go where?" Lùc asked, taking the seat next to Bryan, and glancing curiously between them.

"I know, all right. I know," Bryan repeated, because Eòghann was shaking his head again. "I know, but I'll get you s-so drunk you won't know you've left your house."

The alarm on his stupid watch started to chirp as Eòghann tried to pull deep breaths out of his pinched lungs.

"Can I come?" Lùcas asked, not knowing or caring where to.

"Aye, if you can help me convince him."

"Come on, Eòghann," Lùc joined in. "Of course you must go, it'll be a grand adventure," he teased, echoing Eòghann's own words back to him. "An adventure before my adventure?" he urged. "Where are we going anyway?"

"Tennessee," Bryan answered.

"Is that in Africa?" Lùc asked, and Eòghann coughed out a laugh that finally loosed the boa constrictor around his chest.

"What did they teach you in school?"

Lùc shrugged. "I didn't take geography A levels."

A voice on Bryan's video caught Eòghann's attention, soft and musical like a chime in a summer breeze. "One step at a time," she said, and then the camera panned shakily over to Wes, and the whole world seemed to freeze in rapture at her beauty, and Eòghann's chest loosened a tiny bit more.

"Ohh, Tennessee," Lùcas said, turning the phone towards himself and playing it again. Time hadn't frozen after all, Grace's video had simply ended.

Eòghann wiped his sweaty palms from knee to thigh, over and over, and he glanced up to meet Bryan's gaze once more.

A small smile tugged at his cousin's lips. The bastard knew he wouldn't be able to say no after seeing Wes on that video.

Eòghann nodded once, shakily. "It's going to take something stronger than this bloody ale."

Chapter Six

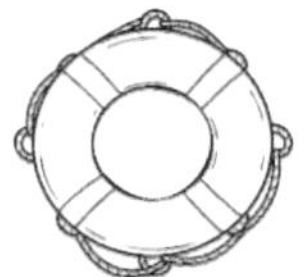

STRATFORD, TENNESSEE

That evening, Wesley's thoughts strayed back to Barra as she washed up in Grandma Ruth's kitchen, back to stormy green eyes and dirty blonde hair, a soft beard and a wry sense of humor. Something about the shape of the Scottish musician's lips reminded her of Eòghann. Maybe it was a Scottish thing?

Or maybe she was down bad just like Grace.

She really needed to get laid.

But she wasn't about to try a vacation fling with a father of three. Should she have said yes when Kevin from work asked her out? As a general rule she shied away from office hookups. It would've made things weird at work and all the weirder when she next texted Eòghann. *Forgive me, Father, for I have really messed up this time...*

If she ever heard from him again.

"If you scrub that any longer you'll take the enamel off it," Grandma Ruth teased, sidling up to her elbow.

"Just thinking," Wes said rinsing the crockery and setting it in a rack to dry.

"Oh?"

"I wish they didn't feel obligated to come to our rescue," she said, turning her thoughts back to safer territory. "But I have to admit, everything feels a bit more manageable with them along for the ride."

"You don't always need to do everything yourself," Grandma reminded her.

"That's what I keep trying to tell her," Grace piped up from the kitchen table, where she was having a cup of delightful-smelling tea.

"Says the woman who didn't call me to ask for help when she got scammed?"

"Stop changing the subject," Grandma Ruth grumbled. "I think it's lovely your friends are here."

"Listen, I'm not proud of myself. But I've been on my own a long time. Old habits, and all that."

Her grandmother regarded her for a moment, but instead of arguing she said, "You've managed to assemble a cracker jack team."

"Someone did anyway," Wes replied, joining Grace at the table and pouring her own cup of tea.

"You're welcome." Grace offered her an angelic smile.

Wes slid her iPad across the table. "I think I got a pretty good idea of where everything should go when we walked the grounds earlier," she began. "I drew up a sketch—not to scale or anything, but it should help us get started."

Grace studied the map and nodded. "How big do you want the stages? The boys can pick up lumber tomorrow morning."

"They don't have to do that."

"Are you and Grandma Ruth going to do it?"

"She has a point," Grandma said.

Wesley scowled in response. Best friends they might be, but it was bad enough they had all rushed to Tennessee. She couldn't ask them to do manual labor in the heat whether they'd volunteered or not. "Maybe we could hire someone."

"We can. We can hire Jack and Andy. I hear they come cheap."

Wes rolled her eyes.

"They're here," Grace insisted. "Where's the harm in putting them to work?"

"Are you sure about the stages, Grandma? You don't think it might hurt the..." She swallowed. "The resale value?"

"If buyers don't like it, they can tear them down again," Grandma scoffed.

Wes loved her fire, and who was she to argue? She wasn't her mother. She could let it go. To prove it, she pointed to the map. "How many vendors do you suppose we can fit along here? I envisioned a sort of alley—booths along both sides with a lane down the middle. But that's assuming we can find enough vendors."

"Merchant's Close," Grace mused, trying out the name for Wesley's alley. "I wonder if Exemplary Boiled Events invited any vendors at all."

"Maybe, but who knows what date they said to show up, given how early Spencer got here," Wes pointed out.

"True. Sadie's making her own list of sellers to invite," Grace said. "If more show up..."

"We'll find somewhere to put them, don't you worry," Grandma Ruth said.

Wes checked off vendors for the time being. "I'll send out a notice to local food trucks. Did you have any specific types in mind?"

"I told the events people they could do whatever they wanted as long as there were turkey legs and fish 'n chips.

What's a seven letter word for idiot?" she asked, looking up from her crossword puzzle, where that definitely wasn't a real clue.

"If it's dumbass, it better not be," Wes told her. "I can't promise turkey legs, but none of this is your fault."

Sipping her tea, she allowed herself to be transported back to last summer's carefree vacation once more. She wondered what Eòghann would've made of this whole situation. She could imagine his eyes twinkling with mirth—once everything was under control.

And everything would be under control soon. It would all be fine.

"Oh look!" Wes said. "There's a database where you can list your event and let food trucks contact you! I guess we need a website."

"You don't need a website," Andy argued, entering the kitchen. "Just create a Facebook event."

"I abhor Facebook."

"Sadie can help," he suggested.

"I don't need help. I simply despise everything Meta stands for."

"Make an exception? For Grandma Ruth?" he said, squeezing Grandma's shoulder. "Part of running a business is dealing with—"

"The devil?"

"—with things like Facebook."

Wes sighed her disdain.

Grandma patted Andy's hand still resting on her shoulder. "Adnan," she said, using his formal Syrian name instead of his nickname. "I think your telescope might still be out in my garage somewhere."

A faraway smile crossed his face, like he hadn't thought about the little blue telescope in years. "I'll look for it later," he promised. "Gall called some friends—The West Highland

Tarriers. They're a sort of Celtic rock fusion band. They can be here by June."

"His name is really Gall? The hot dad?" Wes whispered to Grace.

"Short for Gallifrey."

"But, again, what the hell kind of name is Gallifrey?" Wes asked, and Grace shrugged.

"Anyway, that's two bands, plus Jack and me," Andy went on, picking up a clementine and an apple from the fruit bowl on the table, tossing them into the air, and juggling them.

"Do you really juggle fire while you tell jokes?" Wes asked, wrinkling her nose in concern. She loved her friends, but the last thing she needed was to be held responsible for smoke in the Smoky Mountains.

"Only a little," he answered, tossing the clementine to Grace and biting into the apple. "Need anything from the hardware store while we're out tomorrow?"

"A hunky, tight-jeans wearing handyman?" Grandma Ruth asked, looking up from her crossword once more.

"I'll see what I can do," Andy said, tossing her a wink.

"Take my credit card. It's there in my pocket book," Grandma said, pointing towards the foyer, but Andy waved her off.

"You don't need to go at all," Wes told him. "Seriously, we can—"

"We got this," he said, planting a kiss on the top of Wesley's head. "Let us take this one thing off your plate," he added before heading out.

"I like that one," Grandma Ruth said, studying Wes. "He's a good egg."

"Don't start, Grandma. That one's not for me."

"I wasn't born yesterday. I know he's had an unrequited thing about Jack for—"

"Ever," Grace piped up.

Grandma nodded. "But I've always liked him."

"Me too," Wes agreed, turning back to her iPad list. "Do you think we should go on the news and tell people not to show up this weekend?"

"Wait, if there's no website how were they selling tickets?"

"Through one of those event sites," Grandma answered. "And there *is* a website, but it's full of malarkey."

Wes and Grace stared at each other a minute, but then a quick internet search brought up a page for the Stratford Renayzants Faire.

"They can't spell Renaissance but they got the *e* in faire?" Grace murmured.

A photoshopped picture of Grandma's house was right there on the landing page, along with creepy, plastic-realistic photos of armor-clad jousters, kiddie rides, winged vendors, six-fingered musicians, the works.

"What in the AI fever dream?" Grace whispered.

Wes clicked on the link for tickets, and it took her to a second site which showed two thousand people following the event. She glanced at Grace who was wide-eyed, trying to do the mental math.

"So if ten percent of them bought tickets at thirty-five dollars a pop..."

"Seven thousand dollars," Wes whispered.

"Hopefully they're willing to come back in a few weeks. Definitely go on the news."

Wes took a deep breath and then another, trying to silence the voice in her head, which was screeching one long drawn-out word: *Fuuuuuuuuuuuuck.*

"I wonder if we could find these assholes through the website," Grace mused.

Wes shrugged. She didn't even know how to set up a

Facebook event. There wasn't time to play internet Nancy Drew.

"I bet Beatrix could find them," Grace muttered.

"Don't involve Bea. What would be the point? This kind of stuff happens all the time. It'll be their word against Grandma's. They'll say she knew what she agreed to. They'll make her look silly."

"I already look silly."

"Did you pay them by check or credit card?" Wes asked.

"Check," Grandma said.

"Have you tried to stop payment on it?" Grace suggested.

"It's too late. The one thing they *did* do was cash the check."

Grace frowned. "What about a dispute or fraud claim with the bank?"

"I can do that?"

"I think so," Grace assured her.

"I'll go to the bank tomorrow. Suppose it'll make Maude's day to laugh at me."

"I'm sorry this happened." Wes squeezed her grandma's hand.

"Personally, I say it's all the more reason to track them down," Grace insisted. "We need to stop them from doing this to other people."

"I'll drink to that," Grandma Ruth agreed.

"What we need is to get this website shut down." Wes scrolled to the bottom of the page and clicked REPORT EVENT.

"Where are two thousand people going to park?" Grace wondered. "Were you serious about the front yard?"

Wes looked to her grandma. "We could fit a lot if we parked them all the way back to the road."

Grandma nodded. "If we're going to pack that many in, we're going to need a lot more than two bands and a comedy act, no matter how charming they are."

Wes took a gulp of tea to wet her parched throat. Maybe she had bitten off more than she was ready to chew. She added parking volunteers to the list.

"I'll need a court," Grandma said.

"You want to take the event people to court?"

"Ladies in waiting. If I'm going to be the Queen, the Queen needs to hold court."

"Of course," Grace agreed. "Can I be in your court?"

"Do you have a costume?"

"I know where I could get one."

"Welcome to my court, Lady Gray."

Grace grinned and whispered, "Lady Gray," to herself.

"We should have human chess!" Grandma suggested. "And maypole dancing. And a joust!"

"I'm not sure I can manage a maypole," Wes said, heart breaking a little. It had always been their very favorite part of any faire, but it seemed like a tall order—no pun intended. "There could still be dancing though?" she suggested. "Even without a pole?"

Grandma Ruth nodded slowly. "Don't forget the joust."

"Jousting, Grandma?"

"Fine, skip the joust," she pouted. "How about axe throwing? And archery?"

Wes took another deep breath. Surely that would require a lot of insurance. "Think they'd settle for a dartboard or two inside the barn?"

"That old red barn?"

"Is there another one?" Wes asked. "I thought maybe we could use it for the pub instead of renting a tent."

Grandma pointed. "Under the sink. Rubber gloves and masks. Whoever goes in that barn is going to need them."

Wes swallowed. She'd definitely bitten off more than she could chew, but when had that ever stopped her?

THAT NIGHT SHE COULDN'T SLEEP. THERE WAS STILL NO reply from Eòghann, and she knew she was being ridiculous, knew Bryan would tell Grace immediately if something bad had happened, but what if he'd been hiking and fallen off a cliff and no one had noticed?

She scrolled back through their messages again. He'd asked about Thanksgiving, and she'd told him about convincing her mom and Grandma Ruth to go out to eat instead of cooking. Then she had texted him about the winter solstice. She hadn't realized it was the solstice until Grace had mentioned it, probably after talking to Bryan. He'd seemed off that night. Not quite his usual teasing self.

DECEMBER 21

Wes
Happy Solstice. Have they put you in the
corner at the ceilidh again?

Eòghann
Skipped the ceilidh. I prefer a quieter, less
social acknowledgement of midwinter.

Wes
Fair. It's cold and dark. Were you hibernating
like a Hebridean bear all on your own?

Eòghann
Hiked up to the standing stone near Brevig
with Bryan and Lùc to watch the sun come up
and go down again.

Wes
How long was it up?

Eòghann
About an hour. We shared a dram.

Poured one out for cousin Pòl, Uncle Rob,
Great Uncle Cormac, and my da.

> **Wes**
> How positively pagan of you!

Eòghann
It's meant to be a symbol of death and rebirth,
but I've always tended to focus on embracing
the darkness and letting go of the past.

> **Wes**
> And have you?

Eòghann
Can't say letting go is really my forte, but the
ritual is comforting. I embraced the darkness
with both arms.

> **Wes**
> Because tomorrow there'll be more light?

Eòghann
Look at you, speaking of pagan. Careful, or
you'll be dancing naked around a fire before
you know it.

> **Wes**
> Gray and I are helping our friend Rebecca
> celebrate her divorce. Naked dancing is next
> on the list!

Eòghann
Definitely a sort of rebirth. Very nice.

> **Wes**
> It HAS been nice. Her ex was a dick, and her
> brother Andy is in town. We baked cookies
> and stuffed our faces and burned pictures of
> Marshall-fucking-Majors in effigy.

Eòghann
The ancestors would approve.

She hadn't taken any extra time off for Christmas, but they had texted nearly every day while she was working. At times he was a little less flirty and a little more philosophical, which she supposed went with the priestly territory, but she lived for their daily banter.

JANUARY 1

Eòghann
Happy Hogmanay, American.

> **Wes**
> Happy New Year. Tell me all your resolutions.

Eòghann
No.

> **Wes**
> Yes. I insist.

Eòghann
Such a bossy breeches.

> **Wes**
> ...I'm waiting.

Eòghann
Not a resolution, exactly. But I'm trying to live more boldly.

> **Wes**
>
> A worthy endeavor.

Eòghann
What's yours then?

Wes
Ehh.

Eòghann
Come on. Fair's fair.

> **Wes**
> I know, but mine feels shitty to say after yours.

Eòghann
?

Wes

Eòghann
You've resolved to wear a levitating light tiara?

> **Wes**
> I mean, I'd look amazing.

Eòghann
Obviously.

You've resolved to sing with a heavenly choir?

> **Wes**
> Have you forgotten hearing me sing at
> karaoke?

Eòghann
Brat.

> **Wes**
> UGH. Fine. A long time ago I resolved to stop
> making New Year's resolutions.

Eòghann

> **Wes**
> I think they're mostly sort of awful. All they do
> is pit you against yourself, with impossible
> goals that set you up to be disappointed.

Eòghann
I mean, yes. That's what they're for. How else can you get your annual dose of self-loathing in one quick and easy fix?

> **Wes**
> But yours isn't like that. It's great! It seems totally doable.

Eòghann
Oh totally...

> > **Wes**
> > I believe in you, Padre.

Eòghann
...

> **Wes**
> I'm not blowing smoke. If you try, then you succeed because trying at all is "living more boldly." I love it. Honestly.

Eòghann
Thanks, Wes.

> **Wes**
> Maybe I should try to live more boldly too.

Eòghann
Doubt the world's ready for that.

She liked that he saw her as already bold. She'd never really thought about it before their exchange, but she supposed it was true.

Maybe she took after her parents—though she couldn't see herself flying into battle no matter how many demons she needed to exorcise. Maybe, then, her own brand of boldness had skipped a generation and instead she took after Grandma Ruth.

Chapter Seven

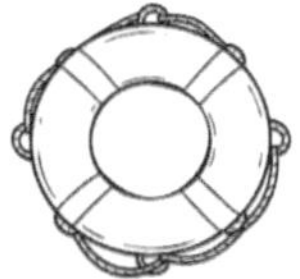

BARRA, SCOTLAND

Bryan purchased plane tickets right there in the pub, so Eòghann couldn't *shite it*, as though Eòghann wasn't perfectly capable of telling him to sod off and paying him back for the tickets when he failed to show. Though, given their flights left tomorrow, he was a little afraid to see the price tag.

After cramming whatever clothes were clean into a holdall, he spent the night sweating and vomiting and trying not to replay his every interaction with Wesley Teal on a loop, though focusing on her instead of the ocean he'd soon be flying over seemed to lower his panic from eleven to a cold, shivery but respectable six and a half for whole entire minutes at a time before he spiraled again.

Over the past year, he'd texted her when he felt anxious or gloomy, and every time he hit send he felt calmer. She made his heart speed up, but still there was something about the blonde American he found soothing. He wished he hadn't lost his phone so could text her now.

Last summer they had palled around together for weeks while Bryan was renovating his cottage and Grace was writing her book. Eòghann had shown Wesley all the sights, and she'd seemed eager to see every last one.

He'd helped her find the ruins of the ancient church at Borve, and he'd taken her to the best spots for admiring puffins and seals. She'd managed to convince him to swallow down his anxiety and join her at a party on the beach—more than once! A minor miracle. At the time, he'd almost believed he could follow her anywhere. He took comfort in how laid back she always seemed, never taking herself or anything else too seriously. She'd been absolutely determined to enjoy every last second of her visit, not bothered at all when they got caught in the rain while hiking or had to wait ages to buy a souvenir. *Vacation is for food and orgasms*, she had giggled, eyes wide as she stared down a decadent raspberry pavlova. *And sometimes both at once!*

At first, his favorite part was how little she actually knew about him, as though—with her—he could become a different version of himself, the person he wished to be. Later on, he began to appreciate how clearly she understood the parts of him he kept hidden inside. The way she teased him, and brought out his teasing. How his heart sped up each time she called him *Padre*. Why was that so hot?

Because no one had ever given him a nickname before, or not a nice one, anyway. During a pirate phase when they were ten, Marcus Beasley dubbed him Lily-livered Landlubber—Lily, for short, when adults were nearby. That one stuck around for years. But Padre was simple. Affectionate. A reminder of their first meeting that fateful day inside the church, and he liked it very much.

And soon he'd get to hear it in her sultry, Southern lilt because the image of her on Bryan's phone had filled him with longing and pushed him over the line into agreeing to the trip.

Because he liked to think if he had it to do over again, last summer would have turned out differently.

Wes had made it abundantly clear she'd be game to take things further if he wanted. But she'd left it up to him, never crossing any lines as they rambled around the whole island for days on end. He had meant to explain why he could never leave the day they hiked up Heaval to see the Madonna and Child statue, Our Lady of the Sea. Instead, he'd offered her a mere kernel of truth.

She had gazed out across the ocean as tourists particularly liked to do, and he'd been trying to avoid the view without making it weird.

"I never get tired of this," she admitted, glancing at him with a small, self-conscious shrug. "I grew up mostly landlocked except for the lake behind my grandmother's house. But I guess you take all this for granted, seeing it every minute of the day your whole life."

"I suppose," he had agreed. "Thing is..." He took a deep breath. "I don't really care for the water."

"Too much of a good thing," she laughed.

"My father loved it. He could never get enough. Acted like he was damn Poseidon most of the time."

Wes had eyed him carefully then, and he tried not to squirm under her scrutiny.

"That must have made things awkward."

Eòghann nodded. "He was a fisherman. And his whole personality was just fish. Boats. The water. If there was anything more to him, I never saw it. He wanted me to be a fisherman too, and I..."

"Had a different calling?"

"Aye, sure. I couldn't understand his passion, and he never understood my indifference," Eòghann had said, putting it mildly.

The truth was, they'd been equally passionate in opposite directions. He loathed his father's one great love—the sea—and it had driven a wedge between them.

"When did you lose him?" she asked.

"About six years back."

She'd smiled sadly then. "Goes to show... I always felt like I never quite knew my dad because I didn't have enough time. But I guess sometimes a whole lifetime isn't enough."

Eòghann nodded.

"Is it weird that makes me feel a little better?"

Her eyes had turned wistful and far away.

" 'Tisn't weird," Eòghann assured her. "You have to find peace where you can."

"I was nine when mine died, but I'd hardly seen him in the three years before that. I guess I don't know my mom all that well either. If your dad was all *fish* my mom's personality is top secret science. She plays her cards close to the vest. I suppose I should make more of an effort."

"You've always been petty well on your own?" Eòghann had asked, his heart splintering a little.

Wes nodded. "It's not so bad," she said, impulsively taking his arm for balance as they trekked back down to sea level.

Eòghann relished the closeness, all the little innocuous ways she found to touch him.

"Grace is constantly trying to earn her parents' approval, you know? Even now. After winning one of the most prestigious awards—maybe *the* most prestigious award—in her field. That shit'll do your head in."

"It will," Eòghann agreed, and she gave him a sidelong look but didn't pry, which he appreciated.

Because Eòghann got on fine with his mother. She was warm and kind and everything a mother ought to be. Only, he'd always craved more from her—explicit proof she didn't blame him for what happened to Pòl. Proof of her forgiveness. For his whole life he'd wanted to see her take his side against his father, but if she ever did, she did so in private. Otherwise, like the darkest of festering secrets, the accident was never mentioned at all. And now it was long since too late.

"Parents, am I right?" Wes had teased, squeezing his hand, but he caught her gazing out towards Kisimul, the castle ruin in the middle of the bay, where she'd tried to go exploring in Auntie Eilidh's old wreck of a dinghy and got caught in a storm.

His heart began to pound remembering that terrifying day once more, and he was off again, drowning in a whirlpool of panic, on and on the whole night long.

THE THREE COUSINS HAD PLANNED TO MEET AT BRYAN'S place, but there was one stop Eòghann needed to make first, and he was dreading it almost as much as stepping aboard Teàrlach's plane.

It had been too late to stop by his mother's cottage when he left the pub the night before, and besides that, he'd been completely foxed. He wasn't entirely sure he was sober now. He could certainly still smell the alcohol, as though it were coming out his every pore despite having showered.

She opened the front door before he could knock, almost as though she'd been waiting up all night for him to return after missing curfew.

"I'm meeting Mal for pilates in a bit," she explained. "She said Bryan convinced you to visit his American girl?" Ma tried to mask the concern in her voice with the enthusiasm any mother of any adult son would feel about him traveling abroad.

He and Bryan were in agreement not to mention Alec—not

until they knew if he'd welcome their visit and wouldn't mind coming back into the fold.

"I'm sorry to be leaving you," Eòghann whispered. "I don't know when I'll be back."

She smiled as he studied her beautiful, freckled face. There were a few more wrinkles around her eyes than he remembered. She was pushing seventy and widowed these last six years. How could he tell her he was half afraid if he made it off the island he'd never make it back again at all?

"I could cancel if you need me here. Bryan'd understand. Besides, he's got wee Lùcas."

She shook her head. "It's about time you went on a proper adventure, my boy. I'm proud of you."

"I've had plenty of adventures," he murmured. He wasn't exactly the adventuring kind.

"I said a proper adventure." She patted his cheek and nodded, holding his gaze. She understood exactly what he was thinking, as she always had. "Don't be sorry," she said gently. "I'm sorry—"

"Ma."

"I am," she said, her voice growing hard as her eyes went soft and she ran a thumb back and forth along his cheek. "For never giving your da the kick in the pants he deserved. He was too hard on you. We all knew it." She sighed. "Maybe if I'd set him straight when you were a wee lad, you wouldn't have been trapped here so long."

"Ma—"

"I can't say I'm sorry I've gotten the time we've had. But I'm glad to see you go."

Eòghann's throat was too tight to reply. Hearing her say it after all these years, a part of him felt like *of course*. Like he'd always known deep down she didn't blame him. Like he should have known. And a part of him didn't believe her at all—the part that wanted to press her on why she'd never spoken up before now.

"Thank you," he whispered instead.

"I'll be here when you come back." His frown must have deepened, because she added, "And if you don't come back, I've always wanted to see America. I'm not too old for my own adventure, you know." She squeezed his hand, giving him her blessing, and with it, revoking any excuse to back out on Bryan and Lùc.

"You look like hell," Teàrlach said when he welcomed the trio of cousins aboard his plane.

Eòghann smiled weakly, a smile he was pretty sure was actually a grimace and saluted the pilot with the travel mug Bryan had brought him filled with more whisky than coffee.

"What did you do to him?" Teàrlach whispered accusingly to Bryan, who looked him steadily in the eye, but didn't say a word.

Lùcas snickered.

Eòghann felt woozy.

"You sure about this, mate?" Teàrlach asked.

"Not even a little."

"But you're going to do it anyway?"

"My ma's proud of me, so."

Teàrlach shook his head and gestured for Bryan to lean down close. "If he's visibly drunk—"

He wasn't. Was he?

"—they won't let him board the next flight. Sober him up when you get to Glasgow."

The thought of flying sober made Eòghann's insides want to rebel, but he pushed it down and took a seat in the front row of the tiny plane, beach-side. *Water? What water?*

Bryan took the seat next to him and Lùcas sat across the aisle, as a handful of other passengers filed aboard. It was the Barra Barrachd Air festival, so while every seat would be taken on the way to the island, precious few were heading back to the mainland with them.

"Mask," Bryan said, holding out a satiny sleep mask that looked like something you'd get with a pair of sexy pajamas. He caught Eòghann's amused glance and shrugged, but before Eòghann pulled the mask over his eyes, his cousin stopped him. "One more thing."

Bryan held out his multi-colored worry stone, and heat rushed to the surface of Eòghann's fraught nerves.

"Go on. I think Grandad Mac would be very p—he'd be proud of you."

Bryan's Grandad Mac was Eòghann's Uncle Rob, and he'd always been very kind about Eòghann's anxiety, despite everything that happened. So Eòghann accepted the stone, clenching it tight in his fist, and he pulled the sleep mask over his eyes and pretended he was someone else, someone who could enjoy his first flight, could revel in the push and pull of gravity and the fact it was his baby cousin piloting the plane. He pretended they were simply flying over land. Easy as lying.

Then he sat back, relaxed, and prayed the Hail Mary in three languages.

He didn't consider himself particularly religious, but he thought—why not? Just in case? When he finished praying it in English, he ran through it in Gaelic too, for good measure.

Fàilte dhut, a Mhoire, tha thu làn de na gràsan...

When he finished that, it became an exercise in distraction to remember his Welsh.

Henffych well, Mair, llawn o nas...

He ran through each version over and over until they were wheels down in Glasgow.

Eòghann was the last one off the plane, not quite ready to peel himself out of his seat for a good few minutes, but he sent Bryan and Lùc on ahead. "Need a moment to catch my breath," he told them as cheerfully as he could muster.

Teàrlach met him, emerging from the cockpit after transferring to the tiny fold-up wheelchair that barely fit down the aisle.

"It was a great flight," Eòghann told him, not masking the pride in his voice. "Very smooth. "You're a wonderful pilot."

Teàrlach smiled. "You've been saying as much for years."

"I could tell it was true, watching you from the ground. But it was nice to experience it for myself."

"You don't have to go any further," his cousin said. "I can take you back home."

Eòghann shrugged. "I've come this far."

Teàrlach grinned at him, big and toothy and proud. "Yeah you fucking did. I should give you a pair of pin-on wings."

"Next time," Eòghann agreed, still not convinced there would ever be a next time.

As though he understood that possibility, Teàrlach nodded. "Promise," he agreed. "If you need anything, wherever you are in the world, call me. I'll come get you, whatever it takes."

Eòghann made his mouth smile, but his eyes felt hot again. He was the oldest. He was supposed to take care of the lot of them, not the other way around. After clearing his throat he rasped, "Lost my phone."

"Borrow Lùc's then. It'd give me a nice break from the memes he usually sends."

A laugh bubbled its way up his chest, and Eòghann embraced his cousin before heading off the plane and into Glasgow airport—where all at once the world became vastly bigger and faster and noisier than it had ever been in his life.

Chapter Eight

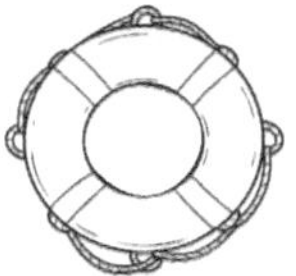

LONDON, ENGLAND

The flight from Glasgow to London was relatively uneventful, but if Eòghann thought Glasgow Airport was overstimulating, Heathrow was like Hogmanay and Disneyland all rolled into one, or so he imagined. It was bright and loud, a constant stream of people, of chatter, of languages and noise and smells bombarding him from every direction. Shops and restaurants, music and televisions, and yelling—so much yelling.

Lùc absorbed it all in wide-eyed wonder, but it made Eòghann's head-pounding hangover worse.

When they passed through the heavily perfumed Duty Free area, Lùc's eyes almost fell out of his head at all the items on offer: gallons of cologne, and special edition whisky, and chocolate bars as big as he was.

"This is amazing," he whispered.

"This is a living nightmare," Eòghann replied.

Taking pity on him, Bryan navigated them both into the back corner of a dimly lit, exorbitantly expensive restaurant, where they ordered coffee and steaks to soak up the leftover booze and make Eòghann feel almost human again.

Before long they were boarding their third plane of the day. The jet was about fifty times the size of Teàrlach's little plane, with two separate aisles and a row of seats down the middle.

Lùc continued to be delighted by everything, from the size of the overhead bins to the plastic bag with a blanket and pillow in his seat. Even Eòghann felt, if not excited, at least eager to get in the air and get things over with.

He was holding it together fairly well, *thank you very much*, until the flight crew mentioned the possible event of a water evacuation and demonstrated how to inflate your own life vest. Teàrlach had spared him that little speech, and taking off from Glasgow, Lùc had distracted him by showing him a video on his phone. This time Eòghann wished the oxygen masks would go ahead and fall, as his chest began to constrict.

"They're required to s-say all this," Bryan assured him, rubbing his arm, bringing him back. "For insurance. It's going to be fine."

"Course it is," Eòghann agreed, nodding a little too vigorously.

Bryan had booked three seats together in the center section, to keep Eòghann as far away from the windows as possible, which was damned thoughtful of him, but once the plane was in the air, Eòghann was tall enough to see out other people's windows and he couldn't find his silly satin sleep mask. Mostly he caught the occasional glimpse of sky and clouds—until the plane rolled enough to offer views of cresting ocean waves.

He took a deep breath. The air was so heavy inside the cabin.

"Watch a film?" Bryan suggested, but when he turned on the screen in the back of the headrest it defaulted to a flight tracking app that showed their position over the middle of the

North Atlantic—water, water everywhere, not a spec of land in sight.

Bryan quickly slapped at the screen until the movie menu appeared.

Eòghann turned on some inane comedy, but his mind wouldn't stop spinning through worst case scenarios. Possibly worse than crashing would be an emergency landing on a remote island, requiring him to board yet another plane—or, heaven forbid, a boat—to get back home.

And in the event of a water evacuation, what if his vest didn't inflate? Had it been tested? Recently? What if rats had chewed a hole in it after testing? Bryan could swim. He'd probably insist Eòghann take *his* vest while he clung to a floating piece of wreckage for as long as he could manage.

Or what if they survived the whole wretched flight, and then the guy in the video wasn't actually Alec, or worse, he *was* Alec but he wanted nothing to do with Eòghann and didn't hesitate to tell everyone the reason why? Sides would be chosen and lines drawn, and Wesley wouldn't want to text with Eòghann anymore, let alone do anything else, not after learning the truth. And Eòghann would be left all alone.

He'd probably wind up wandering the whole of the big, brash United States getting into fights with cowboys and being chased by hungry bears.

Bryan elbowed him.

"A drink, sir?" the flight attendant asked loudly, as though not for the first time.

Eòghann looked to either side and found both of his cousins nursing beers, so he gestured for the same. Then Bryan spoke softly to the young man who smiled sympathetically at Eòghann and gave him a small bottle of whisky, too.

"Ta," he managed gratefully.

They brought food next, and Eòghann lost track of how

many drinks he put down before they turned out the lights, effectively putting all the passengers down for a nap.

But the dark wasn't soothing.

The eerie emergency lighting reminded him of looking up from the darkness beneath the surface of the ocean towards the murky sky above. All around him people's movies ended and were replaced by the flight-tracking screen saver. Good news—they were still on course, somewhere over the godforsaken Atlantic.

"Big old ocean, innit?" he muttered as his head began to swim.

The alcohol had been a bad idea.

It was so hot. He fiddled with the air vent above his head, but it was blowing its hardest, and he was still too hot to breathe. Shouldn't it be colder inside a metal tube hurtling through the atmosphere? But perhaps, like Icarus, they were flying too close to the sun. Any minute now their wings would melt off, and they'd plunge straight down into the icy Atlantic, sinking like lead, never to be seen again. At least he wouldn't be so damn hot anymore.

The monitor on his watch began to beep as his heart started racing.

I am safe, he told himself, picturing his bed back at home.

The fuck you are, his brain replied, shattering any pretense of illusion.

He tried to imagine Wesley beside him. She'd take his hand and crack wise about her latest so-called sins. He would call her naughty and watch her eyes burn with lust, and then he'd apologize for playing it safe last summer.

When imaginary Wesley opened her mouth to reply, she demanded, "Safe? What're you so afraid of, ye jessie?" in his father's cruel sneer. Then she laughed at him, not her ethereal wind chime laugh but the mean-girl laugh of Annie Murray when Eòghann's father forced him to show up at her twelfth birthday party at the community pool.

Everyone knew Eòghann didn't swim. He didn't even own trunks. When Annie passed around the cupcakes, they ran one short. At first, he assumed it was a mistake. Of course, no one believed his ma when she RSVP'd on his behalf. It was a pool party after all—rude of him to defy expectations.

But then, "Oops," Annie had said, pointing to a single dessert floating on a plastic frisbee way out in the middle of the pool. "Looks like yours got away, Lily."

They all laughed: kids. Parents. Life guards.

"Happy Birthday, Annie," he told her before shoving her backwards into the pool.

His father had made sure he couldn't sit down for two days after that, but her furious scream had been worth it as she splashed about in her ruined pink party dress.

For years after, Eòghann had wondered whether his momentary rebellion and the shame it brought his father was why his old man dragged him out on the ill-fated fishing trip a few weeks later.

From the safety of 51 E, Eòghann tried to gulp in a deep breath and focus on literally anything else, but it was so hot and he couldn't get his lungs to remember how to inflate, and he needed to get off this plane. Crashing into the ocean would almost be worth it to make the nightmare end.

Climbing over a sleeping Bryan, Eòghann hurtled towards the toilet, barely getting the weird little folding door open in time.

The lavatory was cramped and sticky, far worse than his seat had been, but after emptying his stomach he was frozen in place, as though whatever stickiness coated the floor now trapped him like fly paper, and he began to shiver as his ears filled with buzzing cotton wool.

He was going to die in here in this hot, smelly tomb. He was fairly certain of it, as he slid to the floor and rocked back and forth, trying desperately to catch his breath. This was ridiculous. *He* was ridiculous. Irrational. He needed to go back to his seat and sit down like the grown-arse adult he was and stop acting like a child.

There was a banging sound from somewhere, either the blood beating in his ears or maybe an albatross had been sucked into an engine and they were actually going down, but how could one bird, no matter how large, make so much racket?

Then the lights went out, because Eòghann truly was in hell.

An eternity later, or maybe only a moment, the door was wrenched open and the dim light from the galley spilled in as the worried faces of Bryan and two strangers peered down at him.

They were going to pull the plane over and drag him off it now for sure, but he'd already be dead by then because he couldn't fucking breathe!

Slowly, gently, a flight attendant squatted down to Eòghann's level. His name tag was too blurry to read, but he said, "My name's Paulo," and of course it fucking was, like the ghost of his cousin Pòl had come to save him one more time. Eòghann's eyes felt hot and damp, like maybe they were bleeding. Did that happen when you were deprived of oxygen too long in an airplane lavatory?

"Eòghann?" Paulo asked, looking from him, back to Bryan, who nodded.

"Are you having trouble breathing?" Paulo asked, and this time Eòghann managed to nod himself. "Is there any chance it's anaphylaxis?"

He shook his head no.

"Good." Paulo smiled. "Last time someone needed epinephrine I stabbed it into my own thumb."

Eòghann choked out a tiny laugh, and it cracked the stranglehold on his lungs a little.

"Okay, Eòghann, what we're going to do is, we're going to breathe through this together, all right, my friend? Can you breathe with me? In through your nose—don't mind the smell. Means you're alive. Good. And out, slowly, through your mouth. You're doing great. One more for me?"

Paulo demonstrated a deep inhale that Eòghann tried to mimic.

"Well done, my friend. Breathe in for a count of four. Good, and then hold for seven. Five—six—seven, and out for eight. Good boy," he said, which was almost funny, since Paulo was probably half Eòghann's age, so why was it such a comfort to be called a good boy?

His heart rate slowed and the trembling began to subside, leaving Eòghann feeling almost too wrung out to be ashamed.

Almost.

"Can you stand?"

Paulo offered him a strong arm to pull himself up off the disgusting floor. His leg had gone to sleep, but Bryan took his other arm, and they helped him over to a fold-down flight attendant seat.

"I'm going to check your vitals, all right, my friend?" Paulo said, and Eòghann realized his stupid watch was still beeping.

"I don't know how to turn it off," he murmured apologetically.

"Are you afraid of flying?" Paulo asked gently as he wrapped a blood pressure cuff around Eòghann's arm.

"Not exactly," he rasped.

"It's the water," Bryan explained.

"That's good news then," Paulo said, removing the cuff and

handing Eòghann a cup of ginger ale to drink. "That's very good news, cause we aren't going anywhere near the water. If we did, the airline would try to claim we used up our PTO playing at the beach," he teased.

Eòghann took a tiny sip of the sweet drink. "I'm sorry," he whispered, the full force of his mortification beginning to catch up with him.

Paulo shook his head. "Happens all the time," he said, giving Eòghann's shoulder a friendly squeeze.

And whether it was true or not, Eòghann desperately appreciated him saying so. He almost wished he could pack calm, friendly Paulo up in his carryall and take him along to Knoxville, Tennessee.

Chapter Nine

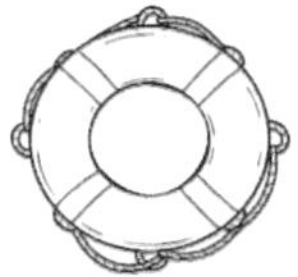

STRATFORD, TENNESSEE

Friday was a veritable hive of activity.

Grace had reached out to a former student who was interning with the local news station, and the girl put a bug in the right person's ear. They wanted to send a truck to Warwick Hall that afternoon.

Meanwhile the boys had taken measurements and headed out to buy lumber for the stages, while Wesley set about scrubbing the house from top to bottom.

"They're coming to do a piece about the faire, Wes. I don't think they're going to check for dust or examine the kitchen grout," Grace teased her.

"But what if they want to interview Grandma in her natural habitat? Or come inside to pee?"

"No interviews," Grandma Ruth grumbled.

"What?" Wes asked, scanning her face for signs of a joke.

"I don't want to end up on the Tube."

The Tube? Grace mouthed.

Wes had thought they'd all agreed to the same plan. "The

news van will be here in a few hours, Grandma. It's a little late to be worried about YouTube."

"I'll put on my Queen Lizzie dress and smile for the camera, but that's my final offer."

"But someone has to explain what's happened," Wes argued.

Her grandmother stared back at her, refusing to budge.

"Right," Wes said, realizing a moment later *she* was the *someone*.

"You can put the vacuum away," Grace urged.

"I'll give the toilet a quick scrub just in case," Wes said, sneaking a peek at her phone. Still nothing. Might as well clean.

Clearly Eòghann was sending a message by *not* sending one. By not reading the last one. Did that mean he'd blocked her number? The last few months, the tone of their correspondence had changed again, each of them continually suggesting the other should come for a visit, and yet neither seemed willing to commit to travel. What were they even doing?

FEBRUARY 10

Wes
Confession: I've never watched so much hockey in my life. Men's. Women's. Sled. I want it all.

Eòghann
Ice hockey?

Wes
Olympics and Paralympics, Baby!

Eòghann
Of course. Are we in it?

Wes
No. Do your people play hockey?

Eòghann
I think...yes? I feel like there was a national
team when I was a lad.

Are you winning?

Wes
Depends on who you mean by "you"

Eòghann
Are you not pulling for the USA?

Wes
Truth? I keep catching myself rooting for
Canada instead. 😳

Eòghann

Wes
I KNOW, MAN!! I KNOW!

I can't help it.

Eòghann
Be sure to scrub these unpatriotic messages
from your phone before you come over to see
me, or they might not let you back in.

Wes
I thought we established you're coming here?

Eòghann
No, you should come here.

Wes
Neutral territory? Meet at a cottage in
Canada? 🍁

The reference had sailed right over his head, she thought,
but not the inference. Unsurprisingly, he hadn't taken the bait.

MARCH 15

Eòghann
Beware the Ides of March, American.

Wes
Et tu, Brutus?

Eòghann
Your Latin needs work.

Wes
Rude! We can't all spend our waking hours in church.

Eòghann
Mea culpa. How are you?

Wes
Bored. In need of adventure.

Eòghann
Any summer trips planned?

Wes
Rome, perhaps.

Eòghann
Maybe stay away from the Theatre of Pompey.

Wes
Rats. Guess I'll have to scrap the whole thing.

(That was a bit. I was never going to Rome. My Italian is worse than my Latin.)

Eòghann
I hear it's lovely but doesn't hold a candle to Barra. Is Grace coming here this summer?

Wes
Probably. Unless she can convince the Stoic Scot to visit TN.

Eòghann
Think you'll join her if she does come?

> **Wes**
> Padre! Does this mean you miss me?

Eòghann
There's no one else tall enough to partner me
at the midsummer ceilidh.

> **Wes**
> Oh, in that case, I'm on my way. 🏃 Seriously
> though. Where would you go, if you could
> travel anywhere in the world?

Eòghann
Dunno.

> **Wes**
> Bucket list. Cost and whatever else don't
> matter.

Eòghann
I've never thought about it.

> **Wes**
> What?! Come on, Padre. Don't hold out on me
> now. The Holy Land? Paris? Rome?

Eòghann
Why stop there? Why not Outer Space?

> **Wes**
> Ooh. Bold choice. I like it! Let's meet on the
> moon.

Eòghann
I'll pack a panic.

*picnic

> **Wes**
> Green cheese and astronaut ice cream only.

And MOON PIES! I'll bring Moon Pies!

Eòghann
Wes?

Wes
Padre?

Eòghann
What the hell are Moon Pies?

Wes
They're only a Tennessee delicacy! Honestly it sounds like you need to come here before you plan on going ANYWHERE else. I'll take you on a tour of old churches. They'll look brand-new to you.

Eòghann
I'll take it under advisement.

Wes
See that you do.

She didn't know why she was pushing him so hard to come here, or why she was so resistant to going back to Barra. Flirting over text was fun and all, but in person they could have *much* more fun—a thrilling prospect—except if she planned a whole trip to go see him it would either be the world's most expensive booty call or it would mean their *situationship* was something more than she cared to admit. Maybe he felt exactly as both-ways about it as she did, and he was ghosting her as his way of putting this thing to rest.

By lunchtime her nervouscitement had spilled over onto everyone else, and they were all as ready for the news team as they were apt to get. Andy and Jack had set out their piles of lumber and chalked where both stages were meant to go. In their ratty blue jeans and t-shirts, they looked far more capable than Wes had ever imagined either of them to be, and she realized that although they were her best friends, she hardly knew these grown-up adults the Shakespeare Syndicate had turned into.

She still thought of them as gawky twenty-year-old boys wandering around like randy lost lambs on stilts—bumping into everything that moved and almost as many things that didn't. And though it wasn't surprising to find Andy ready to jump in feet first and help, despite years of evidence to the contrary she rather expected the opposite from Jack. Cool and aloof and *almost* disengaged had been his MO in the old days, so it was a little unsettling to see him wield a saw like he knew which end of it to hold.

"When did the boys get a little bit hot?" she murmured to Grace.

"Gross. Around the same time you entered your long dry spell," Grace retorted, making a face like the very suggestion their friends might be attractive was appalling, though Sadie had been dating Jack for a decade.

"I'm just saying. Maybe when the news van arrives we ask one of them to take their shirt off and let the cameras roll."

"Focus," Grace ordered. "Have you thought about what you're going to say?"

"No, because I thought Grandma Ruth was going to say it."

"Then you better figure it out."

"Misunderstanding, yadda yadda yadda, please don't come this weekend. We'll be ready the first Saturday in June."

Grace scowled. There were few linguistic expressions the author hated more than yadda yadda. "I think we should hang Exemplary Boiled Events out to dry."

"To what end? All that would do is make it one hundred percent clear we threw the whole thing together last minute."

"Okay first of all, I resent that. Everyone's working hard and it'll be amazing. But secondly, I'm also not sure it's ever a bad thing to set expectations in advance."

"So you do want them to know we threw it together last minute?" Wes grumbled under her breath.

"I want to make sure those jerks don't swindle anyone else," Grace pressed, but the news van had already parked in the driveway, so there was no time to continue arguing. "Ready?" Grace trilled, as a Black woman and a white man stepped out of the van.

"Not at all," Wes replied.

"Go get 'em, tiger," Grace whispered, shoving Wes forward to meet the news crew.

"Welcome to Warwick Hall," Wes called, pulling on her cheerleader mask.

"I thought we'd film some B roll first, if that's okay," LaTonya Devlin, the segment host and producer, told Wesley. "Some enticing snippets to draw viewers in, starting with a shot of this amazing house. It's your"—she checked her notes—"grandmother's house?"

"Yes. She's around here somewhere in a fabulous costume."

"Love it."

"And the bathroom's clean," Wes blurted out. "Just, you know, FYI."

LaTonya smiled. "I appreciate that. It'll make the ride back to the studio a lot more pleasant. This is Eddie," she added, nodding to the man as he hoisted a camera onto his shoulder.

She directed him to get a shot of the house and to include Duncan, as the raven circled suspiciously overhead.

"Red alert," it sounded like the bird was cawing down at them.

"This isn't live, but we don't do much editing," LaTonya went on. "If there's anything you don't want to include, let Eddie know. Likewise if you can think of anything we *should* include."

"Like a kid playing bagpipes down by the lake?"

"Exactly like that, Miss Teal. Are you coming for my job?" LaTonya teased.

So Wes led them through the still-sparse fairgrounds, explaining what would soon be set up, while LaTonya pointed out additional shots she wanted Eddie to capture as they walked, lingering a little longer than strictly necessary on Andy and Jack, their bulging muscles on full display. They had, it appeared, misplaced their t-shirts after all.

When they found Jarrod, he was happy enough to play. "But can you not show my face?" he asked Eddie.

"No problem, man," Eddie agreed, and instead he filmed from the back as Jarrod played a rousing verse of "Scotland the Brave" while standing on the picturesque bank staring out at the water.

They filmed an action shot of Rory in full pirate gear, charging through the woods towards the camera. At the last second he dodged to the side, revealing a regal-looking Grandma Ruth in the Elizabethan dress. Her long white hair was styled in beach wave curls with a small, sideways French braid around her crown like a halo.

"The Tube," she explained when she caught Wesley studying her intricate hairdo.

Next, Jack and Andy took a break from their carpentry to

juggle a little bit of fire, still sans shirts. It was mesmerizing. LaTonya and Eddie seemed suitably impressed.

WES AND LATONYA DECIDED TO SIT SIDE BY SIDE ON THE front porch swing for the interview.

"I understand your grandma was scammed?" LaTonya asked before they started rolling, her face filled with concern.

"Um, yes, but it's not what I was hoping to focus on, if that's okay."

"Whatever you're comfortable with. But it's happening more and more these days. If you prefer, we can say she hired a company that failed to meet important benchmarks, and so they parted ways before she reached out to friends of the family who are experts in the business?"

Wesley appreciated the approach, but hearing it out loud, it sounded a little too corporate for her liking. Maybe LaTonya and Grace were right about sharing the whole truth.

"What's your goal with the segment?" LaTonya asked.

"To get the word out. Stop people from showing up tomorrow—and get them to come back in a couple of weeks."

LaTonya nodded. "Honestly? I think you should tell them about the scam. It'll resonate. Make the story more memorable."

Wes nodded. She'd been worried about embarrassing Grandma Ruth, but she'd said herself Grandma shouldn't be ashamed. "It could happen to anyone right?"

"And probably will again," LaTonya agreed. I'll ask a few softball questions about what guests can expect, and then we'll be out of your hair."

"Thank you so much for doing this, and on such short notice," Wes told her.

"Let us come back to do a story on opening day, and we'll call it even. Can you take your sunglasses off?"

Wes faltered. She really shouldn't be out in the bright sun without them. "Um, I can, but..."

LaTonya waved her off. "Leave them on if you're more comfortable. You ready?"

"No," Wes laughed sheepishly.

"You'll be great. Eddie's going to count down from three. You can look right into the camera while I introduce you, and then we'll chat. Easy breezy."

"Got it."

LaTonya turned and smiled at the camera so she'd be ready the moment Eddie began rolling.

"I'm here today with Wesley Teal in front of her Grandma Ruth's beautiful Tudor home in Stratford, Tennessee, where Wes and her grandmother are planning to host a Renaissance faire—right here on the property?"

"That's right, LaTonya. It's going to be the first Saturday in June, and we couldn't be more excited."

"Is it true that holding this faire has been your grandma's lifelong dream?"

"It has—more than any of us realized. She and my grandad bought Warwick Hall thirty-five years ago when he retired from the Air Force, and she never told him so, but from the moment she saw the place she wanted to host her own Renaissance faire on the grounds.

LaTonya put her hand to her chest like she couldn't stand how precious Grandma Ruth was, and Wes had to agree.

"What a beautiful dream," LaTonya said. "And it's finally coming true."

"It is." Wes couldn't help smiling and feeling a little bit proud.

"You and your friends are making it come true. But she originally hired a company to help her, is that right?"

"She did. She paid a pretty hefty downpayment to a group

she thought was legitimate, but they did very little besides sell tickets—at least we think they sold tickets—and now they've disappeared."

"And so you and your friends stepped in to save the day. Originally the faire was going to be *this* weekend?"

"It was. So now we're asking people if you did buy tickets: please, *please* come back the first Saturday in June. All tickets will be honored, but we need a little bit more time to prepare."

"What can visitors expect when they do show up in June?"

"We've got Celtic bands and period-focused musicians—including a wandering minstrel who's around here somewhere," Wesley answered, making a show of looking around for Spencer, and LaTonya grinned. "He plays a very unique instrument you might've heard but never seen before. And we've got fire-juggling comedians and a wonderful variety of vendors."

"Ohh, what's for sale?"

"A little bit of everything, really. Leather goods, handmade jewelry, historical romance novels. And of course, there'll be games for the kids and local food trucks."

"Wow. Y'all have certainly been busy. It sounds like a ton of fun for all ages."

"Absolutely," Wes agreed. "We're very sorry we can't open this weekend, but I promise it will be worth the wait."

"You heard her, folks," LaTonya said, turning back to the camera. "Make sure and come out to Warwick Hall on the first Saturday in June for Stratford's inaugural Renaissance faire—there'll be something to delight the whole family."

Eddie held up two fingers, then one. "And out," he said.

"You were perfect! It will air on the 6:oo news tonight, and we'll post it on all of our socials. Tell your friends and family to watch!" LaTonya said, giving Wesley a hug before they loaded up the van and headed off down the drive, back to the studio in Knoxville.

Wes only hoped it worked. Something about LaTonya's parting words made her a little bit wary and a little bit sad. Not that she didn't have friends and family who'd watch, but everyone who mattered was here with her already.

And she certainly didn't want to watch *herself* on the news —how mortifying. But she couldn't help wondering what Eòghann would think. Would Grace record it to show Bryan? Would the Stoic Scot share it with his cousin? And would it entice the Padre to actually text her back?

Chapter Ten

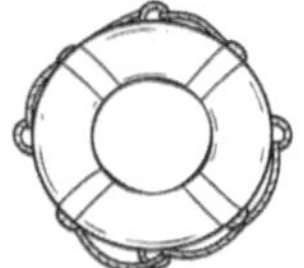

MIDDLE OF THE GODFORSAKEN ATLANTIC

After the walk of shame back to Eòghann's seat, where half the passengers who were still awake stared openly at him and the other half pretended not to, he slid into the middle seat damp and nauseated from the reek of his own perspiration.

Bryan didn't acknowledge what had happened. He took out a small orange sack of hexagonal tiles stamped with the shapes of different insects. "Remember how to play?" he asked softly.

They'd spent hours playing down at the pub when Bryan was deep in his feelings after Grace had gone home last summer, so Eòghann nodded gratefully, and they began to take turns attempting to surround each other's queen bee as they built out the hive.

They played in silence for several rounds before Eòghann whispered, "Sorry about all that."

The words came out so hushed he wasn't sure Bryan could hear him over the whir of the jet engines, until his cousin frowned and shook his head.

"It was wrong of me to force you to come along."

"You didn't *force* me, Bry," Eòghann replied.

Bryan shook his head again and they resumed their silent play, calm and soothing, until the lights came up and the attendants came around with more snacks.

THEY LANDED IN NASHVILLE IN THE LATE AFTERNOON, AND though he'd never been more thankful to set foot anywhere, Eòghann's anxiety began to ratchet up again as they waited their turn to clear customs. What if there was a problem with his visa? What if they put him right back on the plane?

He could feel Bryan's eyes on him as he tried to remain calm. Five years younger, his cousin had looked up to Eòghann since they were children, but the episode on the plane had clearly shaken him.

Bryan was only wee the day Eòghann had nearly drowned after hitting his head at the community pool. He'd grown up most of his life knowing Eòghann avoided the water out of fear, but he'd been away such a long time, and knowing a thing in the abstract was quite different to witnessing it firsthand.

He could see in Bryan's eyes as they flicked over him and then quickly away that the flight had changed how Bryan saw him, and not for the better.

Lùc may not have noticed his distress—everything was new and different and maybe a touch overwhelming to him—but Bryan must think Eòghann a completely ridiculous, over-dramatic wanker, because honestly, what was the difference between flying in a plane above the water and living on an island surrounded by it?

Eòghann wished he could explain the very real difference in his brain.

"What's the purpose of your visit?" the immigration agent asked, and Eòghann's mouth turned to sawdust.

"We're visiting my girl," Bryan explained.

"All of you?"

"She's our friend," Eòghann rasped, his voice dry from the recycled air inside the plane.

"Ee-oh-guh-han?" the agent asked, looking up from Eòghann's passport with hooded eyes. "What kind of name is that?"

"Gaelic," Eòghann grunted.

"Gch-oh-gch-an?" the agent tried again, making sounds like he was clearing his throat of phlegm. "Is that it?"

"You can just say Owen."

"Is that what you say?"

Eòghann nodded.

"Why don't you spell it that way then?"

Eòghann shrugged. "My Ma's side is Irish."

The agent stared at him, unblinking. "What do you do for a living?" he asked, turning back to Bryan.

"I make whisky."

"Bring any with you?"

"Couple of bottles. Why, would you like a taste?"

"Is that a bribe?" the agent asked, his tone stone cold, and Eòghann's watch began to beep as his heart rate spiked.

He scrambled to silence it as Bryan stammered, "Not a b-b-bribe, s-sir. It was a joke."

"Unless you want it to be," Lùc piped up, and Bryan stepped on his foot hard. "Kidding," Lùc yelped.

"I never get British humor," the agent grumbled.

Completely deadpan, Bryan replied, "Neither do I," and now Eòghann wanted to stomp on *his* foot.

Bryan and the agent stared at each other for a long moment.

"Your girlfriend think you're funny?"

"Rarely."

"She live in Nashville?"

"Knoxville."

"What does she do?"

"She's a librarian. And an author," he added, his chest puffing up with pride.

"She's won an award!" Lùc volunteered.

"Anything I'd have read?"

"Probably not," Bryan said, and Eòghann died a little, worried the agent would hear the deliberate insult—that Bryan was suggesting the man didn't know how to read.

"Yeah, probably not," the agent agreed, handing them back their passports.

Minutes later they were walking through the bustling airport, and Bryan was reminding Eòghann to breathe.

As they waited at the rental car kiosk, Bryan checked the time on his phone. "Nearly six."

"AM or PM?" Lùc asked.

"PM. I'm tired. I'm hungry. And it's another two and a half hours to Knoxville."

"Is it?" Lùc asked, watching a group of boisterous young women in boots and pink cowboy hats argue about which way to go to catch their ride. They all wore sparkly t-shirts proclaiming them BRIDESMAIDS, save the bride, who wore a white sash and white boots.

At her side stood the only young man in the group, wearing the shortest shorts of all and a t-shirt that said MAID OF HONOR, a dress bag slung over his shoulder. He tossed a dimpled smile and a wink their way, showing off his glittery eyeliner. Lùc went red as beetroot, before turning back towards the rental counter, away from the hen do.

"Want to get a hotel tonight and head east tomorrow?" Bryan asked.

Eòghann nodded enthusiastically. He needed a shower. He needed a thousand showers.

"Can we go out for a bit then?" Lùc asked, taking one last glance over his shoulder at the departing group of young people.

Bryan sagged a little but acquiesced. "Course, if you like. But you aren't old enough to drink."

"I drink all the time!" Lùc protested.

"Not here."

The rental agent gave Bryan keys to a black Nissan Rogue along with vague directions to the hotel he'd picked out.

Within minutes they pulled into a car park not far from the airport, and when Eòghann stepped out into the warm, humid air he was overwhelmed by a sweet, familiar scent that took his breath away. He'd always thought Wesley smelled of honeysuckle and sunshine and something else, some subtle, sweet, mysterious fragrance that was all her own. Looking around in awe he wondered if she simply smelled like Tennessee.

Bryan slapped him on the shoulder and handed him his bag, so he reluctantly abandoned the sweet smelling outdoors for the over-air conditioned lobby of the hotel and headed up to their shared accommodation with two large beds and a fold-out couch for Lùc.

"Any chance you want to come with us?" Bryan asked, as Lùc changed into a clean vest and trousers.

Eòghann felt guilty to bail when Bryan was clearly exhausted after staying awake most of the flight babysitting him, but before he could answer, his cousin read his face and patted his shoulder.

"We won't be late. I wrote my mobile number on the pad by the phone—"

"I know your number."

"You have to dial the country codes, don't forget. If you get hungry—"

"I won't—"

"—call down for room service."

"I'm fine, Bry," Eòghann insisted.

Bryan caught his gaze and held it for a long moment as if to say *Are you, though?*

"Go enjoy yourselves."

"Get some rest," Bryan told him, and then they left Eòghann in blessed peace.

For probably fifteen minutes he simply stood there, alone, in the middle of the room, silent except for the chilly blast of the air conditioner. He was caught in a conundrum—entirely too filthy to sit down or touch a single surface, but at the same time, an actual shower (or a thousand) felt beyond him.

He needed to wash, but he didn't want to turn on the water, so he kept standing there until he realized he wouldn't be able to stand much longer.

He sat on the side of the tub and did his breathing exercises as the water warmed up, and then he peeled off his clothes and washed as quickly as he could, barely making it into one of the beds before he fell deeply asleep.

WHEN HE WOKE THE NEXT MORNING IT WAS DARK OUTSIDE, and his watch said 3 AM. He was pretty sure that was Tennessee time, and though he was still exhausted, he was also wide awake as if it were 9. Which he supposed it might be, back on Barra.

Bryan was snoring lightly in the other bed, and Lùc was passed out fully dressed on the un-pulled-out couch, so Eòghann slipped a paperback from his carryall and wandered down to the lobby in search of a quiet place to read.

· · ·

SEVERAL HOURS LATER, HE WAS DEEPLY ENGROSSED IN HIS novel when a rumpled and bleary-eyed Bryan approached the comfy chair Eòghann had found in a secluded corner of the lobby.

"There you are," Bryan said, audible relief flooding his voice.

"Did you think I'd flown back to Scotland?"

"Thought you were sssleepwalking maybe," he said, stumbling into a neighboring chair. "You all right?"

Eòghann nodded. He didn't want to talk about yesterday though. "Are you?"

Bryan sighed and rubbed the bridge of his nose. "The next time Lùc has some grand idea, remind me I'm not equipped to keep up with an eighteen-year-old."

"Welcome to the old timer's club," Eòghann chuckled, lifting his paper cup of tepid tea in salute.

Bryan groaned.

"What time did you get back?"

"Around 1:30."

"If he's underage for drinking, what on earth did you find to do all that time?"

"We walked around a lot. And there were places he could go in without being served. He was... enthusiastic. It was cute."

"Was his enthusiasm contagious?"

"Maybe a little." Bryan groaned. "Och, jet lag's a bitch. Right—I'm going to get a cup of coffee and go wake up the kid," Bryan announced, but he didn't move from his chair.

"Silly question," Eòghann began, and his cousin rolled his head sideways to look at him. "Grace knows we're coming, right?" It had been nagging at him since they left the airport.

Bryan sighed again, his lips forming a thin flat line.

"Really, Bry?" He didn't know how he felt about surprising Wes with his sudden appearance.

"I didn't want to try to explain about Alec over text."

"Or a video call?"

"Or that either. It'll be fine. A happy sssurprise."

"And if it's not?"

Bryan rubbed the back of his neck and offered a shrug.

"Here," Eòghann said, handing back Uncle Rob's worry stone. "You might need this more than I do now."

Bryan grinned sheepishly and dropped the smooth, flat, rainbow colored stone in his pajama pocket, and got up to find his coffee.

Chapter Eleven

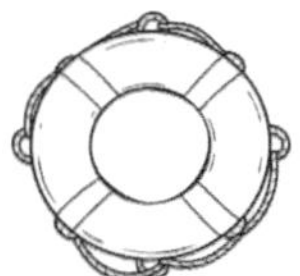

STRATFORD, TENNESSEE

Saturday dawned without a cloud in the sky, but it was already 80 degrees before 7 AM.

"June's going to be terrible," Wes worried. "What if no one comes because it's too hot."

"It'll be fine," Grace assured her. "People will be having too much fun to notice the heat."

"Ha. Maybe we should set up one of those splash pads, or like a tent with misting sprinklers inside?"

"You and all your genius ideas."

"If only I knew how to make them a reality."

Using the vacant barn as a pub may have been one of Wesley's less ingenious ideas. When she pried open the door yesterday afternoon she discovered it was chock full of rusty, old farm equipment and had evidently been inhabited by numerous feral critters in the decades since her grandfather passed, not to mention a family of mice still in residence.

"Grandma Ruth was right," she told Grace. "Let's forget it."

"No," Grace insisted. "No, it was a good idea. Just needs a little elbow grease."

"It's a bio hazard, Gray."

"A lot of elbow grease."

"Fine, but no one goes inside without a mask and gloves. And a hazmat suit," she added under her breath.

"It could be worse," Sadie mused, surveying the barn from behind her own mask.

Wes turned to ask how, but Grace said, "Could be skunks," and Sadie nodded in agreement.

Before Wes could reply, there came a commotion of shouting and cursing from nearby where Andy and Jack were constructing the first stage.

The three girls popped out of the barn in time to see the platform actually collapsing on Jack's legs as Andy danced around wringing his hand in the air and swearing like a sailor.

"I'm fine," Andy yelped.

"Everything's fine," Jack agreed.

"Looks fine," Wes whispered.

"Totally fine," Grace agreed.

"This is their process," Sadie told them.

"You hit your thumb with the hammer again, didn't you?" the musician's oldest son, Daniel asked.

Andy pointed at him to shut up.

"Come on, Darwish," Wes said. "I'll get you an ice pack. Need an ice pack, Jack?" she called, but Jack waved her off.

"I'm fine," Andy protested again.

"Can you juggle fire if your thumbnail falls off?"

"Will ice keep it from falling off?" he asked, catching up with her.

"I have no idea."

They walked around to the front of the house, where Grandma Ruth was decked out in her Queen Elizabeth I costume preparing to royally wave away any guests who hadn't seen Wesley on the evening news, and sure enough, a car was already heading up the driveway.

"Moment of truth," Grace said to Grandma.

"I believe in us," Spencer added to no one in particular, stepping out of the shadows of the vine-covered hydrangea bush like some kind of medieval poltergeist.

"That's real creepy, Spence," Wes breathed.

"Intruders!" Duncan the raven screamed.

"Can't you teach him to say something nice like, *Welcome lords and ladies?*" Wes asked her grandmother, only half teasing.

"He's his own bird," she replied.

As the car neared, Grace shaded her eyes and began to bounce excitedly on her heels. "Wait, is that—did you know they were coming?"

"Who?" Wesley asked, squinting as the car drew nearer. Pretty much everyone she knew was already there except Beatrix and Andy's sister Rebecca. But Bea lived up north, and Becca drove something smaller.

Grace waved for the SUV to park on the wide driveway near the house, right behind her Subaru. When the front two doors opened, Wes had trouble making sense of what she was seeing.

First a tall, broad-shouldered man, and then a gangly one, exited the vehicle. Grace squealed and ran to the driver, and Wes realized it must be the ginger-haired Stoic Scot when he swept her up in his arms and spun her around. The other one stretched and took in the house with a sense of awe.

"Blimey," muttered the MacNeil boys' cousin Lùc.

So they'd left the priest at home. Fine. Good. Fine. It was for the best, to be honest, after the extremely vivid and inappropriate dreams she'd been having in her childhood bed. The thing was, she could almost smell his cologne, and God what was wrong with her? Was she having a stroke? And also how very dare? Hallucinations had no right smelling so good.

Lùc tapped on the open back window. "Wake up, Sleepy Time Tea, we're here," he called to a third passenger in the back seat, and for a moment Wesley held her breath.

Then the door opened and he was there, like a mirage, unfolding all six feet of himself onto the pavement, looking devilishly rumpled and running a hand through his blonde hair and down over his short beard. She remembered perfectly how both were shot through with exactly the right amount of grey. Father What-a-Waste indeed.

She took a few steps closer and shoved her sunglasses on top of her head. He was somehow more handsome than she'd dared to remember, and her tummy did a little cartwheel.

"Eòghann MacNeil, as I live and breathe," she murmured.

He squinted into the sunshine like someone fighting a hangover, and then his blinking eyes found Wes and turned positively molten. This time her stomach did a gigantic swoop like the raven. She wanted him every bit as much as she had last year. Maybe more so. She caught herself licking her lips—because of the heat, obviously—and made a mental note to buy a lip balm.

"What're you doing here?" Grace asked, bewildered. "How was your flight?"

"Mmm-hmm," Bryan replied, noncommittally. He walked around the back of the car, one arm pinning Grace firmly to his side. With the other, he tossed Lùcas the car keys, then patted Eòghann on the chest. Grace gave both of the other cousins a quick hug before returning to Bryan's side and disappearing into the house.

Andy watched the entire interaction, then turned back to Wes, bemused.

"Friends," Wes told him, because it was all she could

manage while staring at Eòghann, right there in front of her after all this time.

Andy and Lùc sized each other up, still waiting for a proper introduction, but Wesley's brain was short circuiting at the sight of Eòghann, as though her jealousy and horny longing had combined in some kind of powerful dark magic to conjure him before her eyes. She couldn't look away lest he disappear. He was exactly how she remembered, if a little tired and travel-frayed around the edges.

After a moment, Andy cleared his throat. "Adnan Darwish," he said, stepping forward and offering his hand to Lùc, along with his legal name.

"Lùcas Buchanan," the boy replied in kind, shaking his hand with relief that someone was acting normal, probably.

Eòghann studied Wes with hungry eyes, and honestly she'd never felt sexier. Thank goodness the heat had driven her to throw on her favorite blue and white sundress that morning instead of a ratty tank top and cargo shorts. She exhaled, and it came out sounding a bit like a growl, which felt appropriately feral.

"I need a minute," Wes announced, grabbing Eòghann's hand. "There's ice in the kitchen for your thumb," she added to Andy. "You know your way around."

She led Father What-a-Waste towards the front door of Grandma's house the same way Grace had dragged Bryan off, just a couple of cave women today, apparently.

"Be gentle with him," Lùcas called after her.

"I only want to talk," she tossed over her shoulder.

"Right. I'll show myself around then, shall I?" Lùc replied.

"I'm happy to see you," she called back.

"I'm Spencer," the resident minstrel said, and Wes almost felt bad for abandoning the kid, but Andy and Grandma Ruth would protect him.

There was no sign of Grace or Bryan as Wes led Eòghann into the living room where she pulled him down to sit on the couch. For a moment all she could do was drink in the sight of him—memorizing his beautiful face, his mussy hair and tidy beard—and damn, he smelled divine. His scent alone left her completely addled.

"What brings you here?" she demanded, then held up a hand. "Wait. Don't answer that."

If he told her he saw her text about the faire and hopped straight on a plane to help—if he opened his big, stupid, beautiful mouth and confessed to dragging his cousins halfway around the world to rescue her—she would actually scream. But man, she'd missed him *so* much. She hadn't realized quite how much, and now he was here, and she didn't want to turn him down or send him away or scream before she had time to enjoy their reunion.

And she wanted to *thoroughly* enjoy their reunion.

"Is this where you grew up?" he asked, looking around at the well-loved room and the pictures on the wall.

"Sure. You want the tour?"

She stood up again, still holding his hand, and bless his heart he followed her without a word, up the stairs and down the hall to her bedroom, which thankfully didn't share a wall with Grace.

Wes closed the door and pushed Eòghann back against it, kissing him the way she'd done after the midsummer ceilidh last year—the same bold way that might have scared him off that night, but she couldn't help it. He tasted like cinnamon and ginger and honey. She missed the sweet, smoky flavor of whisky on his breath, but he smelled exactly the same—an intoxicating blend of teakwood, patchouli, and island musk. She could drown in his scent and go straight to heaven. Or perhaps she'd go straight to hell. Honestly, she wasn't fussy.

Tearing her mouth away from his sinfully delightful lips, she kissed his neck and behind his ear, losing herself in the cologne. "God, you smell so good," she murmured.

"*You* do," he rasped, kissing her back. "I'm glad I at least smell better than I look."

"A fisher of compliments, rather than a fisher of men, Padre?" she teased. "You *look* amazing too," she promised, and when he scoffed, she leaned back, turning her head to study him better in her periphery. It wasn't only his black button-down and his hair that were rumpled. His eyes were red, with deep bruises beneath them betraying a lack of sleep. "This isn't eye shadow," she whispered, tracing his cheek bone lightly with her thumb, and he sank into her palm as though he'd never been caressed in all his life. It made her stomach shiver with delight.

He shook his head to answer her question, before tilting it so he could kiss her fingers, which sent another little jolt directly down her arm and between her legs.

Holding both sides of his face so she could feel the soft scruff of his beard, she kissed his lips again—such very fine lips—and the sigh that escaped them was a little bit shaky, as though he'd thought of nothing else but her kisses in the three hundred and however many days they'd been apart.

That little sigh altered Wesley's brain chemistry. She was never going to be the same again.

Grasping her wrists, which still caressed his face, he pivoted so now it was her back against the door, his weight keeping her there. And that little touch of dominance nearly brought her to her knees.

His arms were huge. She'd forgotten the reality of them, but being pressed between them now, Wes remembered the same realization she'd had the first time she ever saw him, after he'd taken off the sweater she was never giving back: with arms like those he could hold a girl up for hours while he railed her against a castle wall. Or an old church wall. Or her own bedroom wall. Again, she really wasn't picky.

Eòghann perked up, deepening the kiss as though discovering a second wind, his tongue battling hers like a drowning man fighting for a life preserver. An alarm on his watch started to beep until he yanked it off and shoved it in the pocket of his black jeans.

Despite having spent the past year feasting on memories of their first kiss back on Barra, she'd forgotten quite how nice kissing him truly was. Now it all came flooding back—how, after weeks of barely contained desire they had finally given in and made out under a cool, twilit sky, until his conscience caught up and he made some excuse to disappear.

Wes was on her best behavior again after that, up until Grace's birthday party, when she had kissed him platonically on the cheek, and he'd melted into her touch exactly like now, like a man starved, both of them filled with regret because they knew it was goodbye.

Then, as now, kissing Eòghann had awakened something in Wes—a knowing, a longing—a sudden awareness of what kissing was supposed to be like: a whole conversation without the trouble of pesky, elusive words. A dance. A give and take of lips and tongues and fingers, of murmurs and sighs. It was sparks tripping down your backbone, and fire tickling your belly. It was breathing the same air until you were so in tandem that you shared one single breath, one single heartbeat, fast or slow.

No one in her life had kissed Wes like Eòghann had, and she'd long suspected from the way he kissed that he couldn't help but be a generous and attentive lover, slow and sensual and in the moment rather than needy and rough or rushed. As in every part of his life, she suspected he put himself second and gave more than he received, if ever he was allowed.

That had been her perception of him back on Barra anyway, and god damn how she wanted to find out if she was right.

Wes pushed him, holding his shirt bunched in her fists so he couldn't get too far away from her, and he took the hint and walked backwards until he tumbled onto the bed undoing his shirt buttons, while she straddled him, kissing down the column of his throat to his collar bone.

He grunted, and pitched them sideways a little, reaching under his hip and holding up Pablo—the vibrator. She hadn't meant to leave it right out there on the bed.

"Oops," she said, snatching the toy out of his hand so she could move it to the bedside table.

"Wait," he said, taking it back from her, and she raised an eyebrow, intrigued, as he placed it next to them on the bed, without the trace of embarrassment she might've expected from a priest. Was this a bolder, more reckless version of Eòghann than the guarded man she'd met last summer? She supposed now it was his turn to be on vacation.

"Can I help you with that?" she asked, gesturing to his belt. When he nodded, she fumbled with the buckle, but it was so tight she growled—actually *growled*—in frustration.

"Slow down. Take your time," he murmured.

And why did those words make her fall a tiny bit in love with him? How often had she wanted to slow down, pause time, kiss for hours? But her lovers always grew impatient or bored and so, like every other aspect of *her* life, Wes learned to rush, always in a hurry, afraid to run out of time, maybe a little worried that if she didn't come quickly she wouldn't come at all.

"We don't have to," she assured him, meaning both that they didn't have to slow down if he didn't want to, and also that they didn't need to do anything at all.

"So for the record, you're not mad I showed up unannounced?" he teased.

"As long as you're here because you missed me, and you thought about me constantly, and you've been meaning to text me back, I'm good," she said, running her hands up his torso. "Is this okay?" she asked, as she continued down over his denim-covered crotch.

His breath grew ragged as he nodded enthusiastically. She wanted to bottle that sound and play it back whenever she was alone at night.

"I missed you, and I thought of you everyday," he gasped. "And I wanted to text you back, but I lost my phone."

"Liar," Wes teased, running her hands back up his chest, making his shirt pocket crinkle.

He closed his eyes as she reached inside, wiggling out the condom triumphantly.

She truly only meant to talk when she'd dragged him into the house, but his cologne always did something to her. Her increasing regret over leaving him behind on Barra had been screaming at her not to let another chance slip away, and then he'd melted into her every touch, and honestly what was a priest doing with a condom in his pocket? Had Bryan put it there? And with encouragement like that, how could she hold back? It seemed cruel to deny him. Or herself. Being wanted—sincerely, desperately wanted after such a long time—it was a powerful drug.

Wes leaned back on her haunches, straddling him, and he huffed out another strained breath. She loved all his different little sighs. How disgustingly smitten was she? She wiggled her bottom to see if she could elicit yet another one. Through his jeans she could feel him, hard as steel, and she wasn't disappointed. This time he drew a shuddering inhale, though he was trying his hardest to play it cool.

"This is pretty," he gasped, toying with the hem of her sundress.

Wes shrugged coyly. "It was too hot for anything else."

He nodded. "Are you too hot now?" he rasped.

"Boiling." Wes was happy to play along, stripping the dress up and over her head in one fluid motion, leaving her in nothing but a lacy blue bra and butterfly panties.

Eòghann licked his lips and then swallowed hard. "Feel better?" he asked, shrugging out of his shirt, leaving him in a sleeveless undershirt, also black, and dear lord his shoulders matched his massive arms.

"Still sweltering," she said, unhooking the bra and letting it fall away, her nipples instantly pebbling in the chilly air conditioning.

"Oh no," he said before sitting up and taking her right nipple into his mouth, warming it but sending wave after wave of goosebumps down the rest of her. "Now you're cold," he said, scooting backwards to sit against the pillows at her headboard. "Let me warm you up."

A knock sounded at the door, and they both froze, turning in horror. Had she locked it? She crossed her arms over her chest, covering her aching nipples.

"Wes?" Grandma called. "I need to get some bandages out of your bathroom, dear."

"One second, Grandma," Wes called, scrambling off Eòghann and throwing her dress back on without taking time to find her bra. After a glance at her partner in crime and a shrug about how he could hide his erection, she opened the door and wrapped her arms around herself once more. "What do you need bandages for? Are you okay?" she asked, scanning her grandmother from head to foot, though she'd been fine ten minutes ago on the lawn.

"Not for me," Grandma Ruth said, and Wes realized Pirate Rory stood behind her, bleeding from a deep gash above his eye.

"Oh!" she exclaimed. "What happened to you?"

"Duel," he replied, as if that explained everything rather than raising infinitely more questions.

"You forgot to introduce your guest," Grandma chided, letting her gaze travel appreciatively over Eòghann, who held a decorative pillow awkwardly in front of his groin.

"Did I? Sorry. This is Gray's long-distance boyfriend's cousin," she explained, stepping back to allow her grandmother in to find whatever first aid she needed.

Grandma Ruth looked him over again with a wicked gleam in her eye that made Wes half-wonder if she'd been the one to bash Rory's head in as an excuse to visit the guest bathroom.

"Welcome," Grandma Ruth said. "Any cousin of Lady Gray's long-distance boyfriend is a cousin of mine."

"I'm obliged to you ma'am. I don't think I could manage that flight again for quite some time."

"The more the merrier...?"

"Eòghann," he supplied, holding something of a staring contest with Rory, like he couldn't quite look away from the boy, who stared back at him equally curious.

"Ruth. Are you here to help with our faire?" Grandma asked.

"No," Wes jumped in before he could answer.

Grandma Ruth sniffed. "Too bad. I bet you look strapping in a kilt."

"He does," Wes admitted, clearing her throat.

"I'm afraid I left my kilt back on Barra," he said.

"That's a shame," Grandma sniffed. "But I'm sure there's one or two lying around here somewhere."

"Kilt or no kilt, we don't need help," Wes jumped in.

"Yes, yes, everything's under control," Grandma Ruth said,

tilting Rory's chin and dabbing an alcohol swab on his cut, making him hiss and jerk his face away, though she moved it right back where she wanted it. "That's why Adnan raided my icebox and this one's covered in blood. Because everything's under control. Can you sing, Eòghann?"

"Och, no. Bryan and Lùc are the karaoke fiends. Where *is* Lùc?" he asked, as though suddenly remembering his cousin existed.

"The young Scottish fellow with the dashing eyes? Adnan took him to get more wood."

Wes coughed at the unintentional innuendo and busied herself opening a bandage for her grandmother to slather with ointment before pressing it to Rory's brow.

"I'm not quite sure those boys know what they're doing building my stages," Grandma went on.

"Did both of them fall down?" Grace asked, peeking around the door with Bryan in tow, both of them looking far too pleased with themselves.

"It'll be fine, Grandma," Wes assured her.

"Eòghann could probably help, couldn't you?" Grace suggested. "He's a regular Mr. Fix-It back on Barra."

"And what am I?" Bryan demanded, scowling down at her as though affronted.

Grace turned back to him and threw her arms around his neck. "You're *my* Mr. Fix-It, Mr. Bee," she assured him, standing on tip toe for a kiss until Rory made a gagging noise.

Bryan grunted his acceptance and leaned in for more PDA.

Wes rolled her eyes at the pair of them, but it was nice to see them reunited.

"You must be the Stoic Scot," Grandma Ruth said, and Bryan turned his scowl on Wesley, before offering his hand to her grandma.

"Glad to meet you, ma'am."

"Are you guys real Scots? Not fake ones like my brother?" Rory piped up.

Though he and Daniel's accents weren't as pronounced as their middle brother's, their midwestern American had more of a lilt than he seemed to realize.

Bryan's eyes went soft, as though noticing the boy for the first time. His mouth opened, but no words came out.

"Aye," Eòghann replied in a strangled sounding voice. "Real as they come."

"What were you guys doing in here, anyway?" Rory piped up. "Having a pillow fight?"

"All done!" Grandma exclaimed. "Who wants lemonade?" she asked, tossing Wes a meaningful look and herding Rory out, taking the first aid kit with her as Wes closed the door behind them.

Chapter Twelve

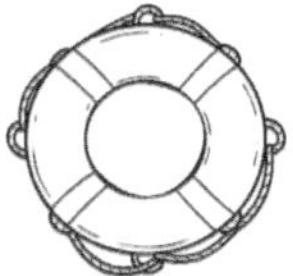

Nothing about the past five minutes matched how Eòghann had imagined meeting Wesley's family.

She leaned back against the closed door and puffed out a breath, but her eyes were dancing when she looked at him.

"To be continued?" he suggested.

"I can't believe I almost committed the seven deadly sins with my grandmother right outside."

"What all seven?" he teased, liking the sound of it a little too much, even though he couldn't name all seven if he tried.

"You tell me," she teased, smiling self-consciously. "What are you doing here anyway?"

"Thought you didn't want to know," he said, a little shy now that the initial adrenaline was subsiding.

"I didn't want you to open your handsome mouth and ruin the moment."

"You think my mouth is handsome?" he asked, unable to resist teasing her as a flush of heat warmed his cheeks.

Wes rolled her eyes and turned away to slip her bra back on, but she tossed him a smile over her shoulder like a damn life preserver.

"Alas the moment has been ruined."

Eòghann looked around the room, soaking in every aspect, the way the sunlight filtered through the blinds, painting the purple walls like a sunset. "Do you live here with your gran?" he asked.

"No, I'm here because of the faire. Are you actually claiming you didn't read my text and immediately jump on a plane to try and be some kind of knight in shining armor?"

"I saw a text from you," he admitted. "I lost my phone before I could read it."

"Lost it?"

"Long story."

"Okay. But if you're not here to rescue me—which I *don't* need, for the record—then why are you here? Unannounced?"

Eòghann sighed and slumped down on the foot of the bed. "Grace sent Bryan a video," he admitted.

Wesley's eyes narrowed. "Do I want to know what kind of video?"

"Your musician," he said, fiddling with his watch to avoid having to look her in the eye while they talked about Alec.

"Spencer?" she asked, studying his reflection in the mirror where she'd been plaiting her hair.

He almost said, *You don't see the resemblance?* But then he caught himself. Maybe she couldn't see the resemblance because of her vision loss, he didn't know. Either way it would seem horribly insensitive to ask, and besides, what if there was no actual resemblance to see? What if it was all the power of suggestion and a byproduct of Bryan's wishful thinking?

"The guy out front when you got here?"

"I don't think so," Eòghann said, trying to remember anyone

but her standing outside when he'd emerged from the rental car. "Father of the rascal with the bash on his forehead."

"Oh—the Scottish guy?" she asked. "Is that a real accent then? It's not as good as yours. Wait, is he a wanted serial killer back in Glasgow or something? Cause I'm pretty sure I listened to that podcast, and the guy didn't have kids."

She searched around the bureau, holding the end of her plait between two fingers.

Eòghann spotted a hair band off to the side and got up to hand it to her, their fingers sparking when they touched. She smiled, and he almost forgot what they'd been talking about.

"So the musician?"

He blinked. "It was a grainy video, but we think—that is, Bryan's fairly certain—he's our cousin Alec."

Wes let out a breath she'd been holding and sagged against the bureau. "Wow. You genuinely aren't here to try and help me with the faire," she said, almost to herself.

Eòghann took a step back, almost surprised that her world wasn't as rocked by the revelation of his cousin as his had been, but why would it be? She didn't know the whole story. "You said it was in hand, but if you need something I'd be happy to—"

"No," she said, shaking her head as a grin spread across her face. "It is in hand, and you have a long-lost cousin. Because of course you do. How long has he been missing?"

Had he been missing, exactly? Or had he simply severed ties? The last time they'd spoken was shortly before Alec had moved to the States. He'd been accepted to medical school in Minnesota, but he was torn up over the idea of leaving his girlfriend behind in Glasgow.

"Do you love her?" Eòghann had asked.

The question was met with a long, silent pause until Alec said, "I thought I did. But if that were true, would I have applied to the Mayo Clinic in the first place?"

"It's okay to want things. Besides, it's only America. 'Tisn't the moon," Eòghann had replied. "Have you asked her to go with you?"

"Her whole life is here," Alec whined, certain the girl would say no.

"Ask her," Eòghann had pressed him.

The next thing he knew they were packing up to move halfway around the world together, leaving Bryan bereft in Glasgow, with young Teàrlach and his footballer friend for company.

"He lost touch with everyone not long after he started medical school," Eòghann explained to Wes.

"He's a doctor?"

"I assume so."

"Named Alec?"

"Why, what name does he go by?" Eòghann asked, a surge of dread rising in his gut. Maybe it was all a case of mistaken identity after all. But the little imp with the head wound had looked *so much* like Alec at the same age.

"Andy calls him Gall—Gallifrey—but that can't be his real name," she answered, clearly confused by the whole situation.

"Gallifrey?" he laughed. "Then it must be him."

"Is it like an old family name or something?"

"No, it's a *Dr. Who* reference, innit?"

"The guy with the scarf?" Wes wrinkled her nose, even more perplexed.

How was it possible for her to be so much cuter than he remembered? He wanted to kiss that little scrunch between her eyes, but he reined himself in and nodded. "Aye, the guy with the scarf."

"Because he's a doctor?"

"Exactly, and also a massive *Dr. Who* fan. The children are his?"

"Yeah. I mean, it's only the four of them so unless he rented them on musical-kids-dot-com, in which case he should ask for a partial refund on the youngest—sorry. Sorry. Inside thoughts. I know he's your nephew or whatever, but he seems like a tiny tyrant."

Eòghann shook his head so she'd know he wasn't bothered, but his thoughts were spinning in a hundred different directions. Where was their mother? And was she the same girl who'd run away to Minnesota with Alec all those years ago?

"Med school, huh? That means you haven't seen him in...?"

"Twenty-two years. Haven't spoken in about eighteen."

"Guess you'll be staying awhile then."

He couldn't tell if she was happy about it or not.

"Is there a hotel close by?"

"Don't be ridiculous. We have room."

He nodded. "Your grandmother won't mind?"

"Oh, she'll eat you up like a tasty snack," Wes told him. "I hope you brought some lighter weight clothes though," she added, eyeing his jeans in a way that made them feel extra tight. "You're not used to our heat."

"I'll survive," he rasped.

"Come here," she said, tugging on the pocket of his jeans and opening her arms. "I want to bury myself in your cologne one more time."

Eòghann didn't need to be told twice. He went to her and let her fold him up in her long, lithe arms and nuzzle into his neck.

She smelled exactly how he remembered—all honeysuckle sweetness mixed with that bit of Tennessee he'd noticed at the hotel. Holding her in his arms, breathing her in, for the first time in a very long time he felt... peaceful.

"Mmm," she murmured, making his stomach start to spin. He

felt pathetic admitting it to himself but being held and touched the way Wes held and touched him, her fingers threading through the hair at the nape of his neck—it made him want to weep.

He hadn't imagined it last year, then. Everything about her felt like coming home.

When she pulled away he cleared his throat and looked around, noticing a crack in the drywall near the door. He tilted his head, running a finger along the crack.

"Oh. Yeah. Grandma's planning to sell this place soon because she can't keep up with the repairs. She says the house is going to rack and ruin."

"I could fix this up in a jiffy. Windowsill too," he said, nodding to the window beside the bed which had obvious water damage.

Wes frowned and shook her head. "Told you," she said. "I don't need help."

Eòghann felt vaguely like he was treading into deep water he didn't understand and couldn't see the bottom of. "With your faire, you said."

"With anything. Grandma's going to sell, and that'll be that." Her voice sounded tight despite her nonchalant shrug.

"Won't it be easier to sell if I do a few quick repairs? It's no trouble. I'd be honored to help your grandmother out."

Wes eyed him suspiciously.

"I've got to earn my keep somehow." He tried to say it like a joke, like a shrug, but it was the truth, wasn't it? Why was he there if he couldn't help somehow?

Wesley pursed her lips, and a wicked gleam in her eye told him exactly how she'd allow him to earn his keep.

Flames licked up the back of his neck and his mouth went dry.

"Come on," she said. "Let's go find your long-lost cousin."

Ouᴛsɪᴅᴇ, ᴛʜᴇʏ ᴡᴇʀᴇ ᴍᴇᴛ ᴡɪᴛʜ ᴀ ᴅᴀᴍᴘ ᴡᴀʟʟ ᴏꜰ ʜᴇᴀᴛ. But rather than feel oppressed by it, after the frigid, blowing air of the hotel and then the rental car, Eòghann welcomed it, warm and comforting like a heavy blanket.

He'd been nervous about showing up on Wesley's doorstep and more than a little anxious about the reception he'd receive from Alec, but with the sun shining on his face and the scent of Wesley floating on a soft breeze, everything else disappeared except for the same voice in his chest he'd first heard in the church last year, once again whispering *home*.

Perhaps, somehow, Stratford, Tennessee was his hiraeth. Or Wesley was.

Eòghann wrapped that feeling around himself along with the heat, like comforting armor, as they joined Bryan and Grace and the little boy who looked like Alec to walk across the back garden towards a wooded area filled with a cacophony of loud music and hammering.

Bryan was vibrating with anticipation once again. Eòghann only hoped their arrival wasn't as jarring and intrusive as it felt. What if seeing Eòghann—introducing him to his new family— was the last thing Alec wanted? Would he turn tail and disappear for another twenty years?

Eòghann lagged behind a little, and Wes let the others go on ahead, waiting for him to catch up. She wound herself around his arm as she'd done when they strolled across Barra together last summer, and he welcomed the closeness. It was as grounding as the heat.

"You okay?" she murmured.

"Course," he said, forcing a little laugh into his reply. "Only jet lag."

Wesley regarded him for a long moment, but she didn't challenge his lie. "Stay hydrated," she said. "I mean it."

"Yes, ma'am," he replied in a bad Southern accent, and a slow, smoldering smile spread across her lips.

They reached a pair of caravans, and the little boy veered off towards an ivory and green one with KISIMUL painted on the back in stylized cursive script.

Eòghann tried to catch Bryan's eye, but he'd locked in on Alec—for it was unquestionably Alec—and the bagpipe player from Grace's video, a lad a few years older than the first one. The boy had traded his pipes for a fiddle and they huddled together, working through an old-sounding ballad about Culloden.

"Rory," Alec called, not looking up from his sheet music. "You decided to join us after all?"

"No," the youngest boy yelled. "They wanted to meet you." Then he promptly escaped into the caravan, letting the door slam shut behind him.

Alec's head jerked up, and all the color drained from his face at the sight of them, as though they were a pair of ghosts. But to Eòghann it was like seeing the spirit of his cousin Pòl made flesh. Pòl was only two years older than Alec was now when he died.

"Alec MacNeil?" Bryan asked. "Of B-Barra?"

"Do you even have to ask?" Eòghann whispered. "He's the spit of you. He's the spit of Pòl."

The boy stopped playing with an unmelodious scratch, darting his wide green eyes back and forth between them and his father, until Alec handed off his guitar, and the next moment he was on his feet, enveloping Bryan in a bear hug.

Eòghann tried to hang back, unobtrusively off to the side, letting them have their moment, but after a few hearty back slaps, Alec yanked him into the cuddle as well.

"What the devil?" Alec asked, pushing them out to arm's length so he could look at them, and then tugging them back in again. "What the bloody devil? When did you two get so damn old?"

"Knew it was you," Bryan gasped. "Can't b-b-believe I actually found you. Never thought I would."

"How did you?" Alec asked, stepping back still holding each of their hands.

"It was Grace," Bryan explained reverently, turning back to where his girlfriend had been standing with Wesley, but the women had drifted away, leaving the three MacNeil cousins to their private reunion. "Doesn't matter," Bryan said. "What're you doing here?"

"Darwish is a good friend. He told us the proprietress needed help, so we came," Alec said, dodging the real question of how a Scottish medical student from Minnesota wound up on the festival circuit in Tennessee. "It's a long story, but the short version is—here we are."

His voice sounded exactly the same, but also somehow different than Eòghann remembered. His Scottish accent had mellowed, broadened, become a bit softer and more nasal.

"Here you are," Bryan repeated. Then he shoved Alec with a little more than playfulness. "Why the hell did you disappear on me?"

"Bry!" Eòghann cautioned, putting a steadying hand on Bryan's shoulder. He didn't want to scare Alec off now they'd found him. He was also a little afraid to hear the answer.

"I..." Shame and sadness swept over Alec's face. "It wasn't deliberate, I... and then I..."

"Didn't know how to come back?" Bryan offered.

Alec gave a tiny nod, and Bryan pulled him into another tight embrace, each clinging to the other. It made Eòghann's eyes burn.

When Bryan stepped back he asked Alec, "You all right?"

The briefest twitch crossed Alec's face, saying *no*, but he nodded once.

"Is it all right we're here?" Eòghann asked, bracing for a similar, negative twitch, smoothly covered over with a wink and a lie.

But Alec's eyes widened with amusement and a broad grin spread across his face. "Of course, you numpty. Lads," he called. "Come and meet your cousins."

He introduced them to the middle boy, the singer with the violin, first. "Jarrod Owen," he said for Eòghann's benefit, his voice full of pride. "He's the backbone of the band. Voice of an angel, and he hasn't met an instrument he can't play."

Jarrod, who Eòghann guessed was about twelve, had set both the fiddle and his father's guitar aside. He bit his lip and shook their hands.

"Lads!" Alec barked again, and this time the oldest and youngest came stumbling out of the caravan.

"Daniel's my oldest," Alec said, nodding towards him as the boys approached. "We named our wee group after him. Danny and the Boys."

The teenager rolled his eyes as only a sixteen-year-old could but reached out. Bryan shook his hand, warmly covering it with his own, clearly touched that Alec's first son had been given his own middle name.

"And it seems you've met the hellion, Rory," Alec said, nodding to the youngest, who jumped forward with a wooden sword yelling, "En grade!"

"Rory, I swear to all that is holy if you don't put that thing away I will put *you* away," Alec warned.

Rory growled at him, baring his teeth, before running off into the woods.

Alec heaved a long-suffering sigh that Eòghann seemed to

recall hearing after some of Teàrlach's more irritating antics back in the day. It was nice to know some things didn't change.

"What did you expect, naming him Ruairidh?" Bryan teased.

"Fifty-fifty, I could've gotten The Gentle instead of The Turbulent," Alec laughed, referencing the ancient Scottish clan chiefs.

"Mmm, I rather think it was always going to be the pirate lord for you," Bryan replied, and they shared another laugh, almost like two decades had never passed them by at all, and the tightness and worry in Eòghann's chest drifted up to the sky, buoyed by their laughter, like those bubbles his therapist was always going on about. Because even though it was his fault Alec had left, maybe he wasn't the whole reason his cousin had stayed away. And maybe he could somehow bring him home.

Chapter Thirteen

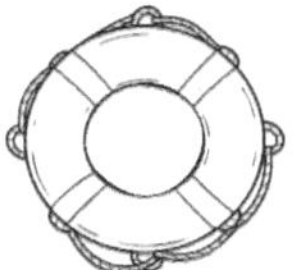

To take her mind off the whole *coitus interruptus* situation, Wes joined Grace and Grandma Ruth in the kitchen for a lunch she already knew wouldn't satisfy her particular brand of hunger.

"Can I make you a sandwich?" her grandmother offered.

"I've got it, thanks," Wes promised, ardently ignoring the questioning looks from Grandma and Grace as they went out of their way to catch her eye.

"She makes a killer one," Grace told her.

"I know."

"She doesn't know, because she's been insisting on making her own since she was seven or eight years old, and that was before I refined my technique."

"Why ask you, when I'm perfectly capable?" Wes said.

"It was nice to see Eòghann again," Grace changed the subject with the finesse of a hatchet.

"Uh huh," Wes replied, setting two slices of bread in to toast—

"Toaster's broken," they chorused at the exact same time.

Wes wasn't sure she liked them being so in sync. She spread

mustard on the cold bread, much more vigorously than was required, and poured a glass of lemonade.

After a moment, Grandma Ruth said, "I finally met the Stoic Scot *and* the Sexy Scot."

"Hey," Grace scolded. "Stoic is also very sexy."

"Right now, I'd say he was also a lot less stoic of the two," Grandma agreed, and Wes snickered, but Grace preened as though taking credit for bringing Bryan out of his shell, oblivious that Grandma was referring to the sounds she'd heard emanating from Gray's bedroom. "What's your fella called again?"

"He's not my fella," Wesley protested, prompting her grandma and her best friend to share an eye roll. "He's not, he's..."

"What?" Grace demanded.

"He's my friend. My pen pal," she settled on, as though she hadn't been trying to jump the poor priest's bones half an hour ago, the interruption of which accounted for her grumpy tone.

"I suppose it has a better ring than *meme pal*," Grace said. "And he's called Eòghann."

"I had a pen pal once," Grandma Ruth said. "I never dragged her into my bedroom by her hair."

Grace snickered.

"Come on, I didn't drag him—look, I know what it looked like," Wes said, because it looked like she'd pretty much dragged him, and she really didn't want to dissect what had happened. Or *not* happened. "Trust me. We just had..."

Grandma and Grace both raised their eyebrows, waiting to hear exactly what she planned to say.

"Words!"

"Words?" Grace asked.

"Yes. Words. To get out of our system."

Grandma cackled.

"Things we'd left unsaid," Wes added testily, "when I came home from vacation last year."

"*He's* why you dumped that crusty baguette Pierre," Grandma exclaimed as though she was Miss Marple solving a murder. "I knew you had your father's brains—which he got from me, by the way."

"I dumped *Pierce* **before** my vacation," Wes told her, rubbing the bridge of her nose to stave off the headache this conversation was promising to cause.

But Grandma's face lit up all the brighter. "You have my ESP too then."

"Cool your jets, Grandma. Nothing's gonna happen with Eòghann." *Father* Eòghann, she repeated to herself because she really shouldn't have climbed him like a cat tree, but even Fleabag eventually got a night with her priest, and she didn't have to wait nearly as long as Wesley had.

Grandma Ruth and Grace exchanged doubtful looks. Some best friend!

"Nothing of significance is going to happen," she amended, trying not to think about the condom in his pocket. "He was a hot island fling, that's it. Not even really a fling, we never got that far. Nothing was ever flung. And even if he wasn't a"—she couldn't bring herself to say priest—"big goofy weirdo," she substituted, feeling mildly disloyal for it, "I'm determined to be a... confirmed bachelorette."

Her whole body cringed at the expression. It sure didn't have the same ring to it as the male version. It evoked images of a white haired party girl taking up an extra seat for her walker on the pedal tavern.

"The term you're looking for is old maid—"

"No," Wes argued, because she refused that term whole heartedly.

"And being alone is overrated," Grandma finished gently.

"Seven out of ten, sometimes recommend," Grace piped up. She hadn't minded being single before meeting Bryan. She'd preferred it, though now they were joined at the hip when they weren't separated by an ocean.

But Wesley's grandfather had passed away when she was a baby, and before that he was a combat veteran. She understood the point her grandma was making.

"Who says I'll end up alone?" Wes countered. "I could have a hot new boy toy every other week if I wanted, my very own personal Kens, if you will."

Grandma cackled again. "That's my girl." Then she turned the full force of her gaze on Grace, who shrank back in alarm. "What about you?"

"What about me?"

"Seven out of ten, my ass. Your Stoic Scot didn't sound too stoic this afternoon."

There it was.

Grace squeaked as red spilled across her cheeks like overturned ink.

"These walls are paper thin, you know."

"Grandma Ruth!" Wes squealed, trying hard to keep her laughter in check for Gray's sake, but her whole body felt like a shaken up Coke about to explode.

"They are," Grandma shrugged.

"Long distance is hard," Grace said in a tiny, meek voice Wes hardly recognized. "I wanted to make sure he knew I missed him."

Now Wesley did burst out laughing.

"Good girl," Grandma said, patting Gray's shoulder and pouring her another glass of lemonade. "But if the hot Scots aren't here to help with the faire, what are they going to get up to while y'all are busy doing my bidding?"

Wes shrugged. "Stand around and look pretty?"

"Oh I'm absolutely putting Bryan and Lùc to work, are you kidding me? After all the noise they made renovating that cottage while I was on deadline? They owe me sweat. And hammering."

"That sounds real filthy, Gray."

Grace grimaced. "They can start by helping Jack and Andy build those stages."

"Speaking of Lùcas, did he and Andy make it back from the hardware store? I'm pretty sure this is his first time off the island."

"Worried Andy's going to corrupt him?"

"More worried he might try to corrupt Andy."

Grandma waved the tongue-in-cheek concern away. "They came back with the name of some cowboy who saw you on the news and volunteered to bushhog the front yard for parking."

Grace and Wesley looked at each other in surprise. "Wow," Wes said.

"It worked! You're a star." Grace mimed checking another thing off their list.

Wes rolled her eyes and took a bite of her ham sandwich. She gagged a little but choked it down so her grandma wouldn't worry the meat had gone bad. Nothing ruined a ham sandwich like unexpected cashew butter where the Dijon mustard was supposed to be.

"Good ham," she said, nodding to answer the question no one had asked. "Savory."

Because if she told the truth, her grandma would've insisted on making her a new sandwich, and Grace would have told her to put on her glasses, and honestly, ham and cashew butter wasn't the worst thing she'd ever choked down.

Chapter Fourteen

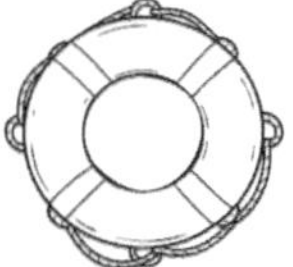

Jet lag was hitting Eòghann like a freight train as they sat before a roaring bonfire that evening, but he was there, off the island, among Wesley's nearest and dearest. And he had Alec back. He wasn't about to beg off and miss a minute. With his luck he'd wake up back on that infernal plane, somewhere over the mid-Atlantic and this would all have been a dream.

Wes flitted from person to person like a fairy godmother, checking in to make certain everyone had enough to eat and drink, teasing them all as she went. Each time she passed Eòghann she squeezed his shoulder or stroked the back of his head, and he found himself leaning into her touch. He hadn't realized how starved for it he was.

Even when she was out of his direct sightline, his body remained acutely aware of her location, the hairs on his arms and the back of his neck following her around the campfire like the needle on a compass. He watched his cousin interacting with the other Americans whose names he mostly couldn't recall, and it was strange to think they all knew Alec better than he did by now. Had they heard stories about his childhood featuring Eòghann?

From what he'd gathered, they were all Wesley's university friends. They performed at these historical themed festivals throughout the country to earn their living, and at some point they'd taken in Alec and the lads as their own. It was one, big, bonded village, and when something had gone wrong with Grandma Ruth's festival, they had flocked in to help like the Renaissance Armada.

Though friendly and engaging with everyone, for his part, Alec seemed desperately sad. Almost hollowed out, in a way. He said all the right things and laughed in the right places, but there was something fragile and heavy about him. Like instead of a twinkle his eyes held back long-bottled tears. Eòghann wanted to ask so many questions, but he didn't feel he'd earned the right.

"Come sit with us, Daniel," Alec called to his eldest, who had piled a plate high with hot dogs and burgers and was heading back towards their caravan.

"Studying," the surly teen grunted, turning away, and Eòghann could swear Alec's shoulders sagged a little deeper.

"Nerd!" Rory yelled after him. "You're so boring. It's summer!"

"It's SAT's," Daniel retorted.

"Boring!"

"Teenagers," Alec huffed, trying to make a joke of it. "Suppose I've only got another year or two before this one can't stand the sight of me either." He nodded to Jarrod, who looked up from his own hotdog like a deer in headlights.

One of the college friends, a pretty Black woman whose name Eòghann thought might begin with 'S' came over to speak with Alec, and an awkwardness settled between Eòghann and his cousin's middle boy.

"So you lot spend the summer traveling around as a band?" he eventually asked the kid. "That's fun."

Jarrod shrugged. "Not only summer. All the time. Ever since..." He trailed off, glancing at his father and shrugged again, driving home the point that after two decades, the things Eòghann didn't know far outweighed the things he did.

"Sounds exciting," he said, realizing how heavy the silence had grown.

"Roddy takes to instruments like a duck to water," Alec said, rejoining their conversation. "Don't you, son?"

Jarrod shrugged.

"How many do you play?" Eòghann asked.

The boy looked thoughtful. "Fiddle, bagpipe, bodhrán, keyboard, and whistle mostly."

"What, no brass?" Eòghann teased.

Alec guffawed. "Don't you start. He's been begging for a trombone the past year."

Jarrod grinned sheepishly.

"Eòghann! Wanna play soccer?" Rory yelled, or maybe he only had one volume and it was always eleven and half.

Eòghann most emphatically did not want to play *soccer*. He rather wanted to lie down and sleep for an age. Being forty-one was for the birds. But he caught Wesley grinning from across the fire and something sizzled between them like he was *in* the fire, and he didn't feel quite so tired anymore.

"That's *Uncle* Eòghann to you," Alec called to his youngest. "Or—I guess you wouldn't be, would you? Hell, you're not *my* uncle, are you?"

"First cousin once removed, I think they call it," Eòghann said, standing up to join Rory a little further away from the fire. To his surprise, Jarrod jumped up to follow.

"Yeah!" Rory pumped his fist and did a silly dance before

racing past another of Wesley's friends, a man with an olive complexion and an injured hand, who was setting up a tripod.

"Careful of the camera," Eòghann warned Rory, as the friend pointed his expensive-looking equipment up at the darkening sky.

"He's fine," the man said loudly.

"Apologies, I..." Eòghann hadn't wanted the whole setup to topple over.

"Appreciate it," the man said more quietly. "But if you tell that one to be careful, he's more likely to knock it over on purpose."

Jarrod laughed. "Andy's right, he would."

"Would what?" Rory said, dribbling the ball back towards them.

Jarrod looked at Eòghann for a second before replying. "Andy would stay up every night trying to shoot the Milky Way if he could."

"Boring! Have you ever seen the Milky Way?" Rory asked Eòghann.

"Aye. It gets especially dark in winter where I come from."

"Where, Scotland?" Rory said, his voice dripping with disdain.

"Indeed. Home of the original Kisimul Castle."

"Alba gu bràth," Rory screamed, *Scotland forever* in Gaelic, though Eòghann doubted he knew what he was saying beyond a battle cry. Then the boy kicked a cracker of a shot aimed right at his bollocks.

Eòghann brought it down deftly with his knee and faked Rory out, passing it sideways to Jarrod, who grinned. "Where I come from, we call this football."

Rory scoffed. "In *real* football you can knock down anyone you want without getting in trouble."

They dribbled and passed for a few minutes, just the three

of them and the—"Glow-worms," he murmured, overwhelmed by the sight of them.

"Worms?" Rory yelled. "You mean fireflies? Kick it high so I can do a header!"

"You already have one plaster on your face," Eòghann protested.

"Plaster," Rory laughed, mimicking his accent. "I'm not scared."

But Eòghann couldn't do it. He'd already imagined it going all wrong—knocking the kid out with a concussion. The flashing lights of an ambulance. What color were they in the States? Were they blue like on the BBC?

"How about keepie-uppie?" Eòghann suggested, juggling the ball between his feet, his knees, his chest, but never letting it hit the ground. "When I was your age, I could do about a hundred. Reckon you can beat me?" he asked, passing the ball back to Rory who immediately started a keepie-uppie juggle of his own.

"I'm *excellent* at keepie-uppie, actually. Once, me and Sully kept it up for two hundred times!" Rory boasted. But, in the blink of an eye, darkness seemed to cross his face, and he let the ball fall. "Even stupid babies can keep a stupid ball in the stupid air," he shouted, turning and punting the football into the trees before storming off in the opposite direction.

What the hell?

Eòghann glanced to Jarrod in confusion, but the middle child simply shrugged. "That was my ball," he said dejectedly, and headed off to find it.

"Shall I come with you?" Eòghann asked, but Jarrod didn't reply, and Eòghann realized he shouldn't have asked, he should've simply followed. A phone with a flashlight sure would come in handy right about now.

He took one step towards the tree line, but a soft, deep voice said, "He'll be fine."

Eòghann turned to see the last of the college friends, who Wes had mentioned was Navajo, his unruly black hair spilling out of his cap as he leaned against another caravan watching the scene.

He took a puff on an e-cigarette and exhaled slowly. "Sullivan was Rory's twin."

Eòghann froze. Twin? "Was?" he repeated.

Jack looked like he wanted to say more, but he swallowed and nodded curtly.

"Jesus. When?"

"Last year."

Another wave of regret and guilt threatened to knock Eòghann sideways. Had a butterfly flapped its wings when Eòghann made Pòl drown, setting in motion every bad thing that ever happened to Alec? No wonder he looked so empty inside.

"Eòghann, right?"

Eòghann nodded, embarrassed to have already forgotten the other man's name. "I'm sorry, the jet lag maybe, I don't..." He shook his head.

The man exhaled another stream of smoke off to the side and then took a step forward, offering his hand for Eòghann to shake. "Jack. Bennally. You're with Wes?"

The sharp left turn threw Eòghann further off balance. "No," he said. Then thinking back to her reaching for his belt buckle in the bedroom he added, "I don't know."

Jack glanced back towards the house like he could read every filthy thought flicking through Eòghann's brain.

"It's casual." Trying to explain their relationship to this veritable stranger who of course knew Wesley better than Eòghann did himself seemed pointless.

One thing they could probably both agree on was that Eòghann didn't deserve her.

"She know it's casual?" Jack asked.

Eòghann nodded because of course she did. Even as she had flirted with him on Barra she put off major non-commitment vibes. Why else was she so hesitant to come back and visit him again?

"She knows," Eòghann said aloud, to convince himself as much as Jack.

"Good. Because if you hurt her..."

"You'll kill me?"

Jack shrugged. "They didn't dub us the Shakespeare Syndicate for nothing."

The what-now? "Why *did* they call you that?" Eòghann asked. They'd quote sonnets while stabbing him in the back like Brutus did to Caesar? Wax poetic while poisoning him like Gertrude and Hamlet?

Jack grinned mysteriously. "Welcome to Tennessee," he said softly. And then he sort of melted into the shadows, as a cold shiver ran down Eòghann's spine.

Chapter Fifteen

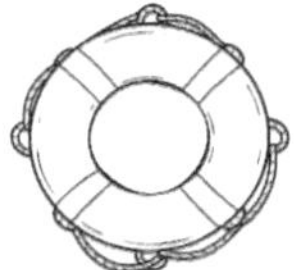

I t was a strange feeling, Wesley's three worlds colliding so spectacularly. Of course, her found family had enjoyed a bonfire with her grandma before, but it had been an awfully long time. And now their motley crew was joined by the boys from Barra, including the man who would likely become the closest thing she'd ever have to a brother-in-law. And his cousin, the man she hadn't stopped thinking about since last summer. A man whose eyes seemed to follow her as she circulated. She couldn't see them in the semi-darkness, but she could feel them, sending frissons of recognition along her skin as though she were being singed by cast off sparks from the fire. And she liked it, damn her. She liked being noticed and appreciated and desired.

She was doing her best to ignore him though, to give him space to visit with his family, to give herself space to avoid pouncing all up on his beautiful biceps, but she couldn't help passing by occasionally to make sure he was all right, touching him every chance she got, simply because he was right there and oh-so-touchable.

It was strange and very unexpected having him show up

here in Stratford, but also somehow perfect. Setting aside the very real and constant tingling between her thighs—a rare enough feat these days that she was happy to know it wasn't dead down there—and despite the fact they'd refunded seven hundred dollars worth of tickets today, she felt content to exist in the same space with all these people. The house had always been a sanctuary, and Grandma Ruth was a real one.

The summer after freshman year Wes had invited Andy to stay for a few weeks. He wanted to get out of his big sister's hair and he hadn't been welcome at his parents' house, so he spent the summer working at the tiny old Stratford drive-in, saving up to buy himself a telescope.

The summer after that, Wes was planning to turn down a design internship in Nashville to help Grandma Ruth after her knee replacement surgery, until Andy convinced her to go while he stayed at Warwick Hall instead. Grandma had taught him how to cook and play bridge, and the house had become his oasis as much as Wesley's. He'd probably feel as bereft to see it go on the market as she would. If only they could scrape up enough money between them to buy it together and keep it in the family.

Between junior and senior years, the whole Shakespeare Syndicate had assembled en masse at Grandma's house. Wes had invited them out for two weeks of what she called Panda-monium, in which they celebrated a bunch of random holidays starting with the births of panda twins at the National Zoo. It definitely had nothing whatsoever to do with Gray's twenty-first birthday, which coincidentally fell during the extravaganza.

As it turned out, Panda-monium had been such a stealthy success that Grace, who was incapable of celebrating herself, still had no idea it was a party for her until last summer when Wesley let it slip during their trip to Scotland.

Anyway, her friends all adored Grandma Ruth, and

Grandma loved having them around, so it was easy to forgive Grace for rallying them to help with the faire no matter how much it made Wesley twitch. As Gray had pointed out, they were in the business, and they wanted to help Grandma Ruth as a way of saying thanks. And, as she'd reminded herself about a hundred times since Wednesday—they weren't a bunch of twelve-year-old boarding school brats. If things went sideways, they wouldn't abandon her.

Adding the Scottish Invasion into the mix somehow also made sense, although having Eòghann around was muddling Wesley's every thought with unhelpful, lust-fueled daydreams.

Right now the priest was chatting with Andy, who'd set up his camera to try and capture the night sky. Perfect. Let him charm her friends. He'd be good for Andy, and the sooner they became allies, the sooner Andy and Jack would tone down their suspicious brother routine.

For all their bluster, they clearly liked Bryan already. Anyone could see how happy he made Grace. Once Eòghann recovered from his jet lag, they'd adore him too—not that he needed to win them over, because he and Wesley weren't in a relationship. Still, she hoped he wasn't overwhelmed. She knew her friends could be a lot, by virtue of there being so many of them.

It was probably a lot for Lùc, too. All of eighteen years old, meeting new people aside from tourists for the first time in who knew how long, watching his cousins rediscover old family who'd left Barra before he was born. Not to mention he was at an awkward age—caught between childhood and adulthood— closer in years to the doctor's three boys than he was to any of his fellow adults.

Wes almost tripped over him, standing in the shadows near the gang's camper, fondly dubbed *The Lair*, listening to Jack tell a story about getting lost on the way to Grandfather Mountain.

"I fixed up a room for you," she told him. "Upstairs, first door on the left."

"Ta for that. Sorry for the trouble."

"So much trouble. I put clean sheets on the bed and everything. You can never possibly repay me so don't bother trying."

He snorted.

"I'm glad you're here," she said, leaning into his shoulder.

"Sort of invited myself along." He smiled sheepishly.

"Hell yeah you did! Good for you. Enjoy yourself—what little there is to enjoy."

He snorted again. "I made Bryan take me out last night."

"In Nashville? Did you have fun?" She couldn't quite imagine Broadway being the Stoic Scot's idea of a good time.

"It was indescribable. Party buses and pedal taverns and hen dos every which way you looked."

"Bet he hated every minute."

"I'm honestly surprised he's still speaking to me."

Wes laughed. "Not much nightlife here, but hopefully the faire will be fun for you."

"I've never been to a Renaissance faire."

"Oh, you're in for a treat. But don't let Grace put you to work. I know she's already threatening to."

"I don't mind."

"Please. You're on vacation. Eat some food. Get to know your cousins."

"You do know they're not *my* cousins, right?"

"They're not?" she asked, confused.

"Wes," he tsked, sounding thoroughly disappointed. "Not everyone on Barra's related to each other."

"I didn't think they were," she lied, although that was exactly the impression she'd gotten last year.

"I'm pure Buchanan. He's pure MacNeil. S'only Eòghann

and Bryan's lot that are mixed up mutts in the middle, related on both sides."

"You really did tag along for the heck of it then?"

He shrugged. "Moral support. Eòghann was a wee bit tetchy about the flight, and I was desperate for something to do."

Had she known Eòghann didn't like flying? Surely that was something she'd have remembered, but then maybe that was why he'd been resistant to the idea of visiting.

"In that case, welcome to Tennessee," she said, patting his arm. "Try not to have too much fun all at once."

"If I get bored can I help?" he asked, tearing his eyes away from Andy's camera and turning to face her.

She could already feel herself losing this battle. "It's under control," she assured him.

He took a long sip of his drink, and she braced herself for whatever argument he was preparing.

"Adnan—your friend," he clarified nodding towards Andy as if there were more than one. "When we went to buy lumber, he said you were going to design some backdrops for the stages?"

"I think that's numbers twelve and thirteen on my to-do list."

He looked down at the ground, chewed his thumbnail. "D'you reckon I could help paint them?"

She was about to gracefully decline, but he rushed on before she had the chance.

"I'd do them up however you want. Only I've never painted anything so large before—unless you count graffitiing my da's shed, which I probably shouldn't since I'll deny it to my dying day."

Until that moment it hadn't occurred to Wes that helping out with the faire could be anything other than a chore to her friends, that for some, like Lùc, it might actually be a chance for personal fulfillment. He was so earnest and pure it almost killed her.

"If you genuinely want to paint, I won't stop you," she said. "But keep it clean." She pointed at him, recalling what she'd heard about his raunchy library book doodles. "No one's getting arrested for public pornography on my watch."

"I wouldn't dare," he laughed. "I just really like to paint."

"I'll let you know when the designs are ready."

"I could help with that too, if you're busy."

"I appreciate the offer but"—she squeezed his shoulder—"I just really like to design."

He grinned at her.

"I'll try to have them for you tomorrow?"

"Deal," he said, holding out his hand to shake on it.

"Wes," Sadie called, approaching them with Grace and Bryan in tow. "Do you want to go into town next week? Maybe hang up some flyers and do a little shopping?"

"Sure. I'll try to finish up the flyers tomorrow," she said. "Backdrop designs first, flyers second," she added for Lùc's benefit. And by finish either one, she definitely meant start them.

"I want to see how much the town has changed," Sadie said. "Should I be scared? Is it going to make me feel old?"

"Probably," Wes laughed. "But we can feel old together."

"Did you all grow up here in Stratford?" Lùc asked.

Sadie shook her head. "Army brat," she said.

"Air Force brat," Wes echoed.

"Just a brat," Grace chimed in with a shrug, and the Stoic Scot burst out with a surprised guffaw.

"How long have you three been working on that bit?" he asked.

Sadie blew out her cheeks, mentally calculating.

"Freshman year?" Grace asked.

Wes nodded. "Certainly by the spring semester."

"Twelve years?" Sadie murmured and they all groaned, feeling older by the minute.

It was nice to be home, to be known and loved, and to have all these jerks show up to help whether she needed them to or not.

Seeming to read her thoughts, the girls piled in for a group hug, and Wesley squeezed them extra tight, reveling in their closeness, as Sadie stroked her hair. Everything was going to work out.

Chapter Sixteen

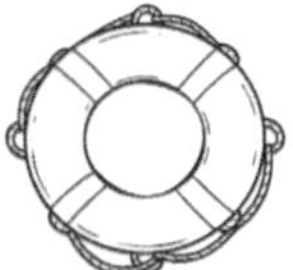

Despite his exhaustion, Eòghann's awareness of Wesley never faded. He tried to be present with Alec and his friends as they caught up on each other's lives in between Grandma Ruth's endless offers of s'mores, but his senses remained tuned to Wes at all times, like some kind of weather radio.

He was staring into the dwindling fire—half asleep, half ruminating on what he'd learned from Jack about his nephews— when he felt her approach. She squeezed his shoulder, setting his nerves on fire, and said, "Come on, Scottish Invasion. Let's get you to bed."

There were snickers from Grace and Bryan's direction, but Eòghann let her drag him to his feet, noticing for the first time that she'd put on a jumper to ward off the refreshing nip in the mountain air. And not any old jumper—the charcoal cable knit she'd pilfered from him last summer.

It made him smile and his heart beat faster to know she still wore it.

As she took his hand and glided back across the garden to

Grandma Ruth's house, more than one pair of eyes watched them go, and Jack's earlier warning rang in his ears.

"I made a room up for you," Wes murmured, interrupting his thoughts, and disappointment nipped at his heels. "If you want it," she added lazily. "You don't have to use it if you're afraid you might get lonely in this big, strange house, in this big, strange country."

"I don't?" he croaked.

She shrugged. "You're a grown man, Padre. And as we've established—you're on vacation."

His stomach tightened at her implication. *Vacation is for food and orgasms.* And both of them had already eaten.

She showed him to the room she'd made up down the hall from her own, flipping on the lights to reveal two double beds and faded blue wallpaper. "If you want it," she said again, almost like she didn't care either way. But she was watching him with eyes of molten cobalt.

"What did yours look like again?" he asked.

Grinning, she took his hand and led him back to her room, which was painted in a soft periwinkle with border paper around the perimeter.

"Oh, right. I think I prefer the blue," he teased, and she jerked him inside and closed the door, leaning up against it to prevent his escape.

"Why are your friends called the Shakespeare Syndicate?" he asked, with an unfamiliar rasp in his voice.

Wes laughed, and it was like a salve to his tired-out soul. "I can't remember who started it. They were all literature majors— Grace, Jack, Sadie. Our friend Beatrix."

"Not you?"

"No. Andy was Jack's randomly assigned roommate and I was Bea's. They sort of adopted us. Him from the physics department and me from the arts."

"And now they do the Shakespeare thing year round?"

"Pretty much. They make decent enough money living their best wild and free, rolling stone lives."

"Jealous?"

"Who me? When I have the privilege of being chained to a desk forty hours a week plus overtime?" She sighed. "I'm not complaining. That desk job gives me health insurance and vacation time to help my grandmother out of this pickle. I'm pretty sure those guys broke a bunch of contracts to be here when Gray called."

"Grace asked them?"

"Didn't even occur to me. I'd never want to impose," she said with a shrug. "If they're rolling stones then I'm a rock and an island. I solve my own problems."

"But you are letting them help?"

"They didn't give me much choice in the matter."

Eòghann thought he understood. She didn't want anyone's help, but there was history there. He didn't know her well enough to impose his own assistance where it wasn't wanted, and a sick sort of dread filled his belly. He wasn't sure he knew how *not* to be useful. He also couldn't bear the idea of being in the way.

"Was it good seeing Alec again?" she asked, breaking into his thoughts with her change of subject.

Good wasn't the first word he'd have chosen. A relief, maybe. Comforting. Also strange and a little bit sad, but he nodded because *good* was expected. *Good* was normal.

"What?" she asked, seeing right through him.

"We're practically strangers. Your friends know more about him than I do."

"He seemed glad to see you."

"His wife—partner? The boys' mother..." he shook his head.

"I wondered about that. You don't know anything?"

"I didn't know he had children until the video Grace recorded," he answered sadly.

"It's okay," she reassured him. "I'm pretty sure there are cousins on my mom's side I've never met. Are you up for some light internet stalking?" She offered him her iPad and snuggled next to him on the bed.

Eòghann hesitated. It felt like an unbearable intrusion. On the other hand, if he asked, Alec would probably tell him, but that risked ripping open old wounds.

"Everyone stalks everyone these days," Wes said, pressing the iPad into his lap.

Reluctantly, he slid on his reading glasses, and she stared at him.

"Go on. You can say it. They make me look old as dust—"

"When did you get slutty little glasses?" she interrupted, embarrassing him for a whole different reason, and he shrugged, trying to suppress a sideways grin.

"Ever since I turned forty I can hardly read without them."

She huffed, and crossed her arms, trying to look away but repeatedly sneaking glances back at him. "I'm behaving," she said, gesturing to the iPad. "Go on with your research."

He'd rather lost interest in internet stalking, but he flipped open the tablet's cover. An art program was already open, displaying a business card for WESLEY TEAL. INTERIOR AND SET DESIGN.

"Oh, here." She reached across him to close the program, her hair falling in a soft curtain of honey-scented gold that left him heady when she leaned back against her pillow.

For a moment he stared at the blinking cursor in the search bar. He wasn't sure the boys' mother was the same girlfriend who'd followed his cousin across the sea. So instead, he found himself searching ***Danny and the Boys Celtic music***.

The search yielded dozens of videos across various social media platforms.

"Try that one," Wes pointed. "You shouldn't need an account."

He cleared his throat, wanting to make a snappy comeback about how he was on all the platforms, thank you very much.

"Are you going to tell me you *do* have an online presence?" she asked.

"Why do you think I haven't?" He might be ten years older than her, but plenty of people in their forties were chronically online these days. Hell, his own ma played in an online mahjong league.

Wes studied him for a moment. "You don't exactly seem like the type to bother with all that." As she said it, he realized she didn't seem the type either. It wasn't an insult or a crack about his age.

"You're right. I'm not," he agreed. He could barely get the hang of scrolling on the touch screen.

Wes grinned triumphantly and reached over to click on one of the videos. Then she rummaged in her side table until she came out with her own glasses—similar to the ones she hated so much she kept trying to lose them last summer.

"Now who's got sexy little glasses?" he teased.

She huffed in disbelief.

It was true, the frames weren't small. They took up two thirds of her face. But he loved them, and if he looked at the right angle they encircled her pretty blue eyes like an adorable owl.

She reached across him to turn up the volume, her hand brushing over his with a spark of static electricity that jump-started his blood.

The video was a few months old. They were all wearing jackets with their kilts, and warm, woolen hats. Alec and Daniel played guitar, and Rory kept time with a shaker, while Jarrod crooned "Wild Mountain Tyne."

Watching it felt so much like peeking into the past and seeing Alec in various stages of his youth.

"They're very talented," Wes murmured.

"Alec was always musical. Got his first guitar when he was about eight, I think."

Eòghann scrolled the comments below the video, which said much the same thing Wesley had—at first.

> **FaireFrenzy77**
> So good.

> **Mitzy-Joy Goddard**
> Beautiful boys.

> **SandraK**
> God bless your sweet family.

But then the tone changed.

> **Singer-Boy-2013**
> I miss Sully :'(

> **Celtic_Crawdad**
> Not as good without Sullivan's sweet
> harmony.

> **Rennie4Life**
> How can they sing Sully's song without him
> there?

Eòghann froze.

"There's always weirdos online," Wes said softly, if a little perplexed. "You should never read the comments."

"Sullivan was Rory's twin," Eòghann explained. "Jack told me."

She didn't have an immediate response to that, but she

rubbed his arm, and he leaned into the touch. Jesus, he was like a dog demanding pets. Why did he need it so much?

The video ended and another began to play.

This one was a couple of years old. It began with Jarrod playing "The Skye Boat Song" on the pipes, accompanied again by both guitars. Rory beat a snare drum, and there was a fourth little boy, mirror image to Rory, who harmonized with Jarrod on vocals, high and sweet if a touch off key.

> **Singer-Boy-2013**
> I miss Sully :'(
>
> **Rennie4Life**
> Justice for Sullivan!!!!!!
>
> **FaireFrenzy77**
> Whatever happened to the twin?
>
> **Singer-Boy-2013**
> He dry-drowned at camp.
>
> **Celtic_Crawdad**
> WTF is dry-drowned?
>
> **Rennie4Life**
> There's no such thing dumbass. It's called secondary drowning.

Bile rose up Eòghann's throat as he read the comments and his heart began to race. Not again. It couldn't have happened to Alec a second time.

"Maybe this was a bad idea," Wes said gently, trying to take the iPad. "I assumed they split up because she couldn't hack it on the faire circuit or something. I didn't realize there was another kid, I—"

"Poor Alec."

Eòghann clutched the tablet so tight his knuckles turned

white, and he clicked back to the browser and typed in ***Sullivan MacNeil camp drowning***.

Immediately, articles came up with variations on the same headline:

Camp Calloway under investigation after 8-year-old's death due to dry drowning

"Eòghann, are you sure?" Wes asked, leaning closer to him, both hands still on the tablet.

"I need to know."

Another wave of nausea washed over him, and he closed his eyes, trying to remember how to breathe the way Paulo the flight attendant had shown him. How ironic that his name was Paulo. For a moment, Eòghann had thought it was a sign, the ghost of his cousin Pòl arriving once more to help him in his moment of need. But if Pòl was going to help anyone, it should've been Sully.

He tried to focus on Wesley—on her warmth and her scent —but the room was spinning around him. "Will you read it to me?"

"Eòghann."

"Please?"

Wes cleared her throat. "Umm, eight-year-old camper Sullivan MacNeil..."

She paused.

"Please, Wes."

Taking his hand, she started again, her voice soft, though stilted. "Eight-year-old camper Sullivan MacNeil died on Tuesday... from complications of pulmonary edema, a side effect of secondary drowning, after his canoe was overturned in Lake Calloway."

Eòghann was no longer on Wesley's bed in Tennessee. He

was in that lake with his cousin's little boy, cold and wet and gasping for breath as water poured into his mouth. The heart rate monitor on his watch began to beep.

Wes ran a hand up and down his back. "I'm so sorry."

"Keep reading," he begged, clawing at his watch, trying to make the beeping stop.

"Eòghann..."

"Wes." He had to know. All of it. Alec had lived it, the least he could do was hear about it.

She sighed but began reading again. "According to the boy's father, musician Alec MacNeil—a performer at the nearby Somerset Celtic Festival—the boy and his twin brother were both expert swimmers."

Eòghann was going to be sick.

He stumbled off the bed, tripping over the rug and making it to the toilet just in time.

Poor Alec. To lose a child the exact same way he lost his own father. It was unthinkable. It was...

"What do you need?" Wes asked, squeezing his shoulder and rubbing his back.

He shook his head, pressing his palms to his eyes as though that would stop everything from going black. Secondary drowning? What did it mean? He should—he needed to pull it together—to get off the bathroom floor and look it up.

Sweat trickled down his back, cold and shivery.

"Eòghann?"

"He lost his *child*," he gasped, "in a brown, muddy lake."

His breath was speeding up again, and instead of being in the lake he was in the frigid, choppy ocean after falling over board at twelve years old, waves splashing in his eyes and mouth while he coughed and cried and trod water for dear life, watching the fishing boat drift further and further away. And then suddenly Pòl was there with the lifebuoy, and Eòghann was saved, and moments later Pòl was gone.

"Pòl! Eòghann!" the others yelled until their names were fused together in one cacophonous scream.

"Eòghann? Eòghann, come back to me."

It was Wes. Her concerned face and forget-me-not eyes full of worry and unshed tears bobbed before him. He wasn't in the water. For the second time in as many days, he was crouched on the floor of a loo, the soft drip of the faucet sounding as loud as a cymbal crash.

At least this time the floor wasn't sticky.

"It's okay, Eòghann," Wes whispered, stroking his hair and placing a cool damp cloth on the back of his neck. "Alec and the boys—they're okay. It's horrible, they lost a piece of themselves, but they've come out the other side."

He nodded, for something to do. Because otherwise his mortification would rip a hole in the earth for him to disappear into.

"Breathe," she whispered, pressing her hand to his chest, grounding him, dragging him back from the depths to dry land. "Breathe."

She helped him to his feet, and he stood there, hunched over the dripping sink for several minutes, telling himself to put his feelings into bubbles or whatever bullshit, until he was at least semi-confident he wouldn't be sick again. Then he washed his face and rinsed his mouth and let her lead him back to the bed.

"Everything's going to be okay," she promised.

And—oh no. He liked this feeling of being taken care of, petted and comforted by her soft, gentle hands. He liked it way too much, and he didn't deserve an ounce of it, so he tried to argue with her.

"You don't understand," he said with a bitter petulance she didn't deserve, which only made him more ashamed.

"You're right, I don't. Not entirely. But they're still here, and you're here now too," she said, taking his glasses and scooting back against the headboard so he could rest on her lap as he curled into himself, shivering, but not from cold.

She pulled the duvet up snug around his shoulders, rubbing his back and stroking his hair until the trembling stopped and sleep mercifully found him—despite his grief, despite the absolute humiliation of it all.

Chapter Seventeen

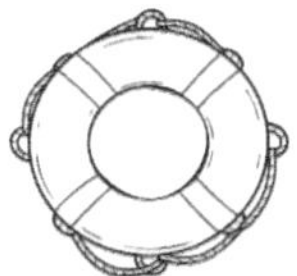

T-MINUS 13 DAYS TO RENAYZANTS FAIRE

When Wesley woke the next morning on the heels of a very filthy dream involving one of those church confessional booths, she found Eòghann's side of the bed cool to the touch, and she sighed. Sleeping next to him had been lovely, but the jet lag must've woken him early and now she was faced with yet another day of organizing the faire while aching to lick him from head to toe.

For half a minute last night, she'd thought he was doing a bit when he pulled out those slutty little reading glasses, and she'd been one hundred percent on board. Realizing he actually needed them to read her tablet somehow tipped her straight into overdrive, despite the crack about his age. He wasn't that old, and besides, she'd always been attracted to older men. It was probably one reason things didn't work out with Pierce. He'd been a blip. A young, immature, not-her-usual-type seven-year blip.

Unfortunately, as always seemed to be the case with Wes and Eòghann, their timing left a lot to be desired. Not that she begrudged him. Last night he'd needed to solve a mystery, and then he'd been understandably distraught over what he learned.

She hoped it was only jet lag rousing him so early, and not more of the anxiety-induced vomiting which had gripped him the night before. It'd been rather terrifying to witness, if she was being honest, the man she thought of as being steady and calm collapsing in a fit of panic.

Maybe she was heartless, but it seemed like a tiny bit of an overreaction, given he hadn't known the boy existed until the same moment he'd found out Sullivan had died, but maybe that was simply Wes being cold and aloof. Maybe it was a *her* problem. She felt sick for him, of course—for all of them—it was a terrible thing, clearly a shock to Eòghann. And she was glad she could be there to hold him as he went to pieces, even if she didn't fully understand it. Circumstances aside, she rather liked being his person, and she kind of loved knowing he could be so empathetic. Still waters run deep and all that.

It was a little bit dangerous.

Unfortunately, despite everything, she was still horny as hell. Groaning into her pillow, she considered calming down with Pablo. She didn't hate the idea of the Sexy Scot walking in on her *in medias res*, as they say, and then deciding to take matters into his own fine hands. But the scent of fresh cinnamon rolls wafted under the bedroom door and her stomach growled, reminding her once more of the long list of things to do today, and neither Pablo nor the Padre was on her list.

After stumbling downstairs, she snagged a gooey pastry and wandered into the living room. There she found Grandma Ruth and Eòghann, who was inexplicably wearing a kilt, huddled together before a built-in bookcase, where the Sexy Scot appeared to be adding a brand new additional shelf.

"Wonderful," Grandma purred. "I've been dying to get

those stacks of books off my bedside table. I was starting to worry they would bury me alive."

"Have you read all these?" Eòghann asked, scanning the old mass market romance novels stacked two deep on the shelf below the one he'd added.

"Oh yes, many times. Does that shock you? I wasn't always old, you know, and they were a welcome distraction when my husband was deployed."

"And now?"

Grandma Ruth smiled wickedly. "Now they're just fun."

"Which are your favorites?" he asked, and she pointed out a few different books, whispering to him, words that made the back of his neck flush and his shoulders shake with laughter.

"Grandma Ruth," Wesley teased. "Are you corrupting the man with your naughty books?"

Grandma turned to Eòghann unapologetically. "Am I?"

The flush on his cheeks deepened. "Erm..." he dissembled. "To be honest, no. I've read a romance novel or two in my day."

"Which two?" Grandma asked.

"More than two."

She cackled. "I knew it! I can clock a happily-ever-after connoisseur at fifty paces. What's your poison? Rivals becoming lovers? Marriage of convenience?"

He shifted, setting the book he'd been examining back on the shelf and rubbing his flaming red neck.

"Not the dark stuff," Grandma went on. "You're much too gentle for all that. And not romantasy either, I don't think."

"No?"

"No." She pointed at him. "You're a historical man. With some contemporary thrown in here and there to keep it fresh."

He nodded his agreement.

"Wait, for real?" Wes asked. "You actually read romance?"

Eòghann shrugged. "Not a terrible way to learn what women like, is it?"

Wesley's brain stuttered like a car with a dead battery because why, exactly, would a priest need to know what women like in bed? To counsel their boorish husbands? To properly assign penance? But then, she supposed he hadn't been born a priest.

As she stared at him, his watch began to beep. He glanced down at it, and then turned back to Grandma, clasping a hand over his wrist to cover the watch and smother the beeping before rocking back on his heels.

"You're all set. This should hold another year's worth of books."

"Feel free to borrow them anytime you like. You too," she added, turning to Wes. "How are the cinnamon rolls?" she asked, winking back at Eòghann.

"Perfection," Wes replied, licking icing off her thumb and trying not to dwell on whatever inside joke her grandma and her *fling* were sharing. "I haven't tasted one of these in years."

"I haven't made them in years, but Eòghann was kind enough to reach my pan down off the shelf above the fridge, right after he fixed the toaster!"

Wes raised an eyebrow. "How accommodating of him."

"You said you didn't need my help with the faire. You didn't say I couldn't help Grandma Ruth around the house."

A technicality she couldn't fault. And why did she get all melty like her cinnamon roll, hearing him talk about her grandmother so familiarly?

Her grandmother, who was beaming up at him like he was one of the models on her romance book covers.

"Busy morning. And in a kilt, no less?" Wes teased.

Eòghann looked down at the blue and yellow plaid a bit sheepishly. "She insisted," he said with a shrug.

"It was your grandfather's. I wanted to see if it would fit."

"Hard for a kilt not to fit," Wes said.

At least he was wearing a shirt. Not that she'd have minded terribly if he wasn't. "You put him in a skirt and made him do chores, Grandma. That's kinda kinky," she added.

"Where do you think you get it from?" Grandma Ruth asked cheekily, and Wes gasped.

"Kilt," he corrected her. "Not a skirt."

"My apologies to the Scottish Invasion."

Eòghann gazed at her, smoldering in a way that almost audibly crackled across the room. Was it hot in there? It was hot in there. Did the A/C break overnight?

Wesley's cheeks burned as his gaze continued to bore into her, and she shoved the too-large final bite of cinnamon roll in her mouth, considering an about face back upstairs to find Pablo after all.

"What's on the menu?" he asked.

Wes choked. "What?"

He nodded towards the iPad under her arm. "Your to-do list of a million and one things you don't need help with?"

"Oh. Cleaning up the old barn to use as a pub. Figuring out seating for the stages. And calling up this farmer Andy and Lùc found to mow the front so we can park cars out there."

Eòghann opened his mouth and then shut it abruptly.

"We do not have a big enough mower for you to try to cut that stuff down yourself," Wes warned him. "And the farmer volunteered."

"Wouldn't dream of interfering."

But despite herself, Wes needed to know what he'd been going to say. "If you were going to dream of interfering, what might you have been about to suggest?"

His lips twitched. "Maybe your farmer could bail the grass into blocks like straw for bench seating around the stages."

Wes was taken aback by the brilliant idea, and she glanced at Grandma who was still gazing adoringly at Eòghann. "Not only a pretty face then," Grandma said, reaching up and patting his cheek affectionately.

"It's what I would suggest. If I were being helpful."

"Your suggestion is noted and appreciated," Wes told him. "If he can do it, I might even let you have a cinnamon roll."

His gazed burned at her once more, in a way that made the cinnamon roll sound like a very dirty double entendre, and she was definitely going to hell for how much she wanted him to lick icing off every inch of her.

His watch started beeping again. Was it some kind of blood sugar monitor? Was he so diabetic that simply thinking about sweets made his glucose spike? That felt like something she'd have remembered about him from last summer, but thinking back, she couldn't recall if she'd seen him eat any sweets during their time together.

"You can have as many cinnamon rolls as you want," Grandma told him, the traitor.

"Ta," he nodded, fiddling with his watch.

"What's with the alarm?" Wes asked. "Do you have somewhere you need to be?"

He gazed at her a moment. "Can't figure out how to turn it off without my phone." Then he swallowed and looked down at his kilt again. "I should change," he said, and made a beeline for the stairs.

Grandma raised her eyebrows at Wes.

She hadn't meant to sound rude. It was the pent up sexual frustration talking.

"Be gentle with him, my dear. That man's a cinnamon roll himself if I ever saw one."

Another wave of heat flushed over Wes. "Barn's not going to

get clean on its own," she said, turning on her heel and heading out the side door.

Chapter Eighteen

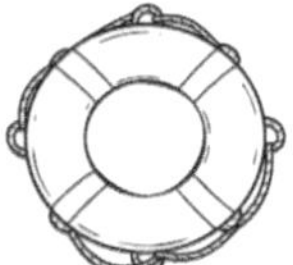

T-MINUS 12 DAYS TO RENAYZANTS FAIRE

It took Wesley, Grace, and Sadie all day Sunday and half of Monday to clear the barn of junk, cobwebs, and suspicious-looking guano, but when they were finally done, it was clean enough to double as a medieval pub.

Wes kind of wanted to collapse into bed and never move again, but she'd promised Sadie a trip into town, and so into town they went to collect her flyers from the little print kiosk inside the General Store and distribute them around town. The only thing on her personal shopping list besides the flyers was condoms, because although the Sexy Scot had taken up residence in the spare room with blue wallpaper last night, if they ever did manage to get another minute alone without a slew of cockblocking friends and relations, she wanted to be prepared.

As they strolled down Main Street looking for shops that might allow them to post their flyers in the windows, they realized none of the shops were open. Without stopping to think why, Wes had noticed an unusual abundance of American flags, and now a melancholy settled over her.

"What day is it?" she asked, already knowing the answer.

"Sunday, I think. Must be why nothing's open," Sadie told her.

"It's Monday," Grace said. "It's um…"

"Memorial Day." Wes could feel them exchanging a look behind her back.

"You know, I'm actually pretty tired," Sadie began. "Maybe we could do this tomorrow."

"I'm fine," Wes assured them. "It's no big deal. And I've got things to pick up."

And it wasn't a big deal, not exactly. The worst thing about Memorial Day were the expectations. She was supposed to feel a certain way and act a certain way and grieve a certain way. And she didn't. Not always.

Yes, her father had been killed on active duty. Yes, it had happened in May, but not on the last Monday in May. It was complicated.

Sadie hugged her, happy to let her be however she needed to be. "Tell me more about these Scottish boys and why you didn't bring one back for me?"

Grace snorted. "Yeah, Jack would've loved us for that," she said sarcastically.

"He probably would."

For a moment Wes pictured her friends in a throuple, but honestly, one man was more than enough trouble in her opinion. "For Grace and Bryan it was love at first sight," she teased.

"It definitely wasn't," Grace argued. "Except for his forearms."

"And his tattoo," Wes reminded her.

"Brandon the bee," Grace whispered with a soft smile.

Sadie grinned.

"They were perfect for each other: the grumpiest pair of grumps who ever grumped," Wes teased.

"Deadlines make people touchy."

"Yeah. It was the deadlines that made you want to touch each other," Wes snorted.

"That's *not* what touchy means!" Grace said, acting scandalized.

"And what about *your* man?" Sadie asked Wes.

"He isn't mine, but I wanted to touch him immediately too. It's complicated."

"Isn't it always? Oh look, the General Store is open."

They dashed across the street and into the shop, which mostly sold souvenirs and snacks. Grace and Sadie were instantly distracted by the window displays, but Wes made a beeline for the back. There were a few household items but not, she was disappointed to realize, condoms. Damn.

"Welcome in. Happy Memorial Day," the bearded proprietor said, when Wes walked up to claim her printed flyers.

"Yeah. Uh. Semper Fi," she told him, noticing his Marine Corps ball cap, and praying he wouldn't want to make further small talk about it.

"This you?" he asked, holding up one of the flyers. When she nodded, he asked, "What's a Renaissance faire, anyway?"

"It's costumes and music and shopping. It's a lot of fun."

"Like the state fair but with Shakespeare cosplay," Sadie called. "Are these candles and ceramics made by someone local?"

The proprietor gave Wes her receipt and went over to answer Sadie's questions about the merchandise, and Wes took her flyers to the community bulletin board in the front of the store.

"Aww, look," Grace said, joining her, and giving her elbow a squeeze. "The local high school did a Shakespeare in the Park fundraiser for their drama club last month," she crooned.

"Welcome to Stratford," Wes said in a sing-song voice.

"Hey, we need volunteers, right? Like for the Queen's court? Human chess? Parking lot attendants?"

Wes heaved a sigh. She hadn't thought about volunteers once after writing them on her list. She hadn't thought about much of anything since the arrival of the Scottish Invasion, except for the single condom in Eòghann's pocket and whether there were more.

"I'll start another list," she told Grace.

"Leave it with me," Grace said. "Our drama club is always looking for stuff to do, and the rising seniors will need service hours for college apps. I bet kids from the local high school might be interested too."

Gratitude flooded through Wesley's veins, but the double edge of gratitude was guilt, especially after Grace had spent so much time cleaning up the barn with her. "If you want to give me their numbers, I can get in touch?" she offered.

"Stop, Wes, it's no big deal. Besides, they'll be more likely to answer if it's me. I'm going to head out, make a few calls. Meet you guys back at the car?"

"Sure."

"You're good, right?" Grace asked, peering into Wesley's face, unable to hide the concern in her own.

"Never better." Wes pasted on a grin.

"If she wasn't our ride, I'd assume she was sneaking off for midday shenanigans with that hunky redhead," Sadie said, making Wesley snort.

"Maybe he's going to meet her behind the hardware store," she teased, and Sadie burst out laughing.

"Oh the honeymoon phase. If only it could last forever."

"Maybe if they keep things long distance it will?"

"Is that the secret sauce?" Sadie wondered.

"Hell if I know. Tell you one thing, I'm not used to feeling jealous of Grace in the relationship department, but Bryan

MacNeil—he's solid. He's good for her. They're good for each other."

"I'm glad. She deserves someone like that. And so do you, by the way." Sadie elbowed her in the ribs.

"You've got to believe in that stuff first," Wes replied with a shrug.

"Do you?" Sadie asked.

Wes wasn't sure whether Sadie was asking *Do you really have to believe in love?* or whether she was asking if Wesley did believe. "It's sort of a prerequisite," she laughed, answering the former as they wandered back to the cash register.

Sadie purchased a candle and a ceramic bowl, and they each picked out a popsicle. "That's all you're getting?" she asked. "My treat."

"You don't gotta."

"I know. Put it on the counter for the man."

"Thanks for the treat," Wes told her, throwing an arm around her friend a few minutes later as they walked down Main Street once more.

"I thought you needed to buy more things?"

"They didn't have what I needed."

"Which was?"

Wes tilted her head back and forth before admitting, "Condoms."

"For your *pen pal?*" Sadie asked, raising one eyebrow. When Wesley shrugged she said, "Then let me treat you twice today because I've got plenty back at the camper."

"I don't want to put you out."

"Please. Use them before they expire. They're *ribbed for her pleasure.*"

And just like that, Wesley's obnoxious brain was off on the beginning of what was sure to be a filthy little fantasy. She barely noticed as they wandered past the stationary shop, or the cute old movie theater, or the bookshop, until she realized Sadie had tucked a rolled-up flyer in each of their door handles.

When they crossed the road to head back down the other side, Sadie's eyes paused on a FOR LEASE sign in the window of an adorable corner shop whose triangle-shaped front reminded Wes of the Flat Iron building in New York. Sadie paused, drinking in the weathered brick and stained glass upper windows.

"I've always loved this building."

"Didn't it use to be a record shop?" Wes asked.

"I've thought about it, you know," Sadie said. "Putting down roots some place."

One military brat to another, Wes totally got that urge. "There's more than one reason I stuck around after college. I'm sure if you talked to Jack—"

Sadie choked back a laugh. "That would go over well. What would we do? None of us have any skills except..." she shrugged.

"Juggling literal fire must be transferable to any number of corporate situations," Wes teased.

Laughing, Sadie shook her head. "Can you imagine?"

"I get it though. Insurance was never supposed to be my career. It was an income—and health insurance—while I got my design business off the ground."

"Oh. I thought..." Sadie trailed off, not wanting to admit she thought Wes had given up on the design dream because of her eyesight, and when it came down to it, that was exactly what she'd done, wasn't it? There was never one specific moment she could point to when she'd decided to let it go, but she had, in a million little indecisions and steps aside.

"Pierce never saw the point, and eventually neither did I."

"In case I haven't said it, good riddance to Pierce," Sadie said, moving away from the vacant storefront to toss her popsicle stick in the garbage. "How is your vision these days?"

"Worse," Wes admitted, but it felt nice to have someone ask outright. Like ripping off a bandage. "I don't like to drive anymore."

Sadie made a sympathetic sound. "That sucks. I'm sorry to hear it."

"It isn't the end of the world. But I do wish I'd made different choices. Hey, it is what it is. I know I'm not the one who called or anything, but I'm so glad you're all here."

This time, Sadie put her arm around Wes as they continued down the street. "Me too. It's been too long."

"I think that's why I got together with Pierce in the first place."

"Because you missed me?" Sadie teased.

"I missed everyone! But you especially," she grinned.

"Obvs," Sadie agreed.

"I went from boarding school to college dorms to our apartment senior year to emptiness," Wes admitted, sobering. "You guys hit the road, Gray doubled down on grad school and her writing. Then along came Pierce with his frat brothers and their girlfriends—a whole built-in community."

"That makes a lot of sense," Sadie said, giving her a squeeze.

"It made sense until it didn't. Until I was lonely even when he was around. I don't know..." It was hard to put into words how isolated she felt as she and Pierce had grown up in different directions. How alone and unsupported she felt when he denigrated her hopes and dreams, exacerbated her fears, and made her feel like she ought to be grateful.

"I get you," Sadie assured her. "We make friends on the road, but even surrounded by people you can still feel lonely."

"How long have you know the MacNeils?"

"Oh gosh. Since their first season, if not their very first faire. Jack and Andy took Alec under their wing. He had no idea what he was doing, but after Miranda died he—I dunno, packed the boys up and ran away from home I guess. The twins couldn't have been more than five. Dan wasn't a surly teenage ball of hormones yet."

"How did she die?"

"Miranda? A car accident, I think. After everything with Sully last year, I was afraid Alec might disappear again, but you know Andy. Darwish holds on tight. He wouldn't allow it."

Wes nodded, grateful for her friends holding on tight to her. They'd been family for so long now, her friends and Grandma Ruth.

"Sometimes I think it's paper clips and bubble gum and Andy keeping Jack and me together," Sadie admitted.

Wes didn't know quite what to say to that. Jack and Sadie had been an institution for almost as long as the Shakespeare Syndicate, but they'd all been so very young way back then. "It's okay to outgrow someone," she said cautiously. "Even someone you still love."

Sadie forced a pained smile. "Come on," she said, nodding down the street. "Gray waited after all. We better get back and make sure the guys haven't burned the place to the ground."

Chapter Nineteen

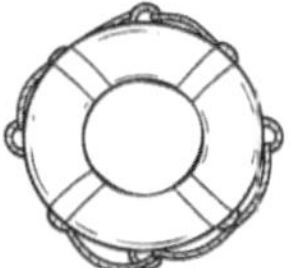

Wesley Teal and her forget-me-not eyes couldn't have been more clear that she didn't want Eòghann to help with her Renaissance faire, and it left him feeling a certain sort of way. On the one hand, he understood. She obviously had some deep-seated aversion to accepting anyone's help, so it wasn't exactly personal. On the other hand, she'd been unable to reject help from her oldest friends—a stark reminder of where he fell in the pecking order. He wasn't a part of the group, which couldn't help feeling deeply personal.

But, of course he wasn't part of her inner circle. She'd known them all since she was eighteen years old, a veritable child like Lùcas. She'd only met *him* a year ago, and most of that time had been little more than flirty text messages. So why did it feel like they shared a deep connection?

Anyway, her forbidding his help wasn't the problem. It was her prerogative to choose and she'd chosen. He was the problem. His entire identity was wrapped up in making himself useful. If he were a Ken doll, his career would be Helper Ken.

He hadn't been joking about earning his keep. Eòghann had

spent his life scratching out a place: in his family, in the community. In the world.

After he'd taken Pòl from them, he'd worked hard to win his way back, and he'd been endeavoring to deserve his place among them ever since. People loved a helper.

Except, apparently, for Wesley Teal, which was pretty damn unfortunate because in most other respects they seemed like a perfect fit.

When he offered to fix things around the house instead of the faire, he could see she wanted to argue, to deny the plain-as-day fact her grandma's house could use a little TLC. But at her core, she was sunshine and stardust, and she hadn't wanted to fight with him about it either, so she bought into his lie about it not being for her but for Grandma Ruth, and then she let herself be swept away by her friends.

This morning, he'd fixed her leaky faucet and the sagging loo door, as well as replacing the rotted-out window frame next to her bed. Now he was determined to get to the root of that particular problem—no pun intended. The English ivy climbing up the north-facing wall had grown too thick and too close to Wesley's window, trapping moisture against the wood every time they got a good rain.

In addition to the English ivy, there was an inundation of another kind Grandma Ruth had called Virginia creeper and boy, had it crept into every crack and cranny. It was climbing the walls, less attractively than the English, he rather hated to admit. But also, along with a few other aggressive weeds, it appeared to be choking the life out of some large, old-growth hydrangea bushes.

After trimming the ivy carefully back from the windows, Eòghann couldn't resist the rather satisfying task of pulling up the Virginia creeper, what seemed like miles and miles of it, and pruning everything back so the hydrangeas could actually breathe.

"Yarr and avast!" Alec's youngest, Rory, jumped out from behind him with a wooden sword, wearing a patch over one eye.

Eòghann put up his hands in surrender, trying hard to stay in the moment and not dwell on what he'd learned about Rory's twin.

Delighted, the boy put his sword to Eòghann's throat, gently raising his chin. "You dare dig for buried gold?"

"Aye," Eòghann played along. "On behalf of the lady herself, for she lost it in this very garden nigh on thirty years ago."

Rory's eyebrows shot up at this news. "And what have ye found, landlubber?"

Landlubber indeed. If only he knew the half of it.

Eòghann shook his head sadly. "Only weeds, I'm afraid. But I've reason to believe if enough are ripped away, the hiding place will reveal itself."

"X marks the spot."

"Precisely, Pirate King."

Rory lowered his sword and nodded gravely. "You speak the truth. Shall I join in your quest?"

"Suit up," Eòghann agreed, tossing him a pair of gardening gloves. They would dwarf his small hands, but it was better than nothing.

"In exchange for half the treasure."

"Half! Nay, good sir, one third."

Rory frowned. "That's less than half. I know my fractions, sir."

"Aye, but the lady makes three. She must have her share. 'Tis only equitable."

Rory considered this a moment, then nodded his agreement and pulled on the gloves, up to his elbows.

"Look how hard you've been working." Grandma Ruth's voice rang out from the front door, and Eòghann turned to find her carrying a tray with a pitcher of lemonade and two cups.

He stood to relieve her of the burden, and she smiled warmly. "I saw your helper, and I thought you both might need some refreshments."

"Ta," Eòghann thanked her, setting the tray on a moss-covered paving stone and pouring a cup for Rory.

"I didn't know there were still hydrangeas under all those weeds!"

"We're going to find out, aren't we, Rory?"

"Yarr," the boy agreed.

"I'm obliged to you," she said. "To all of you. I don't know what I was thinking, trying to host a Renaissance faire at my age."

"You're younger than Shakespeare."

Grandma Ruth laughed. "I was twenty years old when I attended my first faire. It was only Southern California, but that afternoon I felt like I'd been transported to another world."

Her dreamy, faraway smile reminded him of Wesley. He wished Wes would let him help make that dream happen for her Grandma, but helping with the hydrangea was nice too.

"What was your favorite part?" he asked, taking a sip of cool, sweet lemonade.

"The maypole," she answered without missing a beat. "Always the maypole. I loved to dance, you see."

And Eòghann could see, or rather, he could imagine a younger version of Grandma Ruth, one who looked suspiciously like Wesley. Her long golden hair streamed behind her like sunbeams as she ducked and weaved in and out of the other dancers, around and around the pole, braiding their ribbons into a beautiful design.

"Sounds perfect," he told her, and Grandma Ruth nodded.

"All right," she said, clapping her hands. "Lots to do. Keep up the good work out here."

"Thanks for the lemonade," he said, refilling Rory's outstretched cup.

"Ta," Rory said, imitating his Scots slang.

Eòghann laughed and shook his head, pulling his gardening gloves back on.

"You're all my da's cousins?" Rory asked as they resumed their work.

"Bryan and I are, yes. Lùc's from the other side of our family, not related to your da."

Rory nodded wisely. "So that makes you my uncle cousin?"

Eòghann laughed. He rather liked that description. "If you like. Bryan's da and your da's da were brothers, so they're first cousins. If Bryan has kids, you and his kids would be second cousins."

The boy considered this information while Eòghann chided himself for over-sharing. But it was easier than dwelling on the boy who wasn't there.

"Where do you fit?" Rory asked, and hell if that wasn't the question of his life.

Eòghann shook his head, focusing on the weeds in front of him. "My da and their granda were brothers."

"Ohh," Rory said. So his explanation must've been all right. "So you're like super old."

Turning to the kid with mock outrage he sputtered, "Only one year older than your da!"

Rory watched him closely, waiting for his reaction with a cheeky grin. Then he threw his handful of weeds at Eòghann and took off running.

Something in the way the boy looked back told Eòghann he was meant to give chase, so he shoved himself to standing with a particularly loud groan that didn't quite drown out the popping in his knees or put to rest the old man accusations.

His nephew-cousin led him on a merry chase, around the side of the house and into the woods, past a tall birch tree—which could make a perfect maypole if he were one for interfering. They ran all the way to a clearing at the shore of what looked like a swift-moving river.

Skidding to a halt, Eòghann stumbled into Rory, who turned around, putting one finger dramatically to his lips demanding silence, before peering through some large shrubs at his middle brother.

Jarrod sat alone on a log, staring out at the water, strumming a guitar.

Rory frowned. "He only sings Billie Eilish when he's sad," he whispered.

"Should we try and cheer him up?"

"He'd rather be alone."

It was the curse of the MacNeils, perhaps.

"You see that island?" Rory asked, pointing out to the middle of the water.

Eòghann forced himself to look, and then nodded, choking back a wave of nausea.

"How far away do you think it is?"

Ripping his gaze back to the child at his side, Eòghann breathed in and then out for a few counts of eight. "Dunno. Two kilometers, maybe."

"Kilometers," Rory teased, imitating his accent like before. "Bet I could swim all the way out to it."

The thought alone nearly brought Eòghann to his knees, and his heart began to race. His first instinct was to forbid it, to march Rory straight to his father and rat him out. But was that merely his phobia talking? Blowing things out of proportion?

Was swimming two kilometers to a small jungle-like island actually quite a normal feat of daring for young children?

Rory was watching him, waiting for his response.

"Wow," Eòghann said, his voice dry and scratchy. "All the way out there?"

"You don't believe me? How much do you wanna bet?"

Oh hell. How had he managed to turn this into a dare? He swallowed. *You're safe on dry land. And so is Rory. For now.* "If you believe it, I believe it," he assured the boy. "You know yourself better than I do."

Right or wrong, his answer seemed to surprise Rory, who leaned back, giving him a long hard look.

"I've only known you for three days," Eòghann explained.

"How many days are in nine years?"

"Thousands."

Rory nodded at that, and Eòghann gestured for them to head back to the house.

When they reached the front yard, a new car was parked on the long driveway, and a new woman stood beside it, gazing up at the house. Her dark brown hair was pulled up in a ponytail that poked out of a baseball cap, and beneath the brim, her eyes looked shadowed and red-rimmed.

The raven circled overhead screeching, "Intruder! Intruder!" and the woman shrank away like she was going to duck back into her car.

Eòghann whistled through his teeth, and the bird stopped squawking and perched on the roof to watch them.

"En garde," Rory yelled, forgetting he'd left his sword by the hydrangea. "Who're you?"

A little bewildered, the woman pasted on a smile and answered, "I'm Rebecca M-Majors. Heath." She paused, opening and closing her mouth a couple of times before amending, "Just Rebecca."

Her name pinged a memory of solstice divorce cookies and burning pictures of *Marshall-fucking-Majors* in effigy.

She was a few years older than the rest of the university crew, mid-to-late thirties if he had to guess. But wasn't the brother's surname Darwish? "Are you looking for Andy?"

"Yes," she replied, seeming to sag with relief.

"They're around the back. Follow the sounds of hammers and cursing."

Her smile seemed fragile but genuine. "Thank you."

"I'm Eòghann. And this is Pirate Rory."

"*Sir* Pirate Calico Rory, Esquire," the boy corrected.

"Begging your pardon," Eòghann told him.

"Thank you both," Rebecca said, heading off in the direction he'd sent her.

"I didn't know Andy had a wife," Rory said disdainfully as he watched her go.

"It's his sister, ye melon," Eòghann teased.

The boy reared back. "Melon?" he repeated, parroting Eòghann's accent once more.

Laughing, Eòghann ruffled his hair and shoved him back towards the garden, where they both drank another cup of lemonade.

Chapter Twenty

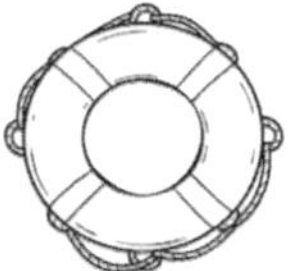

Turning up the long drive of Warwick Hall, Wesley couldn't put her finger on it, but something about the place felt more open and cheerful, like it had when she was a kid.

"Whoa," Grace said. "Did Grandma Ruth hire a groundskeeper?"

That was it—where before, the house looked like something out of a horror movie, being eaten alive by scraggly foliage, now it was tidy and trimmed back, like a certain Scotsman's beard, and she knew exactly which Scotsman she could thank for this. Father Eòghann was making good on his threat to *earn his keep* by helping out Grandma and staying away from the faire preparations.

It shouldn't make her tummy feel like it was full of fizzing champagne, but it did, despite the cloud of Memorial Day hanging over her.

"Looks like she hired *someone*," Sadie murmured appreciatively.

Wes squinted to see the figure Sadie had noticed—namely a

dark-denim clad heinie, bent over and digging in the dirt alongside a small... pirate?

"But if he's the gardener, whose car is that?" Sadie asked, as Grace parked behind another vehicle.

"Knox County plates," Grace said. "Is this Becca's car?"

It certainly *looked* like the same blue shade as Becca's Prius, with a BIGGER ON THE INSIDE bumper magnet. Wes had never understood why that was funny, when the Prius was tiny and cramped on the inside. It was definitely her car, but, "You tell me," she said to Grace.

"I didn't call her!" Grace protested. "I probably should've, but I didn't, I swear."

"I'm sure Andy called her," Sadie reasoned, and of course he would have since he was so rarely in town.

Eòghann and Rory turned in tandem, peering over their shoulders like guilty students caught by the headmaster, as Wes and the girls walked up to the house.

"We haven't found any gold yet," Rory assured them. "Only big, hairy weeds."

As if to prove it, Eòghann held up a fistful of the ivy he'd been pulling up and thank goodness he was wearing gloves.

"That's poison ivy," Grace told him.

His eyes went comically wide as Rory skittered backwards like a crab.

"Poison, you say?" Eòghann asked. "When ingested, d'you mean?"

"Oh no, please tell me you didn't eat it?" Grace exclaimed. To Sadie and Wes she added, "I don't know what would happen if you ate it. If you were allergic, would you die?"

"We didn't eat it. We're not stupid," Rory yelled, and Eòghann shook his head. "If you touch it, you'll get all red and itchy," Rory explained for Eòghann's benefit. "I didn't sign up for poison ivy."

"You've been a massive help, good sir," Eòghann assured him without sounding the least bit facetious, and whether he meant it or not, Wes loved how seriously he managed to take the little heathen.

"Later, Uncle-Cousin," Rory yelled, grabbing a wooden sword from the ground and running away at top speed.

Grace and Sadie headed off in the same direction, presumably to check on their men, but Wes wanted to take in the sight of Eòghann for a little bit longer. His black t-shirt was soaked with sweat around the neck and down the back. How could he stand working in jeans, in this heat? They made his rear look fantastic, but he must be miserable.

"All right?" he asked, wiping his creased brow on his shirt sleeve.

"How're you holding up in the humidity? Have you been out here all day?"

"S'pose it's a bit tropical."

"Come inside and drink some electrolytes."

He regarded her a moment like he wasn't used to be being bossed around, and she supposed he probably wasn't, outside of visiting his Auntie Eilidh. But he didn't argue. In fact, she thought she detected the tiniest quirk in his lips, as he pushed himself up, trying to stifle a soft groan.

In the foyer, an American flag stood rolled up in the corner, and Wes wondered at Grandma having forgotten to hang it up. More likely she'd held off out of misplaced concern over upsetting Wes.

It was a snap decision, but she took the flag outside, unfurled it, and settled it into the holder mounted on one of the porch posts. For a moment the stars and stripes caught a breeze and she stood, frozen in a memory of sitting between her mother and grandmother as another flag, perfectly folded into an impossibly neat triangle, was handed to them.

"Aim high, dad," she whispered. Then, swallowing, she blinked away the memory and turned to find Eòghann still waiting right inside the door.

"It's, uh, Memorial Day," she explained in a raspy voice.

His head tilted to the side for a moment, like a puppy trying to make sense of her words. Then he nodded once and stepped back so she could precede him into the kitchen.

She didn't want to talk about it—any of it—how her vision loss and her father were so inextricably tangled up together in her mind. Most people probably didn't remember the exact date and time of their first misdiagnosis. But then she bet most people weren't sitting in the waiting room of a Valdosta ophthalmologist after an early morning eye exam watching a news segment about adoptable kittens when the national broadcast interrupted to show a plane heading for the south tower of the World Trade Center as smoke billowed from the north.

While the eye doctor gave Wesley's mother the news that she simply needed glasses, Wes sat glued to the TV knowing, in that sinking dread sort of way that scoops out your insides and leaves you hollow—her whole world was about to change. As she sat there, hearing the word *terrorists* batted around, she wondered if she'd get to see her father before he was deployed, and somehow she knew he would die.

It was three more years before his helicopter was shot down over Kandahar, another eight before her macular degeneration became evident enough to finally get her Stargardt diagnosis, but her mind tangled it all up together into a big ball of yarn and dust bunnies that she preferred to keep locked away in a craft bin under the bed.

Rather than explain, she fished out a bottle of Gatorade from the back of Grandma's pantry and poured it over ice for Eòghann without a word.

He eyed the blue drink suspiciously.

"You don't like that flavor?"

"Bit like old lady's toilet water, innit?"

She burst out laughing, and his eyes crinkled as he smiled back at her.

"You've got sweet, fudgy tablet, we've got fancy toilet water electrolytes. Only the best for our guests in Tennessee," she said, laying on the accent extra thick.

He grinned at her and took a sip, but from the way he kept his expression frozen, she could tell he hated it.

"Drink up. You're not used to the heat *or* the humidity."

Eòghann leaned back against the counter and held her gaze as he drank the glass dry right down to its ice cubes, and why did that suddenly make her own mouth feel parched?

She took a gulp straight from the bottle and winced, remembering it wasn't cold. It always tasted better ice cold.

Eòghann held out his glass of ice—a sweet gesture—but Wes refilled it and nodded for him to drink it down again.

Still holding her gaze, he drank that one too, and Wes grinned, taking the glass this time and pouring one for herself.

He stepped closer, invading her space and despite the sweat-soaked shirt, he still smelled so good, like spicy deodorant and cologne and the earth.

She reached out, hooking a finger into his belt loop to pull him closer, and he tilted his head just enough to capture her lips. For the first time all afternoon she could breathe as he shared his breath with her, kissing her softly at first—questioningly—but responding in kind as she deepened the kiss, not looking for gentleness, not today.

His hands moved from the small of her back, down her rump, pulling her closer. Then he lifted her onto the counter and stepped between her legs, stroking up her arms to her shoulders, and smoothing her hair away from her own sweaty face.

"You're so beautiful," he whispered against her lips, and she hooked her legs around his waist, drawing him even closer.

"I heard there were sandwiches in here..." Daniel, the oldest boy, trailed off, the screen door slamming behind him and his middle brother as Eòghann pulled his lips away from Wesley's neck and leaned his forehead against hers, both of them breathing heavily.

Every damn time with these kids.

"Sorry, I think they meant someone else's kitchen," Daniel mumbled, turning his brother around and letting the screen door slam behind them again on their way back out.

But the moment was gone.

Wesley sighed. "Guess I should..." She chucked a thumb over her shoulder.

"Aye. Me too," he agreed, inclining his head back towards the yard.

Poorly-timed interruption aside, Wesley felt somehow lighter as she slipped out back to find and welcome Rebecca to Stratford.

WES HARDLY RECOGNIZED THE WOMAN SHE FOUND attempting to bake sourdough bread in *The Lair*'s tiny oven. Becca had dark circles under her eyes, and someone had tried to give her bangs. Guilt washed over Wesley. She should have checked in on her friend more often post-divorce.

Becca teared up simply hugging her, and her eyes were red, as though that tearing up was a pretty common occurrence these days.

"Thanks for letting me crash your grandma's party," she whispered. "I couldn't stand to sit at home staring at my kitchen curtains for one more minute."

"Are you kidding? You're welcome any time, you know that."

"I didn't want to be in the way," Rebecca told her. "I was going to wait to come until the actual faire, but I've been climbing the walls at home, and I normally channel that into baking, but then the oven went out—"

Wes took her shoulders, to stop her spiraling explanation in its tracks. "Okay, but *that* isn't a real oven. Feel free to use Grandma's all you want."

Rebecca drew a long, shaky breath. "Thanks."

"You can repay me in sourdough."

"I don't remember food being your love language."

"French toast is my love language. And as everyone knows, sourdough makes the best French toast."

"I actually didn't know that fact," Rebecca said, kneading the dough on the little dinette table.

"No? Huh. Well, that's what the recipe I've been making since I was eight said. And it must be true because my French toast is so good it can save marriages and end wars."

Rebecca laughed, genuinely, if a bit sad.

Wes immediately felt terrible. "You think I'm joking, but I call it Peacemaker French toast."

"That sounds like a lot of pressure for some eggy bread."

"Probably," Wes agreed, sliding onto the dinette bench across from Rebecca and hugging her knees. "My dad was only home for about eight months total, in between deployments after 9/11. By the end, they fought constantly, and I—being eight—thought breakfast could fix anything. So I asked my mom to help me cook it. Mistake number one."

"She burned the toast?"

"Worse. She couldn't be bothered with toast. She wanted a smoothie so we made smoothies, and that was the day I learned my dad was allergic to bananas."

"Oh, Wes!"

Wes made a face in agreement. "That was mistake number two. Dad accused her of trying to make him sick, and she accused him of being over dramatic." She shook her head. "It was a whole thing."

"Sounds like it."

"While they were screaming their faces off, I looked up a French toast recipe and made it myself. When it was done, they stopped fighting and for half an hour peace reigned in the Teal household."

"Miracle toast," Rebecca whispered.

"I'm just saying. When my dad redeployed for the last time, I sent my recipe to Laura Bush and told her, quite confidently, it had the power to save lives. I even offered to bake it for George W and Al-Qaeda."

"How have I never heard this story before?"

"I guess I haven't thought about it in a while. How's work?" Wes asked cautiously, deflecting the conversation away from her fucked-up family. Rebecca was a child psychologist. She'd see right through all of Wesley's barriers. She also couldn't exactly skive off whenever she wanted to.

Her friend kneaded the dough harder. "You know. It's work. It's a little slow right now. Clients are starting to leave on vacation, and I realized I haven't taken a vacation in seven years. And I really wanted to see my stupid baby brother."

"And now you're in here. Baking. Alone," Wes pointed out gently.

Rebecca paused like she was going to say more, but instead she said, "He doesn't like it when I hover."

"Ah."

"And there's a lot of people here."

"Yeah," Wes agreed. "I take it you've met the Scottish Invasion."

She nodded.

"Bring your bread up to the house. No one'll mind if you hover as long as you don't tell Grandma Ruth the answers to her crossword puzzle until she asks."

"I don't want to be in the way."

"Come on. Nothing makes a house smell better than warm, fresh bread and Grandma Ruth will be thrilled to meet you at last. Andy's always been her favorite."

Although Becca had long since become a part of the friend group, at four years older than the rest of them, she'd existed on the periphery when the Shakespeare Syndicate originally formed. Back then she'd been Andy's older sister, who he crashed with when he wasn't in the dorms instead of going back to his parents' house in the Nashville suburbs after they kicked him out for good.

Rebecca was Andy's safe space, and the Syndicate loved Andy, so they loved and welcomed Rebecca, but it wasn't until after college that Wes and Grace had really bonded with her.

"Come on," Wes said, urging her to her feet. "I promise you'll only be disappointed if you try to cook that thing in there."

"Story of my life," Rebecca replied, gathering her dough and following Wesley back up to the house.

Chapter Twenty-One

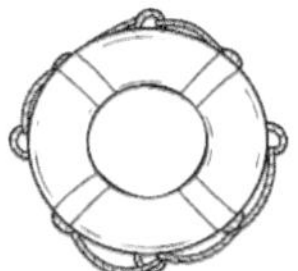

T-MINUS 11 DAYS TO RENAYZANTS FAIRE

By Tuesday, Eòghann had pretty well acclimated to the time zone, if not the weather, because lying alone in the spare room at night there was nothing else to do but either sleep or replay his brief glimpse of Wesley's inner thigh tattoo. He'd only caught a flash that first day: what looked like a slice of pizza, words on a banner he hadn't registered before her dress slid back down over her hips, hiding them from view.

I'll show you mine, if you show me yours, she had teased him last month over text.

As it turned out, she hadn't seen his tattoo at all because of the vest he was wearing, but that quick peek at her thigh had tormented his every waking hour, as if he needed more torment.

The mortifying panic attack wasn't the only reason he was avoiding her, although it was certainly reason enough. She was an irresistible force and he was drawn to her, like a magnet or gravity. And it scared him a little, because how could Helper Ken and Self-Sufficient Barbie ever have any kind of future together?

Dr. Patel would say to be honest with her. To tell her it bothered him that she didn't want his help, that her rejection of his assistance felt like a rejection of his entire being. Made him feel worthless. But if therapy had shown him anything, it was that he couldn't say all those things because his issues were his problem. And because once he started being honest, he might not be able to stop, and the next thing he knew it would be, *I'm a Lily-livered landlubber, and I killed Alec's father when I was twelve.* And then she really would reject him.

Somehow, though, his ridiculous panic attack and self-imposed distance didn't seem to have dampened her interest, if yesterday in the kitchen was any indication.

How the hell did Alec end up with four kids when they were always popping up at the most inopportune moments like feral little bloodhounds?

"You look lost," Grandma Ruth said, stepping into the kitchen where Eòghann's tea had long since gone cold.

Lost was an apt description. The truth was, Eòghann didn't know how to be idle. If he wasn't fixing something or helping someone, what was the point of him? But he knew better than to try to help someone who didn't want to be helped, so where did that leave him?

He forced a smile. "Lost in thought is all."

She regarded him for a moment like she didn't buy it, and he braced himself for the snappy old lady retort his Auntie Eilidh would've dished out.

"Don't let me interrupt," she said instead, crossing to the refrigerator and taking out a pitcher of iced tea. "But next time you want cold tea, help yourself," she added with a smirk.

"Actually can I ask you...?"

She turned, like she'd been expecting this.

"Do you have a chore list? Of things that need doing around

here? For the house, not your faire. Or if you did have one, what would be at the top of it?"

A shadow crossed her face. "That garage," she said, shaking her head sadly. "It's needed cleaning out for a decade. Probably two."

Eòghann perked up. "I can help with that. Would you like me to separate things into piles for you? Things you might want to keep, things to give away, and things to throw out?"

She shook her head, and he deflated.

"I don't want to keep any of it," she said. "Even if it's something I would've wanted if I'd remembered it was out there. I don't want to remember. I've got to downsize this whole place to fit inside one small apartment. Sorting through the things I remember is bad enough." She patted his shoulder as though trying to comfort him over her own heartbreak. "If you find a telescope, it belongs to Adnan. Otherwise do what you think is best. Not having to worry about it at all would be such a load off my mind."

"Consider it done," he said and leaned into the one-armed squeeze she gave him.

Stepping into the garage was a little like stepping inside a time capsule, and the past sure was dusty. Eòghann's first objective was to clear enough space so Grandma Ruth could park her Miata inside. At the moment, the only clear path —a dubious one at best—was from the kitchen door to a small freezer.

An obvious source of space was an old Ford pickup truck that must've belonged to Wesley's grandfather. It would likely need a new battery, but if Eòghann could get it running, and there wasn't a family of rodents to displace from the engine, the truck would make hauling away garbage and donations that much easier. Right now it was half full with crates for recycling —plastic, aluminum, old newspaper, cardboard, and glass—all of it covered in a thick layer of time.

The keys to the Ford had been left in the glove compartment, but when Eòghann tried to start it, the engine merely gave a sad little choke. He could fix it, of course. He could fix pretty much anything. But the garage was the first priority, so he slipped the truck into neutral and pushed it out to the driveway.

"Need a jump?" someone asked, and he glanced over his shoulder to find Alec's oldest lad, Daniel, watching him with mild interest.

"Probably needs more than that," Eòghann admitted.

"I'm pretty okay with engines. I could play around with it."

"Don't you have to study?"

Dan leaned up against the vehicle, arms crossed over his chest. "Took a practice test. Need a break."

"Then welcome to the pit crew," Eòghann said, popping the hood. "There's tools in the garage."

"Cool," the boy said, almost enthusiastic for the first time since Eòghann had met him.

"Grand," Eòghann replied.

With the pickup out of the way, it was easier to see what he was working with inside. A number of boxes and bins were stacked and forgotten. Some were neatly lined up on shelves while others spilled onto the floor. The far wall held a peg board and tools, which Wesley's friends had been picking over as they built whatever all they were constructing out back.

He began by sorting things into two piles—donate and destroy—leaving room for a third, secret pile in case there was something Wes might want, if not Grandma Ruth.

He grinned when he unearthed a box of old toys. It held in-line skates, a jump rope and baseball bat, something called Skip

It, and a small hula hoop. He had no trouble picturing young Wesley with tinsel in her hair, skating backwards down the drive, popping bubble gum and shimmying inside that hoop like it was nothing.

The toys still looked fairly sturdy, so he set them aside for Daniel's brothers, with the exception of the hula hoop. That he tucked away behind the freezer for safe keeping—half an idea forming in the back of his mind.

Another big box was filled with nothing but ceramic vases and old dishes in every color under the sun. Maybe those could come in handy for the faire in some way too. He put them with the toys in the donation-adjacent pile and kept going.

An old wooden chest was filled with handmade blankets.

A couple of once-brightly-colored canoes—*no, thank you*—were tucked away in a corner along with dozens of empty five-gallon paint buckets, and a bicycle with rotted-out tires. He was starting to wonder where the line fell between hoarder and in need of a good spring cleaning, but he chuckled when he found a shelf filled with gardening tools. They would have come in handy yesterday.

He uncovered not one, but two, artificial Christmas trees with what must be hundreds of ornaments and enough twinkle lights to decorate the entire world. Too bad they required an outlet, because those gave him another forbidden idea for interfering with the faire. He might be forced to resort to subterfuge. Or at least put a bug in Bryan's ear.

When he stumbled onto plastic bin after plastic bin of arts and crafts supplies, he knew he'd struck gold. There were yards of fabric scraps, enough yarn to make Auntie Eilidh green with envy, and ribbons—so very many rolls of ribbon—in every width and color. Eòghann grinned, shuffling them aside into his secret stash.

Over the course of several hours, the mess began to coalesce into organized chaos, and by mid-afternoon Eòghann was pleasantly surprised to hear the engine of the old Ford roar to life.

"Well done, lad," he told the kid, patting him on the back. "A veritable auto-whisperer."

Daniel beamed. "You learn a trick or two when you live on the road," he said with the air of someone much older and with a hint of bitterness. "Plus I like mechanical things."

"Me too," Eòghann agreed.

"They're logical. They make sense, unlike people. Where'd you want to go, anyway?"

"Suppose I should haul this lot to the recycling center."

The boy regarded him skeptically, a touch disappointed by the prospect of such a dull outing. "You know which side of the road to drive on?" he asked.

A laugh burst from Eòghann's chest. "I have to stay on the road?"

Daniel smirked. "Does your license actually let you drive here?"

That stopped Eòghann cold. He didn't technically *have* a license. Not having left Barra, he'd never needed one. "Ah," he said, his plan foiled.

Shrugging nonchalantly as he studied the ground, Daniel said, "I'll drive if you want. My license works fine."

"I know better than to turn down a good offer," Eòghann replied. "You sure?"

Daniel shrugged again. "You're family. And you're practically helpless. I can't send you out there alone."

Eòghann burst out laughing again. He probably ought to feel highly insulted, but this sullen teenage cousin was offering to spend time with him. How could he feel insulted by that? "Let's go."

Daniel opened the GPS on his phone, checked his mirrors carefully, and then turned cautiously down the drive.

"Your practice test was for university?" Eòghann asked.

"Don't distract me," Daniel said, watching the traffic before he pulled out onto the main road.

"My apologies."

A few moments of silence passed, and then the boy asked, "Did you go to college?"

"I did not. But Lùc's planning on it."

Daniel nodded.

"What do you want to study?"

"If you'd asked me up until like a year ago, I would've said I wanted to be a veterinarian."

"Not anymore?"

"No. I think I just wanted a pet. I don't want to actually give shots or operate on sick animals or ones that have been hit by cars or whatever."

"What do you prefer now?"

"Some kind of engineering maybe? Like, I read about these kids. High school kids, you know? Who figured out how to get microplastics out of the ocean. One found an organism that actually eats plastic. Another kid invented soap that can cure skin cancer."

"In secondary school?" Eòghann asked, amazed.

"Right? But then, most of them probably go to a real school with clubs and maybe a strong STEM program. Not home school in a camper with their annoying little brothers," he said, not trying to hide the edge in his voice. "But anyway, I want to do something like that."

"I imagine being on the road can get old after a while."

Daniel snorted. "I mean. I guess it was fun at first. Read what you want. Hardly any chores. Like one long holiday. But I don't care much about the music. That's Jarrod and my da's thing."

Eòghann noticed he didn't mention Rory's preference one way or the other.

"When we first started, I used to pretend it was summer vacation. One day we'd go back home, and mom would be there, waiting."

"In Minnesota?"

The boy shrugged. "I don't know where home is anymore. There's nothing left in Minnesota. All our friends have moved on."

Eòghann was struck by the parallels. His years had been spent trapped in one place, while his cousin had been all over the place but still trapped, both of them longing for a home they couldn't reach.

"Have you told your da how you feel?"

"Nah. It'd crush him, I think."

I think he'd want to know, Eòghann wanted to say. But who was he to waltz in and make such assumptions, let alone give them voice?

Chapter Twenty-Two

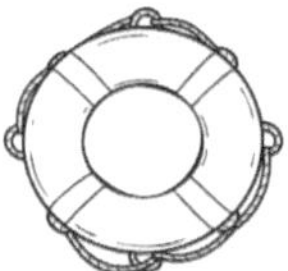

T-MINUS 8 DAYS TO RENAYZANTS FAIRE

After spending the better part of the week calling toilet rental companies across the Tennessee-Kentucky-North Carolina-Virginia service area, on Friday morning Wes finally confirmed that yes, Exemplary Boiled Events had contracted with one. Unfortunately, they'd only booked a single, solitary toilet, which On-the-Go Premium Toilet Rentals had delivered to a very confused homeowner in Stanford, Kentucky.

Wes explained everything, and the rep agreed it was an all-around *shitty situation*, but there was no ready inventory at the moment. No one else seemed to have any either, so at this rate, they were playing a dangerous game of wait-and-see.

"I found two more vendors," Sadie announced with a yawn as she entered the kitchen and made a beeline for the coffee that Grandma Ruth kept perpetually at the ready.

"Really?" Wes flipped back to her list and map. In addition to Jack and Sadie's Ye Olde Lether and Lapis, where they sold handmade leather goods and jewelry, there was a tea shop, delightfully named Et Tu, Brü Té? and a soap maker called Lady MacBeth's Emporium.

"You're going to love it," Sadie said. "Seize the Clay."

"Pottery?"

"You know it!"

"I do love a punny name."

"They supply the General Store. And the candle maker's keen, too," she added, handing Wes a business card for Starlight and Moonshine Candles.

"That's a pretty solid mix of shops, right?"

Sadie nodded. "A little something for everyone, like you said on the news. You should see if Becca would put on a fancy get up and do fortune telling."

"I love it," Wes snorted. "But at this rate she's going to be selling sourdough loaves to the guests."

"Or giving them away." Sadie surveyed the pile of loaves spilling across the kitchen counter. After buttering a slice of bread to go with her coffee, she leaned against the counter, closing her eyes to savor the deliciousness. "The stages are finished. They look like they might actually stay up now that your Barra boys got involved. What's left?"

"Andy's cowboy is coming out to bushhog the front yard later this week, and he *is* going to bale it on site," Wes ticked off on her fingers. "I guess that only leaves beer for the pub. And I need to confirm the food trucks. And, you know, toilets."

"There's still time."

"Eight days."

Sadie shrugged. "Plenty of time."

"Okay but what if it's not?"

"Start digging a trench?" Sadie teased.

"Don't think I haven't thought about it," Wesley said with a grimace. "By the way, how's Andy's hand?"

"Was it hurt?" Sadie asked, as Andy himself stepped inside looking harried. "Andy, did you hurt yourself?"

"Today? I don't think so," he said, glancing down at his arms and legs distractedly. "Have you seen Becca?"

"Not this morning," Wes told him. "But I swear this pile of bread grew since yesterday. I assumed she baked all night and was sleeping it off in *The Lair*. What sparked this particular frenzy anyway?"

He shrugged, seeming to shake off his frazzled state along with her query. "I should be asking *you* the questions."

"About Rebecca?"

"About your Scotsman."

Wes flushed and studied her iPad intently. "He's not *my* Scotsman," she protested.

"So it isn't serious?" he asked, and Sadie raised her eyebrows skeptically.

"It's exactly as serious as I want it to be. What does serious mean anyway?"

Andy gave a low whistle as he took a slice of bread and slathered it in peanut butter.

"It's serious," Sadie confirmed.

"No shit, really?" Andy asked.

"It's **not** serious," Wes repeated. When the two exchanged dubious looks she tried again. "It isn't. I seriously like him. But I don't want a serious relationship."

"You seriously don't?" Andy teased.

"Seriously. No. It feels a little bit illicit, which I'll admit is part of the appeal—"

"I was going to say, since when has illicit ever stopped you?" Andy quipped.

"Excuse you!" Wes trilled, reaching out to—what, smack him? Steal his snack?

He pushed her hand away playfully, so she reached out with the other.

"That's my cue," Sadie said, stepping around them and exiting the kitchen as they pretended to tussle.

"We're just having fun," Wes insisted, snatching the crust of bread from his hand and gobbling it down before she dropped into a chair. "Sit with me?" she asked.

"This feels ominous," Andy said, pulling out another chair to join her. "Do you *want* it to be more than having fun?"

"No! It's…" She slumped forward, propping her head on one hand. "Where's the line? I mean, I'm pretty sure we already crossed it, but—"

"TMI!" Andy whined, putting up his hands to stop her.

"Sorry. But real talk for a minute. Priests are allowed to have friends, right?"

"Wait, time out," Andy said, making a T with his hands like a referee. "Your Scotsman's a priest?"

"Yeah, Darwish, keep up. But, like, even priests are allowed to have deep connections and fellowship, right?"

"Okay, A—if you need someone to help you dispose of a cursed magic ring my feelings will be irreparably hurt if I'm not chosen as part of your posse. I thought that was a base requirement of the Shakespeare Syndicate contract."

"You signed a contract? Sucker."

He laughed but quickly sobered. "And B—are you sure you want to have fellowship with a priest?" he asked cautiously. "Is he a Catholic priest?"

"Is there another kind?"

"Sure. Anglican. Eastern Orthodox."

That felt like information Wes should've looked into last year. "What's the difference?" she asked.

"The other two can get married."

"I don't want to get married! I want to know where to draw the line."

"Wes, I don't..."

"Kissing is obviously okay," she said. *Very okay. More than okay.*

"Is kissing okay with him?"

"He seems into it," she said. *Until he runs away,* she didn't add. "So, touching? Over the clothes or under the clothes?"

Andy took her free hand in both of his. "I love you, but I'm pretty sure I'm the wrong person for this particularly weird discussion."

Wes cocked her head. "Because you did or didn't have a crush on a priest when you were young?"

He shifted uncomfortably. "My parents are religious. I'm... not."

"Oh, right. Yeah, I mean, me neither. Obviously," Wes said. She could probably count on one hand the number of times her mom or dad had taken her to a base chapel.

"But a lot of youth pastors put out some pretty confusing vibes, in and outside of... camp."

"Jeez, sorry." Wes hadn't meant to tread on any trauma in her search for answers. "Did any of them—"

"No."

"Good," Wes told Andy, dropping *that* subject.

Grace peeked in from the living room. "Is this a private palaver?"

"Kinda," Wes said.

At the same time, Andy gave another emphatic, "No."

"What do you think the rules would be, like if I became a nun?" Wes whispered.

"Wes!" he exclaimed.

"You're right. I know. Way too far to go for a friends with benefits situation," she mumbled.

Disappointing, really, because she suspected the benefits could be very nice.

"Are you quoting Shakespeare in here? I thought I heard *anon*," Grace said.

"No Shakespeare. Andy doesn't approve. And I imagine the nuns would frown on my relationship with Pablo, too."

"Pablo?" Andy asked.

"I promise, you don't want to know," Grace said. "Wes, Grandma Ruth's looking for you."

Grace slid open the stuck coaster drawer in search of something, only this time it opened smooth as butter, and she smiled.

"Damn it, he fixed that too?" Wesley found herself exclaiming out loud.

"I think the nuns might frown on your relationship with profanity," Andy told her.

"You'd rather the drawer keep sticking?" Grace asked, being oh-so-reasonable about it as she took out a proper bread knife rather than the steak knife they'd been using to hack at Becca's bread.

"Why does no one get it?" Wes asked the ceiling.

"Because you're ridiculous," Grace told her.

"Rude."

"I know you're Miss Independence, but he's obviously dying to help."

Wes opened her mouth to say, *He only thinks he wants to help*, but Grace didn't give her a chance.

"And speaking of ridiculous, what the hell's going on with your sister?" Grace demanded, turning on Andy.

He sighed. "She's trying to help? And she's super into sourdough?"

"You haven't been gone so long you've forgotten she only bakes like this when she's upset," Grace argued. "Not for the holidays, not because she's bored, not because anyone's hungry. What's going on?"

Andy shifted from one foot to the other, a half-guilty look on his face. "She hasn't been ready to talk about it yet."

"You've asked her?"

He nodded and then sighed. "Don't suppose Gramma Ruth keeps gin lying around?"

"There's a good chance," Wes said, opening cabinets until she found her grandmother's liquor stash and passed over an aqua-colored bottle.

"That's the expensive stuff! I'll pay her back."

"You already have. Go get your sister drunk."

"It's ten o'clock in the morning," Grace pointed out.

"Andy," Wes called him back, opening the fridge to hand him a bottle of orange juice, and passing him a loaf of bread.

"Brunch is good," Grace agreed. "We're making good choices."

"It's five o'clock somewhere. Right?" Wes said with a shrug.

"Moldova? Maybe?"

"Why do you know that?"

"I've researched a lot of weird things for books. Some of it sticks. Anyway, I've got news," she said, sliding into a chair at the kitchen table.

"You found toilets?"

"Was I looking for toilets?" Grace asked, looking crestfallen that she may have forgotten an assignment.

"No. But if you found a magic genie I wouldn't mind if you wished for some."

"Noted."

"What's your news?"

"My co-librarian hooked up with the Stratford High librarian at a state conference—"

"*Hooked up* hooked up?"

"Don't ask questions."

"Yes, ma'am. Sorry, ma'am," Wesley snapped, like Grace was her drill sergeant.

"That's better. Between my school and their school, we've got like forty kids ready to volunteer."

"Do we need that many?"

"Rule number 1, Wes. You can *never* have too many volunteers."

"S'pose not."

"I'm glad you see it my way, so are you really not going to let Eòghann *volunteer* to do *anything*?" she asked, because apparently they weren't done with that whole conversation after all.

"Speaking of volunteers, mind your own business."

"He clearly wants to—" Grace said, cutting her words off when the man himself entered the kitchen. "Lùc clearly wants to help with the painting, so thanks for letting him. I've never seen him so excited," she pivoted.

"How could I say no?" Wes asked, giving Grace a dirty look before turning to Eòghann, still clad in dark jeans and a tight t-shirt, his everyday uniform as she'd begun to think of it. He looked rumpled, disheveled and delicious. Something sparked in his eyes when he glanced over at her, and she shivered. "Hey handsome. Where've you been hiding?" she asked.

"The garage," he said cautiously, which was a very odd answer, but she liked the way he pronounced it, with a long a, like carriage.

"I'm going to make sure Andy doesn't get Becca too drunk," Grace said, heading out the side door.

"It's five o'clock in Moldova!" Wes called after her, but she'd frozen Eòghann with her gaze, and he stood there, staring back at her, half hungry, half guilty. "You should be careful skulking around in the garage," she said. "A pile of junk might topple over, and we wouldn't find you for days."

Eòghann shoved his hands deep in his pockets and rocked back on his heels. "Not when I'm through with it. I'm cleaning it out for Grandma Ruth."

Her traitorous heart warmed at the notion—and the way he called her Grandma Ruth—but she said, "I *thought* I told you to stop working while you're on vacation."

"And I thought I told *you* I have to earn my keep," he protested.

"I think I was pretty clear about how you could earn your keep," she said, with all the subtlety of a LIVE NUDES strip club sign. She desperately needed to locate her chill.

His face flushed adorably, and he opened and closed his mouth, flustered. Remorse washed over Wes, cold and sticky and gross. This sort of behavior was probably why he'd moved out of her room and down the hall.

"Sorry," she said. "That was—"

"No—"

"Sure you haven't been hiding from me because I keep coming on too strong? Like the night of the ceilidh?"

He shook his head but couldn't hold eye contact.

"Maybe I imagined it, but I feel like there's an attraction between us—"

"You didn't imagine it."

"Okay, but I don't understand the rules though. And I want to. If I know the rules, I can play the game. Like, is the celibacy thing strict? I mean, you're still a human being, so it can't mean *never ever*, right? So does it only apply to your congregation? Or are there cheat days?"

"Cheat days?" he repeated, looking up, his face so perplexed she couldn't stand it.

"Nothing. It's stupid. I remember kids used to give up candy for Lent, but Sunday didn't count for some reason, so it was their cheat day." Before the words left her mouth, she knew she was being ridiculous.

He blinked at her. Repeatedly. She may have actually broken him. "Wes..."

"Sorry, I just want to understand where *we* stand, you know?" she said, because her heart had been pounding since the moment he walked in the door, and the rest of her could use a good pounding to go with it.

God. So much for chill.

He slid into the chair Andy had vacated, still blinking, his lips forming words with no sound.

She held her breath and he reached for her hands, and when he held them with his own calloused fingers she felt instantly calm. And warm. And raw, as though his touch were burning off the roughest parts of her.

"You don't actually—" he began. The side door opened, and neither of them moved.

"Ah, Eòghann, there you are," his cousin Alec said. "I heard you found some canoes."

Eòghann's hands flenched in Wesley's as he dragged his gaze up to meet his cousin's. "Canoes?" he rasped.

"Jack and I thought we'd take the lads fishing, and Daniel mentioned some canoes in the garage?"

His palms turned sweaty, and Wes found herself running her thumbs over the backs of his hands in a way she hoped he'd find soothing.

"Fishing," he repeated. "The lads like to fish, do they?" Eòghann asked, clearly uncomfortable with the idea, but Wes supposed it was good parenting for Alec to take them out on the water after everything that had happened, to keep them from developing a fear of it.

Alec shrugged. "Rory will undoubtedly turn the rod into a weapon, and I'm fairly certain Daniel would rather gouge his eyes out with the hooks. But that's parenting innit? Forcing them to form core memories they can complain about for years to come?"

Wes laughed, trying to remember if she had any of those, but nothing came immediately to mind.

"Don't you usually fish from a dock or summat?" Eòghann asked.

"Sometimes," his cousin said, glancing between them as though realizing he'd interrupted something. "I can go have a look myself," he suggested.

"No, I'll show you," Eòghann said, releasing Wesley's hands. "Only, I was about to get rid of them. They're quite old. May not be seaworthy."

"I'll make sure. We'll be careful," his cousin promised, and the two shared a meaningful look.

Eòghann nodded, glancing back at Wes with an apology in his eyes.

"To be continued," she whispered.

He nodded again and led his cousin out to the garage, and Wes sighed, banging her forehand on the kitchen table.

You don't actually—what?

Chapter Twenty-Three

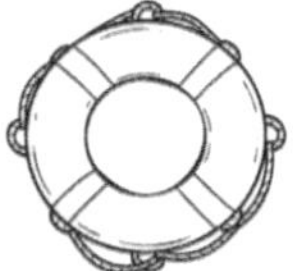

Eòghann was reeling, leading Alec to the garage on wobbly legs like a condemned man walking the plank aboard a ship. All this time, the priest bit—the flirty little jokes about sin and forgiveness—not actually a bit. Some part of her had meant it? When he'd put distance between them to protect his heart, she'd interpreted it as protecting his vows because she genuinely thought he was a priest? How had they gotten their wires so crossed?

"Aye, these'll do fine," Alec said, clapping Eòghann on the shoulder as he admired the ugly canoes that should've been discarded days ago.

Eòghann swallowed. "You sure? Shall—shall I come with you?" he forced himself to offer.

Alec's face gentled. "Next time, aye? Got to save room for the fish."

Exhaling a ragged breath, Eòghann nodded, grateful for the reprieve.

By the time he made it back to the kitchen, Wes was gone, so he threw himself into finishing his garage project, barely aware of his actions as he handed off anything that could be repurposed for the faire to the Shakespeare Syndicate and organized the tools Bryan and Lùc had been using to build their wooden backdrops and photo stand-ins. All the while, his mind was spinning with how he'd explain that he was very much not a man of the cloth.

Meanwhile, Jack and Alec did indeed take the boys out in the canoes for their fishing expedition. They all returned, hearty and hale, with enough trout to feed the 412th Test Wing, as Grandma Ruth liked to say.

"Smells delicious," Eòghann murmured to Wes as they each fixed a plate at dinnertime.

"You smell delicious," she retorted almost aggressively, then she glanced back at him with ravenous eyes, staring for a moment at his lips before unconsciously licking her own.

Eòghann's whole body was pulled tight like a bow with an invisible string running from his throat to his groin.

Suddenly the lightweight red shorts he was wearing were a very bad idea. He turned towards the table, hoping to hide his erection behind the pyramid of corn on the cob.

"Find a kids' ride yet?" Jack asked, giving Wes a hug as he passed behind her to grab extra napkins.

"No, but that reminds me." She turned back to Eòghann. "You haven't run across an old Slip 'N Slide in the garage, have you?"

"A slide?" Eòghann repeated, confused. "I don't think so."

"Wes, no," Grace admonished. "Slip 'N Slide was the most dangerous toy on the planet when we were kids."

"Excuse me. Skateboards and trampolines would like a word," Wes argued.

"I know a kid who lost an eye playing with those marble-munching hippos," Jack said.

Wes raised an arm as if Jack had illustrated her point for her. "We've got to have something for the kids and it's going to be a million degrees out, so Slip 'N Slide might actually be the safest part of the faire if it keeps them from getting heat stroke."

"I don't like it," Grace grumbled. "You better have insurance and a paramedic on hand, and make their parents sign a liability waiver longer than a drugstore receipt."

Wes scowled.

"I don't think there was anything like that in the garage," Eòghann said still not entirely sure what they were talking about.

Shrugging, Wes pasted on a smile. She was good at that— pulling one on like a mask over whatever she was feeling. "Oh well. It was probably a dumb idea anyway."

"I don't think you're capable of dumb ideas," he replied, hearing exactly how trite he sounded, and holding her gaze so she'd know the sentiment was genuine. When she swallowed, the delicate movement of her throat made his mouth go dry, and he realized Grandma Ruth's romance novels would accuse him of smoldering at her, but he couldn't look away.

"You smell so good," she said softly.

"Can't figure out what you smell like," he admitted, and her lips tugged down like she couldn't decide whether to laugh or be offended. "I mean—"

"I'm pretty tired," Wes said, signaling, that either he'd offended her or she'd glimpsed his arousal in the scandalous red shorts and he should stand down, as it were. "I think I'll eat in my room," she added.

His cheeks burned as he nodded that he understood. For a moment he thought she'd been coming on to him about how good he smelled, but he must've misunderstood her tone. He might need to eat standing here in front of the buffet table, though surely the humiliation would rectify his situation any moment. If not, he supposed he could shift his messenger bag around front to hide it.

Wes cleared her throat, but Eòghann couldn't face her. "Enjoy," he murmured. "I'll be fine. See you later."

"You can't help but be fine," she agreed.

And no, it definitely sounded like flirting. Was it a cultural miscue then?

"Aren't you pretty tired too?" she asked.

He nodded.

"I'm sure I'd enjoy this trout a lot more if I had company. You can eat in my room with me if you want. We can *be tired* together? If you want."

Oh. *OH*.

His eyes snapped to hers and she was grinning mischievously. Her eyebrows raised in question, and his todger jerked up to meet them.

Glancing down at his predicament, Eòghann tried to figure out the best way to extricate himself from the buffet table with his dignity intact.

Eyes dancing, Wesley seemed to grasp the situation and took mercy on him. "Here," she said, reaching for his food. "I'll carry your plate if you bring some extra napkins and that bag of malt vinegar chips."

"The whole bag?" he asked.

"There's plenty of stuff out here. You need them more," she added, nodding to his predicament.

Eòghann didn't need a second invitation. He grabbed the crisps and hurried back to the house, with Wesley following along behind.

"I haven't seen you wear shorts before," she murmured appreciatively. "I haven't seen you wear *color* before!"

"You were right about my trousers being miserably inappropriate—"

"Yeah they were."

"—for the climate. I picked these up when I was out with Daniel the other day."

"They suit you," she said.

He'd have preferred black or grey, but the red shorts with khaki trim were all that was on offer besides camo or some horrendous ones with bald eagles and American flags printed on them that would probably cause his passport to be revoked if he was caught with them at the airport.

Upstairs, she passed by her room, heading for his instead. "So this is where you've been hiding all week," she said, looking around as though she'd never seen the place before. "Look at you, you even made the bed," she purred.

She toed off her shoes, moaning in a way that should frankly be illegal, and plopped down on one of the beds with her food. "God, my feet hurt. Sorry," she added, presumably for saying, *God*, rather than the million different ways she'd pushed and prodded his libido towards the edge in the last ten minutes.

Eòghann needed to take a breath before he mauled her like a randy, rampant lion. She was obviously hungry, as well as tired and sore. The least he could do was let her relax and eat her food without being plagued by his raging hard-on.

Placing his dinner on the dresser and his bag on the floor, he sat at the foot of her bed instead of the opposite one, picking up her feet and putting them in his lap. "Can I rub them for you?"

She swallowed a bite of fish, eyes heavy with desire. He could see she wanted to turn down his offer. But she wanted to say yes, too.

After slowly pulling off her left ankle sock, he began to knead her heel and the ball of her foot, and she moaned again, shooting another jolt of adrenaline straight to his crotch. "Well," she gasped. "If you ever decide to quit being a priest, I have a suggestion for your next career."

And there it was, the opening he needed. All he had to do was walk through the door. Would she be relieved? Embarrassed? Disappointed?

"Someday you're going to tell me why a priest is so good at this. Seriously is there anything you can't do?"

She meant it rhetorically, but if only she knew how very many things he couldn't do—most of them involving water.

"What?" she asked, noting his falter and frown. "Please don't say exorcisms. I'll be heartbroken if that movie isn't real."

He laughed then, and the laugh broke through the growing tightness in his chest, which had been keeping him tongue tied. "I dunno how real they are, but no. I cannot perform exorcisms. Or baptisms, or reconciliation for that matter."

She cocked her head at him, frowning, trying to make his words make sense.

He took a deep breath. "I'm not a priest, Wesley. I'm only a very boring man who wears too much black and haunts old churches like some kind of... sad ghost."

Bracing himself, he was prepared for her to kick him, and he held her foot very loosely in case she wanted to, but she merely stared at him for a long moment with inscrutable eyes, right through him like she was replaying their every interaction as he'd done that morning.

"You're not a priest," she repeated, with no emotion in her voice, like she was stunned.

"No."

"This isn't a joke?"

"No," he replied, unable to look her in the eye, focusing instead on continuing to massage her feet.

"So all those times—all those *forgive me, Father's*—"

"I thought it was a bit."

"*I can't actually grant you absolution,*" she quoted one of their text exchanges.

"At first I thought it was a crack about my age—you had a daddy kink, maybe—you did say you liked old things. Then I thought it was a role-play thing. You mentioned watching that show with the priest. Say something, please, so I can stop talking."

"Fuck me, Padre," she said, but it didn't sound much like an invitation. "Shit, can I still call you Padre?"

"I hope you will." He looked up at her then, and there was a naughty gleam in her eye.

"Kinky."

He shrugged. "I like the way you say it."

She nodded. She didn't look angry, but she wasn't exactly laughing either, which he'd kind of hoped for. Eòghann let go of her foot and moved her half-finished plate next to his on the dresser so he could reach for her hand.

"God," she whispered. "Sorry." Then, "No, I guess I'm *not* sorry, because you aren't a fucking priest."

"You seem angry about it," he said cautiously. He had hoped she'd be relieved.

Cheeks flushed, she opened her mouth like she was going to deny it, then jerked her head to the side, not exactly a no.

"I'm sorry," he said. For what? He hadn't lied. He hadn't known. "For being too dim to catch on."

She held up a hand to silence him. "I'm not mad, I'm processing," she said angrily. "I'm going to..." She chucked a thumb over her shoulder, and when he nodded, she got up and left the room.

And it occurred to Eòghann that maybe everything he'd ever been taught, like *honesty is the best policy*, was a load of bull.

Chapter Twenty-Four

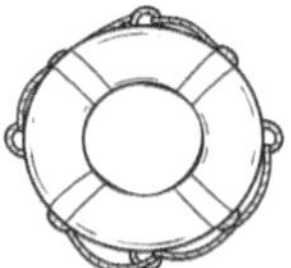

Back in the safety of her own room, Wes sat on the bed, staring blankly at the wall. She'd forgotten to bring her dinner, but she'd lost her appetite anyway, simultaneously nauseated and giddy as her world slipped and slid like a kaleidoscope through shape and shadow before finally snapping into view.

He wasn't actually a priest.

There weren't any rules.

Heavy footsteps tread back up the hallway, and she flew to open the door. Eòghann froze, bending down to place her sneakers to the side of the doorway, where she'd find but not trip over them. He looked up at her, eyes dark with lust and worry, and he swallowed, his Adam's apple bobbing with remorse.

"I feel like a massive idiot," she admitted.

"Please don't. I'm the idiot. I should've realized."

"If you aren't a priest, then why?" She couldn't bring herself to finish the sentence. *Why did you reject me? Why did you run?* "What's been holding you back?" she finally landed on.

He straightened to his full height, still clutching her shoes like they were some kind of floatation device.

"Self-preservation." His voice was a raspy burr that shot straight to her belly. "And a years'-long policy against hooking up with tourists."

That was... fair.

Wes stepped back, holding the door open in invitation, and Eòghann cautiously stepped inside.

Truth be told, finding out he was very much *not* a priest and therefore completely available rather curbed his appeal, but try telling her revved-up libido that. The beauty of Wesley's infatuation had been his pre-existing commitment. Neither one of them would be able to get in too deep if there was a flock for him to shepherd back in Scotland.

Now the casual hookup felt a lot riskier. She hadn't minded putting her own heart in danger, but she'd never meant to risk his.

Still, she'd wanted this man for an entire year, imagined their coupling again and again, and at this point Wes was pretty much a walking clit, raw and needy. Clamping off her ardor would be about as physically impossible as stopping a speeding train with her bare hands.

She wanted to turn off her brain and let her body enjoy the ride, but he was still babbling apologies and she needed him to stop talking.

"I'm so sorry, Wes, I'm such an arse, I—"

"I hear you, Padre," she interrupted. "Now take me to church," she whispered, shoving his t-shirt up and helping him pull it over his head, letting her hands rove down his well-formed torso.

Eòghann stroked a loose hair back behind her ear, and Wes noticed a small tattoo on the ribs under his left arm—so small she'd almost mistaken it for a birthmark. She tilted her head. It looked like a simple semicolon, the kind people used as a personal marker of mental health—of courage or resilience or simply acknowledging they were still here on this earth fighting to live.

She felt her eyes go wide and then soft, but she didn't want to make a thing of it, so she shoved him onto the bed and reached into the side table drawer for a condom, until Eòghann caught her wrist, shaking his head once.

"Not yet," he breathed. Then he grabbed the messenger bag he'd dropped along with her shoes when she shoved him, and he withdrew those slutty little glasses that made her insides go liquid.

"Prefer to do some light reading?" she teased as he slid them up to the bridge of his nose and tilted his head to peer at her through them. Her breath caught. "One of your favorite romance novels, perhaps?"

"I want to examine every inch of you," he answered solemnly, and Wes exhaled a little growl like the revving of her own engine.

She pulled his face down to kiss him again. "Not a priest, *and* the owner of slutty little glasses," she murmured. "It must be my lucky day."

"Let me make it luckier," he whispered, kissing her cheeks and eyebrows and collarbone. "What do you like?"

The question was innocuous enough, and one she should be able to answer easily, but it made her pause. Had a man ever asked her such a thing in bed? Not that she could remember, and surely it was a question she'd remember.

He pulled back a little, studying her face with concern, as though worried he might've said the wrong thing. "Do you want me to guess?"

A slow smile curved her lips.

Normally the answer would be no, but the earnest way he offered made her kind of want to let him. "If I said yes, what would your guess be?"

He gazed steadily at her, the tip of his pink tongue flicking out to wet his lips. "You like to be in control," he said. "I imagine it might be thrilling to have control stripped away."

Wesley's eyes opened wider, and she was about to argue, but she noticed how her own breathing had sped up quite a lot, and her crotch was tingling at the notion, so he might not be as far off base as she immediately thought.

He slipped a few soft cable ties out of the messenger bag.

"I didn't know you brought a bag of tricks. Where'd you get those?"

"Box in the garage," he replied, and her nether region gave a tiny jerk at the idea of him working all day in the hot, stuffy garage, lust fueled by thoughts of her, scavenging those fasteners with naughty optimism.

He lifted her hands over her head and bound them together like handcuffs, then gently lowered her shoulders so she was lying flat on the bed.

"What about my dress?" she asked, wriggling her ass impatiently.

"It's fine for now," he said, leaning down to kiss her neck once more, skimming a hand over first one breast and then the other, both of them aching under too many layers of fabric.

Wesley wiggled again, desperate for more of his touch.

"Patience," he teased, and all she could do was whimper.

Patience might be a virtue, but it had never been one of hers. She tended to be more of a wham-bam-thank-you-ma'am type of lover, though on reflection she couldn't say whether it was by preference or necessity.

One-by-one he undid the buttons down the front of her purple sundress, taking an unbearable amount of time over it— pure, delicious torture as his rough fingers skimmed the underside of her bra and then her belly, until, to her delight, they hooked into the waistband of her panties. "May I?"

She pressed into his touch, desperate for heat and contact as he took the hint and slid them all the way off. Eòghann kissed the inside of her thigh, settling her a little, and she could feel his hot breath, so close, almost there.

"True love," he murmured.

"What?" Wes croaked, trying not to freeze up.

"Pizza is your ain true love?" he asked, brushing a soft, tickling kiss across the tattoo on her left inner thigh.

"Oh!" she laughed, giddy with relief to realize he was reading her tattoo and not professing his own undying affection. "I mean who doesn't love pizza?" she giggled.

He huffed a laugh, hot and breathy enough it ruffled her pubic hair and she tensed in delicious anticipation. Then he kissed his way back up to her lips and she groaned, relishing the hard planes of him pressing her into the bed. She wanted him to hurry. She wanted him to never move again.

"Tormentor," she gasped, bucking her hips, but unwilling to beg for release because in truth, she liked the way he took charge and took his time. It was new. It was a revelation. She closed her eyes and let each touch be a heady surprise that branded her like iron.

He smiled into her kiss and paused to unhook her front clasp bra, pulling the cups aside as he teased first one and then the other nipple with his tongue. Encouraged by her whimpers, he seemed content to stay awhile, tracing lazy circles around her areoles until she was squirming beneath him once more.

"I've wanted to do this for a year," he whispered, and she found herself quite willing to endure it that long. Then he kissed his way down her sternum, nuzzled tantalizing kisses against her tattoo until she was writhing, and lifted her legs over his shoulders at last. He grinned up at her, still wearing those slutty little glasses that made him look cheeky and distinguished and so damn hot. "Is this okay?"

"Hell, yeah," she replied, unwilling to close her eyes on those glasses as he buried his face in the thatch of blonde curls between her legs.

The first flick of his tongue dragged a very unladylike rasp from her throat, and she bucked, involuntarily this time. Hands still lightly bound, Wes managed to maneuver a pillow over her face to stifle the moans as he circled her clit with his tongue. How was it possible she was already on the cusp, already starting to tremble against the rising crescendo, when he'd only just begun?

He wasn't simply going down on her. He was devouring her like a fancy dessert.

And then he stopped.

"Don't stop," she begged, tossing the pillow aside, not caring that it tumbled right off the bed and onto the floor.

"Sit up, please," he said, tugging off those little red shorts that did half the work for him before he'd really gotten started.

Wes found she didn't mind the way he bossed her around in pursuit of her own pleasure, and though she was still short of breath, she wriggled herself up as requested. Eòghann climbed back up the bed towards her, settling himself around her seated form, propping the errant pillow behind his own head.

She leaned against his chest, the hard knot of his erection pressing into her back. Hands still bound, she couldn't reach his crotch, so she raised her arms and brought her wrists down behind his head as he kissed her, her breasts pushing wantonly forward. He fondled them for several minutes, bringing her closer and closer to climax, and then he spread one large, warm hand against her belly as he reached over her, his intoxicating cologne lapping at her like rippling waves as he rummaged in the bedside drawer until he found the cucumber-shaped Pablo.

She craned her neck to smirk over her shoulder at him, and he kissed her nose.

"Turn around," he said, giving her hip a playful smack.

Like Eòghann when she was bossy with the Gatorade, Wesley didn't need to be told twice. She turned around, doing her best to grind her bottom against his barely contained erection as much as possible.

Hissing and clasping her tighter to make her hold still, Eòghann brought the vibrator around and held it against her, and she inhaled sharply. No disrespect to Pablo, but why was this so much hotter with Eòghann doing the driving?

For a moment he held it there, letting Pablo vibrate gently against her core while he kissed her cheek and neck, taking his sweet time about it, every kiss a revelation. Before this moment Wes had always experienced sex as a race against time, but now she found herself melting into each kiss, each touch, till she was hardly more than a puddle to be remade into something new. She was vaguely aware he might be ruining her for all other partners for the rest of time, which was rather inconvenient, all things considered.

"Does it need any—" he began, holding Pablo up for examination, and she knew he was asking about lube.

"Not today," she gasped, desperate to feel it back on her.

Eòghann was excellent at taking directions, and he returned Pablo to her center, adjusting the angle so she could slide down onto it, and the moment she did, Eòghann let his fingers drift from her breast down to her clit.

Wesley gasped, high and sharp, over and over again.

"Is this all right?" he checked in, his voice laced with tender concern.

The only reply she could make was to gasp again, a soft little moan. She was already cresting.

Seeming to understand, Eòghann kissed her neck again and, leaving the vibrator in place, brought his left hand up to fondle her breast instead, eliciting yet another little whimper and a moment later she was clenching down on Pablo, her whole body shaking as she came apart in Eòghann's arms.

"Good girl," he whispered. "Just let go."

It had been so long since a man had properly touched her—since anyone besides herself alone with Pablo had made her orgasm—that she'd forgotten how fun the two-player version could be, how deliciously loud she could get when she relaxed and enjoyed herself.

Once she caught her breath, she rolled over and propped herself up on her elbows to kiss Eòghann some more. That had been amazing, but she wasn't close to sated yet, not after more than a year of wanting, of fantasizing what it would feel like to have him inside her.

"Are you sure?" he asked, when she reached for a condom once more.

"Only if you want to," she replied.

Eòghann's eyes darkened, and he shimmied out of his boxer briefs so fast she didn't have time to prepare for his cock springing free, exactly as perfect as she'd imagined it. She rolled the condom down in one quick, practiced motion despite her hands still being bound and finally, *finally* she was riding him and Jesus he filled her up. It had been so long. In all too brief a few minutes of frenzied thrusting, she was coming apart again right as he began to shudder beneath her, both of them gasping like they'd run a three-minute-mile.

Chapter Twenty-Five

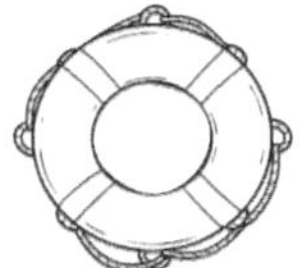

T-MINUS 7 DAYS TO RENAYZANTS FAIRE

Eòghann stayed the entire night in Wesley's bed, alternating between satisfied elation, hunger for more, and dissecting what it would mean for them going forward. Wes talked a big game about vacation and orgasms but eventually vacations had to end.

It was hard to imagine this one ending while he was tangled up in her arms and in her sheets, but regardless, he was sure to fuck it up somehow. And if he couldn't make it right by being helpful, they were doomed.

She woke up smiling and kissed him with closed lips, chasing away his worries behind a cloud.

"It's Saturday," she said, stretching languidly.

"Is it?"

"One week until the faire opens."

"Everything's perfect."

"Except there aren't any toilets."

"Everything *will be* perfect."

"Let's see, shall we?" she said, kissing him again before

climbing out of bed. "I want to get out there and do a walk through in case there's anything I've forgotten."

"Can I show you something first?" Eòghann asked.

One eyebrow ticked up lasciviously, and Wes bit her lip.

"Not that," he replied despite the twitch in his cock at her interest. But there was one final piece of his garage cleanup project he wanted to run by her. He'd been afraid if he showed her before he was done she'd banish him to his room and never allow him to finish.

Not one to turn down an intriguing proposition, Wes followed him down the stairs.

"What kind of Celtic magic happened out here?" she breathed, looking around the tidy space in awe.

Eòghann tried not to preen, but it was clear she was impressed despite his meddling, and that pleased him endlessly.

"I'm not sure Grandma's been able to park in here my whole life!"

"Aye, it's a modern miracle," he teased. "But not what I wanted to show you."

He led her over to the corner where he'd stowed the old cedar chest, and he watched as Wesley's jaw dropped.

"Is that...?" she murmured, falling to her knees and running a hand over the smooth, glossy top. He'd cleaned off at least a decade of dust and taken furniture polish to it the afternoon before.

Reverently, Wes lifted the lid and peered inside, unleashing a puff of cedar and pine needle scent.

"Hello," she whispered.

Inside the trunk there were at least a dozen soft, handmade blankets in an array of colors.

"This was another way she kept busy when my grandad was deployed," she said, running her hand over the burnished orange and brown and gold blanket on top. "Each one tells a story of an era."

She burrowed down through the layers of cotton and wool until she found one done in rippling shades of blue and white and grey.

"She made this one for my dad when he joined the Air Force. I always wrapped myself up in it to watch TV on the couch when I was a little girl. I wonder if she'd let me keep it."

Eòghann could picture her right there in the living room, cozy and close to the memory of her father—while he was deployed, and after—and his heart gave a little tug.

"I think she'd let you keep them all," Eòghann told her. "She said she'd rather get rid of everything out here than be asked to pick and choose."

A faint, sad smile crossed Wesley's lips, and Eòghann wanted to kiss it away. She looked so vulnerable, clutching the blanket tightly to her chest like a lifeline.

"Would you like me to put them in your room?"

She nodded—one quick jerk of her head—as though words and anything else were too much at the moment.

Then she rolled out her shoulders and pulled her mask back on, preparing to begin the day.

WATCHING HER IN ACTION WAS LIKE WATCHING A CYCLONE on a mission. She was a force of nature as she swept through every corner of the upcoming faire. Eòghann admired the hell out of her, even as he held his breath, waiting for her to discover how he'd worked through the others to maneuver around her non-interference rule.

"Okay, so there are six confirmed food trucks lining up over there in the shade," she told Grace and their teenage volunteers.

"Ye Kidd's Craftes right here—oh. What're we going to use for a table?"

"Eòghann found an eight footer in the garage," Grace said.

"You did?" Wes spun around to him, her face alight with pleasure.

He inclined his head in affirmation, bewitched by the way the sunlight made her blue eyes sparkle.

"Convenient. And perfect. Then we have the pub"—she turned towards the barn—"which I know looks fabulous, because I helped."

She paused, squinting at a smaller, second shed not far from the barn. Eòghann had asked Lùc to paint a sign for it, and the bright colors caught her eye.

"We're using the shed too? Isn't it full of…?"

It had been full of all-sorts. Mostly broken down yard equipment—a mower, a blower, a barrow that was missing its wheel. Eòghann had cleaned it out when he finished with the garage, evicting any number of spiders and one small snake.

Wes moved closer, until she could read the sign. "Berserker's Cave?"

"It's pretty ingenious," Lùc jumped in loyally. "One of those rage rooms like the cities have."

Lùc opened the shed door to point out the safety goggles from her grandfather's workbench, and swim goggles too, hanging on pegs. One overturned barrel was set up as a table. An old baseball bat and several golf clubs were mounted on the wall.

"I don't get it."

"For five quid—sorry, dollars—guests can get five minutes to smash the living bollocks out of old dishes and stuff."

"I donated some chipped terracotta pots to the cause," Sadie said with a laugh. "When they're done, we sweep up the pieces, and let the kids use them for mosaic art."

"Your idea?" Wes asked Lùc, a smile spreading slowly across her face.

Lùc shrugged and shook his head, glancing sideways at Eòghann. She fixed him with a firm stare.

"It's a few things from the garage," he said.

"Do we have enough pottery?" Then she held up a hand. "Don't answer that. Grandma Ruth has at least a hundred coffee mugs and she only uses about three on repeat."

"We could try to thrift a few more this week if you're worried, but I think it's plenty," Sadie assured her.

"Perfect." Wes gave Eòghann another suspicious once-over that seemed more thirsty than annoyed, and it zinged straight to his groin.

She led the entourage towards the meadow where a chessboard had been spray painted on the ground for their life-sized match. Drama club students from Gray's high school were practicing their fight choreography with Andy and Jack.

"Looking good over here. Do they need costumes?" she asked.

"They're going to dress in black and white shorts and tees, with hats and masks based on role," Grace explained.

Wes nodded. "Clever. Oh, these turned out amazing," she crooned, pointing to the photo stand-ins with cutout face holes for guests to pose behind.

The first was a minstrel being chased by a fat, little dog, where guests could chose to be either minstrel or dog. The next was reminiscent of the Bremen Town musicians, and then there were a fancy lord and lady, and a court jester.

"Honestly, they turned out beyond my wildest dreams," she admitted, and Eòghann's baby cousin blushed about six shades of red, grinning as though he'd won the lottery, while Bryan rubbed the back of his own neck, equally pleased.

"That's down to you two," he demurred.

"I only painted them. The art was all Wes," Lùc argued.

She smiled and shook her head. "Once again, against my nature, I'm reminded of the value of teamwork. So thank you for your help, truly. Okay, I heard back from Lance and Lottie—they're a knight and dragon themed swing ride. There should be enough space for them to set up alongside the chess, and then artisan alley is here, leading back to the Bard's Stage. I love what you've done with these fairy lights," she added, nodding to the twinkling lights Bryan and Lùc had strung through the woods to create a path and give it a fae quality. "Are they battery powered?"

"Solar," Lùc said.

"Love that."

"Not terribly... bright," Bryan said with a shrug. "They're for ambiance."

"People won't be out here at midnight. They're great," Wes replied. "I guess that's everything. Except the toilets, always the damn toilets," she added, biting her bottom lip in a way that drove Eòghann crazy, when he ought to be trying to find a solution to the toilet issue for her. "I want to thank you all. So much. I mean it. I know I tend to be—"

"Militant?" Jack suggested.

"I was going to say *unwilling* to ask for or accept help. I didn't want it—I never want it—"

"We know!" Andy called out.

"—but I couldn't in a million years have pulled this off without you." Her gaze fell on Eòghann, locking him in place and making his stomach flip-flop. "All of you," she added, heat flaring in her eyes.

"Go team go," Grace cheered. "We love you Wes."

"Yeah you're welcome, I guess," Sadie agreed.

The others joined in, hugging her before drifting back to

their own activities, leaving Eòghann alone with Wes for the first time since they'd rolled out of bed.

She took his hand and turned, strolling casually deeper into the trees.

"You aren't angry?" he asked. "About the rage room?"

"Nope. It's a fun idea."

He warmed all over, and it wasn't only because he was back in jeans in June.

"I know it probably seems weird that I don't want your help..." she began but trailed off.

"You don't need to explain."

He liked her independence, no matter if it clashed with his need to be needed, no matter if it threatened to make them incompatible, because he wasn't sure he could stop helping out if he tried. He loved helping her. But her independence was part of what made her *her*, and he loved her for it. Er. Loved that about her.

She regarded him as though she'd heard every word rattling around inside his head, and the air around them felt heavy and charged, her sweet scent overwhelming him, like it was everywhere, throwing him off kilter.

Wes stepped towards him, shoving him playfully backwards between the branches of a tree, until he stumbled against its broad trunk. The branches were filled with massive, white flowers—bigger than his hand—and he realized their scent was the same as her sweet scent. Before he could ask what they were called, she whispered, "Is it okay if I kiss you?" her mouth a feather's breadth away from his.

"Please," was all he had to say before her lips crashed down, warm and demanding, as she tangled her fingers in his hair.

As usual, she kissed like she was hungry—starving—and only the flick of his tongue and the scrape of his beard could save her. Fuck, it was more intoxicating than the flowers.

"I'm so annoyed you're not a priest," she teased, rocking her hips against him, and he wanted to beg her forgiveness, but his mouth forgot how to form words, forgot how to do anything else but this, as he showed her exactly how mad he wasn't.

He couldn't tell where the tree's perfume ended and her's began as he nuzzled into her neck, kissing behind her ear, the top of her shoulder, her throat, and when she let a tiny, indecent moan escape he turned them around, pushing *her* back against the tree and fisting his hands in her skirt as she ground herself against his erection, tight and urgent inside his jeans.

Thank Christ he wasn't wearing those tiny red shorts. If she didn't stop, he might embarrass himself in a few more minutes, and what if someone saw them through the branches?

"You've got to quit distracting me," she whispered, nipping his bottom lip saucily and inhaling deeply, reveling in his cologne again.

He pressed in closer, letting one hand float along the edge of her bra before dragging it down her ribs and then up her bare thigh underneath the blue and white sundress that she had to know turned her eyes luminescent.

She shivered, despite the heat, and hitched one leg up around his waist. The friction against his aching cock made him gasp, and he had to brace one hand over her head against the smooth tree bark.

"Bombs away," a voice shrieked, and then Eòghann felt the impact of something hitting his head, and the next second came an explosion matching the one building within his trousers— and equally as wet.

"Was that a—?"

"Water balloon," he growled as Rory jumped out of the tree and took off running.

"Little shit has good aim," Wes groaned, water droplets

sprinkling her eyelashes and dripping off her nose. "And terrible timing."

"Aye," Eòghann agreed, stepping back from her a little.

They stared at each other a moment, both breathing heavily, and he gently brushed aside a strand of damp hair that had stuck to her lips.

"Saved by the—"

"Bellend," he interrupted, and Wes snorted with laughter. Oh how he loved to make her laugh.

"Do you want to go change?" she suggested.

"It's hot. I'll dry," he grunted, but the moment was lost once again, and Wes straightened her crumpled dress.

"Back to work then?" she asked.

"Aye," he agreed once more, stepping aside to let her pass and then resting his forehead against the tree, waiting out the erection, which hadn't yet begun to subside. He exhaled hard, pushing the air out between his lips. *Fecking kids.*

ONCE HE CAUGHT HIS BREATH, EÒGHANN WANDERED through the woods. The morning had gone well, and Wes seemed to appreciate his contributions. It felt good to be useful. Maybe it would somehow prove he was worth keeping around.

Stepping out of the woods, he realized he'd managed to find his way back to the secluded bit of beach, hidden from the Troubadour Stage by a grove of trees and shrubs.

Jarrod was there again, like the other day, sitting on his log, strumming the guitar. He was singing softly, like he didn't want anyone to hear. Eòghann could tell the song wasn't part of their usual repertoire, not Celtic or folksy, though his young cousin's voice still sounded earnest and sad as he sang poignant words about longing for home and letting go of the past.

When he finished, Eòghann stepped out onto the beach, doing his level best to focus on Jarrod and not the water.

"That wasn't traditional," he teased.

The boy yanked his head up in alarm but seemed to relax when he saw Eòghann was alone. "Orville Peck."

"South African, isn't he?"

"You know him?" Jarrod asked, surprised and a little pleased.

Eòghann nodded. "I didn't know you played guitar."

"Only a bit," the boy demurred. He played *well*, but Eòghann allowed it.

"Must get boring, singing the same old songs."

Jarrod shrugged one shoulder, his mannerisms so much like his father. After a moment Eòghann realized he was staring, while the kid gave him some pretty epic side-eye.

"Sorry. You must get sick of hearing how much you resemble your da."

Jarrod raised his eyebrows and shook his head. "Do I?"

"It's like stepping through a time machine, lad."

He smiled a little sideways half smile. "You grew up together?"

"Aye."

"How old was he...?" Jarrod began.

A cold shiver ran through Eòghann, settling in his gut.

"When his father died?" he finished for the boy.

Jarrod frowned. "No, umm, when his voice broke? Do you remember?"

Oh. "I'm afraid I don't."

"How old were you?"

"Thirteen. Maybe fourteen. Do you worry about that?"

"No, never," Jarrod answered, immediately sarcastic. "Who would care if it happened on stage? Everyone recording on their phones. I'd be immortal. A social media legend. A meme. It would probably outlive me. Like, share, remix." He shook his head. "I don't worry about it at all."

I can see that, Eòghann wanted to say, but he found himself nodding along instead. "When I was your little brother's age, I pissed myself in a public pool in front of the whole town," he confessed, leaving out the part where seconds before he had hit his head and seconds after he'd nearly drowned.

"Gross," Jarrod said, trying to suppress a small laugh.

"Indeed," Eòghann agreed, and then, miracle of miracles, he laughed, and he realized it may have been the first time in thirty years that thinking about it didn't make his palms go clammy and his chest too tight—until he *realized* it hadn't happened, and then he had to fight to take his next breath.

"Bet it wasn't caught on camera though," Jarrod said, and Eòghann chuckled through the tightness.

"No," he admitted. "It was long before social media. Have you talked to your da about it?"

Jarrod shook his head. "It's fine," he whispered, but they both knew it wasn't true, and once again, Eòghann wished there was some way he could help. "Did you piss yourself this morning?" Jarrod asked, nodding to Eòghann's damp jeans.

"Water balloon," Eòghann explained, and Jarrod nodded with understanding.

"Rory's been hiding in that magnolia tree all day. His aim is a bit too good sometimes," he commiserated, and they both laughed once more.

Chapter Twenty-Six

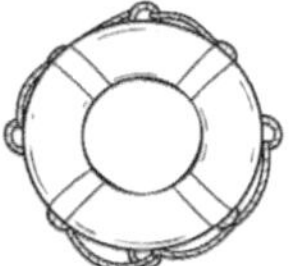

T-MINUS 5 DAYS TO RENAYZANTS FAIRE

When he cut the grass, the hardware store cowboy predicted rain, and it arrived right on cue. Dark clouds rolled in turning the bucolic Tennessee landscape faintly gothic, and so the Shakespeare Syndicate and the Scottish Invasion dragged their photo props and hay bales into the barn for safe keeping, along with basically anything else that wasn't nailed down, including Spencer, who relocated his tent into the barn despite Grandma Ruth's urging him to take one of her spare rooms for the duration.

Everyone else retreated to their own living quarters and hunkered down because once it started, it quickly escalated into a torrential squall.

Wes knew she shouldn't begrudge Grace and Bryan taking full advantage of the weather by holing up in their room and reminding themselves what they liked about each other. She was half tempted to do the same with Eòghann, since she'd decided to ignore her brain waving big red and white dive warning flags now that he wasn't a priest.

Instead, she spent all Monday morning back on the phone with portable toilet providers, trying desperately to find a last minute hookup. By her calculations, they needed twenty for an anticipated crowd of hundreds. Only twenty. There must be twenty toilets available somewhere in the quad-state area, right?

After all, it wasn't just a nice-to-have. "A *necessarium* is the most necessary item on the list," she mumbled with a hopeless chuckle. "Otherwise, we'll be in deep shit."

The rain outside mirrored her darkening mood as this last stumbling block refused to fall, like the sky was weeping on her behalf. *Don't worry*, she thought, making a pact with the sky. She wouldn't allow a shitty lack of shitters to be the thing that stopped her grandma's dreams from coming true.

When the wind picked up, Grandma Ruth turned on the local weather, which seemed to have gone into emergency 24/7 mode already, interrupting the Braves game in progress. Wes was extremely disappointed to see rain predicted all the way out until Friday.

"They don't know anything for sure this far in advance," her grandma scoffed from the kitchen table, where Lùc was teaching her to play some game about bees and bugs he claimed was a more fun version of chess.

Since the meteorologists were predicting the weather might actually clear up by Saturday, Grandma Ruth's skepticism of their accuracy wasn't helpful.

Meanwhile, Eòghann paced from room to room, and his inability to settle was about to make Wes climb out of her own skin. She hadn't noticed it last summer on Barra, but despite being a very capable man, the man seemed quite incapable of sitting still.

While she made her phone calls, he had unloaded Grandma Ruth's dishwasher, swept and mopped the kitchen floor, and asked where the *hoover* was—until Wes had not-so-subtly suggested he go read one of her grandmother's romance novels.

Now, like a caged tiger in a tiny zoo, he was looping a circuit every few minutes from the side door to the front door to the window above the kitchen sink.

"Don't worry about wearing a hole in the rug. I never liked it much anyway. I bet if you check out front again the rain will have let up," Grandma teased him, causing Lùc to snicker.

"You never did like the rain," the boy told his cousin.

"Didn't I?"

"Not so long as I can remember. Like the time we went on a picnic for Auntie Eilidh's birthday? You kept insisting it would rain, and the girls kept insisting it wouldn't."

"And who was right?"

"You, of course. And when it started, they all jumped up screaming, rushing to pack away the food, and you sat there like an angry, wet cat, too put out to bother saying you told them so."

"Some people don't like to get wet," Wes teased, her heart softening at the image of Eòghann turtling down into his shirt collar, much like he was doing now. For once she hadn't intended any innuendo, but his eyes shot to hers in a way that zinged right through her, and she shivered, instantly aroused. Fortunately, *she* didn't mind being wet.

Then a boom of thunder made him duck, severing their connection. Had lightning struck the house? Wes hurried to peek out the front door.

"No, no, no, no!" she yelled, taking off into the rain in her sock feet, with Grace trailing after her like she might need a referee.

The clamor hadn't been thunder or lightning but a driver for On-the-Go Toilets, unloading one single port-o-potty right in the middle of the driveway.

"Sign here," the driver said, handing Wes a clipboard, the name Jimmy printed at the top in neat block letters.

"Look, Jimmy," Wes said. "Is it okay if I call you Jimmy?"

The driver nodded.

"Perfect. Jimmy, like I said on the phone, I don't need toilets until Saturday—"

"*This* Saturday, right? Rental period's Monday to Sunday. "

"Fine. The thing is, we're hosting a large event and we need way more than one toilet."

"One was enough in Kentucky."

"The Kentucky order was wrong."

"Hence being in Kentucky," Grace added with a more light-hearted tone than Wes was managing at the moment.

"There's no cancellations," Jimmy said.

"Great, because I want more, not fewer. I can't hold my event with only one toilet."

"Why didn't you reserve more, then?"

Wes rubbed the bridge of her nose. "I told y'all we got scammed, right?"

"I didn't scam anyone—"

"Not you! I didn't mean you—"

"We know you would never!" Grace exclaimed.

"—the paperwork says *one* toilet. In Kentucky. Two weeks ago. You're lucky I could still fill the order at all. Seems more like you scammed me."

"Thank you, Jimmy. A thousand, million thank yous for this one toilet. Only, the people who hired you charged my grandma for fifteen regular toilets and five handicap ones," she explained, keeping her voice as soft and non-confrontational as she possibly could.

Jimmy shrugged. "I was only paid for one."

"No, I completely understand that," Wes said. "They

ripped us off, and that's on us. We will pay the difference, but we really need the toilets, and not here in the driveway."

"I hear you ma'am, I do. But we don't have any left."

"There aren't *any* at all?"

"Any chance you'll have some before Saturday?" Grace piped up.

Jimmy shook his head. "Rental period's Monday to—"

"Monday to Sunday," Wes supplied.

"They're all out on jobs," Jimmy explained.

"People can come in the house," Grandma Ruth called from the front porch where she was standing in between Eòghann and Bryan.

Wes glowered over her shoulder. "People are going to be over-indulging on greasy food and beer, they absolutely cannot come in the house, Grandma."

She closed her eyes and counted to three.

"Jimmy," she said, turning the sweet, Southern sunshine back on. "If you were throwing an event on Saturday, and you couldn't use your company, who would you call? Is there anyone else within a day's drive, maybe not quite as good, but who you'd recommend?"

Jimmy chewed his cheek for a minute. "I could maybe call up a few buddies, see if there's anything they could do for you."

"Really? That would be amazing, thank you, Jimmy."

"I can't promise anything, but I'll try."

"Thank you."

"All right ma'am. You have a blessed day."

"The only thing that could bless my day is more toilets," Wes told him.

He turned back towards his truck, leaving the potty right there in the driveway, but Wes was willing to choose her battles for now.

"I like your hat," Grace said, following him. "You're a soccer fan?"

Well, if Grace wanted to try to butter him up by talking sports, who was Wes to stop her? She turned back towards the house, squelching through the cold mud in her thoroughly sodden socks.

"I'd tell you to take your shoes off, but it looks like neither of you bothered to put any on," Grandma said, tossing the two girls towels for the floor and to dry themselves off.

"That sounded promising?" Eòghann said, when she reached the porch.

"Promising?" Wes replied, as Grace headed back upstairs. "Sure, as long as Jimmy can beg, borrow, or steal some toilets off a competitor in the next four days."

"Now we wait?"

She sighed. "Now we wait."

"What else is on your list?" he asked, coming over to rub her shoulders, and slowly her tension began to drain away.

"Everything else is done. I feel like I should probably do some work-work," she moped.

"Boo," Lùcas groaned.

"Boo," Wes agreed.

"Not while you're using vacation time."

"I know, Grandma, but they've been calling me."

"Wesley Bernice Teal," Grandma Ruth chided.

Bernice? Lùc mouthed at Eòghann, but he straightened up and looked penitent when he caught Wesley's glower.

"Do you remember when I broke my hip two years ago?" Grandma asked.

Wesley's shoulders tensed again. "Of course," she said. Terrifying didn't begin to describe receiving that phone call in the middle of the night. She'd requested an ambulance immediately, despite Grandma Ruth's protests that it was a whole lot of something over nothing, and then Wes had driven to meet her at the hospital, street lights playing tricks on her eyes the whole way. It was the last time she'd driven any distance at night.

"I'm *still* getting doctor bills and insurance statements."

"All the more reason for me not to fall too far behind—"

"My point is, that business has never moved quickly. Now I agree it should be faster and more efficient, but you working overtime on vacation isn't going to fix it."

Wes sagged back against Eòghann. "What if somebody else's grandma's claim is sitting in my inbox right now? They might disagree."

"Not if they knew you were on vacation, dear. Now please get your Sexy Scot out of my kitchen before he opens a sinkhole right through the floor."

Wes glanced back at Eòghann. A flush crept into his cheeks, which combined with his damp, mussy hair, made him look sexy and bed tousled, and up to no good as he spluttered an apology.

A screeching alert sounded from the TV and Wesley's phone at the exact same time, and upstairs too, followed by scuffling and a muffled, "Fucking hell," from Grace.

"Tornado?" Wes asked, struggling to read the warning that scrolled too quickly across the screen.

"Flash flood warning," Lùcas read.

"Watch or warning?" Grandma Ruth asked.

"Warning. What's the difference?" he replied.

Grandma switched to another channel, where a slicker-clad reporter was standing out in the rain at Volunteer Landing on the Riverfront. "River's at action stage," she told Wes.

"What does that mean?" Eòghann croaked, his hands trembling on her shoulders.

"It means it isn't flooding yet," Wes told him, covering one of his hands with hers. "We'll be fine."

"Is that a river or a lake at the back of the property?"

"A lake," Grandma Ruth said.

At the same time Wes answered, "I mean technically—"

"Technically what?" Eòghann asked.

His voice sounded strained, and for someone who'd lived his whole life on a stormy island, he sure was stressed. What had he told her once? *I don't really care for the water?* Indifferent, he'd said, and Wes was starting to realize it might've been a major understatement.

"Technically...?"

"It's considered a lake, but it's part of the Tennessee River."

"The one that's at action stage?" he asked, failing to keep the mounting panic out of his voice.

Wes halfway shrugged, but she nodded her head at the same time.

"What action do we need to take? Should we evacuate?"

Wes placed both hands on his shoulders, turning him away from the TV to face her. "Breathe," she demanded.

"Am breathing," he gasped.

"Are you?" She smiled.

He nodded, his own brow furrowing.

"We're uphill at a good elevation. I promise we're safe."

"Famous last words."

"Whose last words were those?"

"Some of the animals Noah left behind, probably. Unicorns."

"Come on." She scooped up her iPad and took his hand, leading him towards the stairs. "We'll look up some flood maps or something."

"Can I come?" Lùc asked with mock enthusiasm for flood maps.

"No," Wes, Eòghann, and Grandma Ruth all told him in unison.

Chapter Twenty-Seven

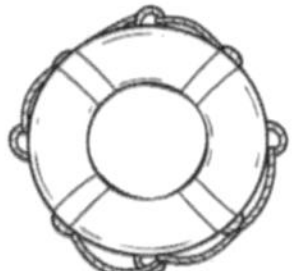

Wes took her time switching on lamps, painting her bedroom in warm, cheerful light and giving Eòghann a minute to settle down and catch his breath. She noticed a discoloration on the wall and leaned in close to examine it.

"Render. Or spackle, you call it," he explained. "To patch the crack. It needs another day to dry before I can sand and paint it.

"You didn't have to do that," she said, feeling her irritation spike. "Or the window, or the leaky faucet or the bathroom door. Or the garage. You've done way too much for someone who's supposed to be on vacation. This is probably why you're so stressed. You're going to need a vacation from your vacation," she quipped, realizing she didn't know what he actually did for a living, since he wasn't a priest.

"We had a deal. I could do whatever I wanted to help out Grandma Ruth."

She raised her eyebrows at him skeptically.

"What? Unless we live here permanently, it wasn't for you, it was for Grandma."

She laughed, unwilling to let her thoughts linger on his use of *we* instead of *you*. "Isn't that the dream? Part of me would love to live here, like those summers when I was a kid, only permanent."

"Why don't you then?"

She scoffed, her voice tinged with a bitter taste. "Because." *I can't mooch off my grandma the rest of my life, and I can't drive from here to my job in the city every day.* "Because this isn't real life, Padre. You and I can shack up and play house, and it's delightful, but it isn't real. Eventually I have to go back to my terrible job and you have to go back to your island paradise. Right?"

"Not unless they invent a teleporter," he muttered.

He seemed... annoyed? Which made no sense. He was on vacation. *She* was on vacation. It was a fun interlude, and it would be great if it could last forever, but it couldn't. Wanting a thing didn't make it possible. Wes wanted to travel the whole world, to be able to eat cinnamon rolls every day and never gain a pound. She wanted 20/20 vision. But wishing didn't make it real, and he was a fully adult man who knew that, so why was he being weird?

"I know it sucks. I'm going to miss you too," she told him. Frankly, the prospect of him leaving was a little devastating.

His face looked so utterly stricken, Wes couldn't stand it. Did he think she was kicking him out tomorrow?

Why did it seem like they were only ever on the same page when they were flirting or hooking up?

"Come on," she said, grabbing him by the waistband of those ridiculously tiny shorts and reaching for his t-shirt. "Let's get you out of these wet clothes," she teased, desperate to get back on the same page again.

"They aren't wet," he halfway protested. "I didn't leave the porch."

"Then maybe that's exactly what you need? Go frolic in the rain to help you remember water is the source of all life? Uisge beatha."

He shook his head. "That's whisky."

"Island Eòghann would be up for it," she teased, scrutinizing him.

"Would he?"

She shrugged. "Seemed like he was up for *most* things at the time," and yes she did put emphasis on most because she was still smarting to learn that his running away had nothing to do with vows, thank you very much.

A flicker of something crossed his face. Shame? Regret?

"Clearly you don't know Island Eòghann very well," he snapped.

"Clearly not, *Padre*," she said, taking a step back and crossing her arms because whose fault was that?

On the other hand, he wasn't the idiot who'd mistaken her for clergy.

"Sorry. I'm sorry," he apologized, staring at the floor.

But he was right. She thought she'd gotten to know him pretty well the past year, but did she actually know him at all? She hadn't known he had a cousin in the States or that he was afraid of flying. She didn't know what he actually did for a living or much about his childhood beyond a messed up relationship with his dad. But his hopes and dreams, his quiet wishes and silent pain—she knew nothing at all.

To be fair, how much of herself had she shared with him? It was only lately she'd spilled her guts over a text message he never even got the opportunity to read.

"Sorry," he whispered again, shaking his head.

Wes took his hand. "No, you're right," she conceded. "I *do* feel like I know you, Eòghann. But there's a lot *about* you that's a mystery."

He nodded.

"Tell me one true thing."

He swallowed and stepped back to sit on the foot of the bed, like he couldn't hold himself upright on his own for a minute longer.

"I'm afraid of drowning," he admitted in a voice so small it nearly broke her and explained, well, maybe everything. "More than afraid. It's a bonafide phobia to be honest."

Somehow the admission felt much bigger than the moment could allow, as the kaleidoscope shifted once more, beginning to form a clear picture.

Wes struggled to react the right way. "I won't let that happen," she promised, taking a seat beside. "I'm 99.9% certain we won't need to evacuate, but if we need to we will. Come here." She gave his hand a squeeze and a tug, and he fell into her arms, resting his cheek on her shoulder.

They held each other like that for a long moment, and then she asked, "Would sex make it better?" and he coughed out a laugh.

It wasn't a no, but before he could say yes, there was a knock at the door and they both huffed out a sigh in tandem.

She threw open the door, startling Jack on the other side.

"Sorry to bother you," he said. Then giving Eòghann the once-over he added, "*Really*, sorry, buddy."

"What's up?" Wes asked, impatient to get back to their discussion.

"Is it the river?" Eòghann rasped.

"No. I was looking for tarps. Grandma Ruth said you'd know if she had any. The barn roof has pretty well caved in."

Wesley's stomach lurched. "Is Spencer okay?"

"He's fine, it's all just very wet."

"There's several tarpaulins in the garage," Eòghann said, drawing a ragged breath. "I'll show you where."

Jack nodded, his hair dripping rain on the rug. They both followed Eòghann down the dark staircase, but when they reached the garage, the light wouldn't turn on.

"That's weird," Wes said, flipping the switch a few times. "Bulb must've blown."

Then she noticed the deathly quiet—not so much as the hum of air conditioning or the outside freezer.

"Grandma?" she called.

"Yep, power's out," Grandma Ruth confirmed, appearing at her elbow with a lit jar candle and a flashlight.

Despite the dim light, Wes was amazed how quickly Eòghann located the tarps, as well as rope and other tie-downs, in what used to be a cluttered labyrinth. To her equal surprise, he didn't hesitate before plunging out into the waterlogged yard behind Jack.

Grabbing a rain jacket off the peg by the door and stepping into a pair of rain boots, Wes hurried to follow them, with Lùcas close on her heels.

THE BARN WAS A DISASTER. SPLINTERED BOARDS STUCK UP from the hole in the roof like a cowlick, while inside, more splintered planks were scattered like confetti. One of the photo stand-ins laid face-down in a pool of muddy water. Another had been snapped in two by a roof beam. They were five days out, and it was beginning to feel entirely hopeless.

"I want you to know, I had nothing to do with it," Spencer said.

"Sure you aren't bad luck, Spence?" Lùc teased.

Together, Jack, Andy, Alec, Lùc, and Eòghann scrambled onto the edges of the old roof and secured the tarps.

"I would help but..." Spencer began.

"You might be bad luck after all?" Wes asked.

"No. I'm afraid of heights."

"I guess I'll call someone to fix it when the rain stops," she grumbled, mentally calculating the cost of hiring a contractor to reroof an old disused barn.

"Bryan and I can fix it, no problem," Lùc assured her.

Wes sighed. "I can't ask you to do that."

"You didn't. I'll volun-tell him to," he said, imitating Gray's accent with a shrug and hurrying back to the house as a fresh peal of thunder tumbled across the sky.

By evening, the rain had slacked up a little, but the power was still out, and Wes found her grandmother standing in the kitchen staring through the mist at her saturated fairgrounds.

"Penny for your thoughts?" Wes asked.

"That's about all they're worth," Grandma Ruth laughed. "I was remembering a joke your grandpa used to make when it would rain like this, about building an ark. And about the four dozen eggs in my refrigerator getting ready to go bad."

"Four dozen?"

"You kids don't eat like you used to."

Wes laughed. "That's too many eggs, Grandma."

"So I noticed."

"Do you own a propane grill?"

"I do. Why? You going to grill eggs?"

Wes grinned. "There's approximately a million loaves of sourdough in here. We make snow day French toast. Why not power outage French toast?"

. . .

LUCKILY, THERE WAS STILL PROPANE IN THE TANK, AND Eòghann got the grill heating while Wesley whisked the eggs. She considered trying to multiply a standard recipe by four dozen eggs, but in the end, she decided to eyeball the spices. She was about to dump in the ground cinnamon, when Eòghann caught her wrist, stopping her. For one heated moment, she flashed back to his clever wrist bindings on the bed, and heat surged through her core.

"Later," she assured him.

His head jerked adorably sideways, and he let go of her arm. But then he said, "Er, no, it's..."

"What?"

He pointed to the bottle of cinnamon in her hand. "I'm no French toast connoisseur, but are you sure you want to use much of that?"

"There can never be too much cinnamon," she protested. "That's a hill I'm willing to die on, so if you disagree, you and me are going to have problems, Padre."

She didn't know why she said it, except his use of the word *we* before had left her looking for a way out of something she wasn't actually sure she was in, and she felt restless and discombobulated.

He frowned. "That's not cinnamon, though. It's chili powder."

She looked at him dumbly for a second and then squinted at the bottle in her hand. Sure enough, she'd grabbed the wrong spice. She tossed the bottle aside and peered at the nutmeg she'd been planning to add next. Cumin. "God what an idiot," she said, as heat licked up her neck. The colors were similar, but were they *that* similar? Or was color blindness creeping in?

"It was dark in there," Eòghann said, giving her an out, but she didn't want his excuses.

She nodded in agreement. "Thank goodness you were here

to save the day," she said, her words holding a bitter edge she hadn't meant to let him hear.

"I only meant, anyone could've made the same mistake."

"*Anyone* didn't. You didn't."

Discomfort spread rapidly across his face, and Wes didn't want it—not his secondhand embarrassment or his absolution, not his sympathy, not his pity, not any of it.

"I'll be right back," she said stalking inside to find her glasses, for what little help they might offer, and to swap out the spices. So much for *Peacemaker* French toast.

He was still standing helplessly beside the grill when she returned, but they didn't speak again. They cooked in silence until they ran out of bread. Then he fixed a plate and took it to Grandma Ruth because of course he did.

"We found some local honey," Bryan said brightly, handing Wes a jar with a label that read BEE-HAVE. "They agreed to set up a tent at the faire," he told her as she piled a stack of toast on her own plate.

"Thank you," she said, drizzling the sweet, fresh honey over her dinner.

Bryan didn't leave. "You okay?" he asked, wrinkling his nose.

Wes found her head weaving in a noncommittal yes/no sort of way and forced it to nod.

Bryan bumped her shoulder. "Lùc and I will fix the roof tomorrow. We can remake the damaged ssstand-in. Repaint the chess board. It'll be fine."

"Point is, you shouldn't have to," she grumbled.

"Roofs are our forte, don't you remember?"

She laughed at the memory of them hammering away installing solar panels at his cottage last summer, and Grace joining them to try and make the noise stop quicker.

"Honestly, we're happy to help," he said.

"I'll try to stay away from the ladder." She'd meant to say it as a joke, but her voice sounded bitter. She was still embarrassed about running into his ladder and breaking her glasses the year before, no matter how much she'd hated wearing them.

Bryan smiled politely, but his eyes flicked across the yard towards Eòghann, and he asked, "That's all that's upset you? The roof?"

"I can't believe you guys never told me he's not a priest," she blurted, and he scrunched up his face in surprise. "I have vision loss. I made a mistake. I could've handled it," she said. "I don't need protecting, especially not from myself."

"I thought you knew. Rios!" he called, and Grace turned to them, her face alight with pleasure. "You never told her Eòghann's not a priest?"

Gray's eyes widened and her mouth formed a little surprised o. "*He* told you. Right? Before you left Barra? I thought..." She searched back into the recesses of her memory. "He didn't tell you?"

"Wait, so your man isn't a priest after all?" Andy piped up.

"As it turns out," Wes grumbled.

Andy's face lit up in congratulations, until he realized she was still very grumpy.

"I apologize, Wes, truly," Bryan told her, tilting his head, his face a picture of concern. "Does it make a difference that he isn't one?"

And that was the million dollar question, wasn't it? Should it? Probably not in the way he meant. But it'd been a convenient excuse to avoid anything too serious. It had allowed her to pretend she was risking her heart alone, because any love on her part could never be requited.

Now she lacked the excuse, and it would appear she hadn't been very deft at avoiding the *anything too serious*, either.

"Thanks for the honey, Mr. Bee," she said, lifting her plate in mock salute and heading towards the quiet stillness of her bedroom.

"Bee-have," the Stoic Scot teased, pointing at her as she left.

"And if you don't, take pictures!" Spencer called after her.

Fumbling in the dark room, Wesley lit some candles and then sat cross-legged on her bed, balancing the plate on her lap.

Eòghann didn't deserve her irritation. He'd seen her about to make a mistake, and he stepped in to prevent it. What did she want, for him to sit back and let her ruin everyone's dinner? That would be entirely ridiculous. She wasn't annoyed with him for helping her this one time, but she also didn't like him trying to manage her feelings—manage her—by walking on egg shells instead of saying, "Hey, bitch, you grabbed the wrong spices."

It was uncomfortable to think he'd noticed and then lay in wait for his chance to swoop in and save the day.

As if on cue, he peeked into the room, and damn, even when she was annoyed and the light was dim he was handsome and smelled delicious. It was honestly rude of him, when all she wanted was to stew in her own feelings.

She tossed a begrudging smile his way and almost immediately his watch started beeping, until he ripped it off and set it on the dresser.

"Do you have a heart condition or something?" she demanded. After all, if she wanted him to be direct about her situation, she should extend the same courtesy.

Eòghann stepped into the bedroom and closed the door, leaning back against it.

"Oh God," she said, her stomach dropping. "Is it very serious? Should you be eating eggs?"

"I'm not *that* old," he protested.

"As we've established, I like old things."

"I don't have a heart condition."

"Then wh—"

"I have a *you* condition," he interrupted.

"What?"

Eòghann squinted up at the ceiling, then rolled his head down to face the floor, looking everywhere but at her. "I got this watch because my family kept complaining I never see their texts when I'm working. Exploring the features, I came across the heart monitor, and I thought of you."

"Me?"

"The first time we met, you told me you were going to lose your sight, and you said the worst part was you wouldn't be able to rely on visual cues to know if a person was into you."

Tears stung the back of Wesley's eyes. She didn't recall her exact words, but it sounded like something she'd say. And he had listened. And remembered.

"Bryan's planning to propose to Grace someday. When he told me, I hoped we might bump into each other again, you and I, and I wanted to make sure you knew what you do to me. But the damn thing's worse than grey jogging bottoms, or those ridiculous red shorts for that matter, and I can't figure out how to turn it off without my phone, which is currently lost at sea."

Wes laughed. "You're not online. How do you know about grey sweatpants?"

"Lùc's constantly sending memes."

As confessions went, it was pretty charming and two sides of Wesley's heart were preparing to do battle against each other. Here was a man who not only asked what she needed, but listened. But he was also already trying to take care of her in ways that no one ever had, and the irony of it all was she didn't want him to.

Because she liked it way too much.

She could get used to someone handy, someone who anticipated her needs before she did, who smoothed the way and watched over her like a second pair of eyes while still letting her do things for herself.

She could get used to it.

And then it could all be ripped away.

It was too easy to become a burden on his kindness. To rely on those constant little sacrifices, the chipping away of himself for her, until he had nothing left to give, until he resented her for being a burden. Until he only stayed out of obligation.

She wanted to tell him he could take his heart monitor and it could join his phone at the bottom of the sea—why was his phone in the sea? She wanted to rebuff his gentle accommodation, but he looked hesitant and vulnerable, and frankly wrung out, and she wasn't one to kick a puppy, even if it peed on the rug.

"That's sweet," she said instead. "You should buy a new phone when you get back from vacation."

He nodded, understanding the implication. This was a holiday fling, and when it was over she expected him to leave and to turn off the ridiculous heart monitor. He picked up his romance novel and glasses from the bedside table and turned to go.

He was leaving like she wanted him to, but with hurt feelings, and panic began to tighten Wesley's chest. She'd never wanted to hurt him. He was supposed to be a priest.

He paused at the door, his back to her. "Why did you really break up with your ex?"

"What?"

"I started reading these novels because you said he was bad in bed, and I wanted to make sure if the opportunity ever presented itself, I wouldn't be. It'd been awhile, you see."

"How long's awhile?" she asked, to keep him talking. To keep him from leaving for a little bit longer.

"Years. When you grow up trapped on an island where all the girls your age are either related to you or have witnessed every humiliating moment of your life, options are a touch limited."

"You could have left," she said, not quite sure why she felt like crying. Not quite sure it was true.

"I couldn't," he argued.

"You did though. You're here."

He smiled sadly over his shoulder. "I didn't have a reason before now. At least not one stronger than my fear."

"Eòghann," she said, stepping closer to him, needing to be near enough to smell his warm skin and intoxicating cologne. She took his hand, not wanting to part on this awkwardness, trying to draw him back to the bed where they could let their hands and sighs and tongues explain where they stood.

"I thought you wanted me to go back," he said.

"Not, like, tonight or anything."

"That's reassuring," he said a little bitterly.

"Why would you stay? What would you do here?" she asked, remembering Sadie's words when Wes suggested her friends settle down.

"Find a job. Live a life."

Her heart stuttered. He actually thought he wanted to stay, to build a life with her.

"My beautiful boy," she said, taking his face and kissing his cheek softly. "I'm so sorry we want different things."

"Do we?"

"You sound like you want forever."

"How could you want anything less?"

"Because wanting less tricks you into not being disappointed when you get it. Forever is a myth."

"It doesn't have to be," he said, holding her gaze until she had to look away. Then he opened the door and disappeared out into the night.

Hours later, as she lay awake, replaying the conversation in her head, she realized he hadn't said, "You want me to go home." He'd said *back*, as though Barra was already no longer his home.

And she definitely didn't feel ready to unpack what that might mean.

You sound like you want forever, she had accused him, expecting him to make a joke or a denial or a deflection as she'd have done.

Instead, he seemed to admit something he hadn't previously admitted to himself, and she wasn't ready to unpack that yet either.

Chapter Twenty-Eight

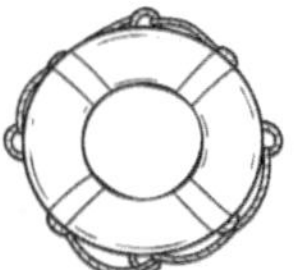

That night Eòghann stayed in his own room, but he didn't exactly sleep. He lay there all night analyzing their argument over and over again, trying to figure out the exact moment it had gone sideways.

Had he really insinuated he wanted to stay here, forever, with her instead of going back to Barra?

It was true, but he hadn't meant to let her know that.

At least he hadn't said the rest—that he'd fallen in love with Wes last summer, and, impossibly, over the past year of heartfelt truths cloaked in flirty banter. The past two weeks had only sealed his fate. It hadn't been a blinding flash or accompanied by fanfare, but it had been building in every quiet moment, in the care she took with her friends and family, in her infectious joy and laughter, and her magnolia and honeysuckle scent.

He hadn't confessed he was in love with her, but she'd guessed as much.

You sound like you want forever.

The unspoken part being she *didn't* want forever. She didn't even want to try, because she believed forever was a myth.

Maybe it was. Maybe he'd been reading too many romance novels.

Or maybe it was only an impossibility for him. Because of what he'd stolen from Alec.

What would you do here?

The more he tried to help, the more she pushed him away. Strip him of his tools and his ability to be useful, and what was left? He brought nothing to the table unless he built the table. Helping was who and what he was. He hadn't been joking about earning his keep except what he meant was earning his place in the world.

Clearly he'd overstayed his welcome. It was time to figure out what came next.

The moment dawn crept over the horizon, Eòghann left his room determined to be out of the way before Wes stirred from her bedroom—no awkward encounters in the hall, no longing looks over coffee.

In the kitchen he found Rebecca aggressively kneading a ball of dough.

"You're up early," he said, trying not to startle her.

She jumped anyway and whirled around. "Sorry. We ate so much bread last night, I thought it couldn't hurt to make more. The power came back on around four. Did I wake you?"

He shook his head, reaching for the easy lie. "Jet lag."

"Right." She nodded, studying him, and he felt too exposed, like he'd put his t-shirt on inside out, revealing the imprint left behind by his broken heart.

"Are you okay?" she asked.

"Are you?"

She shook her head, on the verge of tears.

"No, me neither," he admitted, taking a seat at the table.

She tore her dough ball in half and offered one to him and he accepted it, squeezing the life out of it before imitating her kneading motions.

"Wesley's fear of commitment?" she asked gently.

"Is that what it is? Thought it was maybe an aversion to me."

She chewed her lip, still studying him like she didn't want to be disloyal. They'd both already said too much, but eventually she shook her head. "It isn't you."

His throat felt too tight. "Seems like that should make me feel better. But if it were me, maybe I could find a way to fix it."

Rebecca smiled sympathetically, but her eyes were sad.

"She says we don't want the same things."

"You don't believe her?" she asked, tilting her head to study him again.

"Dunno. Maybe in this case I'm the thing she doesn't want."

Snorting, Rebecca turned back to her dough and punched it. "I'd say I'm in the same boat, but I'm not sure that would make you feel better either."

"Any advice?"

She sighed. "Ask her exactly what it is she doesn't want. And then believe her when she tells you."

That sounded terrifying.

"I was married for ten years. I spent ten years trying to have a baby. We came close a couple of times. But when we didn't, he didn't exactly try to hide his relief."

Eòghann winced.

"Mmpf," she agreed. "I told myself he was scared. He didn't *think* he wanted kids, but he'd change his mind when he had one. Turns out I was right. I bumped into him at the grocery store the other day. He recently became a dad—without actually trying, because the universe has a sense of humor. And he looks... genuinely happy."

"Fuck him," Eòghann growled, and she chuckled. "No, I'm

serious, fuck him. He'll mess that kid up. Maybe not on purpose, but he will. Same as he messed you up. One poorly-timed, perfectly cruel comment, and the kid will need therapy for years."

Rebecca laughed. "And in the meantime, I'm drowning in too much bread."

"No such thing."

"I don't even like sourdough."

Now it was his turn to laugh. "I bet that's because you've never made fairy toast."

"What kind of toast?"

"Och, you're in for a treat," he said, placing two pieces of bread in the toaster.

"I wasted my best years on Marshall Majors," she said, staring at the toaster. "Missed out on the chance to go to Barra with Grace and find a Scotsman of my own."

"I wasted my best years too afraid to leave the place," he replied.

The toast popped up and at his prompting, Rebecca began to spread butter on them, while Eòghann rustled up a jar of candy sprinkles from Grandma Ruth's pantry. He coated the buttered side of each toast in sprinkles and handed one back to Rebecca. "Fairy toast."

She regarded it skeptically and then clinked her slice against his like they were making a different kind of toast. Then she closed her eyes and took a bite.

"Oh my gosh," she said. "You were right. Fairy toast was exactly what I needed."

Eòghann added more bread to the toaster.

Staring bleakly out at the dreich morning, he saw Rory splash across the garden. So Danny and the Boys must be awake. After piling a plate high with more fairy toast, he filled a travel mug with coffee and bid Rebecca good luck with her dough before trudging slowly across the stomach-churning soggy ground to *Kisimul* caravan.

Alec looked genuinely delighted to see him, and the two older boys seemed equally delighted by the fairy toast, which they grabbed on their way out the door into the fresh air, football in hand.

"They're good lads," Eòghann said, watching them splash off towards the woods.

"They are," Alec replied, but his voice sounded melancholy.

"You should be proud."

"I'm not sure what credit I can take. I was hardly ever around before their mother died. Always at the hospital. Always working."

Eòghann was trapped between the wanting to ask and the not wanting to pry. "Can't have been easy," he finally said. "Any of it."

"No. After Miranda... this seemed less hard somehow."

His cousin couldn't meet his eyes, but at the moment, he looked so much like the sad, scared boy whose mother had abandoned him for the mainland and whose father had been taken by the sea.

Back then, the family had worried his ma would turn up to take him back with her, but she never did. Studying Alec's slumped shoulders and furrowed brow, Eòghann wondered if it might not have been better if she had. His Auntie Mal had taken Alec in of course, but it wasn't the same thing. Maybe if his mother had come to get him, he'd have seen Scotland as a safe haven for his grieving children instead of roving the continental U.S. because it was less hard than moving on.

"Because this isn't real life?" Eòghann asked.

"It wasn't supposed to be." Alec's voice was barely a whisper.

I'm so sorry, mate, Eòghann wanted to say, but it was too insufficient and he left the words unsaid.

"I never asked how long you're staying?" Alec changed the subject as though he didn't want to hear the empty platitudes anyway.

Eòghann shook his head. "I think she's ready to have me gone, whether or not I want to stay."

"How long have you been...?"

"It's stupidly complicated."

Alec grinned. "It usually is. Bryan seems happy," he added after a moment.

"Aye. They're making it work despite the distance."

"Is the distance the problem for you and your girl?"

"If anything, the distance would probably help," Eòghann said, shaking his head.

"I don't suppose you'd ever want to join the band?"

"Your band? You've been away a long time, Allie. Don't you remember I have two left vocal cords?"

"I can teach anyone to play guitar." His smile faded. "Almost anyone. Sully was hopelessly tone deaf," he said softly. "Though Roddy managed to make it sound like harmony. Sometimes I think he got Sully's share of the talent."

Eòghann's stomach twisted. "I'm so sorry about what happened."

Alec didn't respond. He cleared his throat and then said, "Dan's going to leave the minute he turns eighteen. I'm honestly surprised he hasn't emancipated himself already, except he's too busy planning his escape to university. I'm fairly certain he blames me for his mother's accident."

"I'm sure he doesn't."

"Are you? Rory absolutely blames me for his brother's. S'pose Roddy's on my side, but it's probably because he's a Libra. He hates conflict. Miranda used to say he'd be a diplomat someday. Och, if you join us, I promise not to be such a stresso depresso on the regular."

"I'll think about it," Eòghann agreed, genuinely touched by the offer.

"Do. The boys would love having you around."

Eòghann snorted.

"As much as they love anything these days," Alec conceded. He reached out, squeezing Eòghann's forearm, and the familiar gesture made a lump form in his throat. "Be almost like old times. The MacNeil Musketeers, aye? Reckon we could convince Bryan to tag along sometimes like when he was wee?"

Eòghann shrugged. "He has a business to run now. He was hoping you'd come home."

"His own distillery." Alec shook his head in awe. "He turned out all right, our baby Bry."

"He did."

"Maybe there's hope for us all."

WALKING BACK TO THE HOUSE, Eòghann's SPIRITS WERE somewhat buoyed by his visit with Alec. Wes might have no use for him, but he could help Alec look after the boys and forge a relationship with them, maybe smooth over some of the rough edges. It was a comforting notion.

"Intruder!" Duncan the raven screamed, so Eòghann headed around to the front of the house, instead of going in the side door.

There he found a sheriff's car parked in the driveway, its khaki-clad occupant making his way up to the front door. The raven called, "Intruder!" a second time, causing the sheriff to glance frantically over his shoulder.

When he spotted Eòghann, he stood up straight, hands moving to rest on his gun belt.

"Everything all right?" Eòghann asked. "Is Ruth okay?"

"You tell me. I know for a fact you're too young to be Ms. Teal's boy."

"Aye. Also he's dead."

"Intruder!" the bird called again, and the sheriff looked like he was thinking about shooting it.

"Got ID on you, son?"

Son? Eòghann wanted to laugh except he was a tiny bit scared. "No. My passport's inside."

"Perfect. I was just about to knock."

But he didn't have to knock, because Grandma Ruth met them at the door and invited the sheriff in.

"What're you doing here, Jerry?" she asked, showing him into the kitchen where Wes was leaning against the counter nibbling toast.

Grandma Ruth put on a fresh pot of coffee, while Wesley offered Eòghann a hesitant smile that nearly wrecked him.

The sheriff settled into a kitchen chair and took off his hat, placing it on the table before helping himself to a slice of toast slathered in jam. "Checking to see you're okay after all the rain."

"Could've used your help when the power went out and I had to cook up four dozen eggs."

The sheriff grunted. "No one's seen you in town for a few weeks. Neighbors said there's been a lot of squatters coming and going—"

"Squatters my ass."

"Old Simeon said he saw Everett's truck at the dump being driven by teenagers."

That *did* make Eòghann laugh.

"My granddaughter and her friends have been staying here,

helping me out. And this lovely young man hauled away some junk."

"Helpful squatters," Sheriff Jerry said, eyeing Eòghann once more.

"You're the only squatter I see, Jerry. I have guests. And the neighbors can mind their own damn business. We're getting ready to open a Renaissance faire, which you'd know if you watched the evening news."

"That so?" the sheriff said, with all the condescension of a man whose child had informed him they were going to open a lemonade stand. "That's what those little fliers in town were all about?"

"Damn right. We open on Saturday."

"Got all your permits and everything in order?"

Wes darted a worried look towards her grandmother.

"You bet. I'll leave a ticket with your name on it at the gate, if you want to come back on Saturday."

"I might do that," he said, finishing off his coffee and hefting himself from the kitchen chair. "You be sure to call us if you need anything now, Ruthie."

"You know I will not, Jerry."

"Ruthie?" Wes asked after the door closed behind him, but her grandmother waved the question away.

"Men like him are a dime a dozen and every last one of them chaps my ass," Grandma Ruth replied, and Wes burst out laughing, but then she slumped against the counter once more, rubbing in between her eyes.

"What's wrong?" Eòghann asked cautiously, then he watched as she rolled her neck and pulled on a smile.

"Nothing."

"The dragon's caught in a hurricane," Grandma said.

Wesley shot her a quelling look. "Lance and Lottie—the ride —their truck broke down, and now they're having to evacuate in the wrong direction because of the hurricane heading for North Carolina. But it's going to be fine, because I'll figure out a backup plan."

"There doesn't have to be a ride, surely."

"People are already asking about ticket refunds if the rain doesn't stop for good. We need to have a ride. We advertised one." Her eyes widened in panic. "And I guess we better figure out those permits the sheriff mentioned."

"How can I help?" Eòghann asked, reaching for her hand.

She let him grasp it for a moment, but she shook her head.

"Maybe I could build some kind of ride. The lads need more lumber to fix up the barn roof anyway."

"No, Eòghann, honestly, you've done more than enough. You're probably right. We don't need a ride."

Being *right* never felt more hollow. "Got it," he said.

Sensing his disappointment she added, "Thank you for the offer. I love... how much you want to help."

He didn't really know how to respond to that. "I love helping," he said with a shrug, but his voice caught in his throat.

Pull yourself together, lad, before I give you something to cry about, his father's words rang in his ears.

"Let me know if you change your mind," he said, and he walked back out the front door the same way he'd come in.

Chapter Twenty-Nine

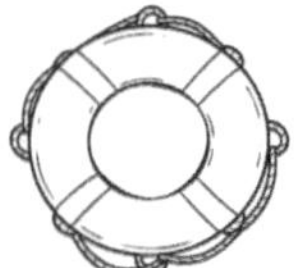

T-MINUS 3 DAYS TO RENAYZANTS FAIRE

Just when everything seemed to be falling into place, it was like a wheel had come off and now it was going spectacularly to pieces. The rain had stopped for the time being, but they were three days out from the faire, and the grounds were as waterlogged as—well, according to Grace, as Bunyan's Swamp of Despair.

The list of problems to solve was growing by the minute: repair the barn roof and photo stand-in, obtain proper permits, sort out the one-potty problem. And on top of everything else, Wes may have well and truly blown things up with Eòghann for good.

He'd been avoiding her ever since their argument the night of the power outage. One minute she'd been angry and embarrassed, the next she'd wanted to jump his bones. Then he'd made some off-hand comment about sticking around, and she'd realized he'd gone and caught feelings, was maybe as down bad as she was, and she'd nipped the whole thing in the bud right there.

You want forever, she'd said, daring him—practically begging him—to contradict her.

But he didn't contradict her.

And now here they were. Hardly looking at each other when they crossed paths, let alone speaking to each other or sleeping together.

"This is why we can't have nice things," Wesley grumbled to herself, *this* simply being *her*.

She should track him down and apologize for being a jerk, except she wasn't being a jerk. She was having honest feelings in response to his honest feelings. For maybe the very first time, all of their cards were on the table, and they were doomed.

The minute she stepped outside she heard Duncan the Raven's shrill, "Intruder!" and she laughed. Leave it to the silly bird to find the boy for her.

"Intruder?" she asked Duncan. "Where?"

"Intruder!" he cried from his rooftop perch. Was *she* the intruder, stomping around her grandma's house ordering everyone to stop helping with her faire?

The bird took off flying, circling around a car heading up the drive. The sheriff was back, and this time, he'd brought a friend in a nice-fitting suit. What was he doing, bringing a lawyer with a cease and desist?

Grandma Ruth followed Wes outside and met Jerry at his car door.

"All of this," the suit said with a sweeping gesture, "needs to be shut down."

There was something familiar about his voice and his tone when he said to shut it down. He turned to look at the house and glare at Duncan swooping overhead, and someone might as well have dumped a bucket of ice water over Wesley's head.

"Pierce?" she called out before she thought better of it.

He whipped comically around to face her like a cartoon

double-take. His sandy brown hair was artfully mussed, and in his skinny tie and loafers, he somehow looked ten years more mature than the day they'd broken up.

"Wessy? What are you doing here?" he asked, and yeah, nope, no, definitely not. He might look good, but the nickname still made her gag.

"Intruder!" Duncan screamed again.

"This is my grandma's house. Which you would know if you'd literally ever come with me to visit her."

"I came," he said defensively. "That one Christmas."

And she supposed he had her there. One Christmas he did tag along, but his nose had been buried in his phone the entire trip.

"Welcome back then, I guess? What the hell do you want?" she demanded, crossing her arms protectively over her chest.

"I..." he shifted uncomfortably. "Permits," he said, and her heart sank.

"Really, Jerry?" Grandma Ruth demanded.

"Now Ruthie, don't blame me. His cousin saw your girl there on the evening news."

Wes and her grandma turned back to Pierce, who was shooting daggers at the sheriff.

"Then, for the record, you're *not* actually surprised to find me here?" Wes asked.

He opened and closed his mouth a few times. "Look, Wessy—"

"It's Wes. Just Wes. Wes-LEY if you can manage two syllables, but you really don't need to."

He cleared his throat. "My cousin mentioned your event, it's true. I checked, and your grandma hasn't filed any permits—"

"You *checked*?"

"I'm the Deputy County Clerk."

"Obviously, she wouldn't have filed them. They'd have been filed by the company she was working with."

"The company that scammed her?" he asked, like she was some kind of idiot.

"They took her money, but they did some of the things."

"There's no permit," he said, and maybe it wasn't his fault, but there was something about the know-it-all condescending way he said it that made Wes kind of want to scream. It was the same tone he used every time he told her there was no point pursuing a career in design, and every time he told her she was lucky he was there to help.

It was the same tone, she realized, as when he suggested she marry him.

"Thank you for confirming that, young man," Grandma Ruth said. "We'll be sure to sort it out right away."

He scoffed—actually scoffed—right in her grandmother's face.

"Impossible. It takes ninety days to get a liquor license," he said, smiling that sweet, dimple-popping, southern boy grin that made Wes fall for him once upon a time. "And have you arranged an on-site medic? The nearest hospital's forty-five minutes away."

"I know very well where the hospital is, young man," Grandma Ruth retorted.

"Then you understand the problem. You can't simply decide to hold a large event because you want to."

"Watch us," Wes said fiercely, all too aware her heat wasn't matching his calm demeanor, but Pierce brought out the worst in her.

He turned that condescending smile her way again. "Why didn't you come to me? I could've helped."

"I forgot you existed," Wes said. Not strictly true, but it

never would have crossed her mind that he was in a position to offer help had she wanted any.

A look of hurt flashed across his face, but Pierce masked it quickly. "Look," he said, stepping closer to Wes and softening his tone. "I don't want to be the bad guy here. Why don't you invite me in? We can talk through your plans and figure out if there's a middle ground."

"A middle ground?"

"Yeah," he shrugged. "We used to be pretty good at that."

"No, you used to be pretty good at framing what you wanted as the middle ground," she said holding the door open for him to come inside anyway.

Grandma Ruth followed behind Pierce and put on a fresh pot of coffee for the sheriff, who made himself at home, spreading jam an inch thick on another slice of sourdough.

They sat at the kitchen table and Pierce spread his hands wide. "First thing's first. Do you own this property?"

"I certainly do," Grandma Ruth assured him.

"Is that good or bad?" Wes asked.

"It's good. You don't need a special event permit."

Well, that was something.

"Is your business license up to date?" he asked, and Wes looked at her grandmother, crestfallen.

"You can't sell tickets without a business license."

"Noted," Wes told him.

"There's tax implications."

"I said we got it."

"And we talked about the liquor license."

"Mmhmm," Wes agreed. Letting him inside had been a mistake. There would be no helpful middle ground.

"You could always pivot to a free, dry event. Have you contacted the health department? Purchased liability insurance? Will the event be ADA compliant?"

Wes resisted the urge to lay her head on the table and cry, but she felt her shoulders sag.

"Everything all right?" a growly Scottish burr asked, as Eòghann stepped into the kitchen, sounding more like the Stoic Scot than his usually charming self.

"Fine." Wes glanced at him. For some reason he was wearing a kilt again, a different one than before, and this time without a shirt. The look was downright rude. She took a deep breath and told him, "Back again about the paperwork we need to file. Thanks for dropping by, Pierce," she said, patting herself on the back for not saying *drop dead*.

Her ex dragged his gaze down Eòghann's chiseled front, and Wes couldn't exactly blame him there.

"Why did you put him back in a kilt?" she whispered to her grandmother.

"I found it in the closet and wanted to see if it brought out the blue in his eyes."

"His eyes are green."

"There's flecks of blue in there," Grandma Ruth insisted, and she wasn't wrong, but Wes was surprised anyone else had noticed them.

"Is *this* what you left me for, Wesley?" Pierce demanded, over enunciating the L in her name. "Event planning—poorly— and cosplay with... him?"

The way he said her name this time was grating, like he was a parent and she an unreasonable child. It was like nails on a chalkboard. She almost hated it more than Wessy. Almost.

"I left because you were bad in bed," she blurted at Pierce, delighted when his head jerked back as though she'd struck him. "You proposed, God knows why, and I realized I couldn't spend the rest of my life eating awful food and sneaking around with Pablo just to have an orgasm."

"Who the fuck is Pablo?" he asked, his voice high and

strained as his face began to redden. "I never heard you complain when we were together."

"You never heard *anything*," she countered. "Turns out, I'm pretty loud when I'm enjoying myself," she added, standing to usher him out the door.

"So you left me for grandpa here?" he demanded, jerking his head towards Eòghann. "Does he need hearing aids to know you're being loud? Jesus, Wesley, I know you lost your dad young, but this is kind of embarrassing. And after everything I did for you..."

There it was. Wes spun around, got right up in his face. "After everything you did for me—what?"

"You..." he floundered.

"Should've been grateful?" Wes demanded. "That's what you want to say, right? After everything you did for me—which I never asked you to do and was kind of the bare minimum if we're both being honest here—but after all that sacrifice, I should've been grateful? I should've condemned myself to a lifetime of complaining and resentment and mediocre sex for which I was expected to say *thank you*?"

"I was willing to take care of you once you—you know."

"Once I what, Pierce? Say it. Once I lost my sight? Guess what—I don't need to be taken care of. You were always *so quick* to tell me what I couldn't do. But you have no idea what I'm capable of, because I don't even know until I do it."

"Fuck yeah," Grace shouted. Wes hadn't realized her friend was in the room.

"Atta girl," Grandma chimed in.

Wes had honestly forgotten she had any kind of an audience, but Eòghann's stupid heart monitor was going off again. Perfect. He was turned on by watching her scream at her ex. Despite the way she'd hurt his feelings, despite the way she'd pushed him away.

"Who are you?" Pierce muttered as he stepped through the door she held open.

Her face was burning. He was right. He never knew her at all. And she probably shouldn't have lost her cool. If he could shut her down, he'd definitely do it now. After seven years together, if Wes knew anything it was how to placate Pierce, and she should've done that, done everything in her power to get him on side—for Grandma Ruth's sake.

The sheriff was looking everywhere but at Pierce, an embarrassed grin on his face as he followed the group outside.

"Will you be needing any help getting your car turned around in the mud?" Eòghann offered.

Pierce huffed. "Shut it down," he told Grandma, before he motioned for the sheriff to get back in the car, at which point he tried to gun it, but his tires spun in the mud until Spencer and Eòghann kind of bounced the back of his car to unstick him, and he sped off down the road, swerving around another car on its way towards them.

"Good riddance," Grandma Ruth said, opening her arms for Wes to fall into.

"Now what?" Wes mumbled, turning to watch the approaching vehicle. If she was forced to issue another refund to an angry ticket holder, she was going to weep.

But it wasn't a ticket holder.

"Diego!" Grace cried, skipping out to meet her brother before he stepped out of the car.

The soccer player picked Grace up and swung her around while she squealed like a little girl, and a part of Wes wished she hadn't grown up an only child.

"Aunt Gray!" her little niece shouted, climbing out of the backseat followed by a more staid older brother of nine or ten years old.

When Grace bent to hug them both, the girl shoved her brother out of the way, keeping her auntie all for herself.

"I can't believe you came," Grace told Diego, ruffling his son's hair. The boy ducked away, too cool for all that, but smiling nonetheless as one of the cochlear processors behind his ears glinted in the sunlight.

"I dragged these two ragamuffins all the way across the country to see a game in Nashville. I'm not going to drive a few extra hours to visit their Tia Gracie?"

She hugged him again.

"Did everything work out with Jimmy?" Grace asked.

Diego nodded. "Your toilet king enjoyed box seats at last night's game. I think the club owner may have been a little surprised, but your johns should be here by three."

"Wait—what's going on?" Wes asked.

"Told you I'd get your potties," Grace crowed.

"Jimmy said there weren't any to be had."

Grace shrugged. "Diego made it worth his while to find some."

"You bribed him?" Wes asked, in awe.

"I gave him a reason to drive to Nashville and pick up what we need."

"Thank you," Wes said, finding herself breathless and on the verge of tears. Grace and Diego had gone to so much trouble to help her, but it wasn't going to matter if her dickhead of an ex shut them down.

WHILE GRACE AND THE OTHERS VISITED WITH DIEGO AND celebrated the arrival of nineteen additional port-o-potties, all placed discretely near the woods, Wes frantically scoured the internet for loopholes in the permit paradox. Giving away alcohol for free without a liquor license was something of a grey area, and what was a Renaissance faire without drinking?

"Take a break," Grace begged, swiping Wesley's iPad and dragging her over to the bonfire that evening. "The weight of the world can wait until tomorrow."

"Anyone up for a hand of poker tonight?" Jack asked.

"Rios?" Bryan glanced at Grace, eyebrow raised, and she replied with a warm smile. "We're in for a hand," he said.

"All right!" Sadie cheered. "Becca?"

"Why not," the sourdough queen answered, having finally run out of flour.

"I'll join too," Alec said, taking a seat next to Rebecca, whose cheeks looked flushed.

"Deal me in," Spencer announced, and Wes wondered if he was an honorary member of the Shakespeare Syndicate now.

"Lùc?" Bryan asked.

"Aye, go on," he agreed. "Grandma Ruth?"

"Sorry kids, I have a date with the new Angi N. Black novel."

"Boo," Lùc complained, and Wes sort of loved how attached he'd grown to her grandmother.

"Captain?" Andy prompted Diego. "Poker?"

"Can't right now," he said. "Bedtime routine," to which his daughter promptly screeched and ran off into the woods chasing Rory.

Wes laughed out loud. When everyone turned to her curiously, she froze. "Sorry. I thought that was a joke. Like washing your hair or something," she babbled. "What—uh—what's a bedtime routine?"

"Pajamas? Teeth? Tuck you in?" Grace said.

"Sing a song. Read a story," Andy added.

"Prayers, sometimes," Sadie said.

So okay, apparently Wes was the asshole. "That's real? Parent's actually do all that? Like on TV?"

"Yours didn't?" Spencer asked, and instantly Wes felt defensive. She figured the guy didn't mean anything by it, but what did it say about her? It was starting to look like Spencer wasn't the weirdo of the group after all.

"No. I mean, once maybe. Why would they? I could put myself to bed."

"We had a bedtime routine," Grandma Ruth protested.

"We caught fireflies until it got too dark and then watched late night movies until I passed out on the couch."

Grandma shrugged. "It was summer. And it worked. The one time I tried to sing to you, you covered my mouth with your hand."

Wesley's friends let out a collective gasp.

"That can't be true," Wes argued.

"Apparently you didn't want to hear, 'It's a Long Way to Tipperary'."

Her words jogged something in Wesley's memory, "Okay, that might be true."

"Wesley, how could you?" Andy teased.

"It's a sad song!" she protested.

The thing was, other than summer visits with Grandma Ruth, Wes mostly grew up as the only child of two single parents. Her mom and dad were married, but one or the other of them was almost always deployed, and whichever one was home was too tired and busy and stressed to worry about much around the apartment.

Wesley started making her own meals when she was seven to take the obvious burden off her mother's plate. Having to deal with a bedtime routine on top of everything else, when Wes was perfectly self-sufficient, would've been silly. She was Wes! *She's so mature for her age. So independent. Wes never makes a fuss.* Most of the time folks hardly remembered she was there.

"Come on, Wes, help us balance out the testosterone party?" Sadie called, but Wes shook her head. Reading the cards by campfire light would be a struggle, and she figured Eòghann would be more likely to stay and hang out if she left them all to it.

"Poker isn't really my game, but have fun," she replied, and wandered off to put herself to bed like she'd done every day of her life.

Chapter Thirty

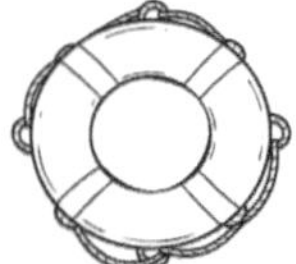

After a few hands of cards, the party broke up. Alec chased his own children off to bed, and the others were tired from working on the barn roof. Even Spencer wandered off to the Berserker's Cave, where he'd relocated his tent after the roof collapse.

Only Andy remained, staring up at the sky for a while before setting up the old telescope Eòghann had found in Grandma Ruth's garage.

"Does it still work?" Eòghann asked, peering up at the moonless sky, his eyes having trouble adjusting to the darkness after gazing into the fire so long. It was still disconcerting, watching the sun fully set on a summer night.

"It seems to work fine."

"Anything to see?"

"Big old universe," Andy replied. "Want a look?"

And strangely, Eòghann found he kind of did want a look, despite never having been compelled before.

Andy fiddled with the focus knob and then stepped back, welcoming Eòghann to the eye piece. He was a bit taller than

Andy, so he needed to hunch to peer through the scope, but when he did, he saw a glowing speck.

"Venus," Andy explained and although the image was somewhat underwhelming, Eòghann felt a tingly sense of awe.

"The planet?"

"Yep."

"I never saw a planet before," he realized.

"They don't have telescopes on Barra?" Andy teased.

"Stays light in the summer and cold in the winter," Eòghann said sheepishly.

"Want to see Jupiter?" Andy asked, and Eòghann stepped back so he could adjust the telescope to a new position.

It took Eòghann a minute to refocus his eyes but then, "Oh my Lord, I can see the stripes and the spot—are those moons?" he whispered.

"They are. Europa, Io, Ganymede, and Callisto."

"That's amazing."

"Not bad for a college kid's toy, huh?" He could hear the grin in Andy's voice.

"You must think I'm ridiculous."

"Nah, it's adorable. I never get tired of looking."

For the next couple of hours, Andy took Eòghann on a tour of the night sky, showing him stars and clusters and he couldn't remember what all, but it was somehow very comforting to be reminded that the universe was vast and infinite and ancient.

"How do you know so much?"

"Astronomy was my first—and only—love," Andy said a little wistfully. "I was a physics major with an astronomy concentration."

"Not Shakespeare?"

"No. I only took one class on Shakespeare. But I didn't have the money for grad school, and I didn't particularly want to teach. And I didn't want to leave Jack. Or Sadie, of course," he added quickly. "Somehow what sounded like a fun way to earn a little money for a couple of years turned into nine."

"And here we are."

"Here we are."

"No camera tonight?" Eòghann asked him.

"We'll see. I don't want to jinx the weather."

Sure enough, right about the time they finally glimpsed the Milky Way—the *actual Milky Way!*—cresting above the trees, more clouds rolled in, obscuring their celestial view.

"You going in?" Andy asked, as he packed up his telescope.

Eòghann sighed. Going in to what? When Diego and the kids arrived, Eòghann had moved his things to Lùc's room so the Rios trio could have the blue one, but he'd sooner spend the night on Grandma Ruth's too-short sofa than face his younger cousin's inquisition. And Wesley was avoiding him.

"I think I'll stay out a bit longer," he said, settling back into a camp chair before the dying embers of the fire.

Andy nodded, and opened his mouth to say something else, before changing his mind.

"Thanks for sharing the stars with me," Eòghann told him.

"Wes—she can be a hard nut to crack. You know, she prides herself on not needing anything from anyone. I've always kind of thought her entire identity was tied up in being low maintenance."

"Putting herself to bed," Eòghann said, recalling the earlier conversation.

Andy nodded. "Hell, man, she sent herself away to boarding school after her dad died."

Eòghann's heart felt so heavy. They had about sixty years of baggage working against them.

"Whereas my entire self-worth is tangled up in making myself useful."

Smiling sympathetically, Andy said, "Love finds a way?"

"Does it?"

"Hell if I know. Night, man."

WHEN HE AWOKE IN THE EARLY MORNING LIGHT, HE FOUND himself draped under the soft blanket crocheted in waterfall shades of Air Force blue. It was a confusing comfort to know Wes had come looking for him sometime during the night and covered him up rather than waking him, but he couldn't begin to guess what it meant.

Had she been awake because she was missing him? Or because she was fretting about her faire? Had she left him to sleep because he'd looked too peaceful to disturb? Or because she couldn't bear to have another conversation with him about forever?

Had she figured out he was in love with her before he'd figured it out for himself?

Despite the early hour, Bryan approached carrying two travel mugs and handed him one filled with strong black coffee. He offered Eòghann a sympathetic grimace and a bottle of Rionnagach to top off the coffee. "Want to talk about it?"

"Talk about what?"

"Why you slept out here under the stars."

"I was watching Andy look for the Milky Way and must've dozed off," Eòghann lied.

"That right?"

Eòghann nodded and took a sip of coffee, as Bryan collapsed into a camp chair beside him.

"A month ago, I thought the only thing in our way was the ocean. That if I could get over it, we might stand a chance."

"Not the fact she thought you were a priest?"

"She thought you were a priest?" Alec asked, taking a seat on Eòghann's other side, reaching out for the whisky bottle to add to his own brightly colored coffee mug, emblazoned with the words JESTERS DO OFT PROVE PROPHETS.

"Aye, well. I wasn't aware of that particular obstacle," Eòghann said. "If the offer still stands to help you out with the lads, I think I'll take you up on it," he told Alec. "If there's room, and you're sure they won't mind."

"There's room," Alec grunted, reminding Eòghann—perhaps reminding them both—there was room because Sullivan was gone.

Bryan frowned but didn't try to talk him out of the decision.

"Do you think you can help me with something first?"

"Of course, whatever you need," Bryan said. "You know that."

"More skulduggery?" Lùcas asked, arriving with Jarrod and Daniel at his heels, each of them munching on fairy toast. "Count me in."

Something popped inside Eòghann, like a balloon of doubt which had been expanding in his chest pushing everything else out. He looked around at their faces, MacNeil and Buchanan alike, and realized that here in Tennessee, however far away he was from Scotland, he was still home.

"The faire must go on," he told them, and they nodded their agreement.

"We fixed the roof and photo prop," Lùc said. "What else is left?"

"A permit for the liquor, apparently. And some kind of ride."

"Piddly stuff then," Alec said, and they all laughed.

"D'you reckon a pony ride would work?" Lùc asked.

"You hiding a horse in your room, are you?" Bryan teased, and Lùc shoved him playfully.

"That farmer who cut the grass? We met him at the hardware store buying salt licks for his ponies."

Bless wee Lùcas. "Ponies, aye? That could work. Kids like ponies, right?" Eòghann asked the lads.

Daniel nodded enthusiastically, but Jarrod looked thoughtful.

"Roddy?" Eòghann encouraged him. "Hit me with it."

"Ponies are good, but maybe you could also get a bounce house? Maybe one shaped like a castle?"

"I love it. Only I'm not allowed to do anything."

"On it," Bryan said. "You call your cowboy. Leave the liquor with me as well. That it?"

"Aye. Except for a business license, an ambulance, and security."

"You don't ask for much do you?" Alec teased.

"Think the sheriff could be persuaded to provide security?" Bryan asked. "He seemed keen on Grandma Ruth."

"Maybe."

"And what exactly did the prick ex-boyfriend say about a business license?"

"Something about taxes."

"You should talk to Sadie," Daniel piped up. Then he seemed to get embarrassed when everyone turned their attention to him. "She's, um, good with paperwork and business stuff," he finished quietly, his cheeks burning.

"True, she is," Alec agreed. "Andy and Jack would've probably fallen apart years ago without her. I'll speak to her if you like. And maybe Andy's sister knows someone with an ambulance?"

"Done and dusted," Lùc said. "Anything else?"

Thunder rumbled in the distance.

"Don't suppose you can control the weather?" Eòghann asked, as the first drops of rain began to fall and everyone hurried to get inside.

"Come in with us for a bit?" Alec asked. It would probably mean walking back to the house in the rain later, but Eòghann agreed.

Inside *Kisimul*, Alec warmed up hot chocolate for Daniel and Jarrod, then casually told them he'd invited Eòghann to join their merry band.

"Do you play any instruments?" Jarrod asked, sounding a little surprised.

"Afraid not. But I can cook and I'm pretty handy."

"Handy enough to keep Rory out of trouble when I'm trying to study?" Daniel asked.

"Aye, at least long enough for you to solve climate change or cure cancer."

"Then I vote yes," Dan laughed.

"I vote yes too," Jarrod agreed. "We go to Connecticut in July. Maryland in August. The Maryland faire is older than Da!"

"Oi!" Alec called.

"I'm looking forward to seeing the country," Eòghann said, ignoring the cracking feeling in his chest at the thought of leaving Wes again, and trying to summon his enthusiasm for adventure.

The caravan door opened. "Good, you're in," Andy said, stepping inside, leading a soaking wet, muddy, and bleeding Rory by the hand.

"What happened this time?" Alec asked, instantly at a level ten.

"Fighting," Andy answered. "With Gray's nephew."

"Jesus Christ, lad, he's only been here five minutes. You better not have broken his cochlears, I swear."

"He started it," Rory yelled, yanking out of Andy's grasp.

"Aye, someone else always does, don't they," Alec yelled back. "That's why we almost got thrown out of Wisconsin, because someone else kept picking fights with you?"

"They did!"

"And what did I tell you would happen if I caught you fighting again?" Alec demanded.

Eòghann shifted uncomfortably, an intruder in this family drama that he'd apparently signed up for.

Rory glared at his father, nostrils flaring, jaw set like stone, but a nervous swallow gave him away.

"What did I tell you?" Alec asked again, his voice level but a thousand years old.

"You'd spank me," Rory yelled, and then he ran into the tiny bathroom and slammed the door with an unsatisfying THWACK.

Alec stared at the floor, seeming to steel his resolve. "Is it raining still? We need a minute."

Dan and Jarrod looked at each other and then hurried out into the rain.

"Don't," Andy said, stepping forward and placing his hand on Alec's arm.

"Well, I shouldn't have said it, but now I've got to make good on it, else he'll never respect me again."

"You really don't." Andy shook his head. "Al, my dad tried to beat the gay out of me, and all it did was make me hate him. I know it isn't the same, but there's a reason I moved in with Becca when I was sixteen, a reason I've been no-contact for half my life and changed my name, and it doesn't matter why."

Alec gritted his teeth. "I don't know what else to do."

"I know," Andy said, squeezing his arm. "But not that."

Maybe if Pòl hadn't died when Alec was eleven, making him an orphan before he hit puberty, he'd feel better equipped to handle his boys now. In a way, this was Eòghann's fault too. Somehow, he needed to make it right.

"Can I try talking to him?" Eòghann asked.

His cousin waved an arm, welcoming him to try.

"Come over for breakfast? Jack's doing a fry up," Andy urged.

Eòghann nodded that Alec should go.

"I do need to talk to Sadie."

Andy nodded his thanks to Eòghann and the two stepped out into the rain.

The ticking clock over the sink was deafening in the sudden silence. And Eòghann had no idea what he was doing.

"You can come out now," he called. "Everyone's gone."

A few minutes later the toilet flushed and Rory peeked outside.

Eòghann slid casually into a booth seat and nodded his head towards the one across from him, but Rory leaned back against the bathroom door frame and crossed his arms.

"Do you want something to eat?" Eòghann asked. The boy shook his head, but Eòghann got up to make him a hot chocolate as his cousin had done for the other two. He rummaged in the freezer until he found an ice pack and wrapped it in a towel. "Put that over your eye," he said gently.

"Aren't you going to yell at me?" Rory asked, but he did as he was bidden.

"Nah," Eòghann said. "Your da..." he shook his head. "Try and cut him some slack, all right? He's been through the same shite as you, and then some."

Rory shrugged, but he accepted the hot chocolate and slid into the booth Eòghann had vacated.

"Do you want to talk about it?" Eòghann asked, Bryan's words from an hour ago rattling in his brain.

The kid shrugged again.

"What was the fight about?"

"Nothing."

"That keeker would suggest otherwise."

"Keeker?"

"Black eye."

"Oh." Rory shrugged. "We just wanted to fight."

Ah. It was like that, was it? Angry feelings with nowhere to go.

"I didn't break his stupid cochlears. He wasn't even wearing them."

"That's good at least. Did it make you feel better?"

"No," the boy replied fiercely.

"Look, I know everything—"

"Fucking sucks?"

Eòghann was proud of himself for not cracking a smile at the little boy's profanity.

"You don't know anything about it," Rory added stubbornly.

"To lose a twin brother and your ma? No, you're right, I don't. But I know what it's like to lose *someone*. And to feel completely gutted. Hollowed out and consumed with rage and fear. And guilt?" he added, taking a stab in the dark with his honesty.

The way Rory turned away from him, scowl deepening, he thought maybe he hadn't been too wide of the mark.

"I'd like to say it gets better but... the ache'll dull over time. Mostly. You learn to live with the scars."

"Just shut up," Rory whispered.

"Can I ask you something?"

"No."

"Your da and brothers invited me to join you for a while. Live in the caravan, travel to the next few faires."

"Why?"

"Because I'm lost too. Would it be all right with you?"

Rory shook his head. "Doesn't matter what I want," he said, pushing his no longer hot chocolate away and dragging himself out of the booth and out the door, leaving Eòghann once again alone in a place he didn't belong.

Chapter Thirty-One

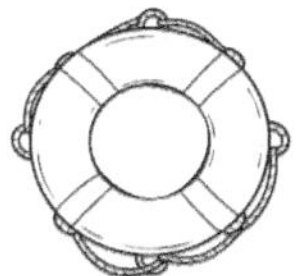

T-MINUS 2 DAYS TO RENAYZANTS FAIRE

Wes had waited up for what felt like hours. She figured eventually the poker game would end and Eòghann would come to her, since he'd vacated his room for Diego and the kids.

She'd held her breath as she listened to the sounds of Grace and Bryan, and later, Lùc, all turning in for the night. But Eòghann had never come.

At some point she succumbed to a fitful sleep, and when she awoke in the pre-dawn hours, still alone, she figured he must've crashed with Lùcas or else on the living room couch.

She had dragged herself downstairs to check on him, wrapped in her dad's soft old blue-and-grey blanket, but the living room was empty. He was probably with Lùc but fear gripped her by the throat—what were the odds he'd caught a ride to the airport and headed back to Barra without so much as saying goodbye?

After returning to her room, she was unable to shake the sense of dread growing in her belly that she'd ruined a truly good thing. It wasn't fair to keep him around for flirting at arm's length, but she was selfish, and she didn't want to let him go.

Staring out the window at the soon-to-be faire grounds, she thought she saw a silhouette in the moonlight, huddled before the dead campfire.

Maybe it was her mind playing tricks, but she needed to be sure, and sure enough, he had slept outside all night, his tall frame slouched into a camp chair rather than share the same bed as her because she didn't believe in forever.

After so many days of rain, there was a nip in the air, and so Wes had tucked her dad's blanket gently around him, relieved when he hadn't woken up. Disappointed, too.

When she arose again hours later, the house was eerily silent, and Eòghann still hadn't come.

None of the upstairs guests were around, nor were they hanging out in the living room when she found the courage to venture down and make a cup of tea. She cut a thick slice of sourdough and sat down for who knew how long, staring into the mug until her tea went cold and probably long enough for the bread to go stale.

"Out with it, Blondie," Grandma Ruth said, sitting down across from her.

"Where is everyone?"

"Grace and her brother took the kids to the zoo. The Barra boys went off on some errand or other. What's eating you?"

Wesley shrugged. Where to begin? "I probably should've thought to start with the business license and liquor permit," she said.

"Pah. I'm not worried. Whatever happens on Saturday, putting together my faire has been a wonderful adventure. Doing it with you has been the joy of my lifetime."

Wes chuckled and shook her head at the same time. How

was it possible for Grandma to be so go-with-the-flow about absolutely everything? Even things that actually mattered?

"What's going on with your Sexy Scot?"

Wes frowned.

"Are you mad at me for putting him back in a kilt?" Grandma asked.

Now she had to laugh. "Who could be mad about that?" Wes teased.

"Some people might."

"No, Grandma. Eòghann's a grown-ass man. I don't imagine he'd wear it if he didn't want to. And he belongs in a kilt 24/7."

"And what did the grown-ass man do that has you down in the dumps?"

Wesley's frown returned. "Nothing." She sighed, shaking her head adamantly. She didn't want her grandma to think ill of Eòghann when he'd been perfect by any normal person's standards. By her own, to be honest.

Grandma Ruth studied her shrewdly. "What did *you* do then?"

"Rude."

Grandma raised an eyebrow at her.

"I told him the truth. It was a fling. It was never going to work out."

"Did it upset you? Seeing Pierce again?"

Wes nodded. "It did. I wasted too many years with him."

"I never liked him."

"You didn't?" Wes asked, genuinely surprised her grandmother had formed an opinion of her ex one way or the other. She'd never come out and admitted she disliked anyone Wes had dated before Pierce. Not even the stuck up guy in college who wouldn't answer a single question about himself.

"He never saw you."

Wes nodded. "He saw a problem to solve."

"*He* was the problem," her grandma said fiercely. "He never respected you. And he had unkind eyes."

"Not sure I ever noticed."

"You noticed. Whether you realized it or not. So what happened?"

"He really was bad in bed," Wes repeated the line emphatically. It maybe wasn't a reason to break up, but shallow as it sounded, it'd been her wakeup call.

Grandma stared down her nose at Wes. "You could have fooled me," she said, obviously referring to Eòghann when Wes had meant Pierce.

"God Grandma! Eòghann and I—we don't align."

Grandma Ruth gave her another skeptical look that made her cheeks burn, and she sighed deeply. "I thought we were having fun. He thought we could build a life."

"The two aren't mutually exclusive."

"I should've realized it sooner, but I thought he was a priest. Which I found very convenient."

"Because you're afraid to commit."

"I'm not *afraid*, but it would never work. It's like he has some kind of pathological need to be helpful. To be needed."

"What a terrible fate," Grandma said gently, without a trace of sarcasm, "for someone who doesn't want to need anyone, ever."

She looked up and Grandma held her gaze until Wes had to look away.

"I mean of course it's been nice having him around. Doing things for us."

"He seems very capable. Of doing *things*."

"*Grandma.*"

"But?"

Wes shook her head. "You can't build a relationship on that. You can't build a life on it."

"Who says?"

"The minute you let yourself need someone, you become dependent on them. You want them to keep doing those things, and you stop being able to do them for yourself. You become an *obligation*. And I won't let that happen. I—" she almost said *love him too much*, but she caught herself. "I care too much about him to put him in that situation. And believe it or not, I have too much self-respect to let myself be hurt that way again."

"Are you here out of obligation?"

"No, of course not! It's different."

"How?"

"It's just different." She didn't know how to explain the things that made perfect sense in her head, but she went on, "Pierce was a terrible cook. I might occasionally mix up the cinnamon and chili powder, but I'm still better than he was. He hated cooking, but he insisted on doing it all the time because *one day* I wouldn't be able to."

"Bah!" Grandma scoffed.

"I know! It was ridiculous. I could've come up with creative solutions as my vision declined, but I think every time he looked at me he saw the Robin Hood fox dressed as a blind pauper and forgot it was Robin Hood in disguise."

"Wes..." Grandma Ruth said, covering Wesley's hand with her own, her skin soft and warm.

"He never asked what I needed or wanted. He assumed I wouldn't be able to adapt. And he *helped me*"—she made air quotes with her fingers—"by doing the cooking. Out of obligation. Until it felt ungrateful not to let him *help*. And I ate his shitty food out of my own warped sense of obligation, and I was thankful for it. Out of obligation. And the whole time he resented me for the help I never asked for and didn't need, and honestly I resented him right back."

"Eòghann isn't Pierce," Grandma said.

"No, but I love him too much to become his obligation."

Grandma Ruth sat back like she was seeing Wesley for the first time.

"What?" Wes asked, not sure she was ready to hear the answer.

"I never understood why you wanted to go away to boarding school. Honestly, I always believed your mother put the idea in your head."

Wes shook her head. "I didn't want to be a bother."

"Oh, my girl," Grandma said, shaking her head as she stroked Wesley's cheek. "How desperately we all failed you."

"You didn't."

"You stopped coming around here. For the same reason? You didn't want to be a bother?"

Wesley's instinct was to say no, of course not. To shelter her grandmother from any more uncomfortable feelings the conversation might cause. But Grandma Ruth was piercing her with a stare that demanded honesty. She swallowed.

"Well, yeah. Grandpa had been gone a long time. You deserved to be living your best life, cruising around the world, going out with rich men who drove Mustangs with the top down so they could feel the wind in their hair implants, playing bridge with the ladies, joining book clubs—not catching fireflies and having spa days with an eleven-year-old.

"I hate book club. They always choose such pretentious books."

"Maybe you need to find a different book club."

"Catching fireflies and having spa days and going to Renaissance faires with an eleven-year-old *was* living my best life."

"I was just a dumb kid. My logic may have been skewed."

"And now?"

"I still feel like a dumb kid most of the time."

"I'm sorry—"

"No."

"I'm sorry, Wes. For whatever I did or said that made you feel like the time I had with you was a burden. The only burden was saying goodbye."

"Maybe it wasn't about you, Grandma."

"If it was my son, then that's my fault too. And if it was your mother, I promised my son a long time ago I wouldn't say a word against her."

Wes shook her head again. "I guess we're all a little fucked up, one way or another."

Grandma Ruth went to her and pulled her into a long hug, and when the tears fell they were because she liked that hug a tiny bit more than seemed wise.

She'd felt the same way about Eòghann's hugs. She was a tactile person, and she missed being touched. Being held. Being cared for, but then that was the whole point, wasn't it? She might get used to it. Rely on it. Need more than the people around her could offer. She'd already gotten used to the feel of him, to his little check-ins—his hand pressed to the small of her back when he passed her in the kitchen, his eyes finding hers from across the room and crinkling with warmth and delight.

Damn.

She'd pushed him away for nothing, far too late. She was already in the deep end, and the water was way over her head.

Chapter Thirty-Two

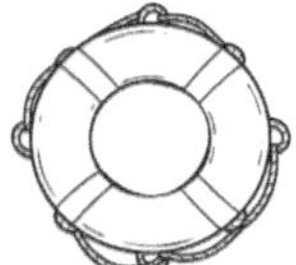

Eòghann took a long walk through the woodlands surrounding Warwick Hall. This adventure wasn't shaping up quite the way he'd expected when he said goodbye to his mother and boarded Teàrlach's plane. But what had he expected? That a year-old infatuation would transform into Happily Ever After before the month was through? He really had been reading too many romance novels.

This was the real world, and he and Wes wanted disparate things—him, because he didn't know what he wanted. Her, because she was happy enough for a fuck, but didn't want a relationship. Between her grandma, Grace, and their college friends, Wes had all the support she needed. It was Eòghann who was drifting and lonely. Eòghann who craved more.

And that was fine. His goal had been to leave the island for Bryan and Grace's eventual wedding, and now he was here. Mission accomplished, way ahead of schedule considering they weren't yet engaged as far as he knew. He'd accomplished it because of the secondary mission: to find Alec. Now it was time to finish that quest and win over his cousins, and then see what else life had in store.

The group had scattered that morning to check off those last few items on Wesley's list. Day after tomorrow the faire would open, and all would be well. Then Wes could go back to her terrible job and Grandma Ruth could sell her home and move into a terrible apartment, and Eòghann would ride off into the sunset, attempting to fill a terrible void with Danny and the Boys. He'd go back to hearing secondhand updates on Wesley by way of Grace and Bryan, and if he was lucky, the occasional text from Wes. He would focus on repairing something old and building something new with Alec and his lads.

The adventure wasn't taking shape at all the way he'd imagined, but it would still be an adventure.

Except wasn't he doing the exact same thing with them as he'd been doing his whole life? Trying to be helpful enough to earn their love and forgiveness?

He tripped over the uneven ground and almost went down, regaining his balance with one hand on that perfect birch tree he'd chased Rory past a week and a half ago.

Where had that thought come from? *Trying to be helpful enough to earn their love and forgiveness?* That wasn't what he was trying to do, was it?

Eòghann glanced at his watch and did the mental math. It was 6 PM on Thursday in Barra. He'd missed his last few appointments with Dr. Patel, not having a phone and all.

Weeks ago, during their second or third appointment, Eòghann had thought they were making idle getting-to-know-you-better small talk. He'd explained to Dr. Patel about doing odd jobs around the island as a lad, turning into a sort of teenage jack-of-all-trades before even leaving school, until one day he was an adult and people started paying him.

He'd never actually chosen it as a career, but it suited him because he liked to be helpful.

Sharing all this with his therapist had made him feel

extremely stable and well-adjusted because how many people were lucky enough to do the thing they'd probably be doing anyway as their actual job?

"Interesting," Dr. Patel had said. "Do you think you equate helpfulness with lovability?"

"What?" Eòghann scoffed, his world starting to spin.

"It isn't an accusation," Dr. Patel replied. "Only I wonder if, as a boy, some part of you, driven by guilt, perhaps felt like you needed to earn love by being helpful?"

"No," Eòghann replied fiercely. "It's what you do when you're part of a community. You're from the city. You wouldn't understand."

They'd said no more about it, but some part of him knew the therapist was right. He'd always felt like if he wasn't helping people, what was the point of him? He enjoyed becoming known around the island as someone who could be relied on, in or out of a pinch, instead of the boy Pòl was trying to rescue when he drowned.

Sliding to the damp, muddy ground, his back against the birch tree, Eòghann thought about those words again.

Do you think you equate helpfulness with lovability?

Hadn't he entertained the very same thought when Wesley declined his assistance with the faire? Uncertain where they stood, he'd wondered how he could ever convince her to fall in love with him when she wouldn't let him help her with anything. He'd said it out loud to himself: he would win Grandma Ruth over to his cause by helping her instead of helping with the faire.

Hell, he'd come on this trip partly because Bryan wanted him to—wanted his help finding and speaking to Alec—and he didn't want Bryan to love him any less if he said no.

And now he was doing it again. He was trying to earn back Alec's love by helping with the boys, to win Daniel by keeping

Rory out of mischief, to win Jarrod with home-cooked dinners and fairy toast. To win Rory by being on his side.

Because deep down, he didn't see why anyone would love him on his own merit. What was there to love?

He should probably borrow someone's laptop and show up to his therapy session next Tuesday. Would Dr. Patel be proud of him for admitting all this out loud?

Jesus, now he was trying to win his therapist's approval.

But where did all this leave him with Wes? Understanding his patterns didn't mean he was any closer to changing them.

He pushed himself to his feet and looked up at the birch tree. It was the perfect tree, straight and tall and smooth. He'd meant to turn it into a maypole for her. He thought she and Grandma Ruth would both be thrilled by it. But would that be one more pathetic attempt to make her love him?

Eòghann didn't feel sure of anything anymore.

Shoving his hands deep in his pockets, he turned his back on the tree and kept walking.

Without meaning to, he found his way to the lakeshore. It sure didn't look like a lake to him. It was vast, the current swift, the water brown with mud after so many days of rain.

If he weren't a coward he'd take a canoe and row over to the island that so fascinated Rory. He would cut down the overgrown weeds and build a castle out of brick, a replica of his very own Kisimul here in Stratford. They could punt faire guests back and forth in search of the Loch Tennessee Monster.

Like that one.

He blinked and rubbed his eyes, thinking he'd glimpsed something red in the water, but it was gone. He stared hard at the spot, despite the mounting nausea. And there it was again.

Oh hell.

Someone was in the water.

Racing onto the beach, he found where Alec had left the old

canoes after their fishing trip a few days back. Before everything went sideways. But if both canoes were on the beach, Rory must've made good on his threat to swim out to the island. What was he trying to prove?

Eòghann took several deep breaths, which, if he were being honest, weren't deep at all, but at least they were breaths.

What was it Dr. Patel always told him to do? Name what he was feeling and imagine putting them into bubbles?

"I feel terrified," he admitted, picturing sticky yellow sludge inside a glimmering bubble as it struggled to float up into the sky.

"I feel ashamed." That one was a dark, inky red, like the blood of a blush. The bubble hung heavy in the air beside him.

"I feel disgusted," he said, shoving the orange canoe into the water as a bubble filled with grey-green duck poo floated by.

"I feel unworthy." He pushed off from the shore as an empty bubble followed him. "I feel like I'm going to be sick."

Squinting through the fogginess that threatened to envelop his mind, he could see that the boy was in distress, fighting against the current with one arm and periodically slipping under the water.

"Help!" Eòghann roared, paddling with all his strength. "Help!"

Why hadn't he gone to find someone else instead of charging in after the kid? What was he thinking? He tried to yell again, but his lungs wouldn't open and the shout was sequestered within his chest. Closing his eyes against the encroaching darkness, he tried to picture himself somewhere safe and dry, but the only thing that came to mind was Wesley's bedroom, and he wasn't welcome there anymore. He tried to gasp for breath, frozen, the paddle stuck as though the current had turned to concrete, and then everything went black.

Chapter Thirty-Three

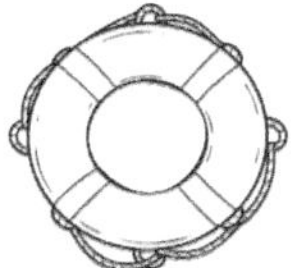

Wesley's cuddle with Grandma Ruth was cut short when Sadie slipped inside looking smart in a fitted purple suit.

"Ready to go Gram?" she asked.

"Let me get my pocket book."

"Go where?" Wes wondered.

"Don't worry about it," Grandma replied, relishing the air of mystery. "We don't need any help."

"We're going to go talk to someone about the paperwork," Sadie replied.

"Someone who? Pierce?"

"Not Pierce."

"Should I come too?" Wes asked, looking down at her cable knit sweater and pajama pants. "I can change real fast."

"It's cool," Sadie said. "We got this."

"Okay..."

Wes walked them to the door, wondering if they were excluding her from helping them because she'd been so rude to Pierce or maybe as a dose of her own medicine, which—fair.

She sat on the front porch awhile, trying to figure out what she wanted to say the next time she saw Eòghann, until she noticed the hydrangea bush. The one she had planted with Grandma Ruth twenty years ago. The one Eòghann had rescued from Virginia creeper. For the first time in as long as she could remember, it had finally bloomed.

Maybe it was all the rain, or maybe it was Eòghann's TLC, but the defiant little cluster of pink flowers kind of broke her heart.

"I'm going to miss it here," Spencer said as if reading her mind as he plopped down next to her on the swing.

"Yeah? Where are you from, Spence?" she asked, to keep from asking *where the heck did you pop up from?*

"Saskatchewan," he said, causing her to turn and look at him in surprise.

"Wow," she said. "Long way from home."

He looked tired and maybe a little homesick. She wondered what kind of life he led. "You should take one of Grandma Ruth's blankets when you go. What's your favorite color?"

"Elephant's Breath. Either the 1880 or the 1909. I'm not ashamed to admit I lean more towards the 1909 if forced to choose."

"Noted," she said, having no idea what color Elephant's Breath of either year was meant to represent. "I'm restless. I need to walk. Come with me? Maybe we'll see something close to that color."

Spencer perked up. "Maybe some fungi after all this rain!" he said, falling into step beside her as they squelched off across the waterlogged grounds, taking in all that Wesley's friends had built for her in the last few weeks—not because she'd asked or because they felt obligated to, but because they wanted to. The Shakespeare Syndicate had shown up because Grandma Ruth was a haven for each of them in the past, and they wanted to reflect back her love and kindness. Danny and the Boys had come along too because they'd rather be together with Andy, Jack, and Sadie, having fun and working towards something meaningful, than traveling between whatever gigs they otherwise had planned.

No amount of protesting from Wesley could dissuade them because they didn't see her as a burden. They wanted to be there. Honestly, that probably should've been her first clue. Any time she'd offered Pierce an out, he'd taken it—gladly. *How had she never noticed that before?*

Now Eòghann was doing the same thing, taking the out, avoiding her like she had the actual bubonic plague that kicked off the Renaissance.

No. That wasn't fair. She had more than given him an out, she'd pushed, pulled, and dragged him towards the exit. She couldn't blame him for finally stepping through it.

She had no one to blame except herself.

Still, she'd told Grandma Ruth the truth, too. Eòghann was a helper to his core, and she had always been stubbornly independent, and why did opposites have to attract so damn hard?

How could she trust that even a helper like Eòghann wouldn't eventually come to see her as an obligation? She was too old to pack herself off to boarding school a third time, but he would never truly be happy with her, not as long as she tried to do everything herself. And she'd feel like shit for constantly telling him to butt out.

"Help!"

The strangled cry interrupted her thoughts and she turned to Spencer. "That sounded—"

"Like the Sexy Scot?" he asked.

A shiver ran down her spine. It did sound a bit like Eòghann's voice, if distorted and unnatural.

"Help!" the shout came again, and a shadow crossed overhead as a large, black bird circled the trees. "Help!"

"Duncan?"

The bird landed on Spencer's shoulder and looked Wes right in the eye. "Help! Family!" it cawed, then it took off flying in the direction of the lake, with Wes and Spencer scrambling to follow.

They skidded to a halt at the water's edge, trying to make sense of the scene. There was a blurry figure in a stationary, bright orange canoe about halfway to the island in the middle of the stream. Nearer the island, she could barely make out the dark form of Duncan circling and diving—at what, she couldn't say.

"Oh fuck," Wes muttered. "Duncan!"

The bird flew back to her, almost frantic as it squawked, "Help! Family!"

"Yes. Help. Good bird. Go find more family," she begged, pointing back the way they'd come.

"Family," Duncan screamed, and flew off.

Wes patted her pockets. "Do you have a phone?" she asked Spencer.

"No."

"I must've left mine in the kitchen. Go call 911."

Somehow Wes knew, without being able to see clearly, that the distressed figure in the canoe was Eòghann, attempting some kind of rescue. With sick dread growing in her belly, she refused to imagine the possibilities. Hadn't Grandma Ruth said all the children went to the zoo?

Kicking off her shoes and stripping down to her tank top and underwear, she grabbed a little paddle board from inside the green canoe and waded out into the muddy water. It was high after all the rain, and the current was swift. She had to fight hard to reach the orange boat, which was thankfully caught in a barricade of flood debris. Otherwise, it probably would've washed downstream already, and, with Eòghann's luck, he'd be heading over the dam at Fort Loudon.

He sat slumped forward, eyes wide open but unseeing as he struggled to breathe.

"Eòghann?" Wes yelled, treading water against the fierce current but keeping away from the canoe lest she dislodge it from its anchor. "You okay? What happened?" She couldn't tell if this was another panic attack or some kind of medical emergency.

Had his line about having a *her* problem been merely that—a line—and he actually needed the heart monitor?

"Eòghann? Look at me, sweetheart. It's Wes. Can you look at me, Padre?"

Maybe she was imagining it, but she thought his eyes shifted infinitesimally in her direction.

"Help!" Duncan cried, flying past her and swooping once more. Wes still couldn't make out what the bird was diving at, but she had to make a choice.

"Hang on, Padre, I'll be right back," she promised, taking off again before she grew too tired to fight the upstream current.

When she reached Duncan, her worst fear was confirmed.

Rory was bobbing in the water, trapped somehow by yet more brush that must've been swept into the river during the storms, one arm floating uselessly at his side. His eyes were closed, and he wasn't struggling against the current, but his head was tipped back to keep his nose above the water. His teeth were chattering, though, which seemed like a good sign.

Taking a deep breath, Wes plunged into the murky water to try and assess the situation.

The leg was bent at a funny angle, and it was hopelessly caught up in a tangle of tree branches. Why hadn't she brought so much as a knife with her?

When she surfaced for air, Rory's eyes flickered open.

"You're okay, kid. I've got you."

He coughed. "Tell Da I'm sorry."

"No chance," she argued. "That one's on you." Then she plunged back under the water, unwilling to imagine an outcome where Alec lost a second twin to drowning.

It was delicate work—impossible to see much, and like Eòghann's canoe, she didn't want to dislodge the wrong thing and send the whole pile rushing downriver with Rory still caught in its grasp.

She was forced to surface for air again before making any headway, but this time Jack was there at her side, offering her a knife. Together they managed to cut and pull and wriggle the little boy free.

Wes caught him while Jack scrambled into the green canoe alongside Alec, and together they lifted the shivering boy into the tiny boat. It wasn't built for four, but Jack reached for Wesley's arm to pull her up.

"You go on. I'll get Eòghann," she told them, and before they could argue, she swam off, letting the current carry her back downstream to the bright orange canoe.

This time, she gave the vessel an almighty shove and shimmied herself onto the back as it broke away from the brush. She didn't have the strength to fully fight the current, so she let it drift them a little further down the beach, but when she reached the shallow water, she jumped out, dragging the canoe behind her, and then collapsed on her back, gasping for breath.

Further up the beach, Alec and Jack had laid Rory on the sand, while Rebecca and a uniformed medic hurried towards them.

Everything was going to be okay.

The EMT, a young Chinese woman, finished with Rory and ran over to Wes and Eòghann. "Are you okay?"

"I'm fine. He's afraid of the water," she panted, the full

weight of what Eòghann had attempted hitting her all at once. "Also he might have a heart condition. I don't know. I didn't want to move him, I didn't know what to do."

"You did great," the medic assured her, leaning over Eòghann to check his vitals. "Do you know his name?"

"Eòghann."

"Eòghann? Can you hear me? How are you feeling? You're going to be fine, okay?" the EMT assured them both, and Wes really hoped she was right because she couldn't bear to lose him, and she'd be furious forever if she didn't get a chance to slap him silly for not asking someone for help.

Chapter Thirty-Four

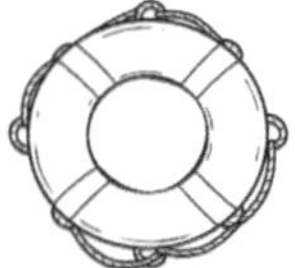

Numb. Every part of Eòghann was simply numb. Not from the cold of the water. Not even from the panic attack his phobia had brought on. Or, maybe that too. But his mind and soul were numb with grief, with worry, with despair. Rory could've died—still could, probably—because of him. Because he'd been unable to help when every second counted.

Wesley draped a heated blanket over him. "You were shivering," she explained when he looked up.

Quivering, more like, recalling those harrowing moments in the water. But the warm blanket was nice. Solid. A tether to the hospital bed, reminding him he was safe and dry.

Rebecca entered the exam room and spoke softly to Wes, but Eòghann couldn't make his brain process her hushed words.

"Hear that?" Wes whispered. "The EMT thinks Rory's going to be okay. His vitals were stable."

"No thanks to me."

She squeezed his arm and rubbed his neck. He didn't deserve the kindness or the comfort. He wanted to pull away but found himself leaning into it instead. "All that matters is he'll live," she said.

"That isn't all that matters," he argued bitterly. She ought to be accusing him. Demanding to know why he would attempt to go after Rory when he knew—of course he *knew*—what would happen because it happened every fucking time. And the answer was that he'd been too scared to think straight, too afraid to leave Rory alone, and too selfish to do the right thing. He had wanted to be the one to save his little cousin, as though it could somehow be his redemption.

Wesley sighed. "Have you ever treated a patient with a phobia?" she whispered.

"A few," Rebecca replied.

"Will you talk to him?"

"If he wants to talk to me. But professionally I'm only licensed to work with children."

"I probably needed one as a child," Eòghann said, and they both turned, as though surprised to remember he was lying right there, hearing every word. "My mother always said I was born drowning."

Wes started to get up so Rebecca could take her seat, giving Eòghann his privacy, but he caught her hand. He didn't want her to go. And anyway, she deserved to hear it too. Instead, Rebecca pulled a second chair closer.

"Wet lungs, the midwife called it. I never knew until later. When I was eight, I hit my head going into the swimming pool. Drowned again that day. That's when my phobia began."

"Phobia is a perfectly normal reaction to a near death experience," Rebecca gently assured him. "It's your brain's way of trying to protect you."

"My father didn't think so. We come from generations of fishermen. No son of his was going to be a big jessie, scared of water on land or in the sea."

"Did he force you to go back in before you were ready?"

His breathing began to speed up and he felt lightheaded again.

"Eòghann," Rebecca said, clawing back the darkness. "I want you to focus on your breathing."

"Trying..."

"Not the fact that you *can't* breathe. Count with me? Inhale-two-three-four-five, and out-two-three. In and out. Good."

"By the time I was twelve, he'd had enough." Eòghann paused to take another shaky deep breath. "He insisted I go out with him and my Uncle Rob and cousin Pòl to draw the nets. The water was rough, and I was... overcome. I was boking over the side when... I dunno. There was a swell, and one minute I was in the boat, and the next I was in the water."

He felt, rather than heard, Wesley's breath hitch, and she ran her thumb up and down the back of his hand.

"The current was strong, and I was so afraid. I couldn't do what I was trained to do. Pòl jumped in after me. I don't know what happened next," he admitted, his eyes filling with tears, his throat threatening to close. "He got me in the lifebuoy, and they dragged me back to the boat, but somehow he was swept away. They found his body three days later."

Wesley and Rebecca were both silent as he lifted a trembling hand to swipe away his tears.

"Alec was left an orphan—because of me. His da died saving me. So when I saw Rory out there today, I didn't think. Only, I couldn't let it happen to him again. I couldn't do that to him again. But I should have—I should have gone for help. I should've known I couldn't save him, and if Rory dies, it'll be my fault. I'll have done to him all over again."

"No," Wes said. No excuses, no supplication. Simply no. She wasn't having it.

"You didn't do it to me the first time," Alec said from the doorway.

Eòghann froze. How much had his cousin heard?

"Rory's a tough wee shite. He's going to be fine."

"What about secondary drowning?" Eòghann rasped. Saying the words out loud made his stomach turn.

"That's—whatever you read, that's not really a thing. And they're monitoring him. It won't happen. Not this time."

Relief washed over Eòghann and with it, more tears. Rebecca gave Alec her seat and he leaned forward, taking both Eòghann's hands. "I never blamed you for my da. Not for one minute."

"It was my fault."

"You were a child. The only child on the boat. You had no business being out there that day. My da knew it, that's why he went along. Because your da was a stubborn old mule and wouldn't be talked out of it."

"How do you know?"

"Uncle Cam told me. He was there too. And nothing that happened was your fault, Eòghann. You were twelve years old, a wee lad, same as my Jarrod."

Eòghann's whole body was shaking now, wracked with sobs he couldn't hold back, and he crumpled into a ball. Alec leaned closer, stroking his hair.

"I'd say you're forgiven if I thought it would help. But I don't want to because there's nothing to forgive. What happened to my da was a tragedy, but it wasn't your fault. It's the risk of life on the sea. It's why I wanted a different one—for me, for my family. Turns out tragedy has a way of finding you."

"I'm sorry," Eòghann whispered. "I'm so sorry, Alec. I took him from you."

"No," Alec said, pushing Eòghann back so they could look at each other through their tears. "No. He gave you back to me.

I'm sorry for not honoring that better, for disappearing for so long."

Then he pulled Eòghann into a smothering hug that smelled like campfire and lake water and days' old sweat and held him tight until his breathing slowed.

"Rory's okay?" Wes asked, when Eòghann finally sat back in bed, utterly exhausted.

"Aye. He's got a knot on his head, and his leg was broken by the debris. Wrist too. He won't be playing bodhrán for a while," Alec added with a forced chuckle. "But he'll be all right."

"What was he doing out there?" Wes asked.

"He said he wanted to swim across it for Sullivan." Alec's voice hitched and his brow furrowed even deeper. "Got it into his head Sully might be waiting for him on that island."

"And there's truly no worry about water in his lungs?" Eòghann rasped. "They've checked?"

"They're monitoring him, but he says he didn't swallow any and they think he's out of danger. He's already asked for something to eat."

Eòghann inhaled, sharp and deep, his own lungs fully expanding for what felt like the first time in days. Maybe years.

"The others are back from the zoo. I asked Jarrod to call the West Highland Tarriers. They're nearly here. They'll cover our sets, so there won't be any empty stage time," Alec told Wes.

"Oh," she nodded. "Thanks. You didn't have to."

"The show must go on," he said wryly. "I'm going to get back in there," he added, squeezing Eòghann's shoulder.

When Alec stood, Rebecca did too. "I need to call Andy back," she said, stepping away to leave Eòghann and Wesley alone.

"For a minute there I thought I lost you," Wes said, her voice wobbly with emotion.

Eòghann didn't dare hope those words meant she cared for

him as anything more than a very dear friend, but it was nice to hear. "I'm sorry," he said. He never meant to worry her.

"No, *I'm* sorry. For pushing you away. I guess I've been more stressed about this whole thing than I wanted to admit."

"Of course," he rasped.

"The house—Warwick Hall, and Grandma Ruth—they were basically the only constants in my life growing up. No matter where I was going to school or where my parents were stationed or deployed, every summer for two months it was me and Grandma and Warwick Hall. I *hate* the idea of her selling it to strangers and moving anywhere else. But she's an old lady, and she deserves to make her own decisions, and I so wanted to make her dream come true first."

"You have."

"Who cares anymore?"

He thought she probably still cared, but he didn't have the energy to say so.

She sighed. "No. That's a lie."

"Which part?"

Wes took a deep breath. "I didn't push you away because I was stressed about the faire," she said. "Or the house."

"Was it because I'm a monster?" he asked, only half teasing.

"No, Caliban. It was because I was falling in love with you, and I didn't exactly want to. And I know that's some kind of Darcy-level shitty thing to say, but it's time to be honest, and honestly, I'm afraid to fall in love with anyone, but especially you."

"Afraid?"

She nodded, slowly, like she was coming to terms with what she wanted to say.

"The whole bedtime routine thing? My dad put me to bed once."

"Once?" He couldn't imagine being a father and not tucking his child into bed every single night.

"I think I must've been sick or something. He read me a story. Sang me a song. It was *nice*. And then the next night, I couldn't fall asleep. I kept thinking about how cozy it had been, all cuddled up together with his five o'clock shadow in my hair and the smell of dry cleaning still clinging to his uniform. I didn't *need* him to read to me or tuck the covers under my chin, but I'd gotten a taste of it, and I wanted more. I loved feeling taken care of."

Eòghann's heart ached, and he knew exactly how she felt.

"Eventually I got out of bed and asked him if he'd do it again, but he couldn't. I don't remember why. I could tell he was spent. He had nothing left to give that day. I remember thinking something bad must've happened to his friends back in Afghanistan, and there I was, one more obligation. I remember the pain in his eyes when he told me no. I shouldn't have put him in that position over something I didn't really need. I was the easy kid. My own problem solver. *Wes is so grown up, so dependable, so independent.* That's what I heard my whole life. So that's who I became. But you—you're a helper."

"I am a helper," he agreed.

"And that's extraordinary. Despite my best efforts, I've enjoyed having your help," she said, and why didn't that make him feel any better? "But I don't want to become your obligation. I love you too much to one day ask more from you than you want or are able to give. To see the pain in your eyes when you tell me you can't, or worse—to have you resent me instead of saying no."

He wanted to promise her it would never happen, but the fiasco in the river today was evidence he couldn't promise anything. She loved him, even now, even though he hadn't been the one to help, even when he'd been the one in need of rescuing. But it still wasn't enough, and Eòghann turned away, hoping she wouldn't see the heartbreak in his eyes.

Chapter Thirty-Five

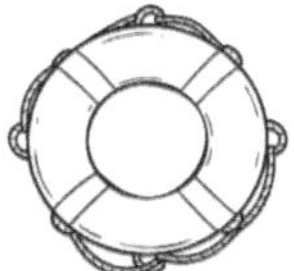

T-MINUS 1 DAY TO RENAYZANTS FAIRE

Rebecca drove Wes and Eòghann back to Warwick Hall, all of them silently lost in thought, only the mechanical voice of the GPS to disturb them while they crawled through rainy, rush hour traffic heading out of Knoxville.

As they made their way up the long and winding driveway to Grandma Ruth's, Wes could see it all play out again in her mind: Alec and Jack, squelching through the sodden grass with Rory on a stretcher between them. The EMTs walking slowly with Eòghann and then opening the back of the ambulance for them all to climb inside. The boxy truck's wheels spinning in the wet, muddy ground until Alec, Jack and Spencer, possessed of a super human strength, joined forces to push the vehicle back on the gravel drive while its lights flashed orange and white in eerie silence. The wail of the siren as it finally pulled away with Rory, Eòghann, and Alec inside.

Grief washed over Wes at the realization of what might've happened if fate had flipped heads instead of tails, and she began to shake. Eòghann reached forward to rub her shoulder from the back seat.

"Shock," Rebecca murmured. "You need rest."

Inside the house, Wes slipped back into caregiver mode, her shivers forgotten. She'd made a hash of her confession in the hospital, trying to explain but somehow creating more distance between them. Now, at least, she could show him how she felt, show him he was wanted.

Eòghann allowed her to lead him upstairs and tuck him straight into bed. Despite the summer heat, she spread her father's blue-and-grey blanket around him to keep him safe and then force fed him chicken noodle soup, which he swallowed without a word of complaint. She brought him a stack of Grandma's historical romance novels and sat on the edge of the bed, still in her pajamas from that morning, trying to find the words to ask him to stay with her, reminding herself all the while that now was not the time.

But he laced his fingers through hers, and it felt like he was asking her the same thing, so she tumbled into bed beside him, and soon they fell asleep, clinging tightly to each other like they were both afraid of drowning.

SOMETIME DURING THE NIGHT, WESLEY WOKE WITH A start. Eòghann was breathing in short, shallow gasps, his body twitching as he cried out incomprehensible words.

"Shh," she murmured, nuzzling closer to him and stroking his hair. "You're safe, Padre. It's only a nightmare." She kissed his temple and rubbed his chest, continuing to whisper soft words until he woke with a jerk and a shout.

"It's all right. You were dreaming," she whispered, kissing his fevered brow as his breaths deepened and tears leaked from the corners of his eyes. "It's okay. Everyone's safe and dry. I'm here, Eòghann. I'm right here."

"Why are you?" he asked, rolling to face her, and somehow she knew his words were merely self-recrimination before he added, "I wouldn't be."

"Of course you would," she told him, running her fingers through his hair and pressing his head to her chest. "You already are. I've pushed you and pushed you away, but you're still here."

She kissed the top of his head, continuing to stroke him affectionately, this man who needed to know his own value. "I'm here because I love you, Eòghann MacNeil," she whispered.

Her other hand was clasped tightly in his, and he brought it to his lips. It was more than a kiss, it was fealty and gratitude. It was forever.

She kissed his forehead, and then his lips, because she wanted him to know—needed him to know how much she meant those words and that she understood what he was telling her in return—that he loved her too.

"You shouldn't love me. I don't deserve it."

"You deserve everything."

"I don't."

"Of course you do, and anyway, I tried not to, and look what happened?"

He sighed, so full of anguish it killed her.

"Look, I know I suck at accepting help. So, maybe we start by me helping you. And then we help each other. Equally. You can be as afraid and broken as you need to. I've got you. I'll hold all the pieces so you don't lose any when you come apart."

He chuckled, a little bitterly. "Promise?"

"Promise. You were brave, trying to help Rory today. For a minute, I thought I'd lost you. And right now, I don't know if seeing where this goes is brave or cowardly, I just know I'm not ready to let you go. Because I love you when you're scared, and when you're funny. I love you when you're climbing the walls, and when you're fixing them. I loved you when I thought you were a priest. I loved you when I really didn't want to love anyone."

He claimed her mouth after that, kissing her into silence, and when she smiled, her lips parting, he deepened the kiss, letting his tongue say what words could not. Words seemed beyond him at the moment, and that was fine. Who needed words? She'd said all she needed to say.

It felt like they became one person as they kissed, limbs all tangled up together, her head resting on his outstretched arm like a pillow, closer than close. He seemed to crave nearness and touch, and lord knew she did too, so she kept stroking his hair, his back, his face, as he clung to her. As they clung to each other.

Gradually his posture relaxed and his breathing evened out, and the kissing became less frantic. More sensual. Wes kept trying to tell her libido to stand down. Now was not the time. But he smelled so good, and she could feel him stiffen beneath her crotch as they lay face to face, rocking gently, just kissing, just comforting, just holding on for dear life.

Wes snuggled closer, and Eòghann ran his hand down her back and over her rump, setting her nerve endings alight.

"Sorry," he whispered.

"For what?" she asked, sliding his other hand over her breast —permission, if he wanted it. He took the hint and thumbed her nipple lightly, making her whimper into his neck. She allowed her own hand to stray down his back to his very fine bottom, pulled him closer, and threw her left leg over his hip as they kissed, slowly, luxuriously, reveling in each other's taste and scent and breath.

Wes ground lazily against the rigid bundle nearly bursting from his boxer briefs, and almost as though they shared a single mind—for she couldn't say who moved first—she shimmed out of her bottoms and he out of his, rolling on a condom before he slid into her, still lying on their sides facing each other, still kissing, as they rocked gently together, two half pieces coming together to make a whole.

It was so achingly tender, and Wesley didn't ever want it to end. She took a calming breath and allowed herself the pleasure of not being hurried. She kissed his neck, his cheek, his lips, her hands running up and down his back as they rocked, slowly, until her climax snuck up on her.

When he kissed away her tears, she realized she'd been crying—at how cared for, how seen, how completely loved she felt. Sex before Eòghann had always been a frenzied affair, chasing that O, as many and as fast as she could manage—or, when she wasn't expecting one at all, trying to get through to the other side so she could go watch TV. But this had been something else entirely, almost spiritual, and somehow healing for her ragged soul.

Eòghann's arms tightened around her as his breathing changed, cresting his own orgasm, and Wesley didn't want him to ever let her go.

When she emerged from her bedroom late Friday morning, Wes sat alone on the kitchen counter staring bleakly out at the soggy landscape. They'd come so close to achieving Grandma Ruth's dream, but in the end, they had failed, and at what cost to Rory and Eòghann?

"Penny for your thoughts?" Grandma asked, shuffling into the kitchen wearing fuzzy turquoise slippers, and setting to work filling the coffee pot.

She shook her head. "You should charge me to hear them."

"How's your Sexy Scot?" Grandma asked, and a flush shot through Wesley's cheeks remembering the night before. Strange how a near catastrophe and a nightmare had led to the most satisfying sex of her life.

"Still sleeping," she said with a smile.

Grandma nodded, not commenting on Wesley's failure to deny he was *her* Scot this time.

"Do you remember the summer when you were eleven and you took the canoe all the way out to that island on your own?"

"I didn't want to leave."

"I should have told you I was planning to sell."

"It's your house," Wes said with a shrug.

"That's true." Grandma nodded. "I still should've told you sooner."

"What happened with the paperwork yesterday?"

"That Sadie, she's a sharp one. While you were off rescuing the love of your life, she took me to Knoxville, and we sweet talked our way into a meeting or two."

"And?"

"We need a business license to sell tickets, like Pierre said, but non-profits can accept donations."

"Pay what you want?"

"You got it, toots," Grandma said, raising a cup of coffee in salute.

"But we aren't a non-profit."

"That's true, we're not. But your grandpa used to be active with a group in the city called Knights of the Sky."

"They help out Air Force widows and orphans, don't they?" Wes asked, tears stinging her eyes.

"They do. And they are now our co-host. They get every cent after we recoup our money."

"And if we don't recoup it?"

"Then they get half of whatever we do bring in."

"And the liquor license?"

"That was our second stop. The liquor board remembered seeing you on the news and expedited approval of our application."

"I thought Pierce said it would take ninety days."

"Maybe for him. We batted our eyes and said pretty please."

"So we need to go buy Miller Lite after all?"

"Don't you dare. Gray's Stoic Scot was busy yesterday too. He has a brewery, a distillery, and a winery coming out tomorrow."

Genius. Wes would have to remember to give Bryan a big, sloppy kiss on the cheek for figuring that one out.

"And the health department—?"

"Will be here in the morning. I told you, Blondie, it all came together."

Wes swallowed against the lump growing in her throat. While she'd been moping around, her friends had pulled off the impossible.

"That's amazing."

"But?"

"But the ground is so waterlogged. We can't ask people to park in a cranberry bog. They'll get stuck like the ambulance did." Her voice wavered on the world *ambulance*, and she cleared her throat.

"Maybe you're right. Sure has been fun to put together though," Grandma said, kissing her on the head and retreating to her bedroom with her coffee.

Wes wasn't usually the Negative Nancy of her friend group. *Aim high... Fly, Fight, Win*, had been drilled into her from the time she was small. She much preferred to bull her way through than to surrender. But this time, she couldn't see a path forward. Unless the ambulance had been unlucky and found the one low spot where they shouldn't let people park?

Pulling on her grandmother's too-small rain boots, she went out into the yard to get the lay of the land and come up with a plan. Close to the house, it was every bit as bad as she remembered, and worse. The water was practically up to her ankles, the ground soft and squishy beneath.

She sloshed across the lawn, all the way back to the main road. Further away from the house it was better. A downward slope helped drain some of the water away. But it still wasn't good.

Pulling her hands inside the sleeves of Eòghann's old sweater, she tried to think of options. Start bailing? Ha. They could try bussing people in, but from where? Using what bus? Could they dismantle the hay bale benches and spread the hay around? It had come from this field, so in theory it should be enough to re-cover the area, right? People could stand to watch the shows?

"Wes?"

Eòghann was on the front porch when she schlepped back to the house. If anyone would know how to fix this, it was Eòghann. All she needed to do was ask, but it went against her nature and her nurture and her whole entire being.

"What's wrong, love?"

She laughed, but it sounded more like a sob. "We got so close. But we can't let people park out here, not like this."

Eòghann nodded sympathetically and opened his arms for her, settling his chin on top of her head, as she buried her face in his cologne.

She took a deep breath, letting his scent settle her nerves. He loved her. He loved to help. He wouldn't see her as a burden, he would never. "I know I have no right to ask it—and I'll love you even if the answer is no. But can you please help me try to figure out what to do?"

For a moment his eyes lit up, but then he frowned. Probably

sick of the whole faire affair entirely. He ought to tell her needy ass no after being repeatedly assured his assistance was neither required nor appreciated.

"What?" she asked, swallowing her trepidation.

"I'm afraid it won't work."

"Then we're no worse off than we already are."

He nodded. "We could try to sump-pump it," he suggested.

"Sump-pump?"

"Saw something similar on *Scrapheap Challenge* years ago," he said, growing more and more animated as he thought it through. There's loads of useful bits and bobs in the garage still. Big paint buckets and motors from different tools."

Wes stood on her tip toes to kiss him hard on the mouth.

"It probably won't work," he said warily.

"I love you whether it works or not," she said, and a slow smile spread across his face like maybe he believed her. "I love you for trying. Where do we start?"

First, they dug large holes to hold the giant paint buckets connected to hoses. Once the buckets filled with enough water, small motors began to pump the water away. While the sump-pumps worked, Eòghann kept digging, making trenches twelve feet apart to give the rest of the water somewhere else to go.

Exhausted and aching, Wes did as he suggested, and looked online for anyone nearby selling wood chips. She found a guy one county over who was giving them away for free to get them out of his backyard. He was so excited to get rid of them that after helping Eòghann and his cousins load up Alec's truck and Jack's truck and her grandfather's old truck, he and his buddy loaded up their two trucks as well, and they all spent the rest of the day spreading chopped up Bradford pear trees around the pumped-out lawn and along the pathways of the faire.

It was going to work. It had to.

And then Wes would beg Eòghann to stay because she'd realized somewhere between the island and the shore that she could never let him go.

Chapter Thirty-Six

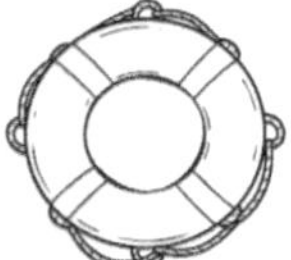

The sun dawned early on Saturday morning, not a rain cloud in sight. The day of the faire was upon them, and Eòghann awoke with Wesley in his arms. Her hair still smelled of last night's shampoo and honeysuckle and the flower he now knew was called magnolia.

"Ready?" he asked, kissing behind her ear.

She moaned softly, snuggling against him. "Do we have to?"

"It's Grandma Ruth's dream," he said, delighting in the little smile that played across her lips.

"Let her deal with it then."

"You've worked so hard."

"*You* have. You must be exhausted. I was asleep before you ever came to bed."

He was *plum tuckered out*, as Grandma Ruth would say, but he shook his head, brushing the hair out of Wesley's eyes. He'd stayed out late working on one finishing piece for the faire and it would be worth it.

"Something else is working hard," she teased, grinding against him, drawing a growl from deep in his throat that he hadn't realized was in there. "What time is it?" she asked.

"Half seven."

"Plenty of time. Don't move."

She scrambled out of bed and into the loo, returning a few minutes later with fresh breath and fresh enthusiasm when she pounced on him.

"Be right back." He rolled away from her to do the same, being sure to add a touch of cologne before he climbed back into bed.

"Ugh, you always smell *so* good," Wes said, settling herself on top of him and kissing him senseless.

She trailed fiery kisses down his neck, each one setting off a tiny explosion in his synapses, before returning hungrily to his lips. His heart rate monitor began to beep and Wesley laughed. "There it is. Confirmation I'm doing something right," she said, as he took the watch off and buried it in the side table before rolling her onto her back and kissing the same pattern into her skin as she'd used to brand him.

"It's going to be a very long day," he whispered in between kisses.

"Yes," she agreed, her brow furrowing adorably.

"How many orgasms do you reckon you need to power through such a very long day?"

A wicked smile curled her lips. "Three at least."

"All at once? Or spread out?"

"Ohh, an excellent question."

"Perhaps we should start with three this morning and see where the day takes us?" he suggested, as she stripped off her t-shirt. Then he began kissing his way down her throat, pausing to give overdue attention to each rosy nipple.

Wesley's breathing hitched, and she squirmed beneath him.

"Only if you're up for it, old man."

He raised an eyebrow at her and continued kissing his way down her belly until he could situate himself between her thighs. "You do like old things," he reminded her before kissing her tattoo in a way that he knew would make her squirm with anticipation.

"I absolutely do," she panted.

Lifting a leg over each shoulder he set to work, licking and lapping and sucking the bundle of nerves until she was shaking and panting, a surge of salty fluid flooding his tongue.

"One," he whispered, as he kissed his way back up her torso while she caught her breath.

"One and a half, at least," she gasped, and he laughed into her neck, pulling her close.

"I want you inside me," she whispered.

"That is the plan."

"Now," she said, rolling on top of him. "But only if you want to."

"More than anything," he replied, passing her a condom.

With that encouragement, she made quick work of the sheath and then slid down on to him, and they both gasped as though it were the first time. Wes had a way of riding him that was the sexiest goddamn thing he'd ever experienced, sitting up enough that he could fondle her gorgeous breasts, whimpering at each stroke of his fingers, while also somehow pulling him almost all the way out with each thrust before plunging back down on his aching, needy cock, finding her own pleasure, inside and out, and returning his tenfold. This morning, she took charge and went slowly, savoring every moment, almost stopping time.

It was hungry, yet patient, rhythmic, but somehow still unexpected, tender and demanding and soon he was hurtling towards the edge.

"I'm so close," he whispered, wanting to reach for her clit to help her along, but she caught both his wrists and pressed them into the mattress above his head, lying closer to him—moaning as she ground herself against his pubic bone after each thrust, and when he thought he couldn't hold back another second, she cried out and shuddered against him.

Eòghann wrapped his arms around her and surrendered to his own cataclysmic orgasm until they both lay boneless and senseless, panting in each other's arms.

When he could finally speak again he whispered, "Two."

"Two and three quarters at least," she purred, nuzzling into his neck like she could stay there for a lifetime.

He didn't want to jinx it, but he sure hoped she would.

"I can't imagine what you've got planned for number three," she teased, sucking his ear lobe and throwing one leg over his.

He smacked her bum playfully, eliciting a sound resembling a purr. "You've noticed I don't spend an excess amount of time in the shower?"

She pulled back from him so he could see her face, all traces of silliness gone as she nodded.

"When I was young, even bathing gave me panic attacks. That's when I started wearing cologne. It's not so bad now, but I don't love it the way most people do," he admitted. "One thing that makes it easier is if I imagine you in there with me. Helping me forget about the water altogether."

She nodded seriously and licked her lips. "How long do you need?" she asked, glancing down towards his used-up cock.

"More time than we have right now," he laughed. "But you..."

"Whatever I can do to help," she murmured, coming in for another kiss before taking his hand and leading him off to the shower.

Wes took her time scrubbing him down, bringing him back to life surprisingly quickly until he spun her around, and pulled her tight against his chest. He kissed the her neck to make her shiver, enjoying the feel of her bum torturing his groin while he teased her nipples and let his fingers go to work between her legs until she was a limp rag in his arms.

"Can't we stay in here all day?" she begged.

"No. But it was quite the most enjoyable shower of my life," he assured her, kissing her deeply and wrapping her up in a towel.

Chapter Thirty-Seven

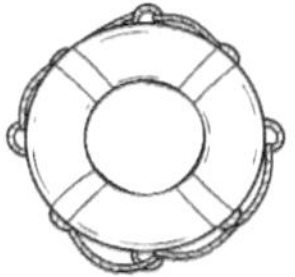

Stepping outside that morning felt like entering another world. Wes wasn't at her Grandma's house in Tennessee anymore. She'd been transported through time and space. All the rain had brought fog and cooler temperatures which would undoubtedly burn off quickly as the sun rose in a cloudless, cerulean sky.

Grandma Ruth had loaned Wesley an old, lilac-colored dress that was blousy and flowy and clung to her curves in all the right places if she said so herself. She finished her look with a ring of flowers for her hair—and fairy wings because when in faux Rome—and she topped it off with her snazziest pair of sunglasses.

It was giving nerdy elf, but Wes didn't mind. She looked like someone whose partner might wear slutty little reading glasses with his kilt, and her mouth watered at the idea of seeing him later in those glasses and absolutely nothing else.

Grandma looked resplendent in her Elizabethan gown, grinning gleefully in the dappled morning sun. People were already arriving by the time Wes joined her out front, the line of cars stretching all the way down the driveway to the road. Sheriff Jerry would probably have something to say about that.

"We did it, Blondie," Grandma Ruth whispered, squeezing her hand.

Wes nodded. "It was a team effort."

"Welcome! Welcome!" Duncan cawed, circling overhead as teenage volunteers directed visitors to their parking spaces on the lawn.

"Did you teach him that?" Grace asked.

Grandma shrugged. "He's his own bird," she said, with her usual air of mystery.

Eòghann joined them, wearing one of Grandma's kilts as promised, and he stood with his hand at Wesley's low back as they greeted guests.

When the news van arrived, Wes nudged her grandma forward. "Your turn."

Wes hugged LaTonya and Eddie, and waved at Lian, the EMT who'd agreed to come back on her day off and work the faire. Then, hand in hand, she led Eòghann into the crowd of guests heading around the back of the house to explore their faire.

"The wood chips were a stroke of genius," she told him. "But where did this rubber sidewalk come from?" she asked, as a girl in a wheel chair moved easily along the little path.

"We were spreading the chips around, and I remembered how much trouble Teàrlach had on the beach before he got a special chair for it. Lùc's cowboy mentioned there were rolls of this stuff at the hardware store."

Wesley's heart flooded with warmth. "It's difficult for me to admit this, but I do love how you solve problems before it occurs to me they might be problems,"

"We're a team," he said, leaning over to kiss her cheek, and they turned down vendor alley, browsing each and every stall.

Wes wanted to buy everything—tea and candles, books and bobbles, leather and jewels. The air smelled like short bread and fish 'n chips, and she could hear bagpipes and Spencer's hurdy-gurdy, and somewhere there was a campfire burning to create sweetly scented smoke for ambience.

The world felt magical—like Wesley's first faire as a little kid—more magical than she'd have ever imagined possible in her grandmother's own backyard.

"It all came together," she whispered.

"Are you pleased?" Eòghann asked, and she nodded, unable to express quite how happy she was.

"Can I show you something?" He took her hand with a sly little grin, not waiting for a reply.

"What did you do?" she teased, instantly alert—and excited.

"Close your eyes," he ordered, and when he used that low, growly burr, Wes had no choice but to comply.

Eyes shut, she clung to his arm, relishing the scents and sounds and closeness as he led her wherever it was he wanted her to go.

"Alright, you can open them," he whispered, his lips brushing the shell of her ear and making her shiver.

When she opened her eyes, they were standing in a clearing where a lone birch tree had somehow been transformed into a Renaissance maypole.

"Oh my word," Grandma Ruth whispered, stepping into the clearing behind them, and gazing up at the colorful ribbons in awe, her whole face lit up like a little kid seeing their first sky full of fireworks.

"Look what he did for you," Wes breathed, wrapping her arms around her grandma, each of them holding tight to the other as they gazed up at Eòghann's creation, breathing new life into the old birch tree.

"Yes," she replied. "Aren't I lucky?"

"How?" Wes asked Eòghann, who was watching her anxiously.

"An old hula hoop and other things from the garage. It was a treasure trove."

"I recognize this fabric," Grandma Ruth said, taking hold of a long strip of yellow cloth patterned with daisies that had been cut to make a ribbon. "I made you a sundress out of this when you were eight, do you remember?"

Wes did remember. The dress had been her very favorite—she'd worn it for years until it fell apart.

"D'you like it?" Eòghann asked, his face as earnest as she'd ever seen.

"It's perfect," she replied, kissing his cheek. "Absolute perfection. Somebody find Spencer. I want to dance."

"Milady," Spencer replied, popping up out of nowhere like he had a knack for doing, and they each took up a ribbon, Grace and Bryan, Lùc and Sadie, Wes and Eòghann, and Grandma Ruth of course, as they laughed and danced together.

When it was over, Wes jumped into Eòghann's arms, and he spun her around.

"I'm definitely going to need number four," she whispered, and he turned about a thousand shades of red beneath his beard.

"Now, or...?"

"I suppose it'd be in poor taste to disappear before lunch," Wes whined, rolling her eyes at the absolute imposition their guests were putting on them. "Can I buy you fish and chips?"

Eòghann smiled and let her take his hand and guide him back onto the path towards the food trucks, but when she turned, she came face to face with Pierce. *Now what?*

They blinked at each other for a moment, and he slid his gaze over Eòghann, whose hand had moved protectively to Wesley's lower back once more.

"You pulled it off," Pierce mumbled.

"We pulled it off," she agreed. "Completely above board, so if you're here to—"

"Relax. I'm here with my cousin, not to shut you down."

Wes rolled her shoulders, forcing her adrenaline down. "In that case, welcome. I hope you have fun."

Pierce nodded. "I'm sorry I couldn't help."

"You did help. You told us what we couldn't do." *Like always*, she didn't add. She should win an award for being on her best behavior.

He glared past her at Eòghann, like he wanted to say more.

Wes glanced back at the Scot, who raised his eyebrows for confirmation. Did she want him to disappear for a minute? She gave a tiny nod. She'd be all right.

"I'll go order those fish and chips," he said, kissing her on the cheek.

"Malt vinegar, please," she replied, squeezing his hand as he walked away, leaving the two of them to stand like awkward strangers.

"You said your cousin's here?" Wes finally asked, looking around, trying to remember if she'd ever met any of his cousins.

"Yeah, she's in line for the rage room."

Wes nodded.

"I did love you, you know," he blurted out.

She nodded again. "I loved you too."

"Until you didn't. Because I was bad in bed."

"Because you were selfish. In and out of bed."

"Selfish!" Pierce exclaimed, taking a step back like she'd stepped on a nerve. "I cooked, I cleaned. Sometimes. I was willing to do everything!"

"I believe you think so. But you didn't *want* to do any of those things."

"No one wants to clean!"

"Fair enough. No one wants to be with a martyr, either.

Come on, Pierce. You didn't want to get married. Believing you had to was easier than starting over."

He stared at the ground, processing what she'd said. "You seem happier."

"I am. I hope you are."

Shrugging, Pierce huffed out a sigh that he tried to turn into a laugh. "I still have to cook."

Wes didn't laugh.

"And the guy in the kilt? He's a generous lover?"

She was absolutely not going to answer that, but she couldn't help thinking back to Eòghann in the shower that morning.

"Got it," Pierce snapped, reading her face. "Any tips?"

Grimacing, she said, "Maybe ask her what she likes. Take care of yourself, Pierce," she added, turning towards the food trucks and feeling about a million pounds lighter as she walked away.

Chapter Thirty-Eight

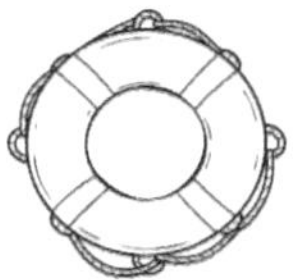

The look on Wesley's face when she saw the two-level bouncy castle Andy and Bryan had tracked down was priceless. She squealed as joyfully as the children jumping their wee hearts out.

"Pony rides *and* a bouncy castle? Move over, Lance and Lottie," she teased. "Your idea?"

"Jarrod's actually."

"Good kid."

"He is. They all are," Eòghann agreed, and a wave of grief washed over him because the boys were at the hospital with their brother, instead of all three running amok at the faire. Somehow in these few short weeks he'd come to love his cousin's lads as if he'd known them from the day they were born. He hated how much he'd already missed.

"Do you think they'll keep traveling?" Wes asked.

"The kids don't want to."

"And your cousin?"

Eòghann shook his head. "I'm not sure Alec knows what he wants." He took a deep breath. "He invited me to go with them —on to Maryland or wherever the next faire is. Before Rory's accident." Wesley stiffened at his side, and the tiny betrayal of her disappointment made him feel hope for their shared future.

"What did you say?"

"I said yes. Before."

She nodded. "It sounds like fun."

Eòghann nodded too. He'd given his word. He would go if they still wanted him, but it felt good to know she wasn't in such a hurry to get rid of him anymore.

"You should probably get a new phone," she said softly.

"Should I?"

"People might want to keep in touch with you."

"People?"

"Sure. Didn't you hear that guy over there raving about the Berserker's Cave?"

"Oh, that guy? I paid that guy to say those things," he teased.

"*I* might also want to keep in touch with you," she said, turning to face him. She ran her hands down his t-shirt, as though smoothing non-existent wrinkles. "And if they don't go back on the road, maybe you could stay with me awhile."

Eòghann grinned and leaned in for a kiss, but the second their lips met, someone called out, "Wes!"

She squeezed his hand and peered around him.

"Nadine," the woman said. "From Et Tu, Brü Té."

"I love the name of your shop," Wes told her.

"Thanks. We have fun. And I wanted to say, on behalf of all of us vendors—thank you so much for letting us be a part of this. I hope next year you do the whole month, but even if it's only a day, I'd love to come back."

Wesley's smile faltered a little, but she hugged Nadine.

"I wish we *could* do it again," Wes murmured as they walked back to the house at sunset.

While the last cars headed down the drive, glow-worms

came out to flit and float. More than once, Rory had reminded Eòghann that here among the civilized, they were called fireflies —and Grandma Ruth had countered that Stratford was far from civilized, and they were actually lightning bugs. Eòghann didn't care what they were called. He couldn't get enough of them.

Duncan flew overhead calling, "Farewell friends! Farewell!" and Wes paused to soak it all in.

"Thanks for helping make it a perfect day."

Eòghann turned and offered her a small box he'd collected on his way back with the wood chips yesterday.

She hesitated a moment, biting her lip.

"It isn't what you think," he promised.

So she opened the box. Inside was another box, and she opened that one with a curious chuckle. It held one hundred square business cards—the same design he'd found on her iPad that first night. She sighed and bit her lip, staring down at her own artwork in her hand.

"You're so talented," he said. "At art and design and executing an ambitious vision. You shouldn't waste another second in that job you hate."

"It pays the bills."

"So could a small business grant. Sadie told me. Look, you don't want this house to go up for sale. And I don't think Grandma Ruth truly wants to leave. What if you did move in with her? Cut down on expenses and give your dream a real Shakespeare Syndicate try?"

She laughed so hard she snorted, but there were tears in her eyes too. "I'm not sure the two of us together could maintain it very long on our own."

"S'pose that's where I come in. If you'll have me." When he looked up, her eyes were sparkling.

"What about Alec and the boys? Your promise to them?"

"That was never going to be forever. If they go back out

after Rory heals up, I could do both. Spend time with them, spend time with you. I'm a man of many talents."

"*Huge* talent," she said, waggling her eyebrows lasciviously, but then she sobered. "I don't know if Grandma Ruth would agree to it. She might be looking forward to learning pickleball and having experienced bridge partners."

"She is not," Grandma said, stepping up behind them, carrying her skirts to keep them out of the mud.

Wesley swirled around, prepared to protest, but Grandma didn't let her.

"How would I make sure I win, if I play against people who know what they're doing? Now, I didn't hear everything your Sexy Scot said, but I heard enough to get the gist of it, and if you two don't mind living with an eccentric old lady, then I'm one hundred percent on board. I promise to let you have your independence as long as you let me have mine."

"I dunno, Grandma. I could get kind of used to being part of a team sometimes."

"Only on Tuesdays and alternating Thursdays," Grandma Ruth agreed.

Wesley beamed at Eòghann, and he spun first her, and then Grandma Ruth around, both of them squealing like children.

"All right, all right," Grandma said when he set her down and steadied her elbow. "You two go ahead and kiss to make it official. I want to put my feet up and drink a cold gin and tonic."

And so, as Wesley's grandmother made her way back to the house, kiss was exactly what they did.

Epilogue

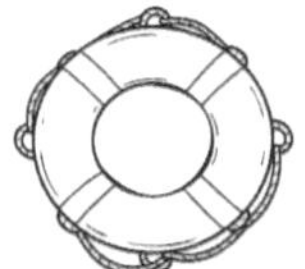

2 MONTHS LATER… STRATFORD

Wes sat on the front porch in the not-yet-stifling August heat. Next to her, Simon Clifton, the Artistic Director of the Smoky Mountain Repertory Theater, sipped a glass of ice cold lemonade.

"This is beautiful land," he said, looking out across the lawn. "How long has your grandmother owned it?"

"About thirty-five years."

"Will you host the Stratford Ren Faire again next year?" he asked.

"I hope so," Wes said, trying to be patient with the conversation, though she was dying to know why he was there. "With more time to plan, we might stay open all of May, who knows."

"I hope you do. Knox County needs more events like this one."

"You're doing your part at the Rep."

"That's actually why I'm here," he said, finally working his way around to the point. "The backdrops for the stages—they were very clever. Whimsical. I was told you were responsible for the designs?"

"I sketched them. But I have to confess my former house guests built and painted them."

"To your specifications?"

"Yes."

"Your vision."

She laughed. "Yes, I suppose so."

"We do six shows a season at the Rep. Do you think you could design sets for all six?"

"Me?" she asked, turning to him in surprise.

He looked at her steadily, waiting for an answer.

"I'd love to."

"Excellent."

"Let me get you a business card so you don't have to drive all the way out here next time."

She hurried into the foyer, where she knew she'd left a few business cards in her purse. Ignoring the playful squabble coming from the living room she stepped back outside to trade the yellow card for Mr. Clifton's empty lemonade glass.

"Perfect," he said. "Our season opens in September with *The Tempest*, so I'll be in touch soon."

After he drove off, Wes re-entered the house in a daze. She didn't have *landing her first set design gig* on her bingo card when she woke up that morning.

"If you have a club, you're supposed to play a club," Jarrod chided Rory.

"I didn't want to play a club," Rory argued.

"That's not how it works," Jarrod said in the even voice of a long-suffering older brother.

"Tell him I can play whichever suit I want to, Grandma Ruth," Rory whined.

"Sure can, if you're a cheater," Grandma agreed. "Has your

guest left already?" she asked Wes, following her into the kitchen while the boys continued to bicker.

"He offered me a job," Wes said, still in disbelief. "Designing sets for the Rep."

"I love that theater."

"I can't quite believe it." Wes hugged her grandmother around the waist, proving to herself that everything was real. "First Bea tracked down those jerks who scammed you, and now this?"

"Everything's going according to plan."

"A lawsuit, three interior design consultations, and now sets for six shows? I don't think I could've planned this in my wildest dreams. Suppose I'll need a ride into Knoxville on occasion."

"I think that can be arranged." Grandma Ruth squeezed her again. "When's that Sexy Scot of yours going to get his license?"

"He'll need to go back home eventually, but he's trying to figure out what can be done from here before he leaves. It's a lot of water to fly over."

"That's why the good Lord invented Xanax."

Wes laughed.

"Are they back?" Jarrod asked, entering the kitchen and helping himself to a glass of lemonade.

"Not yet," Wes told him. "But unless they made a detour to Dollywood, they should be here any minute."

Rory looked forlorn as he clomped up wearing the boot cast he'd transitioned to while his tibia fracture continued to heal, his wrist and forearm still incased in a plaster cast as well. "They wouldn't go to Dollywood without us," he said softly.

"I'm sure you're right," Wes agreed. "Maybe they stopped for snacks. Are you a Takis or a beef jerky man?"

"Chocolate."

"Ah, the purest currency of fourth grade."

"Is it?" he asked, doing his best to hide any nerves about

starting public school next week, after being homeschooled his whole life.

"Sorry kid, I dunno. When I was in fourth grade it was Pokémon."

"Family!" Duncan cawed moments before Alec's truck came into view out the kitchen window, "Welcome, family!" This time instead of a camper, a U-Haul was hitched to the back.

Alec and the boys had stayed at Grandma Ruth's until after Rory's wrist surgery. When he asked what they wanted to do next, they all agreed it was time to stop running, so he found a three bedroom apartment in Knoxville not too far from Grace, and he enrolled the boys in school for the fall semester.

Daniel was ecstatic to spend senior year amongst his peers, racking up the extracurriculars he felt he'd been missing.

Soon as school was settled, Wes and Grandma Ruth had agreed to entertain Jarrod and Rory while Alec, Eòghann, and Daniel drove back to Minnesota to empty out their old storage unit.

As promised, Eòghann had bought a new phone before they left town, and from what he'd told Wes, Alec intended to start practicing medicine again. Wes hoped the relocation would be the fresh start they all craved—and an added inducement to stick around if Eòghann needed one.

As for Eòghann... Wesley's tummy flip-flopped as she waited for the truck to stop and let him out. She'd missed him the past week, and she hadn't told him, but she'd been learning the ins and outs of visas so that as soon as he was ready, he could come back again to stay.

Jarrod ran out to meet his father and brother, with Rory stumping along after him. For a long moment they all held each other close.

Grandma Ruth invited them to stay for dinner, but Wes didn't hear the answer. She only had eyes and ears for Eòghann.

As she took his hand and led him up to the bedroom she whispered, "Forgive me, Padre, for I have sinned. It's been a week and a bit since my last confession."

Once in her room, she shut the door and pushed him back against it, inhaling his cologne and gobbling up the sight of him, a little rumpled and sleepy from the road, but settled. Happy.

"What could you possibly have done in such a short amount of time, ye wee devil?" he teased, his lips quirking up into a sideways smile.

"I've had *so many* impure thoughts," she confessed, rising on her toes to capture his lips and prevent him from naming her penance.

Acknowledgments

When I first decided to plan out a multi-book contemporary romance series, I knew I wanted to revisit a world of characters I had created many years ago, a group of friends who performed at Renaissance faires around the country. And so the first romance book I ever tried (and failed) to write became the foundation for the world of Stratford, Tennessee and Grandma Ruth's very own Renaissance faire. Precious little of that early story made its way into this book, and the main players mostly stand on the sidelines, but visiting with them and finally bringing their stories into 2026 felt a bit like visiting with old friends who you haven't seen in years.

Still, some books are easier than others to write. This one found me in a period when I already hadn't written for six months because of things going on in my life and the world. And then, after finishing one draft, I was seized by the ghost of another story, and held hostage until it was complete.

But finally—like Grandma Ruth's dream—my own faire has come to life. All of this to say, I needed a lot of cheerleaders to get to this point. So, Sarah Blair, this book pretty much owes its life to you. For being its champion and mine, every minute of every day, for patiently talking me off the ledge more times than I can count, and for loving my little glasses-wearing idiots as much as I do. Thank you. I don't think I would've finished without you.

Thank you to Jenni Ritz and Jessie Parker as well. You are both too good to me, for reading early drafts and answering endless questions. To my editor, Angi Black. My failure to plan was not your crisis, but you finished in record time and were instrumental in the final version. And to the incredibly talented Jessica Khoury, who designed this beautiful cover and brought Wesley and Eòghann to life.

My contemporary stories don't always require the same amount of research as my historical, but sometimes a book will surprise you. This one required quite a bit. Many thanks are owed to Kyndra Brewer at the City of Knoxville for patiently answering my questions about the licenses and legal hoops required to hold a large event, and to Lianne Walker, for advising me on Gaelic name pronunciations. Also, the members of the Stargardt community who have shared their experiences with vision-loss online.

To my Writerly community, which grows more every year. I don't know what I would do without you all, and watching you flourish and excel has been such an immeasurable joy.

To my 'Canes friends, who introduced me to my very first Ren faire at Deerfield Beach, Florida—while the members of the Shakespeare Syndicate aren't based on any of you individually, the bond between them is very much based on my love for all of you, and I hope we can see each other soon.

To my mom, for going to my second Ren faire with me way back when, and to my dad for playing Hive with me last Christmas—thank you both for letting me borrow aspects of your mothers and mash them together into one fictional Grandma to rule them all.

And to DJ, for all the reasons, too many to enumerate, but mostly for listening to me, and believing in me, and never doubting for a minute that I would finish the thing. And if I may quote *Hamlet*, "Doubt thou the stars are fire, doubt that the sun doth move, doubt truth to be a liar, but never doubt I love."

About the Author

Rose Prendeville is a librarian living in Middle Tennessee with her husband, the world's cutest dog, and a garden full of bees, writing stories about found families and flawed people doing their best. The award winning author of *Last Blue Christmas* and the Brides of Chattan historical series is passionate about books with happy endings and their ability to brighten a sometimes dismal world.

If you enjoyed this book, please consider leaving a review at your favorite marketplace.

To stay up-to-date on this series and other news, scan the QR code and sign up for Rose's newsletter or visit:

    roseprendeville.com

Books by Rose Prendeville

Last Blue Christmas

The Unknown Birds

Brides of Chattan Series

Mistress Mackintosh and the Shaw Wretch

Lady Len and the Mysterious Mac

Maggie and the Pirate's Son

Tennessee Hebrides Series

Grace on the Rocks

A Faire Affair

www.ingramcontent.com/pod-product-compliance
Lightning Source LLC
Chambersburg PA
CBHW020902060726
47591CB00004B/1053